Gangsta Twist 1

D0170258

Gangsta Twist 1

Clifford Johnson

www.urbanbooks.net

Urban Books, LLC
78 East Industry Court
Deer Park, NY 11729

Gangsta Twist 1 Copyright © 2011 Clifford Johnson

ISBN 13: 978-1-60162-457-4
ISBN 10: 1-60162-457-3

First Printing July 2011
Printed in the United States of America

10 9 8 7 6 5 4 3 2

Distributed by Kensington Publishing Corp.
Submit Wholesale Orders to:
Kensington Publishing Corp.
C/O Penguin Group (USA) Inc.
Attention: Order Processing
405 Murray Hill Parkway
East Rutherford, NJ 07073-2316
Phone: 1-800-526-0275
Fax: 1-800-227-9604

Chapter One

Once the flight reached it's cruising altitude, Taz watched as Keno reached under his seat, grabbed his carry-on bag, and pulled out his portable DVD player. Keno smiled at Taz as he inserted his *Scarface* DVD into his Toshiba SD-P2800. He loved that movie. Every time they went on a mission out of town, he repeatedly watched that DVD. Taz shook his head from side to side as he watched his partner plug his headphones into the DVD player.

Keno noticed him staring and asked, "Are you trying to watch *'Face* with me, dog?"

Taz shook his head no and said, "I'm chillin', fool. I'm thinking about what I'm going to get into when we get back home. I'm so fuckin' tired of the same ol' shit we be doing. Either it's the club or riding around town, flossin' and shit. I think I'm going out to Norman and spend some time with Tazneema. It's been way too long since I chilled with her."

"Yeah, that's straight, but tonight we're still going to the club and get our floss on. We gots to let the haters hate," Keno said with a smile on his face.

With a smile of his own, Taz said, "Yeah, I know." He sat back and reclined in his chair and started thinking about the mission they had just completed out in Seattle. As usual, everything went as planned. Hell, nothing ever went wrong whenever Won put something together. They had just successfully robbed some dope boys for over 1.5 million dollars, not including the jewelry and drugs that they took. Taz and his five comrades didn't fuck with drugs; all they took for themselves was the money. Won would look out for them with the jewels and keep the drugs for himself. That way, everyone would be happy, especially Taz and the crew. As long as they continued to maintain their strict and orderly ways, he didn't foresee any future problems with how they were earning their money.

It felt real good to be financially secure, but it felt even better to know that no matter what happened, it was highly unlikely that they would ever go back to broke. That was something that just simply could not happen. They were all millionaires. *Millionaires! Robbin' punk-ass dope boys has made us all fuckin' millionaires. Now, ain't that somethin'!* he thought as he closed his eyes.

As the plane was making it's final decent into Will Rogers Airport in Oklahoma City, one of the flight attendants lightly shook Taz and told him that he had to put his seat in the upright position for the landing. He opened his eyes, did as she had asked, and turned towards Keno.

Keno was smiling as he watched Al Pacino shooting up a bunch of Colombian hit men in his mansion. "Get 'em, 'Face! Don't go out by yourself, baby!" he said as if this was his first time ever watching the movie.

Taz tapped him on his shoulder, and Keno pulled the headphones out of the DVD. Taz told him, "Dog, turn that shit off. We're about to land."

"Hold the fuck up. It's almost over. You know this is my favorite part of the flick. 'Face is about to get smashed, but he's going out like a warrior, for real."

Taz stared at Keno briefly, shook his head again, and closed his eyes.

When their flight pulled up to the gate, Taz told Keno, "Call the others to make sure that they're on schedule."

Keno reached into his pocket, pulled out a thin cell phone, and started dialing. After a few seconds he asked someone on the other line, "Are y'all straight? . . . That's cool. We just got in too. We'll be at the house in about thirty to forty minutes. Have you gotten at Bo-Pete and Wild Bill yet? . . . Get at them and let them know everything is everything. By the time y'all make it in from Tulsa and they get in from Dallas, it'll be time to hit the club. So make sure y'all's gear is up to par. It's time to party, my nigga! . . . 'All right, I'll tell him. Out!" Keno closed his cell phone. "Bob and Red just got to Tulsa, and they're on their way in now. By the time we get to the house and get dressed and shit, Bo-Pete and Wild Bill should be there too. Dog, I hate all of this separate flying shit. Why we gots to get down like that every time we bounce?"

Taz frowned at Keno but remained silent as they left the plane. As they walked through the terminal, Taz noticed two of the three undercover airport security officers staring at them. He wasn't worried because all they had on them was a small amount of money. *Thanks to Won, we never have to worry about petty shit,* he said to himself as he led the way out of the airport.

Once they were outside, they climbed into one of the airport shuttle vans and rode in silence to the long-term parking area. After they were inside of Taz's all-black 2005 Denali, he answered Keno's question. "Dog, ever since we've been getting down, we've always maintained our discipline, right?"

"Yeah."

"So, why would you ask me some stupid shit? You know Won has it set up for us to move in sets of twos. That's how we move when we're at home, and that's how we move when we're on a mission. I swear, sometimes you just don't think before you run that mouth of yours! Bob was right. You be too damn anxious to get into shit. You need to relax a li'l, homey."

"Ain't that a bitch! That nigga Bob be just as anxious as I am. Shit, I ain't even talkin' about gettin' into shit. I was just thinking, like, damn! This shit always slows us down a little. Fuck! After we get paid, it's all about relaxing and having a good time, my nigga. You need to get off your ass and try it sometimes."

"What you talkin' 'bout, fool? I go out every time y'all go out."

"Yeah, I know. You go out with us, but you don't be trying to have a good time. All you do is post up and let a few bitches holla. But on the real, you don't be trying to holla back. It's like you're just passing the time, my nigga."

Taz knew Keno was right, but how could he explain that he just wasn't into that bullshit-ass club scene? How could he tell one of his lifelong friends that all he wanted to do was continue to make sure that their rental houses around the city were straight, and enjoy the fruits of their work by staying in his big-ass house and working out in his home gym? How could he explain how lonely he really was? Those were things that he kept close to his chest, because no one would ever understand the pain that he felt and lived with daily... *no one!* "Whatever, nigga! You just make sure that you get real fly tonight, 'cause I'm bustin' out the burgundy chinchilla."

Smiling, Keno said, "Oh, so we're sportin' the minks, huh? That's cool, 'cause I ordered a tight-ass creme chinchilla a few weeks ago. I've been waiting for it to get kind of chilly to sport that bitch. So it's on and poppin' tonight, nigga. You better be careful!"

"What are you talkin' 'bout now, fool?" Taz asked as he pulled into the circular driveway of Keno's mini-mansion.

"That chinchilla be making them hoes fiend, and you know you ain't with that much female attention." Keno started laughing as he got out of the truck. Taz smiled and gave him the finger as he pulled out of the driveway once he saw Keno go inside of his home.

By the time Taz made it to his home, Wild Bill, Bo-Pete, Red and Bob were all standing beside Bob's all-black Escalade. Bo-Pete's all-black Navigator was parked behind Bob's truck. They turned towards Taz as he jumped out of his truck.

"What up, fools? I'm glad to see y'all made it. Come on in so we can hit Won and check on everything," he said as he led the way into his 15,000-square-foot mini-mansion. Even though he stayed alone, he loved all of the space he had. Staying way out on the outskirts of the City made him feel secure. His whereabouts and safety were two things that were very important to him. But more importantly, he just loved being secluded.

Once they were inside, he led them to one of his two dens so they could all relax. Bob went to the bar and poured himself a shot of Rémy Martin, while Bo-Pete and Wild Bill pulled the cover back to Taz's pool table and started a game. Red turned on Taz's 60-inch plasma screen and turned the channel to ESPN. Taz went upstairs to his bedroom and set his bag down. He grabbed the phone and left a text message for Won. After that, he walked back downstairs and rejoined his comrades.

The plushness of his home was so amazing that one would swear that a woman had decorated. The two dens were both identical; soft brown Italian leather sectional sofas, with a pool table in each, the same color as his furniture. Plasma screen televisions and the most sophisticated entertainment system money could buy gave his dens the feel as if one was in a high-tech arcade or something. The other ten rooms were just as tasteful, as were the four bathrooms, for that matter. Taz left no stone unturned when it came to his home. After all, he was a millionaire.

Just as Taz was about to speak, there was a loud knock at the front door. He sighed and said, "Man, go let that fool Keno in, please."

Red got up and went and let Keno inside. A minute later, he returned followed by Keno. Keno was dressed to impress. He had on a pair of creme-colored Azzure jeans with matching colored Timberland boots. You couldn't see his shirt because his creme-colored chinchilla mink was zipped all the way up. He smiled as he unzipped his coat and said, "What up, my peoples?"

"Damn, nigga! When you get that?" asked Bo-Pete.

Before Keno could answer him, Taz said, "He ordered it a few weeks ago. Now, sit down so we can take care of this shit. We need to get this out of the way." Taz sat down, flipped open his laptop, and quickly started tapping on the keys. After a few minutes of this he stopped, smiled, and said, "Now that's what I'm talkin' 'bout!"

"It's all there?" asked Red.

"Yep. Here, check your account," Taz said as he passed the small computer to Red.

Red quickly punched in his password and pulled up his account in the Cayman Islands. After a few minutes he, too, smiled and said, "Oh yeah! I'm loving that shit!"

After passing the laptop around, each member of the six-man crew saw that their accounts in the islands had an additional two hundred and fifty thousand dollars, profit from their short trip to Seattle. Not bad for twenty-four hours of work. Not bad at all.

Wild Bill closed the laptop and said, "Well, that's that. Let's go get something to eat before we hit the club. I'm hungry."

Laughing loudly, Bob said, "Nigga, for a li'l nigga, you always hungry. But I feel you, gee. I'm starving my damn self. That airline food ain't nothin' nice."

Taz's cell rang. He quickly flipped it open and said, "What up, Won?"

"What's up with you, Babyboy? I see y'all made it back safely."

"Yeah, we're good. How 'bout your end? You straight?"

"Always. Have you checked your accounts yet?"

"Yeah, we just finished. Everything is everything. Good lookin' on the jewels and shit."

"No problem. I tried to get y'all as much as I could for them. I'm glad you're satisfied. Now, check this. I'm on the move, so stay ready because you and the troops will definitely have to stay on standby for this next one. It could happen as soon as next week—possibly sooner."

"Don't trip. We got you. All we need is the call. As long as you set it up, we'll be ready," Taz replied confidently.

"I know, Babyboy. That's why you're my man. Now, tell them knuckleheads with you that I said enjoy, be merry, and most of all, be good! Out!"

Taz closed his phone and gave Won's message to the crew. They all laughed.

Taz then ran upstairs and changed into his gear for the night. He put on a pair of black Rocawear jeans and a black T-shirt; then he grabbed his black Timbs and his burgundy chinchilla. He stepped towards the bedroom mirror and smiled. The lights shined brightly against his one-hundred-and-fifty-thousand-dollar platinum and diamond fronts. He reached into his drawer and pulled out his Rolex, then his two-hundred-and-fifty gram platinum chain and put it around his neck. The diamonds in his Jesus piece sparkled in the lighting as he adjusted it around his neck. "Now that's what a nigga calls bling-bling!" he said aloud as he grabbed his wallet and went back downstairs. "Time to go clubbin'!"

Chapter Two

Sacha Carbajal stepped out of the office building of Johnson & Whitney, the law firm she was working for, feeling extremely excited. She had just been told by the partners that she was next in line for a partnership. Finally, after six years of hard work, it was about to happen for her. She smiled happily as she strolled towards her brand-new 2006 BMW 325i. She was on her way to the top, and it felt great! Once she was inside of her car, she pulled out her cell phone and called her best friend, Gwen.

Gwen answered her phone after the third ring. "Hello?"

"What it do, bitch!" yelled Sacha.

"What it do, ho? Did you get it?" asked Gwen.

"I think so, girl. I'll know for sure sometime next week. Mr. Whitney told me that I was definitely next in line, and as long as nothing drastic occurs, I should be a partner soon."

"I'm so happy for you, girl! Congratulations!"

"Save that shit for later. Nothing is written in stone yet, but I'm still feeling giddy all over. We need to go out tonight. Do you have any plans?"

"Nope. What, you want to hit Bricktown and hang out a little?"

"Uh-uh. I'm trying to kick it with my peoples tonight. Let's go to that club you told me about a couple of months back."

"Bitch, I know you ain't talking about Club Cancun, the same club that has nothing but hoochie hoes and wannabe ballers!" Gwen said sarcastically.

"Alright, so I wasn't feeling it at first, but I'm in the mood to party with my peoples. I'm tired of hanging with the squares and those uppity-ass white people."

Laughing, Gwen said, "Now, ain't that something! Bitch, you're just as square as those uppity-ass white people! The only reason you still have a little hood left in your ass is because of me. Sometimes I think you've forgotten where you came from. But I ain't tripping. If you want to do the club, I'm with it. But we're going to have to go get some gear for tonight, 'cause I know you ain't got nothing in that uppity-ass closet of yours."

"Yeah, you're right. Meet me at Penn Square Mall in thirty, ho."

"Gotcha, bitch," Gwen said, and hung up the phone.

Gwen and Sacha had been best friends for over twenty years. They both graduated at the top of their classes in high school; then they went to Oklahoma State and graduated at the top of their classes there too. That's when their paths seemed to split. While Sacha went on to law school, Gwen got pregnant and had her son, Remel. Sacha tried her best to get Gwen to go back to school so she could follow her dreams, but the love bug had bitten her best friend too hard. Nothing anyone could say would deter Gwen from the love of her life. William had walked into Gwen's life and changed her forever.

Thinking back about the past almost caused tears to fill Sacha's eyes as she drove towards the mall. *Life just wasn't fair sometimes,* she thought as she remembered the day Gwen's life got turned completely upside down.

It had been raining all day and Gwen didn't feel like doing anything, so she had asked William to pick up

Remel from day care after he got off of work. The rainy day had her in a funky mood, so she chose to sit back and relax a little. She began to doze off, and eventually fell asleep.

The next thing Gwen remembered was being awakened by banging at her front door. She got up groggily and went to see who was beating on her door like they were out of their damn minds. When she saw that it was her girl, Sacha, she smiled and opened the door. As soon as she saw Sacha's face, she knew that something was wrong. Her makeup was smeared, and she was shaking uncontrollably. "What's wrong, Sacha?" she asked as she brought her into her home and sat her down in her living room.

Tears rolled silently down Sacha's cheeks as she gathered the nerve to tell her best friend in the world that her son and husband were dead.

Sacha remembered Gwen's screams as if it were yesterday. She prayed to the Almighty that she'd never hear another person scream like that ever again. After calming Gwen down a little, she explained what had happened and how she came to be at the horrible scene.

William was pulling out of the driveway of the daycare center when he was hit head-on by a drunk driver. The drunk driver, William, and baby Remel all died instantly. Sacha was on her way home and just so happened to see everything. When she realized that William and Remel were inside of the car and Gwen wasn't, she remembered feeling slightly relieved. The guilt of that thought still haunted her to this very day. She jumped back into her car and drove as fast as she could to her best friend's home.

As Sacha pulled into the mall's parking lot, she smiled sadly as she thought about how her girl got herself back together from such a devastating loss. Gwen was never one to mope. As hard as it was for her, she got back on her feet, went back to school and got her bachelor's degree, as well as her master's. Her original goal was to be an attorney just like Sacha, but after losing her baby and the love of her life, she chose psychology as her major. She wanted to help people. She opened her own office and started helping others and healing herself all at the same time. She'd never blamed that drunk driver for taking her family away from her; she always blamed herself for being too lazy that day. She felt that if she had gone and picked up Remel like she always did, her family would be with her to this very day. She didn't use that as an excuse; she used that to motivate herself.

She was the most driven woman that Sacha had ever known, and it was her strength that helped Sacha continue on at Johnson & Whitney, Attorneys at Law. Many times she had considered quitting and joining another law firm because she felt as if her talents were being overlooked. But Gwen rode her hard and told her to never quit. "Stay down, girl. Everything will be all right, and don't you give up on me, bitch!" Gwen yelled at her every time she felt weak. And now, finally after six years, the hard work was finally paying off, and Sacha owed it all to her girl, the strongest woman alive. So, it was only fitting that they spend the evening together, having a good time.

As she got out of her car, she smiled as Gwen's thick ass strolled to meet her at the front of the Dillard's department store in the mall. *She's living her life to the fullest after all of the pain she's been through, damnit! I'm about to start doing the same damn thing,* she said to herself as she stepped towards her best friend.

"What's up, bitch? Come on, I got an idea of what we're going to wear tonight," Gwen said as she pulled Sacha into the mall.

"I don't need your ass picking out my clothes, ho. I know what I like, and it damn sure ain't that hoochie shit you be liking to wear."

"Humph! That's why your ass don't have a man now. Look at you, with that power suit and power look. Bitch, you ain't at court! Yo' wanna be Johnny Cochran ass gots to loosen up. Tonight, we're gonna let this city see exactly what you're working with. And I ain't talking about no slutty shit . . . well, a little slutty . . . but with class, baby. Now, come on." Gwen took Sacha into the Buckle, a small store in the mall, and led her straight to a bunch of skimpy dresses.

Sacha stared at some of the dresses and started shaking her head. "Uh-uh! I know you don't think you're about to get me into any of that! Ho, you gots to be out of your fucking mind! It's too damn cold to be wearing that type of shit, Gwen!"

"Would you shut the fuck up? It ain't that damn cold, bitch. Look at this. Now tell me this ain't a fly-ass mini hookup," she said as she held up a one-piece Apple Bottoms skirt. It was all black, with the words "Apple Bottoms" going across the middle in gold lettering. "Bitch, if Melyssa can sport this bitch, so can you. If you want to turn some heads tonight, then this is the bad boy to do it in."

"Who said anything about turning some damn heads? All I want to do is go out and have some fun, and I don't need no damn man to do that."

"You see, that's what I'm talking about. Your ass is in denial. Has that square-ass nigga at your firm gotten up the nerve to get at you yet?"

"Who are you talking about? Clifford?"

"Who else could I be talking about, bitch? Stop playing with me!"

"Well, I still catch him peeking at me during meetings and stuff, but actually, I think he's lost interest."

"Good. That nerdy nigga ain't worthy anyway. But back to this. Get this skirt so we can go to Nine West and see if they have some tight pumps to match."

"You're really serious, huh?"

"You damn skippy! Now go try it on so we can see how it looks."

Sacha did as she was told. After putting on the skimpy dress, she couldn't deny it, she looked damn good. She came out of the dressing room and spun around slowly and asked Gwen, "How does it look?"

"Bitch, you already looked in the mirror! You know how good it looks, so I don't have to tell your ass!"

Sacha stood in front of the mirror outside of the dressing room, smiled, and said, "My legs are too thick for this."

"Shut the fuck up, bitch! Your legs are just right for that skirt. Go put your clothes back on so we can get you some pumps."

They both started laughing as Sacha went and changed back into her clothes. She couldn't argue and win with her girl, so she said to hell with it and bought the dress. They went to a few shoe stores and finally decided on a pair of black Prada pumps that matched the dress to a tee. Gwen bought herself a Coogi denim skirt with a matching top, and some colorful pumps by Jimmy Choo.

After getting all of their stuff together, they decided to go to Red Lobster for dinner. As they were being led to their table, Sacha noticed several different guys peeping at them. She knew she was looking tired, and she self-consciously tried to straighten herself out. She stood a little under five-five and weighed between 125 and 130 pounds. She was thick in all the right places.

She had small hips, nice C-cup sized breasts, and an ass to make a grown man cry. But what made her stand out was the exotic look she possessed. She looked as if she had just flown in from the islands somewhere. Her skin tone was bronze-like. She looked as if she stayed in Florida or California somewhere. Her shoulder-length hair completed the island look she possessed. Even dressed in a navy blue pant suit, she still turned heads.

After they were seated, Gwen said, "Look at you, still turning heads wherever we go. I swear, sometimes I hate you, bitch!"

"You the one that got all the men in your life. Shit, how do you know the heads that are turning ain't looking at your hoochie mama hot ass?" They laughed as they gave their orders to the waiter.

After the waiter had left to go get them their salads, Gwen said, "We're going to do the damn thing tonight, bitch. And I swear, you're going to have the club shut the fuck down in that skirt."

"Whatever!"

"I'm serious, bitch. You gon' have every nigga on your ass."

"Whatever!"

Gwen sipped her water and shook her head as she stared at her best friend. Gwen knew she was no slouch when it came to men. Shit, she knew she could have any nigga she wanted for real. She just chose to fuck and go as she pleased. There was only one man who owned her heart, and he was in Heaven, so ain't no need trying to fake it. *It is what it is,* she thought as she continued to smile at her friend.

Gwen was the same height as Sacha, but thinner. She had that ghetto booty to make men's mouths water, but she was short in the breast department. Her little

A-cups constantly frustrated her. She was dying to get a boob job, but was just too scared to go through with it. She knew that if she told Sacha about it, she would laugh her out of the house. But she was definitely eye candy. Her hazel eyes matched her light brown skin to perfection. God wasn't playing when he blessed her with her looks. But with William gone to Heaven, to her it was all moot.

After they finished their meal, Sacha smiled and said, "All right, girl, I'm about to head on home and take a hot bath so I can get ready for this wild night. I hope I don't look like no damn fool in this hoochie out-fit you got me wearing."

"Trust me, bitch. The club and any nigga you want will be yours tonight."

They kissed each other on the cheek and parted ways.

Sacha made it home a little after eight p.m. She took her new clothes to her room and went and ran her bath-water. While the water was running, she checked a few e-mails from some of her clients. Since it was the week-end and she didn't have any court dates next week, she decided to put everything else on hold. She was focused on having a good time tonight. She stripped out of her pant suit, walked into her bathroom, and got into the steaming tub full of hot water. As she relaxed in the water, she smiled and said, "Time to go clubbin'!"

Chapter Three

The parking lot of Club Cancun was packed as Taz and the crew pulled into the parking lot. Keno was driving Taz's Denali, and he had the doors to the truck open as they pulled into the parking lot, followed by Bo-Pete, who was driving his truck, and Bob, who was bringing up the rear. Since Taz's Denali had a vertical door conversion kit, all eyes were on them as they parked.

The line to get inside was crazy long, but that didn't bother Keno as he stepped out of the truck and struck a pose for all of the ladies that were staring at them . . . oh, and for the haters also.

Taz climbed out of his truck, smiled, and said, "Damn, nigga! You love this shit, huh?"

After calmly zipping up his chinchilla, Keno said, "Dog, this town is ours, and it's only right that everyone knows it. Look at all of these window-shopping ass bustas staring at us. Look at the hoes. I'm telling you, my nigga, this is *our* town!"

Bob, Red, Bo-Pete, and Wild Bill stepped next to the truck, and Keno asked them, "Are y'all ready?"

"You know it!" replied Bo-Pete.

"Then do you. You know the drill," Keno said as he fired up the purple haze.

Bo-Pete and Wild Bill walked straight towards the front door and were not bothered by the security as they entered the club.

Bo-Pete smiled at a few ladies as he passed them, and gave a soft nod to a few fellas from around the way. The confidence he possessed showed as he casually strolled into the club. Bo-Pete may be only five-eleven, but he felt like a king every time they went to the club. His chocolate brown skin was smooth as can be, and he knew he looked good. He felt that he made the clothes he wore look good, instead of the other way around. He kept his hair cut low and even all the way around, and sported a neat, well-kept goatee. His muscular frame spoke volumes to the women. They could tell that he always kept himself in tip-top condition.

Wild Bill, Bo-Pete's partner and road dog, was like the complete opposite of Bo-Pete. Bill's hair was extremely long. He kept it permed and combed to the back in a long ponytail. He was a short man, but just as muscular as Bo-Pete. He wore gold-rimmed glasses and if you paid close attention, you could tell that he was damn near blind. But he, too, possessed that confident stroll as he followed Bo-Pete into the club.

Inside of the club, Katrina and Paquita were having their normal conversation about who was doing what to whom, and what other females were wearing and whatnot. They both were regulars at the club, and were well known 'round-the-way girls. In other words, they were "hood rats."

". . . Girl, I'm telling you, I saw Latanya's scandalous ass at the mall earlier, taking everything as if it was free. I mean, she wasn't even trying to be low! She's a bold bitch for real!" Paquita yelled excitedly.

"Shit, you know how that freak bitch get down. I don't know why your ass is shocked," replied Katrina as she straightened her too-tight, too-small miniskirt.

"Ooh, girl! Look who just came into the club!" Paquita said as she slung her micro-braids over her shoulder.

After taking a long look around the club and not noticing anyone of importance, Katrina asked, "Who, bitch? I don't see nobody."

"Over there by the front! It's Bo-Pete and Wild Bill!"

"So? What's so damn special about Bo-Pete and Wild Bill?"

"Girl, whenever you see them come into the club, that can only mean one thing."

"And what's that?"

Smiling broadly, Paquita said, "That means Taz is here!"

"Stop playing! Where he at?"

"Wait, and you'll see. Look, they're checking out the club to make sure that everything is straight for Taz to come in here. You know how he is about his surroundings."

"Nah, I don't know shit about it. But I do know that Taz is one fine-ass nigga, and sooner or later I'm gon' get me some of that dick," Katrina replied confidently.

"Well, bitch, you better get in line, 'cause damn near every bitch in this club has tried to get with him. You know I know my shit. And to my knowledge, ain't no ho in the City been successful. Oooh, ooh! I knew I was right, bitch! Look, there goes Red and Bob too. Watch. You see how Bo-Pete and Wild Bill went to the left of the club and posted up?"

"Yeah, so what?"

"Now Red and Bob are going to look around real quick. Then they're going to go to the right of the club. Then, I'll give it three to five minutes before we see Keno and Taz's fine asses come in here. Taz is going to stand in the entrance and look around. Then, he's going to go to the bar and hold up two fingers, and Winky, the bartender, is going to pour him a double shot of that expensive ass Courvoiser XO—you know, that three hundred a bottle type shit."

"Damn, bitch! How you know so much about Taz?"

"I told you, I know what I'm talkin' about! I've been about fuckin' that nigga since back in the day. I would have had action, too, if I wouldn't have done the goofy and started fucking with that whack-ass nigga Clarence. That's back when Taz was sociable. Ever since he . . . oh, never mind, bitch! What did I tell you? Here he comes now!"

At that moment, Paquita was right. Taz and Keno stood in the entranceway of the club and took a good look around until their eyes locked with Bo-Pete's and Wild Bill's, who were standing to their left. Then they let their eyes roam some more until they locked eyes with Red and Bob, who were posted up on the right side of the club. Then, Taz did exactly what Paquita said he would. He stepped to the bar and held up two fingers. Winky, the bartender, quickly poured Taz a double shot of XO into a brandy snifter and passed it to him. Taz sipped his drink and gave Winky a slight nod of his head.

Keno unzipped his chinchilla and smiled at a few ladies who were standing close to them.

Taz noticed how everybody was taking peeks their way, and he shook his head. *These broke mothafuckas are always hating. Look at all these soft-ass niggas! I swear, I don't know why I keep coming to this lame-ass spot,* he said to himself as he took another sip of his drink.

As if reading Taz's mind, Keno said, "Don't trip, my nigga. This may not be your scene, but for us, it is what it is. You straight? 'cause I'm about to do me."

"Yeah, I'm good. Go on, 'Floss King'! Do you!"

Keno smiled as he took a quick look at his Presidential Rolex and said, "Yep, it's about that time."

As if they had been standing right by Taz and Keno and heard their conversation, Bo-Pete and Wild Bill went to the back bar and got themselves a drink, and Red and Bob had stopped a waitress and had her bring them both some Rémy Martin.

Bob's bald head was sweaty, so he wiped himself with a napkin. His decision to wear all black gave him a sinister look. His dark clothing and dark-skinned complexion made a few females around them a little nervous. But what really made Bob stand out was the knot on his forehead. It stood out about four inches and was an oval shape. People in the know knew never to play with Bob about his knot. But Taz and the crew clowned him about it all of the time. He was the same height as Bo-Pete, Taz, and Keno, but he was the wildest one out of the crew. Once that liquor got into him, he was going to start acting up. Red knew this, so he said, "Don't get too faded tonight, dog. I really don't feel like carrying your ass outta here."

"What's wrong, big boy? All those muscles and you worried about picking up your homeboy?"

"It ain't that, fool. That shit's embarrassing. Just don't over fucking do it," said Red as he lit up a Black & Mild cigar.

Red was the biggest in the crew. He stood between six-two and six-three, and he was the only light-skinned member. He kept his hair long and braided in tight French braids going towards the back of his head. To say he was muscular like Taz, Bo-Pete, and the rest of the crew would be an understatement. He was fucking huge! He could easily pass for Mr. Universe or some shit. He had muscles popping out of everywhere. His laid-back demeanor shocked those who got to know him, because you would swear he was one of those cocky, conceited niggas. Actually, he was the coolest member of the crew . . . except when he became angry. Then, watch out, 'cause all hell would break loose when that happened.

Back by the front bar, Taz stood and watched as Keno did his thing on the dance floor with a cute little female.

Keno, at five-eleven, was Taz's heart. No one knew Taz better, and Taz loved him like a brother. But for the life of him, Taz just couldn't figure out why Keno loved to floss so damn much. Yeah, it was cool sometimes, but every time they came out to play, Keno had to make sure that he shined the most. Though they were both the same height, they were completely different from each other. Where Taz was solid and thick, Keno was just as muscular but had a thinner lower body. Keno's hair was long and kept in braids like Red's, whereas Taz's hair was longer and kept in individual plaits.

What made Taz stand out the most were his eyes. His dark brown eyes could show you so much love, but at the snap of a finger they could show you much hate. You could read his every expression by looking into his eyes.

Keno's outgoing personality was irritating at times to Taz, but he loved him all the same. He chalked it up to Keno being the yin to his yang. Taz never let anyone too close, especially women. Keno, on the other hand, fell in love damn near every other day, and was very open about things, especially his personal life. That was definitely a no-no in Taz's book, and he had to constantly stay on Keno's ass about certain things. Taz was not going for any of that shit when it came to his personal life.

Katrina and Paquita finally built up enough nerve to approach Taz.

Taz smiled as they slowly came toward him. *I know these two crazy-ass hoes don't think they got a shot at the title! This is about to be some funny shit,* he told himself.

Once they were standing in front of him, Paquita took charge. "What's up, Taz? How ya been, baby?"

"Laid back. You know how I get down, 'Quita. What's up with you?"

"The same ol', same ol'. Just trying to make it out here in this cold, cold world."

"Is that right? What's up, Katrina? What, the cat got your tongue tonight?"

"Uh-uh. But you can have it if you want it, Taz."

Smiling, Taz asked, "Can I have *everything* I want?"

Stepping back slightly so that Taz could take a good look at her voluptuous figure, Katrina smiled and said, "It's yours for the taking, baby. You name it, you got it, Taz!"

He was sipping his drink as she said this, and he damn near spit a mouthful of his expensive cognac all over her. He caught himself and said, "I'll have to take a rain check on you this time, boo. You know I'm saving myself for that special lady."

"That's fucked up, Taz! Why you trying to clown a sista? You know I've been wanting to get with your fine ass!" whined Katrina.

With a shrug of his shoulders, Taz smiled and said, "Baby, I guess it just ain't meant to be. Look, let me buy you two a drink or somethin', huh?"

"That's cool, but can you do me a favor, Taz, please?"

Sighing, he asked, "What is it, 'Quita?"

With a bright smile on her face, Paquita asked him, "Can you smile for me, Daddy?"

That got a smile out of him because he knew what she wanted to see. So, he smiled brightly and let her get a good look at the diamonds in his grille.

"Damn, baby! You the shit and you know it, huh?"

"Nah, 'Quita, I'm just good ol' Taz, baby girl. Look, y'all go on and tell Winky to give y'all whatever y'all want. And make sure you keep this 'tiger' out of trouble, 'Quita," he said, referring to Katrina.

"I will, Taz. Come on, girl. Let's go get our drink on."

As they were walking away, Katrina put an extra swish into her big hips, and Taz started shaking his head and laughing at the same time. He turned around to check and see what his partners were getting into and noticed the baddest female that he'd seen in a very long time. I mean, just by looking at her, he felt himself stir down below. *Who the fuck is that?* he asked himself as he watched the sexy female enter the club with another female. *Damn, she's sexy as hell!* he thought as he sipped his drink and continued to stare at her.

As Sacha and Gwen entered the club, Sacha could actually feel all of the eyes on her. *Oh, my God! Why did I let this girl talk me into wearing this hoochie outfit? I feel damn near naked!* she thought to herself as they found a table by the back bar. After they sat down, a waitress came to their table and asked if they wanted anything to drink. They both ordered apple martinis. While the waitress went to get them their drinks, they both took a look around the club.

Sacha could see a bunch of the fake wannabe ballers flossing around the club and acting like they owned the place. She also saw a few good-looking men here and there. As her eyes continued to scan the club, they stopped when they came to Taz. *Damn! Who's that fine-ass specimen of a man?* she asked herself as she took a real good look at Taz and what he was wearing. *Hmmm. A thug with taste, huh? Gots to be. He's wearing that chinchilla like it was made especially for him. Nice jewelry, expensive too. Not too much, but just enough. I like them braids too. Damn, that nigga is sexy!* she thought to herself as she turned back to face Gwen.

Gwen, who had followed her friend's eyes and saw the same thing that she had seen, said, "That is one bad man, bitch! You peep that chinchilla he has on?"

"Umm-hmm! He's definitely at the top of his game, ho. Probably the biggest dope dealer in the city. I'll probably be representing his ass in federal court one day." They both started laughing as the waitress came and set their drinks on the table.

While the ladies were sipping their drinks, Taz continued to watch them. *I gots to meet that broad. Ain't no way in hell I can let her leave this spot without me gettin' at her. But how? I don't get down like that. Shit! Bitches get at Taz. Taz don't get at bitches.* "Fuck it!" he said as he turned back towards the bar.

Someone came up behind him, tapped him lightly on his shoulder, and said, "Excuse me, Taz. Can I holla at ya for a sec?"

Taz turned around and faced a tall, brown-skinned brother with a few muscles showing under his white tee. "What up, dog? Do I know you?"

"Not personally, but you probably know my big brother, KK."

"Yeah, I remember him. Is he still on lock?"

"Yeah, he got twenty in the feds. I be looking out for him, though."

"That's straight. So, what's up?"

"Man, Taz, a nigga was trying to see how he could be down."

With a confused expression on his face, Taz asked, "Down with what, gee?"

"You know, down with you. I'm trying to eat big like you and your crew. I ain't no sucka nigga, and I'm vertical all the way, baby, straight up and down. I got a few traps around the way, and I'm moving shit. I just don't have no real plug, you know what I'm saying?"

"Hold the fuck up, youngsta! Are you talkin' 'bout some dope?"

"Yeah. Everyone knows you got the town on lock. I just want to be down."

Taz set his drink on the bar and said, "Check this, you li'l mark, ass nigga! I don't fuck with dope boys, nor do I fuck with dope, period! So, whoever told you that punk shit, you really need to check they ass, 'cause if you ever come near me again talking about some dope, I'm going to beat the fuck outta your punk ass! Do...you...under...stand...me...D...Boy?" Taz said as he stabbed his index finger into the youngster's chest with each syllable to make his point.

The youngster was so shocked that he couldn't speak; he just turned and went to where his homeboys were seated. As soon as he sat down at his table, one of his homies asked him, "So, is he going to hook you up or what?"

"Yeah, he told me to get with him in a few weeks," lied the youngster. "But fuck that shit! We gots to eat. I ain't trying to be waiting on that nigga."

"But, nigga, I thought you said he has the town on lock," said his homey.

"So what? He ain't the only nigga in this town eating. Change the fuckin' subject, nigga."

Taz was so irritated now that his mood was border-line volatile. He turned and waved for Keno.

Keno saw him and quickly walked toward him. "What up, gee? You straight?"

"Nah, I'm ready to bounce."

"What? Dog, it's just starting to get crackin' in this bitch! Don't do me like that, baby!"

"I'm out. Tell them niggas that you'll be back. I want you to drop me off at the pad. I'm about to go out to Moore and lay it down for a minute. Since I'm going to spend the day with Tazneema tomorrow, I might as well be out that way."

"Nigga, go on with that shit! You want some ass, so you're going to your li'l chickie's pad. That's fucked up, dog, but I ain't trippin'. Let's roll so I can hurry up and get back to doing me."

After letting the others know that they were leaving, Taz took one last glance at the cutie in the Apple Bottoms outfit, shook his head sadly, and left. *If it's meant to be, I'll see her again,* he told himself as he followed Keno out of the club.

Keno drove like a madman all of the way out to Taz's home. Once he pulled into the driveway, he jumped out of Taz's truck and said, "I'm out, my nigga. I'll holla at you sometime tomorrow."

"That's straight," said Taz as he watched Keno jump into his Range Rover and pull out of his driveway. Taz then got into the driver's seat of his truck and slowly pulled out of his driveway. He grabbed his cell and made a call. As soon as the other line was answered, he said, "What's up, sexy? I'm on my way."

"Whatever, Taz. You know you don't have to call me every time you come out here. I was sleeping soundly."

"Sorry about that, baby. What, you don't want to see me tonight?"

"Stop being silly. I'm always ready to see you, baby. Now, hurry up," she said before hanging up the phone.

Twenty minutes later, Taz pulled into the driveway of a modest home on the southeast side of Oklahoma City. He jumped out of his truck and walked straight into the house. He knew Tari would have left the door unlocked for him as she always did. He walked through the house and made sure that there wasn't anyone lurking around.

"Taz, would you bring your ass in here! You know damn well there isn't anyone else in this house!" yelled Tari from the back bedroom.

He smiled as he walked into the bedroom. Tari was sitting at the edge of her bed, taking off her thong. "You know how I get down, Tari. You never know. One day you might decide to change the rules to the game."

Tari pulled her long blond hair into a ponytail and said, "Come get some of your pussy, Daddy." She sat back on her bed, opened her long legs, and said, "I'd never do anything to put you in harm's way, Taz. I'm here for you whenever you want me, baby. You know that."

As he walked slowly towards the bed, he said, "Yeah, I know, but I'll never change my ways, so stop trying to get me to, and continue to play your part."

"My part? That's all I'm doing, Taz? Playing a part?"

With his eyes softening slightly, he said, "You know what I mean, Tari. Everybody has a role to play in my life." He got on the bed with her.

"And what's my particular role, Mr. Taz?"

"You are my blue-eyed devil, and your role is to always be here to satisfy me," he said as he grabbed her hands to stop her from swinging at him. "I'm just clowning, baby. Come here."

Tari slid into his embrace and they shared a brief kiss. She pulled out of his embrace and said, "M—m—m! I kinda like playing this role, Daddy." She then slid down towards his manhood and put it into her mouth.

Taz smiled and said, "I do too, baby!"

Chapter Four

The next morning, Tari woke Taz and gave him break-fast in bed. Taz opened his eyes and said, "Damn, Tari! Why you always got to wake a nigga up so damn early?"

"Stop using that word, Taz! You know I hate that shit. Now, sit up so you can eat your breakfast. And to answer your question, you know I have to be at work early, and I'm not about to leave you without making sure that I've taken the very best care of you. Now eat!" After setting everything in front of him, she turned and went into the bathroom to finish getting ready for her shift at the hospital.

Taz smiled as he began eating his breakfast of pan-cakes, bacon, and orange juice. *For a white girl, Tari could cook her ass off*, he thought as he ate his food.

Tari came out of the bathroom fully dressed in her nurse's uniform. She was tall—almost six feet bare-footed—and had a body that made sisters hate. She had curves in all the right places, as well as an ass that was just too damn phat. Her bright blue eyes and her sweet personality made Taz feel comfortable whenever he came over to her place. She was his escape from everyone. Whenever he felt the need to release some sexual energy, or whenever he felt the need to talk, her home was where he went. Tari was the only person who knew his personal dreams and his darkest nightmares. She was his confidante, lover, and friend all rolled into one beautiful package. Even though he knew that she wanted more out of their relationship, she accepted the fact that Taz just wasn't the type to ever love a woman the way she wanted to be loved.

"So, what are your plans for the day, lover boy?" Tari asked as she took the tray away from him and set it on the floor next to the bed.

"I'm going to go spend some time with Tazneema. It's been too long since we chilled together."

"That's good, but why do you do that to that darling little girl? You know she cherishes the ground you walk on, Taz."

"Come on with that shit, Tee! You know how I get down. Plus, she ain't no damn darling li'l girl. She's a grown-ass woman. You must have forgotten that she's now a freshman in college."

"I know how old she is, silly. You must have forgotten that she loves you more than anything in this world. Anyway, what do you have planned for her today?"

"Man, I don't know. I might take her to the mall and let her do her thing. After that, maybe lunch or some shit . . . whatever she wants to get into."

"Does she know that you're coming to spend the day with her?"

"Nope. I was going to, like, surprise her. Tari shook her head from side to side, and he asked, "What, you think I should call her and let her know I'm coming out there?"

"That would be wise. What if she already has plans, Taz? You never know what a young college student might have planned on a Saturday afternoon. I swear, sometimes you amaze me with your Neanderthal way of thinking!"

"My Neander-*what*? Gon' with that shit, Tee! I thought it would be cool if I popped up on her and surprised her, that's all."

Shaking her head no, Tari said, "No, you didn't. You think you're slick. You planned on popping up on her in hopes of catching her off guard. That way you might catch her doing something. Call her, Taz." Tari grabbed the cordless phone and placed it into his hands, then bent over and grabbed the tray that had held Taz's breakfast. Taz slapped her on her butt and smiled when she yelled, "Ouch!"

While Tari was in the kitchen, cleaning up, Taz did as he was told and gave Tazneema a call. She answered the phone on the second ring. "Hello?"

"What's up, baby girl? You straight?" he asked.

"Taz! I'm fine. What's up with you?"

"Just chillin'. How's the school thing coming along?"

"It's cool. I'm getting ready for the holidays. Mama-Mama wants me to come spend Christmas break with her, but I'd really rather go to Houston and spend the holidays with my roommate and her family. Do you think you could talk to Mama-Mama for me, Taz?"

"I don't know. You know how Mama-Mama is when she has her mind made up."

"But, Taz, it's going to be off the chain in Houston over the holidays. Ple—e—ease?"

"I'll see what I can do, but I ain't making no promises."

"Okay, just try real hard for me, okay?"

Laughing, he said, "Whatever, girl! But look, I was thinking about coming out that way and spending a li'l time with you today. Is that cool, or do you have plans already?"

"I was going to go to the mall with my roommate and finish up my Christmas shopping."

"Who is this damn roommate?"

"Her name is Lyla, and she's real cool, Taz."

"All right, this is what we'll do. I'm about to get up and get dressed. I should be out there in about thirty minutes. We'll go shopping and have some lunch. Cool?"

"That's cool, but make it an hour. We just got up about ten minutes ago. We kinda had a late night last night."

"Stop! I really don't need to be hearing any of that, especially if you plan on spending the holiday in H-Town."

"Oops! My bad! See you in an hour or so. Bye!" she said and quickly hung up the phone.

Taz started laughing as he hung up the phone.

Tari came back into the bedroom and asked, "What's so funny, baby?"

"That girl is something else. Now she wants to go spend the holiday in Houston with her roommate."

"What's wrong with that?"

"I don't have a problem with it, but I don't think Mama-Mama is going to go for it. 'Neema wants me to try to convince Mama-Mama to let her go."

"Mama-Mama will let her go if you okay it. You know she's a big old softy when it comes to you."

"Yeah, I know, but I'm wondering whether I should okay it or not."

"Why?"

"Do you really think it'll be wise to let 'Neema go running off to Houston, doing only God knows what?"

"Taz, Tazneema is eighteen years old. Technically, she doesn't need consent from you *or* Mama-Mama. She's legal now."

"Don't remind me! I feel old enough as it is!"

Tari smiled and said, "Ooh, my baby is feeling old now? You didn't act like an old man last night—or should I say this morning."

"I never feel old when I'm chillin' with you, baby. Come here," he said as he grabbed her and they shared a kiss.

After a minute or so, Tari pulled from his embrace and said, "Now, let me go. I have to go to work. Will I be blessed with your presence later on?"

"Ain't no tellin'. Don't wait up, though. I'll have to check and see what the boys are getting into later on. I'll hit you up when I know something."

"Okay. Bye, baby!" she said after giving him another quick kiss.

After Tari left, Taz got up and went into the guest room and grabbed some clothes out of the closet. He always kept a few outfits at Tari's. After taking a long hot shower, he got dressed and made himself a cup of coffee. As he sipped his coffee, he grabbed the phone and called Keno. "What up, fool? What you gettin' into today?" he asked when Keno answered the phone.

"Ain't shit. I just got up, nigga. I don't know what the fuck I'm doing later, but right now I'm about to go check on the house in the North Highlands."

"Which one?"

"The one on 83rd Street. The plumbing is tripping again. I'm about to call Al and have him meet me over there."

"What's up with the boys?"

"Ain't no tellin'. Bob got bent and started trippin' last night. Red had to carry that nigga up outta the club. Wild Bill came up with a bad bitch, so most likely he's still laid up with her. Bo-Pete told me that he was going out to the south side to check on the houses over that way. What's up with you? You still going out to Norman?"

"Yeah, I'm about to bounce that way in a minute. Make sure you get at everybody and let them know to keep them phones open. Won may hit us at any given time."

"Don't trip. They know already. Hit me when you're through out that way."

"For sho'. Out!"

"Out!" Keno said and hung up.

Taz grabbed his keys and left the house. During the short drive out to the city of Norman, he was thinking about Tazneema. It seemed as if she was starting to get a little wild. He hoped and prayed that he would be able to calm her ass down. He knew that he had spoiled her too much, but hell, he really didn't have a choice. *Mama-Mama is just as much to blame as I am,* he thought to himself as he pulled in front of her apartment building. Eighteen years old, and she refused to live in the dorm building with the rest of the freshman females that attended the University of Oklahoma. Tazneema had to have her own apartment. Taz smiled as he remembered her begging him and Mama-Mama to let her move in with her roommate. Once Mama-Mama gave in, she knew Taz wouldn't object, and now look at her, wanting to spend the holiday out of town. *Ain't no way Mama-Mama is gon' go for that*, he thought as he climbed out of his truck.

When he made it to the front door, he could hear the music blasting from the other side. He shook his head and began to knock on the door. After about three minutes of waiting, he started banging on the door loudly. Finally, after another two minutes, a pretty little white girl opened the door and said, "Hi! You must be Taz. I'm Lyla. Please, come in. I'm sorry we didn't hear you. I was in the back room, and Tee is still in the shower."

Taz followed her inside and gave the living room a quick once-over. The apartment was neat and orderly. That made him feel a little bit better as he sat down on the sofa. He smiled at Lyla and asked, "So, how's school going for you two?"

"It's cool, but kinda boring because we have to go through the freshman thing and all . . . you know, silly pranks and whatnot."

Lyla was a small female but built nicely. She had firm breasts, and Taz could tell that she was trying her best to make him notice them. She sat at the dining room table and smiled seductively towards him as she talked. Her long brown hair fell past her shoulders, and he couldn't help but to think about Tari. He shook the thought off and asked, "Are you sure your parents won't mind having another mouth to feed over the holidays?"

"Mommy and Daddy both adore Tazneema. They met when we first moved in here. As a matter of fact, it was Mommy's idea to invite her. You are going to let her come, aren't you?"

"That's up to Mama-Mama. We'll have to wait and see. You better go on and get dressed. You're joining us, right?"

"Yeah, I'm ready, see?" she said as she turned around in her short little outfit. She was wearing a tiny pair of Baby Phat shorts, with a cut-off Baby Phat T-shirt showing off her nice abs. She was sockless in a pair of DKNY tennis shoes. Her slim legs looked very inviting to Taz. She noticed that he was staring at her legs and asked, "Taz, do you mind if we went out on a date?"

Taz smiled calmly and said, "A what? Lyla, baby, when you're able to buy liquor, holla at your boy. Until then, baby girl, look at me as your older brother."

"That sucks. You know I—"

"Girl, I know you ain't in here trying to get your mack on!" said Tazneema as she came into the room to give Taz a hug and a kiss on his cheek.

"Come on, Tee-Tee! You know how much I'm digging your brother."

Tazneema and Taz shared a smile with each other, and then Tazneema said, "Girl, stop! Taz is not about to waste his time on a li'l girl."

"Taz, do I look like a li'l girl to you?" Lyla asked as she did her li'l twirl for him again.

Once again, Taz took notice of her sexy legs and said, "Baby girl, you are tempting, but I have to stand on my word. So, get at me in, like, three more years and you just might have a shot."

Pouting slightly, Lyla said, "Well, hell! That's a bummer!"

They all laughed as the girls went and grabbed their purses.

Taz had a headache as he sat down outside one of the dressing rooms in the Gap store. It felt as if they had been in every store in the damn mall. He gave Tazneema and Lyla his Black Card, and those two little freshmen went crazy shopping. Shoes, shoes, and more shoes were their first purchases, and after that, they then started looking for clothes to match the shoes. He had made so many trips back to his truck, putting up their stuff, that he'd lost count. It was now close to noon and they hadn't even shown the least bit of slowing down.

He pulled out his cell and called Tari at work. As soon as she answered her cell, he said, "Help! These girls are killing me!"

Laughing, Tari said, "Aw-w-w! Poor baby! Where are you all at?"

"We're at the mall. These two crazy-ass girls are trying to buy everything in every fuckin' store! Please, talk to me and tell me something that will stop me from losing my mind!"

"Well, I wish I could, but as you well know, I'm currently at work right now, and I'm kinda busy. So, you're going to have to deal with this one solo, buddy, 'cause, I gots to go. Bye-e-e-e, boo!" she said and hung up the phone.

"Ain't that a bitch!" Taz said to himself as Lyla and Tazneema both came out of the dressing room wearing matching Gap jeans and tops.

"Tell me, Taz. Do you like how I look in these jeans?" asked Lyla as she did her twirl for him, showing her nice little booty.

Taz nodded his head and said, "You straight. But look, ladies. I'm getting tired of all of this shopping. Can we take a break and go have some lunch somewhere, please?"

They both started laughing. "Alright, we can go get some Leo's Barbeque," said Tazneema.

"What? I ain't trying to go way back down to the City to get no damn Leo's!" said Taz.

"Taz, there's a Leo's out here in Norman. It's right down the street from here. See, we can go get something to eat, then come back here so I can finish doing my Christmas shopping."

"You mean to tell me that you're not finished yet?!"

Laughing, Tazneema said, "Uh-uh. I've gotten my stuff out of the way. Now I have to get gifts for you, Mama-Mama, and Lyla's parents. Come on, Taz. You said you wanted to spend the day with me."

He smiled and said, "Yeah, I did. I stuck my foot in my mouth this time, didn't I?"

Smiling brightly, Tazneema said, "Yep, you sure did!" She turned and went back into the dressing room to change back into her clothes.

Lyla, on the other hand, stayed and smiled at Taz with a sexy look on her face. "Taz, you know I've learned a lot of things since I've been in college."

Not really paying attention to the look in her eyes, Taz asked, "Yeah, like what?"

She stepped up to him and whispered into his ear, "Like how to please an older man."

Taz stepped back, smiled, and said, "Won't you ever give up?"

Smiling brightly, she said, "Not until I've gotten what I want. And, Taz, I *will* get what I want, sooner or later." She shook her small hips seductively as she, too, went back into the dressing room to change.

Taz shook his head and wondered if Tazneema was as horny as her roommate. *God, I hope she ain't!* he thought to himself as he sat back in the chair.

Chapter Five

What a relaxing weekend, thought Sacha as she walked into the office with a bright smile on her face. She spoke to a few other attorneys as she was headed towards her office. Just as she made it to her door, Clifford, another attorney who worked for Johnson & Whitney, stopped her. "How are you doing this morning, Sacha?" he asked with a smile on his face.

Damn! I almost made it! Sacha thought to herself as she turned around, smiled, and said, "Good morning, Cliff. I'm just fine. How about yourself?"

"I'm good. I heard the news about you becoming a partner soon. I guess congratulations are in order."

"Not yet, but hopefully soon," she said as she entered her office, hoping that he wouldn't follow her.

Her hopes were in vain. Clifford followed her into her office, closed her door, and said rather confidently, "Don't you think it's way past time for us to go out on a date, Sacha?"

"Was that a question or a statement, Cliff?"

Smiling, he said, "Both. I know you can tell that I'm interested. Won't you give a hardworking brother a chance?"

Sacha sat down behind her desk and once again took inventory of Clifford Nelson. He was a handsome man with a nice body. He stood a little over six feet and had very broad shoulders. He wasn't muscular like she liked her men, but he wasn't skinny either. He kept his hair cut low, nice and neat. Even though she liked nice trimmed goatees, his clean-shaven face was attractive.

Sacha had been wondering how long it was going to take for him to finally ask her out on a date. He had been eyeing her for some time now. He never made a suggestive comment toward her in the three years he'd been with the firm. Now that he had, she was unsure whether she wanted to go out with him. She thought about what Gwen had said to her repeatedly over the weekend, and decided to see if Cliff really wanted to play. God only knows how long it had been since she'd been on a date. She smiled and asked, "So, you want a chance, brother?"

"Definitely!"

"Okay, when and where?"

"You choose, because I want it to be the perfect date, and I don't want to stick my foot in my mouth and make a bad decision."

"Taking the safe way out, huh?"

"I feel it's best to be safe than sorry . . . for now. So, it's all up to you, lovely lady."

"What if I told you that I like for the man I date to have total control?"

Laughing, he said, "I wouldn't believe you. Don't forget, I've seen some of your work in the courtroom, Ms. Carbajal. There's no weakness in you."

"Why, thank you! But, just because I like my dates to have control doesn't mean I'm a weak woman. I like surprises, Cliff, so if you want to take me out for a pleasurable evening, you're going to have to make all of the decisions."

"Okay, that's fine, but don't say that I didn't give you the opportunity to choose."

"I won't."

"Good. Is Friday good for you?"

"Sure. What time?"

"Say about seven. That should give you enough time to unwind after work."

"Where are we going?" she asked with a smile on her face.

With a boyish grin, he said, "You said you like surprises, right?"

"Yes."

"So, you'll see Friday evening at seven. Have a nice day, Ms. Carbajal!" he said and turned and left her office.

Sacha started laughing as she watched Clifford's nice ass as he walked out of her office. "Not bad, Cliff . . . not bad at all!" she said aloud as she turned on her PC on her desk.

Clifford left Sacha's office feeling as if he'd just hit the lottery. *Yes! I knew my plan of patience would work. Sacha's too damn fine for me to have come at her any other way. Now all I have to do is impress the hell out of her fine ass, and she'll be mine,* he thought to himself as he walked confidently to his office.

Friday came faster than Clifford expected it to. He was sitting down in his den, planning the finishing touches for his date with Sacha. It was ten after six, and he was already dressed and ready for the evening. He was wearing a pair of beige Dockers, a dark brown Lacoste shirt, and low-cut Polo boots.

He told Sacha to dress casually but comfortably for their evening together. He was going to take her out to dinner in Bricktown at his favorite Italian restaurant, and afterwards he was going to take her to the Comedy Store for their late show. And, if everything went his way, they would have a pretty nice evening.

Even though he knew he wanted Sacha in his bed in the worst way, he knew that he would have to continue to be patient. Everything would happen in due time. First, he had to show her that he was everything she was looking for in a man: intelligent, secure financially, mature, and most of all, successful. He figured that was the type of man she was looking for. Not only was he sure of it, he was positive. She was about to be made a partner in one of Oklahoma City's highly successful law firms. She wouldn't settle for just any man, so he had to be on top of his game. He wasn't worried about losing his patience waiting for her to come around. He had plenty of women on his line to bide his time with while he was courting Sacha.

Thinking about that made him smile as he grabbed his cordless phone and made a quick call before he left to go pick her up. After a few rings the other line was answered. "Hello, Cory?" he asked.

"Hey, what's up, Cliff?"

"Nothing much. What's up with you?"

"Just relaxing a little, you know, sipping on a little Absolut Peach."

"Yeah? What are you going to be doing later on?"

"It depends on how much of this Absolut I consume."

Laughing, he said, "Well, if you're still able to function later, say around midnight, I'd love for you to come by and keep me company."

"Ummm, that sounds interesting. Would I be staying the night, or will I have to make a late-night departure?"

"You know I'd never forgive myself if I let you leave me too early."

"Whatever! You need to go on with that shit, playboy! You must have forgotten the countless times you had me get the fuck out after you've handled your business. But, since I don't have anything else planned for the night, I might as well see what kind of mood you're going to be in later on."

"What do you mean by that?"

"Come on, Cliff. You and I both know how you are. If you're in a freaky mood, I'll get broken off real proper like. If you're just horny, I'll get the kitty licked quickly and ran up in even faster."

Her bluntness cracked him up. He was laughing so hard that he damn near dropped the phone. After regaining his composure, he said, "Since you put it like that, I want to assure you that I'm going to be in that freak mode that you seem to desire. Is that cool with you?"

"Definitely, playboy! I'll see you later. Give me a call when you're ready for me."

"Most definitely, sexy. Bye!"

"See ya, playboy!" Cory said and hung up.

With a bright smile on his face, Clifford got up from his sofa, grabbed his wallet and keys, and left to go pick up his date for the evening.

As Clifford pulled into Sacha's driveway, he was impressed. She lived way out on the far north side of Oklahoma City, in a neighborhood called Camelot. Most of the homes were recently built, and the price range was close to three to four hundred thousand. *Yeah, she's doing damn good as far as ends are concerned,* he thought as he got out of his CLS 500 Mercedes.

He strolled confidently to her front door and rang her doorbell. He had already been shocked by her beauty from their first meeting, but when she opened the door, it was as if he had just met her for the first time. She was absolutely gorgeous! She was dressed as he requested, casually and comfortably. She made a simple outfit look as if it was made for Tyra Banks or something. She had on a pair of low-rise Apple Bottoms jeans and a black turtleneck wool sweater. Everything fit her so snugly that it seemed as if he could see her entire body. Her sexy shape made him feel a few twitches down below. He smiled and said, "Hello, Sacha! Are you ready for a very memorable evening?"

She returned his smile and said, "Most definitely, Cliff. Let me grab my purse and I'll be right with you."

She left him standing at her front door, which he thought was rude, but he didn't say anything as he waited for her to return. She came back within a few minutes and followed him outside to his car.

Clifford walked her to the passenger's side of the car and opened the door for her. Once she was inside of the car, he closed the door and got in on the other side. *Hmm! He definitely gets points for being a gentleman,* she thought to herself as she watched him get in the car. "So, where are we dining this evening?"

"I hope you like Italian food, because we're about to have one of the best Italian meals ever made in the City."

"Ummm, you must have read my mind. I was hoping you liked Italian food. That's one of my favorites. You still haven't told me where we're going, though."

"Ravio's out in Bricktown. Have you ever been there before?"

"No, I haven't, but they've received some nice reviews in the paper. I heard their veal is divine. And believe me, I love me some veal."

Love me some veal? Damn! She sounds as if she's straight from the eastside or some shit, he thought to himself. To her, he said, "That's great. I guess I'm starting off on the right foot, then, huh?"

Smiling, she said, "Yes, Cliff, you most definitely are."

After dinner, Clifford took Sacha to the Comedy Store, and they both enjoyed the up-and-coming comedians.

Now that their evening was coming to a close, Clifford realized just how lucky he was. Sacha was not only sexy as hell, but the intelligence she possessed was almost astonishing to him. Earlier, during their meal, they had several discussions on everything, from the war over in Iraq to the terrible state New Orleans was in after Hurricane Katrina. Sacha seemed so compassionate towards the hurricane victims that it was touching. She made him feel guilty for not donating more than he had already. She made him feel good all over, and he couldn't wait for the day when they would become intimate. His loins were actually burning for her at that very moment. *Hold on, big boy! Hold on!* he told himself as he pulled into her driveway. "Well, here we are. I hope you enjoyed this evening as much as I did, Sacha," Clifford said as he turned towards her.

Smiling sincerely, she said, "I really did, Cliff. The meal was excellent, and those comedians almost made me pee on myself, they were so funny! Thank you for a wonderful evening."

"I hope that this was the first of many wonderful evenings that we'll be able to share with each other, Sacha. I really want to get to know you better."

Smiling, she said, "I don't think that will be a problem, Cliff. Let's take it one day at a time and see where it leads us, okay?"

With a bright smile on his face, Clifford said, "That's fine with me."

Sacha leaned over and gave him a kiss on his cheek and said, "Give me a call tomorrow if you're not too busy. Maybe we can get into something."

"That sounds like a plan, then."

"Okay, bye! I'll talk to you tomorrow," she said and slid out of his car.

Clifford watched her as she walked towards her front door, and shook his head from side to side as he stared at her sexy walk. *She did those Apple Bottoms jeans proud with a body like that,* he thought as he watched her disappear into her home.

Once she closed her door, he started his car and pulled out of her driveway. As soon as he was out of Sacha's neighborhood, he grabbed his cell and quickly dialed Cory's number. When Cory answered, he said, "I'm on my way home now, babe. How long will it take for you to get there?"

"I'll be there in about twenty minutes. Is that cool, playboy?"

After a quick glance at his watch, he said, "Yeah, I guess that's cool. But hurry up, okay?"

Laughing loudly, Cory said, "Damn, playboy! Are you that horny tonight?"

"You better believe it! So hurry up, 'cause I promise you're going to love every bit of what I'm going to do to you. You wanted freaky-freaky, and that's exactly what I plan on giving you."

"Bye, playboy! 'cause I'm walking out of the door right now!" she said and hung up the phone.

Chapter Six

Taz was pulling out of Tari's driveway when his cell rang. He flipped it open and saw that there was a picture of Michael Jordan slam-dunking the ball over Patrick Ewing of the New York Knicks. Taz smiled as he closed his cell because he knew it was on. That was Won's signal for them to get ready. Taz called Keno and told him to have everyone meet him at his place within the next thirty minutes. After he was finished talking with Keno, he called Tari at work and said, "Baby, I'm about to be out for a minute. I'm going to need you to make sure everything is straight at the house for me."

"No problem, Taz. Is there anything else?"

"Nah. Just feed the dogs and let them loose so they can roam around while I'm gone."

"How long this time?"

"Ain't no telling, so make sure you keep a line open just in case I need to holla."

"Don't I always? Bye, Mister! Oh, and Taz."

"What up?"

"Be careful."

"All the time, baby," he said and closed his cell phone. Whenever he went out of town, he always told Tari. She was the only person other than the crew that knew what he did for a living. She would make sure that his beloved Dobermans would be fed and taken care of while he was away. Even though he never expected to be gone longer than forty-eight hours, he never left the state without having her check on everything while he was gone. The trust and love he had for her was just as strong as the love he had for his homeboys—unbreakable.

Everything about Taz and the crew was timing. They were all disciplined in a military-type fashion. When it came to their missions, they remained prepared at all times.

Taz smiled as he pulled into his driveway and saw everyone there waiting for him. He jumped out of his truck and said, "Time to go to work, boys." They followed him as he entered his home. He led them to his den, and they watched as he grabbed his laptop computer and punched in several keys.

After about three minutes, he said, "Alright, it's like this. Keno and I are bouncing outta DFW. Bo-Pete and Bill, y'all are out of here this time, so Red, you and Bob gots Tulsa. All three of our flights are to arrive at Atlanta's Hartsfield Airport within twenty minutes of each other. Catch a cab to the Sheraton off of Peach near downtown. As usual, the rooms will already be reserved, so give them your Barney, and everything should be good. Once me and Keno get in, I'll hit the front desk and check to make sure that y'all are in. Then, I'll leave a message for y'all to hit me up in my room. Once we all hook up, we'll then hook up with Won. Any questions?"

"Yeah. How do that fool Won be knowing what Barney we're going to be using?" asked Bob.

"He's made all of the arrangements, Bob. He's the one who takes care of getting us the fake IDs and shit. If it wasn't for him, we wouldn't have any Barneys. We'd be using our real hookups. Anyway, there will be a package left for me at the front desk when we check in. Knowing Won, that package most likely will have our instructions. So, it is what it is, gentlemen. Time to get paid. Let's do it." Taz stood and watched as everyone except Keno left his home. He checked a few more things on his laptop, turned it off, and said, "Since we have to make the ride out to Dallas this time, you're driving."

"That's cool, but you're driving back," Keno said as he followed Taz out of his home.

Once they were inside of Keno's Range Rover, Taz asked, "Do you have everything?"

"I repack my bag as soon as we make it back, dog. Everything I need is in the back."

"I hope you brought a different DVD this time. I'm tired of that damn *Scarface*."

Keno laughed and said, "Come on, dog, don't hate. You know you be loving *'Face*."

Taz moaned as he relaxed back in his seat. It was going to be another long-ass flight. *Damn!*

By the time Taz and Keno had checked into the Sheraton in downtown Atlanta, the sun was setting and the weather was nice and warm. Taz wished they could get to do some things while they were in the ATL, but he knew that was out of the question. They were there to handle their business, and that's exactly what they planned on doing.

After Taz and Keno entered their room, Taz called the front desk and asked for the room numbers of James Jenkins and Walter Johnson. The operator gave him the room numbers and asked if he would like to be connected to one of the rooms. He told her yes, and she transferred him to James Jenkins's room. James Jenkins was Red's alias name.

Red answered the phone on the first ring and said, "What up?"

"Room 3923," Taz said and hung up the phone. He then called Walter Johnson's room, which was Wild Bill's alias. When the phone was answered, he once again said, "Room 3923." After hanging up the phone, he went to the dining room table and opened the package that was left for him at the front desk. Inside of the small package was a DVD and a brief typewritten note. After reading the note, he smiled and said, "Dog, this lick is worth a grip. Look." He passed the note to Keno.

Keno read it quickly, smiled, and said, "I'm loving those figures, my nigga."

Before Taz could reply, there was a soft knock at the door. He went and let the rest of the crew inside.

Wild Bill walked by him and said, "Damn, dog! It's a gang of hoes out here in the ATL! Bitches was choosing like a muthafucka at the airport when we got in. I'm tellin' you, dog, I'm going to have to bounce back this way sometime this summer."

Bo-Pete laughed and said, "Nigga, would you sit your blind ass down so we can get to business? Worry about your dick on your time. I'm trying to make some money right now."

Taz laughed and passed Bo-Pete the note that was inside of the package. Then Bo-Pete passed it to Red, who in turn read it and passed it to Bob. After Bob was finished, he passed it to Wild Bill. Every last member of the six-man crew had smiles on their faces as they all stared at Taz.

Taz grabbed the DVD and went and inserted it into the DVD player sitting under the television in the hotel room. He turned it on, and the first thing that came onto the screen was a picture of Michael Jordan doing a reverse layup against A.C. Green of the Lakers.

After a full minute had passed, Won's voice could be heard. "I'm glad that you all made it safely. Taz, take a

look under the bed in your room and you'll find everything you need necessary for this job. Make sure that
everything is to your liking before you leave. If there
are any problems, hit me on my cell immediately. As
you all know, everything is timed down to the last minute. In exactly one hour, you are to leave your rooms
and meet in the underground parking area. In the B-
Section, you will see an all-black Ford Excursion, Geor-
gia, plates 115 BHB. The doors will be unlocked and the
keys will be inside of the glove box.

"You are then to proceed to a club located right off of
Highway 75, exit right on Butner Avenue. That street
will take you straight to the club. Once you have the
club in your sights, drive one block past it and you'll
see an alley. Make a left turn, and the alley will lead
you right to the back entrance of the club. The back
door of the club will be unlocked, but there will be one
sentry to your immediate left. Once you enter the club,
he must be secured.

"You'll then see the staircase leading to the upstairs
office. There should be no more than four or five people
inside of the office, but to be on the safe side, assume
that there are five. Once you have entered the office
and secured everyone, you will have ten to twelve minutes approximately to clean out the safe.

"Before I continue, Taz, one of y'all might want to
write what I'm about to say down."

While there was a pause in Won's instructions, Taz
quickly grabbed a pen and some writing paper out of
the desk over by the bed. Just as he turned back towards the television, Won continued.

"Okay. Once you're in the office, to your right will be
a wall with a yellow and brown sofa against it. There
will be a thermostat at the left end of the sofa. That's
where you'll go, and move the thermostat's knob to

twenty degrees, then back to zero degrees, then to fifteen degrees, and lastly back to twenty degrees. Again,
that's twenty degrees, back to zero degrees, fifteen degrees, and back to twenty degrees. Once you make that
last turn, the wall will part like the Red Sea, and you'll
see the rest.

"In your bag of goodies under the bed are backpacks
for each one of you. The backpacks, as well as one
ample-sized carryall bag for each, are for what's for
me in the safe. The carryall bags are for the ends. Once
you've cleaned everything out of the safe, double time
it up outta there.

"There shouldn't be any need for violence, but you
know how that goes. So have everything locked and
cocked. Once you've made it safely back to the highway,
head back to your rooms. When you've made it back to
the hotel, leave everything inside the Excursion.

"I wasn't able to get you flights out tonight, so y'all
are going to have to chill and relax for the rest of the
evening. Here are your flight reservations."

The picture of Michael Jordan was replaced with
flight reservations, which Taz quickly wrote down.

A minute passed before Won started speaking again.
"You know the routine once you've made it back to the
City. By the time you get home, check your accounts
and give me a holla. Be safe, and remember, ten to
twelve minutes tops. If you're in there any longer than
that, be prepared to shoot your way up outta there. Be
precise, be prepared, and most of all, be careful. Out!"

The television screen went blank, and Taz went over
to the DVD player, popped out the DVD, and dropped
it onto the floor. He then stepped on it with his Timberland boots. After crushing it, he picked up the pieces
and went out onto the balcony of his room and threw
them over the railing. After that, he came back into the

room and said, "All right, we got about forty-five minutes to get ready. Let's do it."

Keno pulled three large bags out from under the bed and set them on top of the bed. In one bag were their weapons. Each member of the crew had a nine-millimeter Beretta with a silencer already attached to it. There were three magazines full for each, a bulletproof vest for each man, as well as several pairs of plastic hand restraints.

Bo-Pete and Wild Bill put their weapons, vests, and backpacks into their bags and set them down next to where they were standing. Red and Bob did the same, and so did Taz and Keno. Keno pulled out what looked like earplugs and gave one to every man in the hotel room. After each one of them had inserted the earplugs into their ears, they pulled out their cell phones and punched in a three-digit code. Keno then went into the bathroom and said, "Testing, 1, 2 . . . testing 1, 2!"

Back inside the room everyone said, "Good!"

Keno came back into the room, smiled, and said, "Ready!"

Taz checked the time and saw that they had thirty minutes before it was time for them to leave. "Alright, go get changed and meet us at the truck in twenty."

Red, Bob, Bo-Pete, and Wild Bill left the room in single file.

Keno slipped out of his Sean Jean sweat suit and put on a pair of black army fatigue pants and a black, long-sleeved T-shirt. As he was lacing up his black Timberlands, Taz started getting dressed, identically as Keno. They both put on their bulletproof vests and snapped them tightly on each other.

When they were finished, Taz said, "Time!" They smiled at each other briefly; then Taz led the way out of the room. They took the stairs to the parking area and met up with everyone inside of the Excursion. Once everyone was inside of the truck, Keno started the ignition and backed out of the parking space. The mission had begun.

Keno had no problem finding the club as he drove down Butner Avenue. He passed the club and made a left turn down the alley, just like Won had instructed on the DVD. He bypassed the back entrance of the club and made a U-turn onto the next street and returned back towards the club. That way, they were now facing the same way that they had come.

"Fa' sho'. I don't know the terrain that cool, so I figured, why risk it? At least this way I know all I have to do is go straight out the alley and bust a right, and we're on our way back to the hotel," Keno said confidently.

"Do you, baby. I'm always comfortable when you're behind the wheel," Red said as he once again checked his weapon. The only noise you heard inside of the Excursion was the click-clack of the chambers of the nine millimeters that everyone had inside their hands.

After their weapons were checked and the safety buttons were off, Taz said, "Red, you and Bob take the sentry to the left. Once he's secured, bring up the rear. We're not entering until we know y'all are on our ass."

"Gotcha'."

"When we hit the office, y'all know the drill. Two to the right, two to the left, and the last two posted at the door to watch our backs. When everything is secure, I'll hit the thermostat. Once the safe is open, Keno and I will fill up our bags and backpacks. Then, we'll switch with Bo-Pete and Wild Bill. Then they'll switch with Red and Bob. Time check."

They checked their watches and made sure that they were all on the exact same time. One minute off could cost one of them their lives.

They got out of the Excursion, with Red and Bob leading the way towards the back door of the club. Once they were in front of the door, Taz gave Red a nod of his head; then Red and Bob rushed into the club. Just like Won had told them, there was a security guard posted to their left. Red's nine millimeter was aimed directly at the security guard's head as he whispered, "Get the fuck on the ground or die!" The security guard was so scared that he couldn't move. Bob ran up to the guard and slapped him across his forehead. The guard fell to the ground, and Bob quickly restrained him with a pair of his plastic hand restraints. Once Red saw that Bob had the guard secured, he spoke softly and said, "We're good."

Taz heard Red and signaled for the rest to follow him as he entered the club. Taz, Keno, Bo-Pete, and Wild Bill slid past Red and Bob as if they weren't even there. They moved silently up the stairs towards the office. When they were right outside of the office, Taz looked over his shoulder and saw that Red and Bob were right behind Bo-Pete and Wild Bill. He inhaled deeply and slowly turned the doorknob. Once the door was slightly open, he rushed into the office with his gun drawn. "Get the fuck down! Get the fuck down, now!" yelled Taz.

There were four people inside of the office—three men and a female—who were stunned as they watched the six men rush in. They did as they were told and got onto the floor. Taz and Keno quickly put a pair of the hand restraints on two of the men, and Wild Bill and Bo-Pete did the same with the female and the other male in the room. Red and Bob stood at the door, covering them while they restrained everyone.

Red checked his watch and said, "One minute!"

Taz then quickly stepped towards the sofa. Once he was there, he moved the thermostat's knob to the numbers he memorized from Won's briefing. And just like Won had said, the walls parted like the Red Sea. Taz was stunned as he focused on all of the stacks of one-hundred-dollar bills inside of the wall safe. He was even more fascinated by all of the drugs.

Once again, Red's voice came into his ear. "Move, my nigga. We've been here three and a half minutes already." That snapped Taz out of his daze, and he snatched off his backpack and started piling as many of the kilos of cocaine he could into his backpack. Once his backpack was filled to capacity, he strapped it across his back and then started filling up his carry bag. Keno was right by his side, filling up his bags. They both finished at the same time and stepped away from the safe in one fluid motion.

As they moved toward the door, Wild Bill and Bo-Pete ran to the safe and started filling their bags. Red and Bob slid into the position that Wild Bill and Bo-Pete had just left from.

Now it was Taz's turn to watch the clock. He checked his watch and said, "Seven minutes, gentlemen." By the time Bo-Pete and Wild Bill had finished, they had been inside of the office for nine minutes. Red and Bob finished emptying the safe at the eleven-minute mark.

Taz spoke softly and said, "It's time to roll, baby. One minute left and it'll be time for some gunplay." They then ran out of the office just as quickly as they had come in.

As they were descending the stairs, they heard the female that was upstairs start screaming. That gave them an extra pep in their steps as they broke out of the back door and back into the alleyway.

Once they were all inside of the Excursion, Keno started the truck and pulled away smoothly. When he made the right turn back onto Butner Avenue, he noticed several black SUVs as they pulled up in front of the club. Armed men were exiting the SUVs and running into the club. Keno smiled and said, "It's all about the timing, baby!"

Taz relaxed in his seat and said, "You know it! Once again, that fool Won did the damn thang."

"Man, how the fuck does he be knowing all of this shit?" asked Wild Bill from the backseat of the Excursion.

"Ain't no tellin', my nigga. And to tell you the truth, I don't really give a fuck, just as long as he continues to be on point. I'm good," Taz said with a satisfied smile on his face.

"I know that's right, gee!" Wild Bill said as he opened his carry bag and smiled at all of the Benjamin Franklins that were stacked on top of each other.

They made it back to the hotel without incident. Keno locked the doors to the truck, and they went back to their rooms. After they had changed their clothes, they met back up in Taz's and Keno's room. They were relaxing and sipping on some of the liquor out of the minibar of Taz's room when Bob said, "Damn, my nigga! How much dope do you think was in that safe?"

"Dog, I'm not knowing. It had to be over a hundred bricks," said Bo-Pete.

"I know, huh? How much chips you think we took?" asked Red.

"We're clearing two million apiece, so it had to be twelve tickets or more," said Taz as he turned the channel on the television.

"You know what, though? That nigga Won is a muthafucka! You know he be having us watched, right?" asked Keno.

"How do you know that?" asked Wild Bill.

"How else would that fool be able to have that DVD in here done, and be able to tell us that we have one hour to be here and there? He has to be having us peeped at. He would have to know what time we arrived here and shit. Yeah, he knows when we'll touch down at the airport and shit, but how does he know exactly when we've made it to the hotel and shit? That's one smooth nigga, dog. I love fuckin' with that fool."

Taz smiled but didn't say anything as he continued to watch the television. He knew that they were watched whenever they went on a mission for Won. That's how he got down. Won would never leave anything to chance; every move he made was calculated. He'd taught Taz that a long time ago. *Yeah, my man will always be on top of his game. That's why we are all on top of the pile,* he thought as he continued to watch television.

The next morning, Taz and Keno checked out of the hotel and caught a cab to the airport. They were scheduled for a ten a.m. flight back to Dallas Ft. Worth, while Red and Bob's flight had already departed for Tulsa International. Wild Bill and Bo-Pete's flight back to Oklahoma City wasn't due to depart until noon, so they had decided to run to Lenox Square Mall to do a little shopping before they left.

Keno and Taz boarded their flight, and as soon as they were seated, Keno pulled out that damn DVD player and put in that damn *Scarface* DVD. Taz shook his head and said, "I swear, I'm going to take that muthafucka and break it in half before our next trip, Keno! I hate that fuckin' movie now!"

Keno smiled and said, "Don't hate, nigga. You know you love some *'Face.*"

Taz laughed as he closed his eyes. He was glad they were on their way home. Mission completed.

It was a little after ten p.m. when the crew had made it out to Taz's home. They went through their usual routine and checked the laptop to make sure that their financial gains were intact. And as usual, they were. They each had made two million dollars for their day spent in the ATL.

Taz's cell rang, and when he answered it, Won said, "Another job well done, Babyboy."

"You know it, Won. As long as you give it to us raw, we'll handle the rest."

"I know that's right! Have you checked y'all's accounts yet?"

"Yeah, it's all good."

"All righty then. I don't anticipate anything anytime soon, so you know the routine. Enjoy, be merry, and most of all be good! Out!"

"Hold up a minute, Won. Bob has a question for you real quick."

"Put him on."

Taz passed his cell to Bob and sat down and watched as Bob spoke to Won.

Bob accepted the phone, smiled, and said, "What up, Won?"

"What's poppin', Babyboy?"

"Dog, I love how you do your thing and all, but I've been real curious about something ever since we've been fuckin' with you."

"Speak your mind, baby."

"How the fuck do you be knowing the shit you be knowing?"

Won started laughing, then said, "I know what needs to be known, Babyboy, because I'm always on top of my game. Always. Is there anything else?"

"Yeah, I got one more question for you, big homey. Why do they call you 'Won'?"

That made Won start laughing harder than before. After he regained his composure, he said, "A long time ago I was in the game, and I played it with so much vigor that I knew one day I was going to win it. After I did in fact win the game, I changed my name to 'Won'."

"Because you had 'won' the game?"

"Exactly!"

"So, what was your name before you won the game?"

Won started laughing again. Afterwards he simply said, "Win!" And then the line went dead in Bob's ear.

Bob gave the phone back to Taz and said, "Well, I guess that's that. Y'all know what time it is now, huh?"

Taz said, "Yep."

And in unison, they all said, "It's time to go clubbin'!"

Chapter Seven

Sacha was relaxing in her bedroom, wondering what Clifford had in store for their evening together. For the past three weeks, they'd spent almost every evening doing something, whether it was going out to dinner, taking long walks down by the river, walking downtown, going to the movies, or just chilling with each other at either of their homes. She felt comfortable with him, but still there seemed to be something missing. She just couldn't put her finger on it yet. *Maybe I should go on and give him some. God knows I want to,* she thought to herself as she got off of her bed and went into the living room. She plopped onto her sofa and concluded that having sex with Clifford would definitely propel their relationship to the next level. She smiled as she grabbed her cordless phone and gave Clifford a call.

Clifford answered the phone on the first ring. "Hello, pretty lady!" he said before Sacha could speak.

"Hey, Cliff. Were you busy?"

"Not really. I just got out of the shower. I was about to call you and see if you wanted to go down to Bricktown and get into something."

"Actually, I was thinking about just chilling out tonight. Why don't you come over here and keep me company?" she asked in a seductive tone.

Not noticing the tone in her voice, Clifford said, "That's cool. How about I stop at Blockbuster and pick up a few movies?"

"I have a better idea. Why don't you stop at the liquor store and pick us up a bottle of wine? That way when you get here, we'll be able to set this evening off properly. What'd you say about that, handsome?"

Once again not realizing that what he'd been so patiently waiting for was within his grasp, he said, "If it makes you happy, Sacha, I'm here to please. I'll be there in thirty to forty-five minutes."

"That's fine. That'll give me just enough time to get nice and sexy for you. Bye!" she said and hung up the phone.

Clifford hung up the phone feeling really good with the progress he'd made with Sacha. *She's going to be the future Mrs. Nelson. I can feel it,* he thought as he quickly started to get himself dressed.

Sacha went back into her bedroom and chose a sexy black and emerald skirt with a thin black lace top. Her matching black bra and thong completed the look she desired. *If I'm going to give him some, I'm going to make this night one he's never going to forget,* she thought as she went into her bathroom to take a shower.

Clifford arrived at Sacha's home right on time. He was dressed casually, as usual, in a pair of khakis and a long sleeved Polo shirt. While he waited for Sacha to come let him inside of her home, he checked to make sure that he had everything. He did as she requested, and stopped at the liquor store and bought an expensive bottle of Chablis. He also made a quick stop at Blockbuster and rented two DVDs for them to watch. Just being able to spend quality time like this with her made him feel as if there was indeed a perfect world.

Sacha opened the door with one hand and had the other on her hip. The three-inch heels by Giorgio Armani made it seem as if she almost stood eye to eye with Clifford. She smiled seductively and said, "Hi, handsome! Come on in." She turned and led the way into the living room. She could feel Clifford's eyes all over her was she walked. Tiny goose bumps were all over her body as she thought about what she was actually about to do. *Damn! I'm more excited than I thought I'd be,* she thought as she sat down on the sofa.

Clifford followed her into the living room and said, "You never did tell me what you wanted me to rent, so I got us *Diary of a Mad Black Woman* and *Batman Begins*. Is that cool?" he asked as he set the DVDs and the bottle of wine on the coffee table.

No, this nigga didn't! I know he can see what I'm wearing. He can't possibly think I'm trying to watch some damn DVDs! Or is he just nervous? Yeah, that's it. Cliff's a li'l scared. That's so cute! she thought as she slid next to him on the sofa and said, "Baby, I'm not really in the mood to watch any movies. Why don't we open up that bottle of wine and listen to some music and chill?"

"That's cool, baby, but I really want to check out this *Diary of a Mad Black Woman*. Alton down in Entertainment told me that it was definitely worth watching."

Is this man serious? Hold up! He is! She watched as Clifford got up from the sofa and went towards her entertainment center, where her television and DVD player were located. She watched amazingly as he inserted the DVD into the DVD player. *Uh-uh! This ain't even happening!* She got up and said, "Cliff, come here for a minute."

He turned around and faced her and said, "Yeah, babe?"

"Do you like what I have on?"

As if noticing what she was wearing for the first time, he said," Oh, that's sexy, Sacha. I like how your toenails are painted the same color green as your skirt."

"Emerald."

"Huh?"

"I said, emerald. My toenails are emerald, not green."

"My bad. They still look nice."

"Thanks!" she said sarcastically. She sat back down and watched as Clifford went back to turning on the television. *Uh-uh! Not me! Not tonight! If this clown-ass nigga really wants to watch this movie, he's going to be on his own!* she thought to herself as she stood up and said, "Cliff, I'm not in the mood to watch any movies. Let's do something else instead."

He turned toward her and asked, "Like what, Sacha?"

"Let's go to the club and hang out."

"The club? Which one? Birdies down in Bricktown, or that one by the Comedy Store?"

"Neither. Let's go to Club Cancun or to Rhea's."

"What? I know you're not serious! You want to go to one of those 'hood clubs?"

"'Hood clubs? I want to go out and have a good time with my peoples, not a bunch of corny fakes. Is there something wrong with that, Cliff?"

For the first time this evening he seemed to be aware of Sacha and her tone of voice. If he'd only paid closer attention, he would have had his wildest fantasies about her come true. But since he didn't, he was now wondering what had gotten into her. "You mean to tell me that you'd actually be comfortable in a place like that Club Cancun?"

"I'm comfortable whenever I'm around my people."

"Your people? Sacha, what's gotten into you tonight? I thought we were going to chill out and watch some movies."

Shaking her head from side to side, she said, "You know what? Forget it. I'm not in the mood to sit in this house tonight, Cliff. I'm going out. The only question I have for you is, am I going out alone or not?"

"Are you serious?"

"As a heart attack. So, what's your answer?"

Smiling, he said, "Well, I guess we're going to the club!"

Smiling brightly, Sacha said, "That's right, baby! We're about to go clubbin'!"

Club Cancun was packed, as usual, when Clifford and Sacha finally made it inside. They got lucky and found an empty table close to the bar. After they were seated, Sacha asked, "Are you going to have a drink with me, Cliff?"

"Sure. I don't do the heavy stuff, but I'll sip on a glass of wine," he said as he waved at a waitress as she was headed towards the bar.

After ordering a glass of white wine for himself and an apple martini for Sacha, he sat back and took a better look around the club. He noticed several old acquaintances and smiled. *If Sacha only knew!* he thought to himself with a slight smile on his face. *There are some hot, looking females inside of the club. I might have to come back here and check this scene out again,* he thought just as their drinks arrived.

As he sipped his glass of wine, he noticed how Sacha seemed to fit right in at this type of club. That didn't really sit well with him. *She's a top-notch type of lady. No way was she supposed to fit in with a 'hood crowd like this,* he thought as he stared at some of the obvious-looking thug drug dealer types that had passed their table. *Then again, at least she's a little versatile. Maybe that's a good thing.*

Sacha smiled at Clifford and said, "I like their choice of music here. They're not all caught up on that straight hip-hop. They mix it real smooth with R&B. Then they seem to know right when to slow it up for ya. I hope you'll get out there and dance with me before we leave."

"I wouldn't consider myself a gentleman if I didn't, Sacha," he said with a satisfied smile on his face. *Maybe this wasn't a bad idea, after all,* he thought to himself as he took another sip of his drink.

At the opposite side of the bar, Paquita and Katrina were taking inventory of everyone inside of the club. "Girl, that's that broad who had that skimpy-ass Apple Bottoms mini on a few weeks ago," Paquita said as she pointed toward Sacha.

"I wonder who's that fine-ass nigga she's with," said Katrina.

"She's cute. I like how she keeps her hair. I wonder who does her weave."

"Probably Stacey over at Images. You know she's the best in the City."

"Bullshit! Javon does the tightest weaves in the City, bitch. Shit, look at my shit," Katrina said as she patted her micro-braids.

"Yeah, you clownin', bitch, but I'm doin' the damn thing with this new look Javon gave me," Paquita said as she shook her extra long blond weave job. Before Katrina had a chance to speak, Paquita said, "Ooh, bitch! There goes Bo-Pete and Wild Bill!"

Turning toward the front entrance of the club, Katrina smiled and said, "Damn! That means that Taz is on his way! You know what, bitch? I think I'm going to get at that nigga Keno tonight. I'm feelin' that nigga too."

"Well, you go on and do you. I'm not going to stop until I get me some of that fine-ass nigga Taz. He's not going to keep shaking me," Paquita said confidently.

The both of them turned and watched as Wild Bill and Bo-Pete entered the club and walked toward the right of the bar. Five minutes later, Red and Bob came into the club and went and posted up on the far left side of the club. A few minutes after that, Keno and Taz walked inside of the club as if they were royalty.

Keno smiled as they stepped toward the bar. Winky, the bartender, passed Taz his normal drink and smiled after Taz gave him a slight nod of his head. Taz saw Paquita and Katrina staring at them and whispered to Keno, "Dog, why don't you break one of them hoes off so they can get off a nigga's nuts?"

"Who, them rats to the right? Nigga, you gots to be outta your fuckin' mind! Don't get me wrong Katrina is definitely fuckable. But that other one is on some other shit. Plus, she's all yours, big boy. Look how she's staring at your ass!" Keno started laughing as Taz turned and saw Paquita smiling at him from ear to ear.

"Oh, God, let me make it through the night!" he prayed silently as his sipped his Courvoisier XO. As he turned and gave a slight nod toward Red and Bob, then towards Wild Bill and Bo-Pete, he smiled as he watched his crew break loose like a bunch of horny niggas fresh out of prison. He shook his head and started to take another sip of his drink when he saw Sacha sitting at a table with Clifford. He smiled at the square-looking guy she was with and said, "I guess it was meant to be, sexy. I'm not letting you get away from me tonight."

Sacha looked away from Cliff and directly at Taz, as if she had heard the statement he'd just made. She smiled at him and thought, *Oh, my God! That's that sexy somethin'-somethin' I saw the last time I was here. Come on, babe. Don't stare at me like that. You're getting me wet!* She shook herself slightly, turned back toward Clifford, and said, "Do you want to have that dance now, Cliff?"

"Let's do it, sexy," Clifford said as he got up from the table. He grabbed her hand and led her out onto the dance floor.

Taz watched amused as Sacha and Clifford started dancing. He knew she was feeling him because of the nervous glances she kept shooting his way. *I know you want me, boo, and I'm going to make damn sure you know I want you,* he thought to himself as he turned back towards the bar and asked, "Winky, which waitress is working the section to my right?"

Winky smiled and said, "That's Mikki's section, Taz. What's up? Is everything okay?"

"Yeah, everything's straight. Tell Mikki to come get at me when she comes back to the bar."

"Gotcha, Taz," the bartender said, and went back to making someone a drink.

Taz resumed his staring game with Sacha. *Damn, she's fine! She's wearing the hell out of that skirt. She's got class too. I can tell. And that long-ass hair gots to be real. Ain't no way that's a weave,* he thought as he continued to stare at her.

Keno came back to the bar, saw how his homey was staring at Sacha, and said, "Well, I'll be damn! You got your sights locked on that ass, huh?"

Taz smiled and said, "Dog, that's one bad broad. I gots to holla."

"Do you, nigga. What, you gon' let that square cat stand in your way?"

Taz recognized the challenge in his homey's voice, smiled, and said, "Since when have I ever let someone stop me from doing what I want to do?"

"Now that's what I'm talkin' 'bout! My nigga Taz is back in the game! I think I'll drink to that!" Keno said, and he downed the rest of his glass of Hennessy.

The waitress Mikki came up to Taz and asked, "You wanted to see me, Taz?"

"Yeah, I did. What's up, Mikki? How you been?"

"I'm good. Just trying to finish up with school and stuff. I'm trying to get the hell out of the City."

"Is that right? Where you trying to move to?"

"Anywhere, just as long as I'm out of Oklahoma."

Laughing, he said, "I know that's right. But check this out. I need to know what that couple is drinking over there at that table," he said as he pointed towards Sacha and Clifford's table.

Mikki smiled and said, "The female is drinking an apple martini, and the guy has a white wine."

"Do me a favor and take them another round of drinks for me. Make sure it's after they're back and seated. Let the female know that they're from me," he said as he gave Mikki a hundred-dollar bill.

"Taz, why you got to be giving me this big-ass bill? You know Winky's gon' be whining when he sees this."

"Don't trip, Mikki. Keep the change for yourself. Maybe that can help out a li'l."

Smiling brightly, Mikki said, "Thank you Taz! You're so sweet!" She gave him a quick kiss on his cheek and hurried to go do what he'd told her to.

Taz watched as Sacha and Clifford finished dancing. He smiled when he saw Mikki go to their table and give them their drinks. When she pointed towards Taz at the bar, Sacha smiled and raised her drink in thanks. Clifford, on the other hand, frowned and turned his attention back toward Sacha. Taz laughed and said, "Old boy, you're way out of your league on this one."

To say Clifford was agitated would be putting it way too mildly. He was pissed off. "How dare that clown send you a drink over here! I should go over there and have a word with his ass!"

Sacha smiled and said, "Come on, Cliff. He bought the both of us a drink. Why are you tripping?"

"Why am I tripping? I'm tripping because he has blatantly disrespected me. He's trying to get at you on the cool."

"By buying us a drink, he's trying to get at me? Cliff, that's absurd. And even if he is, so what? I'm here with *you!* You should take his gesture as a compliment and stop hating."

That comment irked the hell out of Clifford; he was ready to leave now. "Sacha, it's getting late. Maybe we should leave now."

"Leave? I'm not ready to leave. We haven't been here an hour yet. Come on, don't let that guy ruin our evening. The night's still young, and we have plenty more of it to enjoy. So relax."

Shaking his head no, Clifford said, "Nah, for real, I'm ready to go, Sacha."

Sacha didn't like the tone of his voice, so she said, "Well, I'm not, Cliff. I came out to enjoy myself, and that's exactly what I plan on doing."

"Let's not go through this, Sacha. I said I'm ready to go!"

"And I said I'm not!"

"Don't make me do something I know I'll regret!"

She laughed and said, "Cliff, you're a grown-ass man. You can do whatever you want to. Whether you'll regret it or not is solely on you. I'm a big girl, so if you want to leave, then leave. I'm quite sure I won't have a problem finding a way back home." She turned and shot a seductive smile toward Taz to add emphasis to her statement. That statement hit Clifford right where she figured it would . . . his pride.

"I'm sure you wouldn't! Maybe that thug you seem to be so fascinated by would love to take you home! Wait! I didn't mean that, Sacha. Can't we just leave? I'm no longer enjoying this place."

She couldn't believe how much Clifford sounded like a child. *And to think I was just about to give the li'l baby some ass! Whoa!* she thought. "Cliff, if you want to leave, then I think you should. Like I've already told you, I'm a big girl. I'll be fine." She sipped her drink and said, "As a matter of fact, I think you *should* leave. I'm no longer enjoying your company."

"What? Come on, Sacha. It's not that serious."

"Yes, Cliff, it is. You're trying to ruin a perfectly good evening, and I refuse to let you. So, why don't you just leave?"

"Don't push me, Sacha, 'cause I won't have a problem bouncing up out of this place without you."

She started laughing so hard that she thought she was going to pee on herself. Once she regained her composure, she said, "Have a nice evening, Cliff!" She stood and left him sitting at the table by himself. She put an extra sway in her walk as she passed Taz on her way towards the restroom.

Taz watched and smiled when he saw Clifford storm out of the club. *The first part of my mission has now been completed. Now on to phase two. Taz, do you, boy! Do you!* He turned toward Winky and ordered himself another glass of XO.

By the time Sacha came out of the bathroom, she saw that Clifford had gone, and that sexy-ass, thug-looking guy was boldly sitting at her table. *So, you think you got it like that, huh, Mr. Smooth? Let me see what you're really working with.* She went back to her table.

Once she was standing in front of Taz, she said, "Excuse me, but this is my table."

"I know. Since your date shook you, I thought I'd come keep you company."

"Shook me? What makes you think that he shook me?" she asked as she sat down in her seat.

"Come on, sexy. Ain't no need for game playin'. I saw how he got heated behind the drinks I sent y'all. I didn't mean to interrupt your evening with that squ—uh—guy."

"Is that right? So, what were your intentions when you sent those drinks over to us?"

Staring directly into her sexy brown eyes, he said, "I wanted to get your attention."

"And why is that? You did notice I was with someone, didn't you?"

Taz laughed and said, "Of course! I sent him a drink, too, didn't I?"

Sacha couldn't help herself from laughing. *This cutie is something else,* she thought as she took a sip of her drink. "Well, since you've run my date away, can I at least know your name?"

"My name is Taz."

"Taz . . . hmm . . . I like that. My name is Sacha, Taz."

"Sacha . . . hmm . . . I like that too. Now that the introductions are out of the way, I have a question for you, Sacha."

"What's that, Taz?"

"Will you let me take you back out on that dance floor so we can get our groove on a li'l?"

Smiling, Sacha said, "I don't have a problem with that."

Taz stood up, took one of Sacha's small hands in his, and led her onto the dance floor.

Keno was talking to Bob when he noticed Taz slow dancing with Sacha. "Look, nigga! Taz is back in the game, dog!"

Bob turned and stared in disbelief at what he was seeing and said, "Now ain't that a bitch! What's gotten into that nigga?"

Keno smiled and said, "Fool, if you can't see that he done cracked a bad bitch, then you're one blind mutha-fucka!"

Out on the dance floor, Taz couldn't believe that he was actually dancing with this sexy-ass woman. She felt so good in his arms that he wanted to hold her like this all night long. *Slow down, nigga! You don't even know this broad!* he thought to himself as she held on tightly to his broad shoulders.

Sacha, on the other hand, was just as mesmerized by Taz as he was by her. *I know he's some sort of thug, but he sure as hell smells good,* she thought as she inhaled deeply and savored the smell of his Vera Wang for men.

The slow song came to an end and the DJ switched to some "Laffy Taffy" by D4L, and they started shaking all around the dance floor together, having a real good time.

Paquita and Katrina couldn't believe what they were seeing. "Bitch, Taz don't dance! How the fuck did that stuck-up-looking bitch get him out there?" yelled Paquita.

"I don't know, girl, but look at him! I've never seen Taz smile like that. He's digging that bitch."

"I hate that ho! Where the fuck did she come from any fuckin' way?"

"I don't know, girl, but it looks like he's finally chosen someone."

"That's fucked up!"

"Bitch, why you trippin'?"

"'Cause he didn't choose me!" Paquita said with a hurt expression on her face.

"That's the way the game is, girl. Come on. Let's go get a drink," Katrina said as she led her homegirl towards the bar.

After five or six songs, Taz and Sacha were sweating and tired. He led her back to her table and signaled Mikki to bring them some more drinks. After Mikki had brought their orders and left, he said, "I can't remember the last time I've actually been out on a dance floor. That shit was kinda fun."

"You're kidding, right? You dance too damn good for that."

"I'm serious. I'm not really into this club scene shit."

"So, why do you come to the club then?"

"My homies like to come and unwind here. They're into it more than I am. Usually, I just get me a drink and chill in front of the bar."

"I noticed that the last time I was here. You had a real serious look on your face. You were looking as if you didn't want to be bothered by anyone."

"Yeah, I'm like that at times."

Smiling, she said, "Well, you're sure not like that tonight. What changed?"

Taz sipped his XO and simply said, "You."

Chapter Eight

By the time the club started letting out, Taz had found out through their conversation what Sacha did for a living, as well as confirmed that this was definitely a woman that he wanted to get to know better. "I hope that you'll let me take you to go get some breakfast or something," he asked.

"Or something?" Sacha asked with a raised eyebrow.

Smiling sheepishly, Taz said, "Come on, you know what I mean. I'm really feeling you, and I kinda don't want this night to end right now. Let's go get some Denny's or something."

"I'd prefer IHOP."

"I ain't trippin'. Whatever you want is fine with me."

Before he could continue, Keno, Bo-Pete, Wild Bill, Bob, and Red came to their table. Keno smiled and said, "You ready to shake this spot, gee?"

"Nah, I'm good. Look, Red, take Keno back to my spot so he can get his truck. I'm about to go have breakfast with this lovely lady."

Red laughed and said, "Well, it's about time, dog."

"Whatever! Excuse my rudeness, Sacha. These are my homeboys, Red, Bob, Bo-Pete, Wild Bill, and this clown right here is Keno."

Sacha smiled at the crew and said, "Hello, gentlemen."

They all said their hellos and smiled, but Bob just couldn't help himself. He had to say something slick.

"So, you're the one who has finally been able to get this old fuddy-duddy interested in someone, huh?"

She smiled at Bob and said, "If you say so."

Before their conversation could get any deeper, Taz said, "All right, clowns. Y'all can bounce."

"You sure, gee?" asked Keno.

"Yeah, I'm good. I'll get with y'all at the gym in the morning."

Keno smiled and said, "Yeah, we'll see you at the gym in the morning." Keno and the rest of the crew all started laughing as they left the club.

Taz waited until they were out of the club and said, "Come on, let's go get our eat on."

Sacha smiled as she stood up from the table. She liked what she had seen so far in Taz. *Be careful, girl! You know he's into something illegal,* she warned herself as they were headed towards the exit.

Once they made it outside of the club, Taz led her toward his all-black Denali and pulled out his keys. He hit a button and his alarm chirped twice and the doors to his truck made a "whoosh" sound and opened vertically. Sacha smiled and said, "Men and their toys!"

After Taz made sure that Sacha was safely inside the truck, he went around the other side and climbed in himself. He started the truck and said, "Yeah, you know how it is. We have to have all the go-go gadgets and whatnot. Life wouldn't be that much fun if men couldn't play with their toys."

"Uh-hmm, whatever! I know you have a sound system in this toy of yours. Would you turn on some music, please?"

Taz smiled and said, "Anything to please a lady." He then said, "What would you like to listen to?"

"What do you have?"

"Whatever you want to listen to, I have it."

"Is that right?"

"Yep, that's right."

I got something for this slickster! she told herself. "Okay, I'd like to listen to that new single by Alicia Keys, 'Unbreakable.'"

"Yeah, I like that one too," Taz said with his smile still in place. Then he focused as he pulled his truck out of the club parking lot.

I knew he was just fronting. That's a shame. I really didn't think he was the fake type. Oh, well, at least I'll get me some breakfast out of his ass. Then I'll call Gwen and have her come pick me up from IHOP. I'm not letting this thug know where I live, Sacha thought to herself as she relaxed back in her seat.

Once Taz had slid his truck into traffic, he said, "CD number three, track number one, volume level four, mids three, and highs four, please."

Sacha stared at him as if he'd lost his mind.

A second later, the song "Unbreakable" by Alicia Keys started playing on Taz's sound system. He turned towards Sacha, shrugged his shoulders slightly, and said, "More toys, huh?"

Sacha started laughing and said, "Oh, my God! How much did you pay for something like that?"

"A li'l bit of nothin'. I let Keno talk me into getting that voice-activated system. It's pretty cool, huh?"

"It sure is. Play another song for me, Taz."

"What do you wanna hear?"

"Anything. I just want to see you do that again."

He smiled and said, "So, you *are* impressed by my toys. I guess that's a good thing." His cell phone started ringing and he said, "Excuse me for one minute, Sacha." He flipped opened his cell and said, "What up, Red?"

"Nothin' much, my nigga. Just wanted to make sure that your new girlfriend was treating you alright."

"Fuck you!"

"Aw-w-w, come on, dog. Don't be like that. Tell me, will she be at the gym with you in the morning? I mean, the gym is at your house and all."

Before Taz could reply, he heard Bob in the background telling Red to ask Taz if she had a friend. Taz shook his head and said, "Tell that nigga I said I'll find out for him after I finish eating. Now, can I go please? I am on a date!"

Red started laughing and said, "You know we love this shit, gee. It's been way too long since you really enjoyed yourself. I hope she's the one, my nigga. I really do."

Taz turned toward Sacha and told Red, "I do too, homey. Out!" After he closed his phone, he said, "My homey Bob wants to know if you have a friend."

"Bob was the darker one with the lump on his head, right?"

Taz started laughing and said, "Yeah, that's him."

"Hmm . . . I might. My girl Gwen loves her men dark skinned. Hey, what happened to my other request?"

"Oh, I forgot. Here you go. CD number seven, track six, volume level seven, mids two, and highs three please." It was quiet inside of the truck as his automated sound system changed CDs as it was told to. Then, all of a sudden, Fifty Cent's "Just a Li'l Bit" started playing.

Sacha started laughing and said, "I like it! I like it!"

Taz smiled as he drove on towards IHOP.

By the time they arrived at the restaurant, Sacha had made him play six different songs. She was really impressed with his voice command system.

They entered the restaurant hand in hand, and Taz noticed several people in the crowded restaurant take notice of them. *I hate this part of the game. All of these clowns are going to try and be all up in my business,* Taz thought as he walked straight towards a waitress and said, "Table for two, please."

The waitress stared at Taz as if he was crazy and said, "Sir, there's about a twenty-minute wait. Please give me your name and I'll call you when your turn has come up."

Taz grinned and said, "Tell your manager that Taz said he needs a table for two." He then turned and winked at Sacha.

Sacha stared at him and said, "So you got it like that, huh?"

"I guess we're about to find out."

The waitress Taz had spoken with came back, followed by the manager. When the manager saw Taz, he smiled and said, "Right this way, Taz. I thought Sheila was playing with me when she said your name. How have you been? It's been a while."

"The same ol', same ol'. Staying busy and stuff," Taz replied as they followed the manager as he led them to the back of the restaurant. Once they were seated, Taz said, "Thanks, Donald. I know how busy you are at this time of the morning."

"No problem, Taz. Anything for you, you know that. I'll have another waitress come take your orders in a few minutes."

"That's cool." Taz waited until the manager was out of earshot and asked, "Did that impress you?"

Sacha laughed and turned her small right hand from side to side, saying, "Just a li'l bit."

"Well, I see that you're hard to impress, so I'm going to have to step up my game."

"Don't do that, Taz. Just be yourself. I'm quite sure that will impress me more than enough," she said as she opened up her menu.

I can't believe that I'm actually having breakfast with a broad like this. Shit, what the fuck am I doing? Taz asked himself as he stared at Sacha.

Sacha saw him staring, put down her menu, and asked, "So, tell me something about you that I'd never believe."

"What?"

Smiling, she said, "Tell me something interesting about yourself, Taz."

"Interesting? To be honest, there's really nothing interesting about me. I'm your average businessman. I work out a lot to try and stay in shape, and tend to my businesses the best I can."

"What exactly are some of your businesses?"

"I do a li'l bit of this and a li'l bit of that."

"Uh-uh, slick. That's too evasive. Have you forgotten that I told you I'm an attorney? You've got to come better than that."

Laughing, he said, "A'ight, but can I ask you a question first?"

"Go ahead."

"What kind of businesses do you think I have?"

"To be completely honest with you, you look like a very successful drug dealer to me."

Taz laughed and said, "Well, at least you said 'successful.' But why a brother have to sell drugs?"

"Look at yourself. You got the nice expensive clothing, the high-priced diamonds in your ears. Your grille looks more expensive than that rapper guy, Baby. Your truck has the big, big chrome rims, and the extra loud automated sound system. And, on top of everything else, you got the mean-looking macho crew. Everything about you screams drugs."

With his smile still in place Taz shook his head slowly and said, "First of all, I've never sold drugs in my life. And to tell you the truth, I despise the people who do. I'm a successful businessman, and my crew, as you called them, are my closest friends. We've been together for a very long time. Thugs, yeah, maybe, but it is what it is. We've never forgotten our beginnings and we never will. Just because we made it financially doesn't mean that we have to dress and act all goody-goody. Or do we have to maintain a certain look for certain people?"

"Not really, but—"

"But what? We work for ourselves. Therefore, we don't have to answer to anyone but us."

"Okay, okay, dang! So, what kind of businesses are you all involved in?"

"You're nosy, aren't ya?"

"I'm just trying to get to know the man I'm having breakfast with," she said with a smile on her face.

"Real estate and small food chains."

Sacha started laughing so hard that she almost choked. "Come on, handsome! You got to come better than that! Don't forget, you're talking to an attorney."

Slightly irritated yet amused, Taz said, "So, you're calling me a liar? Let me tell you something, boo. I'm not the type to go around bragging about my accomplishments. That's just not my style. But, as you obviously noticed, I'm a li'l on the flashy side. I'm a thirty-six-year-old man who is set financially for the rest of my life. All I have is a high school diploma from John Marshall, but I've been blessed with enough business sense to make all of the right moves with my money. So have my homies. Answer this for me. Do you think we were able to get this table without a wait just because I'm the big kingpin of the town?"

Smiling, she said, "Maybe. You know the ballers get special treatment wherever they roll."

"True." Staring directly into Sacha's lovely eyes, Taz said, "I like what I see in you so far, Sacha, and I hope you will give me the opportunity to get to know you better. But before I go any further, it is a must that you believe me, as well as in me. I am not a drug dealer. I've never dealt with drugs in my life, and neither have any of my homeboys."

The tone in his voice made her feel that his words were honest, but what really convinced her was the look in his brown eyes. "The eyes never lie. . . . Well, most times they don't," she said. She raised her glass of water to her lips, sipped, and said, "I believe you, Taz. You can't blame me for asking, can you?"

"Nah, I don't. I just want that understood before we go any further."

"What makes you think we'll go any further than this breakfast?"

Smiling, he said, "Like you said, the eyes never lie."

"What's that supposed to mean?"

"You're diggin' me just as much as I'm diggin' you. I can see it in your eyes." Before she could respond, Donald, the manager of IHOP, came back to their table and said, "Sorry about the wait, Taz, but you know how it is after the club lets out. Sheila's running around like crazy back there. Let me take you guys' order."

"That's cool, Donald. What are you having, Sacha?"

"I'll have the Denver omelet and hash browns."

"That sounds good. I'll have the same, Donald. Add a side of bacon and sausage for me also. Will orange juice be cool, boo?"

Blushing slightly, she said, "Yes, that'll be fine."

"A carafe of orange juice, too, Donald."

"Coming right up, Taz."

Before Donald left to go fill their order, Taz stopped him and asked, "Donald, how do this month's profits look? Better than last months, I hope."

Smiling brightly, Donald said, "Everything's great, Taz. I think we're having our best month this year. I sure hope you don't open up another place and cause me more competition."

Taz smiled at Donald and said, "Now, you know that might just be a good idea, Don. I bet that'll keep you on your toes."

"Ah, Taz, you're killin' me!" They both laughed as Donald left to go fill their orders.

Sacha had a smirk on her face as she said, "Showoff!"

"What?"

"You know what, slick! I told you I believed you, Taz!"

"I had to make sure. Like you said, you are an attorney."

"What's that supposed to mean?"

"You need proof beyond a reasonable doubt."

"I'm goin' to get you for that one, slick!" she said with that sexy smile on her face.

"I hope so, boo! I hope so!"

Chapter Nine

Over the next few weeks, Taz and Sacha had become inseparable. Whenever she wasn't at work, she was with him. They enjoyed each other's company tremendously. Sacha found herself daydreaming about Taz whenever they weren't together. She loved the way he took charge when they went anyplace. His strength was a complete turn-on to her. And those eyes! Taz's brown eyes made her heart skip a beat whenever he stared at her.

"I'm telling you, Gwen, I think I'm falling in love."

"Bitch, please! How long have you been dating this Taz? Two weeks?"

"Ho, it'll be a month this Saturday. And I want you to meet him this weekend, so don't make any plans, okay?"

"Whatever! You said he had a crew, huh? Are any of them worth me giving the time of day?"

"Maybe. There are five of them you can choose from. Knowing your whorish ass, you'll be able to pick one or two."

"You got that right, bitch! Look, I have a client coming over. Let me call you later on."

"All right, ho, but if I don't answer the phone, it's because I'm giving Taz some of my goodies tonight."

Laughing, Gwen said, "It's about time you knocked the dust off that coochie, bitch! Bye!"

Sacha was laughing as she hung up the phone. She went into her bathroom and climbed into the tub. Tonight was the night she was going to let Taz take their relationship to the next level. *I hope he doesn't pull that same shit Clifford pulled on me.* The thought of Clifford and how he completely missed a golden opportunity amused the hell out of her. *Thanks to his ass, I got me some Taz!* she said to herself as she let the bubbles in her bath consume her body. "Fuck Calgon! Taz, take me away!" she laughed aloud.

Clifford was lying back on Cory's bed, thinking about Sacha. It had been almost a month since the incident at the club. Ever since, Sacha had made it a point to avoid him. *Damn, I fucked up! How in the hell am I ever going to get back in good with her? All because of that damn wannabe ass thug nigga. Fuck!* he thought to himself as he watched Cory come back into the bedroom from her bathroom. Her slim frame was cool, but she was a straight slouch compared to Sacha.

Cory smiled as she climbed onto the bed and said, "Smile, baby. It can't be that bad."

"What? What are you talking about?"

"You look as if you've lost your best friend, baby."

"Nah, I just got a lot on my mind, that's all."

"Well, maybe I can get your mind on something else," she said as she slid down towards his manhood and put it inside of her mouth.

"Yeah, you just might," Clifford said as he closed his eyes while she did her thing.

Taz was dressed in a pair of light gray Dickies and a plain white tee. He climbed out of his truck and smiled as he walked towards Sacha's front door. *I can't believe how patient I'm being with this broad. I know I could have fucked the first night if I'd wanted to, but instead I chose to play the patient game with her. Why? That's the million-dollar fucking question,* he thought to himself as he knocked on the door.

Sacha came to the door dressed like the "Eye Candy" of the month in *XXL* magazine. She had on a matching bra and panties set covered with a sheer top. Her curvy figure was looking so enticing that it took all of Taz's self-control not to grab her and start making love to her right there in the doorway.

She smiled and said, "I hope you didn't have any plans for us tonight, baby, 'cause as you can see, I have plans for you all night long."

He smiled as he entered her home and said, "Nah. I thought we were going to watch a flick or something, but I see you're tryin' to make your own flick tonight, huh?"

Smiling seductively, she said, "That's right, baby. I want to see if we can make our own magic on the big screen tonight. Now, come here and kiss me, baby." As they shared a long kiss, Sacha couldn't believe that she was being this straightforward. This was completely out of character for her. But she didn't care; all she cared about at that moment was making love to Taz. He had shown her that he could be patient, and she respected that so much, even though she knew that he could have had her that very first night. That thought got her even wetter than she already was. She stepped out of his embrace and said, "Come." She then led him into her bedroom, which was dark except for the three scented candles she had burning.

Taz stopped her and said, "Boo, are you really ready?"

"I've been ready, Taz. Tonight's the night, baby." She sat on her bed and watched as he slowly began to undress. Watching him taking off his clothes got her so hot that she didn't even realize that she had let her right hand slip between her legs. She fondled herself while he took off his clothes.

Taz smiled as he watched her playing with her pussy. *This is one bad-ass female! Damnit, man, it's about to be on!* he said to himself as he stepped to her. "Come here, baby. Let me taste some of that."

She pulled her hand from her sex, put two of her fingers inside of his mouth, and asked, "How does that taste, baby? Is it good? Tell me it tastes good, baby."

Taz sucked her fingers and said, "Mmm! You're just as sweet as I thought you'd be." He then scooped her into his arms and gently laid her onto her bed. He climbed on top of her and began to methodically lick her entire body. When he made it to her toes, he began to suck each one, one at a time.

Sacha moaned as her right hand found it's way back to her pussy. She was on fire from Taz's every touch.

Taz was so hard he felt as if he was about to explode. *I have to get inside of this pussy like now!* he said to himself as he slid back towards her face. They kissed each other passionately until Taz just couldn't take it any longer. He rolled off of her and reached for his wallet.

Sacha smiled as she took the condom he grabbed out of his wallet and opened the wrapper. She then pushed him onto his back and began sucking his dick. Her mouth was so warm and wet!

Damn! I done died and went to heaven! thought Taz as he watched her suck on him. He didn't know when or how she had done it, but somehow she had slid the condom onto his dick while she was sucking him off. The next thing he knew, she was straddled on top of him, riding him as if her life depended on it. He reached up with both of his hands and began to squeeze each of her nipples. They grew hard instantly from his touch. Sacha's hair was all over the place as she continued to ride him harder and harder. Taz didn't think he would be able to hold off any longer. He wanted to be on top when he came, so he pulled her close to him and started kissing her as he rolled on top of her without ever coming out of her sex. He mounted her and took complete control. Through all of this, Sacha remained silent, which he appreciated. He really wasn't with all of that yelling and screaming shit, so it shocked the hell out of him when he heard all of the noise that he was making. "Damn, baby! This pussy is so good . . . it's so good! Is it mine, boo? Tell me it's mine! Tell! Me! It's! Mine!" he screamed.

"It's yours, Taz! It's all yours, baby! It's all yours!" Sacha yelled as she wrapped her legs around his waist and used her vaginal muscles to grip his dick harder. It had been so long since she had had sex that she was extremely tight. Taz was filling her completely, and she was in ecstasy. "Cum with me, baby! Can you do that for me?" she panted. "Cum with me, baby! Let's make this special. Cum! With! Me! Taz!"

"I'm cummin', baby! I'm cummin'!" he screamed as he unloaded his sperm into the condom he was wearing.

Spent, he rolled off of her and sighed. Sacha was still feeling a few aftershocks of their lovemaking as she lay there, still slightly trembling. After a few minutes, she seemed to regain her bearings. She turned towards Taz and knew right then and there that she was in love. She wiped the sweat off of his forehead, smiled, and said, "Get up, baby. I'm not finished with you yet."

She then pulled him to the end of the bed so that his feet were on the floor. She got in front of him and started sucking his dick with so much vigor that Taz felt as if he was going to cum again that fast. Once she had him nice and hard again, she put her feet onto his thighs and turned her body so that her back was against his chest. Using her legs for leverage, she slid herself onto his dick and began to ride him real slow at first, then faster and faster.

All Taz could do was lay back on the bed and watch in amazement as she rode him like she was a sex maniac.

This time when she came, he came also. "Oh! Taz! I'm! Cumming! It feels so go-o-o-od, baby! It feels so-o-o-o good!"

"Ride that dick, baby! Ride that dick!" he screamed.

"Is it mine, Taz? Is it all mine?"

Just as he started to cum, he screamed, "Yeah, boo, it's yours! It's all yours!"

They both fell back onto the bed, completely spent. They were so caught up with their lovemaking that neither of them realized that their second round of sexing was without a condom.

Chapter Ten

The next morning, Sacha got up to find Taz gone. She groggily climbed out of her bed and went to the bathroom, where she was surprised to see Taz soaking in the bathtub. She smiled and said, "Good morning, baby. How long have you been up?"

"Good morning. I got up a li'l after six. I don't like to sleep late. Plus, I knew you would be getting up early to go to work."

Sacha sat down on the toilet and started relieving herself. After she was finished, she smiled and said, "I'm sorry, I couldn't hold that much longer."

Taz laughed and said, "I ain't trippin'. After all, this is your spot."

"Speaking of spots, Mr. Taz, when am I going to be invited to yours? We've been seeing quite a bit of each other, and I don't even know where you live. Don't tell me that you have a wife and kids somewhere stashed on me. I wouldn't take too kindly to that, mister."

Taz climbed out of the tub, wrapped a towel around himself, and said, "Nah, baby, nothin' like that is goin' on in my life. It's all about you, Sacha."

The look in his eyes told her that he was telling the truth. For some reason, she felt that his eyes seemed to speak volumes to her. She smiled and said, "Good. So, when am I going to get to make love to you in your bedroom?"

He laughed and said, "Whenever you want to, baby. I'm about to go get my workout on, and then I'll be free for the rest of the day. What's on your agenda today? Any court appearances?"

"Nope. I have to go to the county jail and visit a client at ten. After that, my day is done. Are we on for some lunch, then heart-stopping sex or what?" she asked with that sexy smile of hers.

"How about the heart-stopping sex, then lunch?"

Laughing, she said, "Either way is fine with me, Mister Taz."

"That's cool. Now, come here and give me a hug." They shared a tight hug and then a passionate kiss. "I'm digging you more than I expected, Sacha," Taz said as he pulled himself from their embrace.

Staring into his eyes, she asked, "Is that good or bad, baby?"

Smiling, he responded, "It's definitely good. I never thought I could feel this strongly for a woman so quickly."

"Why is that?"

"My past just wouldn't let me love easily."

"Love? Are you telling me that you're in love with me?"

He returned her stare briefly, then nodded his head yes. "I fell in love with you the first time I laid my eyes on you, boo. But I refused to let my emotions override my intellect. I knew that if I ever saw you again, you were going to be mine. That's why when I saw you at the club again, I didn't hesitate. That clown you were with didn't have a chance. I was going after what I wanted."

As she pulled Taz out of the bathroom, she said, "You're so damn cocky sometimes! I wish I could say the same, but I wasn't sure about you or your intentions until after I got to know you."

"Yeah, I know. You thought I was Nino Brown."

She punched him lightly on his arm and said, "I'm serious, Taz. I have to be careful. You know I could be disbarred if I got involved with a criminal. But, when we made love last night, I realized that I don't give a damn if you're on the Ten Most Wanted list by the FBI. All I want is for you to love me as much as I love you."

Smiling, he asked, "Love? So, are you telling me that you love me, Sacha?"

"Yes, Taz, I love you."

"I love you, too, Li'l Mama."

"Li'l Mama? Where'd that come from?"

"My mother always told me that she will always be my Big Mama, and any other woman who ever comes into my life will be my Li'l Mama. Now that it's official that you're my woman, you're now my Li'l Mama. So, I guess I have to call Mama-Mama and set up a time for you two to meet."

"Mama-Mama?"

"That's my mother."

"Oh, okay. When will I get to meet her?"

"I'll give her a call after I finish working out this morning. Call me after you come from the county jail, and we'll see then."

"Taz, it's a quarter to eight. I don't have to be at the county jail until ten."

"And I told you I have to go work out. I'm meeting my niggas at the gym in an hour."

Smiling seductively, she said, "Well, that means we still have some time to kill." She pulled him close to her and said, "There are a few more things I didn't get to show you last night."

Smiling, he asked, "And what's that, Li'l Mama?"

She pulled him onto the bed and said, "You'll see!"

***

By the time Taz made it home, the entire crew was parked in his driveway.

Keno smiled as he watched Taz get out of his truck. "Damn, my nigga! Is she really like that? You look like you've been in a fuckin' marathon or some shit."

Taz smiled and said, "Yeah, dog, she's like that!"

They went inside of Taz's home, and Taz said, "Y'all go on downstairs and start warming up. I'll be down after I change." He went upstairs to his bedroom and quickly changed into a pair of sweatpants and a wife-beater. Once he was changed, he went downstairs and joined his homies.

Bob was stretching, while Red and Wild Bill were loosening up their joints by curling one of Taz's curl bars without any weights on it. Bo-Pete and Keno were taking turns warming up their joints by bench-pressing light weight.

Taz's built-in gym was equipped with everything one could imagine. There were over several hundred pounds of free weights. He had dumbbells, shoulder machines, squat machines, even a built-in Olympic-sized swimming pool, not to mention a sauna room and Jacuzzi. He had spent over three hundred thousand dollars on everything. To him, it was money well spent, because he had all the luxuries of a regular gym inside of his home.

"All right, you clowns, let's do this," Taz said as he began to stretch and get loose.

They had a set routine that they did Monday thru Friday. They would start by doing five sets of twenty-five reps with the curl bars. Then they would do some work with the dumbbells. Afterward, they would head to the bench press and do ten sets of twenty reps on the bench. Finally, they would jump into the pool and swim fifty laps. Since they were all over thirty, it was a must that they kept themselves in tip-top shape. And though they had different characteristics physically, they were some very strong men.

After they had finished their workout, Taz told Keno that he was having lunch with Sacha, and that he planned on taking her over to meet Mama-Mama.

"Is that right? Damn, gee! You're really serious about, her huh?"

"Yeah, dog, I love her."

Wild Bill was sipping on a bottled water and damned near spit a mouthful all over Bob's face. "You're *what?* Damn, nigga, you just met the broad!"

"So what? I know when I'm loving a female, nigga. I'm not like your li'l ass. I don't fall in and out of love every other week."

Bob started laughing and said, "I'm happy for you, my nigga. I hope she's been looking for a homegirl for me."

"Bob, she's a attorney, gee. I don't think she has any fuckin' 'homegirls,'" Taz said sarcastically.

"Well, one of her colleagues, then," Bob said with a smile.

"You're a fuckin' clown, nigga, you know that?"

"Don't pay that nigga any attention, homey. Do you. I'm happy for your ass. It's about time you really started living again," Red said seriously.

"I have a question, though. What you gon' do about Tari now that you're all in love and shit?" asked Bo-Pete.

"That, my nigga, is a very good question," Taz said as his sipped his bottled water.

Sacha decided to stop at the office before she went to go visit her client in the county jail. She was feeling extremely giddy as she walked down the hallway towards her office. The smile she had on her face quickly turned to a frown when she saw Clifford coming towards her. He stopped her and said, "Hello, Sacha."

"Good morning, Cliff. How are you?"

"Fine. You're looking stunning this morning."

"Thanks. Could you excuse me? I'm kind of pressed for time. I have to be at County in about twenty minutes," she said as she checked the time on her Rolex.

"Sacha, I know I made a complete ass of myself at the club that night. I hope you can forgive me for my childish behavior."

"Cliff, that's the past. Let's just leave it there, okay?"

Smiling brightly, he said, "Exactly! So, when do you think we could get together and start from scratch?"

She gave him a look as if to ask whether he was serious. When she saw that he was, she said, "Well, Cliff, I'm seeing someone now, and it looks as if it's getting pretty serious."

"Serious? Come on, Sacha! It's barely been a month since we were at the club. How could it be that serious?"

Sighing heavily, she said, "It'll be a month this Saturday, Cliff. And believe me, it is serious, so let it go, okay? Look, like I said, I'm running late. Bye, Cliff," she said as she went inside of her office and grabbed a few of her notes on her new client.

After Sacha was led into the visiting room of the county jail, she sat down at the small table and pulled out her files and started reviewing them. Her new client was being held without bail by the DEA for distribution of crack cocaine. He obviously had plenty of money, since he was able to afford her as an attorney.

She figured the best thing she could do for him was to get him to plea out and hope for the best deal possible, especially since he was caught on tape making a direct drug transaction with an undercover agent.

One of the sheriffs came into the visiting room with her client in handcuffs. After cuffing one of his hands to the small table, the sheriff left them alone inside the visiting room.

"Hello, Mr. Surefield. How are you doing today?"

"I'm hangin' in there. Do you think you'll be able to get me a bail, ma'am?"

"I don't think so, but I'll try when we go to your bail hearing next week."

"*Next week?* Why do we have to wait so damn long?"

"First off, your court date has been set for Tuesday, Mr. Surefield. That's only six days away. And secondly, that's how these things go. Now, tell me, have you ever been in any trouble like this before?"

"Nah, this is my first case. How much time do you think I'm gon' get?"

"That's kind of difficult to say at this point. You do know that you were caught on tape selling crack cocaine to an undercover officer."

"Yeah, I know. You can't tell me what I'm lookin' at?"

"Since this is your first arrest, you might be lucky enough to get ten years."

"*Ten years?* Fuck that shit! I ain't tryin' to do no damn ten years! You gots to get me a better deal than that!"

"Mr. Surefield, the only way we can get you a better deal than that will be for you to tell the DEA something that will want to make them help you out."

"So, in order for me to get less than a dime, I got to tell somethin', huh? Fuck that shit! I ain't no snitch!"

"I understand, Mr. Surefield."

"Call me Tony."

"Okay, Tony. Let's go over everything for the record. You sold two ounces of crack cocaine to an undercover agent on November 10th, 2005. You were unlucky enough to be caught up in a DEA sting operation. Since you sold more than 52 grams of crack, that puts you in the ten to life penalty range."

"Ten to life? I thought you said I was lookin' at ten years!"

"I did. But the federal system doesn't work exactly like that."

"You need to break this shit down for me, ma'am."

"Your deal will most likely be, like I said, ten years to life. But since this is your first arrest, your numbers on the federal guidelines should be relatively low—category one to be exact. It's the decision of the U.S. assistant attorney on exactly how low your numbers will be down the category. If they want to, they could push for more time. It all depends."

"On what?"

"On you, Mr.—excuse me—Tony."

"So, once again you're tellin' me that I should tell them something?"

"No, I'm not telling you to tell them anything, Tony. That decision has to be made by you, and you only. What I am telling you is that you're looking at doing some time, either way. The final decision is solely up to you. If you'd like, I'll speak with the U.S. assistant attorney who has your case, and see what he's actually talking about."

"Yeah, you do that, 'cause if I gots to tell somethin' to get under a dime, then so be it."

Damn! I thought you weren't going to snitch, Sacha thought to herself. To her client, she said, "That's fine, Tony. I'll get right on it, and I'll see you Tuesday in court."

"If I tell somethin', will that help me get a bail?"

"It might. Like I said, it's all up to the U.S. assistant attorney."

"Okay. When you speak with him, make sure that you let him know that I gots a lot to tell. Okay?"

"I'll do that. You do understand that my fee is still the same either way?"

"Yeah, I got your chips. Don't trip on that shit."

"Whom shall I contact for payment?"

"My big brother KK's wife will be getting at you later on today."

"That's fine. Have her take the check to my office and leave it with the receptionist if I'm not there. Well, I guess that's all for now, Tony. I'll give the assistant attorney a call and see exactly where we're at. I'll know more when we get to court Tuesday. If you need to speak with me, give me a call at the office. You can call collect if you have to."

"Thanks."

After they had shaken hands, Sacha gathered her things and put them inside of her leather briefcase and called for the sheriff. She watched as Tony was led back into the county jail. *It's a shame that these young brothers get themselves caught up like this. Now he's about to get more young brothers caught up in the system just because he can't do all of the time he's about to get. This shit is so crazy,* thought Sacha as she left the visiting room.

Clifford was sitting at his desk, steaming. *How could that bitch do me like that? That's some cold-ass shit! After all of the time and energy I've put into her, she's just going to up and get involved with someone else. That's cold!* he said to himself as he stared at the picture he and Sacha had taken in front of the Oklahoma City Bombing memorial. *She's too damn special to lose like that. I'm going to have to find a way to get her away from whomever she's seeing. I have to!* He put the picture back inside of his desk drawer.

Once Sacha was outside of the county jail, she pulled out her cell phone and quickly called Taz. He answered his cell after the third ring. "What up, Li'l Mama?"

She smiled and said, "Hi, baby! Are you through getting your muscles all worked up?"

"Yeah, we just finished. Where are you?"

"I'm leaving County now. I'm going to go back to the house and change into something comfortable. What do you have planned for us?"

"After I take a quick shower, I'm going to give Mama-Mama a call and see if she's busy. If she isn't, I'm going to see if she'd mind cooking us lunch. More than likely she'll tell me to hurry up and get over there. So, I'll give you a call after I get at her. Then I'll come scoop you up."

"That's fine, baby. After we leave from your mother's, are we going to your house to do the nasty some more?"

Laughing, Taz said, "Damn, Li'l Mama! You're a straight sex fiend, huh?"

"I am now! See you in a li'l bit, baby."

Laughing loudly, Taz said, "A'ight then, Li'l Mama."

Chapter Eleven

Sacha stepped out of her home, dressed casually in a pair of brown corduroy pants and a tan sweater. Since it was slightly chilly outside, she hoped she was dressed appropriately to meet Taz's mother.

Taz smiled as he watched Sacha walk towards his truck. "That's one sexy-ass lady!" he said aloud as he continued to stare at her.

Once Sacha was inside of the truck and comfortable, she said, "Hi, baby. Did you have a nice workout?"

"Yeah, it was cool. I got at Mama-Mama. She's expecting us to be there in about twenty minutes."

"That's fine. Do I look okay, baby?"

"You're on point, Li'l Mama. I like those boots you got on. They're tight."

Blushing slightly, she said, "Thanks. I've been having these bad boys for a minute now. I've been waiting for a reason to wear them. I hope your mom will like me. I'm kinda nervous."

"Nervous about what? Baby, you've already impressed the hell outta me, and that's all that matters. I love Mama-Mama, but nothin' and no one will ever change how I feel about you. So relax, 'cause she's goin' to love you, anyway," Taz said seriously as he pulled out of her driveway.

"I hope you're right."

Taz pulled into the long driveway of his mother's home out in the city of Spencer. Spencer is considered the country, since it's about twenty minutes outside of Oklahoma City, and is mostly a rural area with lots and lots of land. Taz's mother's home was a large ranch-style house with plenty of flowers in the front.

Sacha smiled and said, "Oh, I love your mother's flower garden! I wish I had the time to do something like that in front of my house."

"If you'd like, I could come over when I find some time and hook yours up just like it."

"You'd do that?"

"Yep. Why do you look so surprised? I got skills, Li'l Mama," he said as he pushed a button on the door panel and both of their doors opened with a whoosh.

Mama-Mama was standing in her doorway when Taz and Sacha stepped out of the truck. She smiled as she watched her loving child. Finally, after all of these years, he was bringing a girl home for her to meet. *Thank you, Jesus, for letting this boy finally start to live again!* Mama-Mama thought to herself as she stepped out of the doorway. "Well, well, it's about time I got to see my man child! For a minute there, I thought you done forgot about Mama-Mama," she said as she gave Taz a tight hug.

After they finished hugging each other, Taz stepped back and said, "You need to gon' with that, Mama-Mama. You know I be busy and stuff. Anyway, Mama-Mama, this is Sacha. Sacha, this is my mother, Mama-Mama."

Sacha stepped forward, extended her hand, and said, "I'm pleased to meet you, Mrs.—"

Mama-Mama slapped her hand down, gave Sacha a tight hug, and said, "Girl, you gon' with that Mrs. stuff! You call me 'Mama-Mama' just like everybody else, hear?"

Laughing, Sacha said, "Sure, Mama-Mama."

"Good. Now, y'all come on inside so we can sit down and eat. After lunch, we can gets to know each other better."

As they followed Mama-Mama into the house, Taz grabbed Sacha's hand and whispered, "See, I told you! Mama-Mama loves you."

Sacha smiled but remained silent as they went inside. Once they were inside, she smiled because Mama-Mama's home was so comfortable looking. She had a beige sectional in her living room, with a huge glass coffee table sitting in front of it. The house made her think of something out of that old TV show, *Dallas*. It was homey looking as well as expensive. *I bet Taz made sure that Mama-Mama remained well taken care of,* she thought as she stepped to the mantel over the fireplace and stared at some of the pictures that were sitting there. There were pictures of Taz when he was in high school, looking funny in his football uniform. Then there were some of Taz, Mama-Mama, and another little girl who Sacha assumed was Taz's little sister, because they could pass as twins, except that she could see that she was much younger than Taz.

Taz plopped himself onto the sofa and watched Sacha as she was looking at the pictures of him and his family. *Yeah, she's definitely going to be in my life for a long time.*

After a few more minutes, Mama-Mama yelled from the kitchen, "Y'all come on back here! The food's ready now!"

Sacha turned and asked, "Where's your little sister, Taz?"

He smiled and said, "She goes to OU. She lives out by the campus in Norman."

"That's nice. You know you two could pass as twins."

"Yeah, that's what everybody tells me. Come on, before Mama-Mama starts tripping."

"Tripping about what, boy?" Mama-Mama asked, standing in the doorway of the kitchen.

"Nothin'."

"Humph! Y'all come on now before I gets upset and gets my switch!"

They all laughed as they went into the kitchen.

Mama-Mama sat her large frame down and said, "Taz, have you spoken to Tazneema lately?"

Taz was reaching across the table, grabbing himself one of Mama-Mama's buttered rolls, and said, "Yeah, I talked to her a few weeks ago. Why? Is something wrong?"

"Did you know that she wants to go spend the holidays with some white folks way out in Houston?"

"Yeah, she told me. I really don't see nothin' wrong with it, Mama-Mama. She's been doing real good in school, so you might as well let her have some fun."

"Humph! You know how them youngstas are now these days. Especially out there in Houston."

"Come on, Mama-Mama! What do you know about what's goin' on in Houston?"

"Boy, you think I don't know about how they be out there sippin' on that syrup?" The shocked look on both Sacha's and Taz's face answered her question. "Just like I thought. Y'all be thinkin' 'cause I'm an old woman, I don't be knowin' what's goin' on. Well, you're both wrong."

Laughing, Taz asked, "Mama-Mama, what do you know about syrup?"

"Miss Jones's son lives out there in Houston, and he told her all about that there 'lean' they be drankin' down there. She told me it's codeine and pop they be

mixing and stuff. I'm not having my baby out there gettin' mixed up with all of that stuff, ya hear me, Taz?"

"Yes, ma'am. But I doubt if 'Neema would get caught
up with any of that stuff. You need to have more faith
in her, Mama-Mama."

"Faith my ass! Now pass me the corn, boy."

As Taz did as she told him to, she turned toward Sacha and said, "Now, tell me something about yourself,
Sacha. I already knows you're a lawyer, so you can skip
that part."

Sacha laughed nervously and said, "Well, I was born
in the City. I grew up in Bethany. After I graduated
from Putnam North, I went to Oklahoma State and
studied law. I'm an only child, and both of my parents
now live in Florida."

"Florida? What made them want to move way out
that way?"

"After they retired, my mom talked my father into it.
They seem to love it out there, because I hardly ever get
to see them anymore."

"You mean to tell me that they don't come to visit or
nothin'?"

"That's right."

"And you don't go out to visit them neither?"

"Well, with my job it's kind of difficult to find the
time. But I was hoping to go out there this summer."

"That sounds like a lovely idea. You need to make
sure that you take this knucklehead out there with you.
That way, he can meet your folks. They gon' need to
meet their new son-in-law," Mama-Mama said, and
she stuffed a piece of the tender brisket she made inside of her mouth.

Taz almost choked on the corn he had in his mouth.
Sacha laughed as she watched him. "Mama-Mama!
You know you need to quit it!" Taz said and smiled.

"Boy, this is the first woman that you've brought to this house in I don't know how long. And I can tell by the way the both of you look that y'all done fell in love with each other. So don't be tryin' to play like Mama-Mama don't know what she be talkin' 'bout. 'Cause I do!"

"It hasn't even been a whole month since we've been goin' out, Mama-Mama."

"So what, Taz? That ain't squat. Ain't no time limit on love, boy. Look at the both of y'all. If y'all ain't in love with each other, my name ain't Mama-Mama."

They laughed some more and continued to eat the big lunch that Mama-Mama prepared for them.

After spending a couple of hours chatting with Mama-Mama, Taz said, "Well, Mama-Mama, it's time for us to be going. Do you need anything before we leave?"

"Mama-Mama's just fine, boy. I want you to know that I don't agree with that Houston stuff, but I'm gon' go on and let that girl go. But if somethin' crazy happens, I'm gon' blame it all on *you*, Taz!"

Smiling, Taz shook his head and said, "All right, Mama-Mama." He then stepped to her and gave her a tight hug and a kiss on her cheek and said, "I love you, Mama-Mama."

"I love you, too, boy. Now, gon' and get out my way so I can give my daughter-in-law a hug."

They laughed as Sacha stepped into Mama-Mama's warm embrace and gave her a hug. "It was really nice meeting you, Mama-Mama. I hope we can come and do this again real soon," Sacha said sincerely.

"Girl, you're welcome in this home anytime . . . anytime, ya hear?"

"Yes, ma'am," replied Sacha.

Taz turned towards Sacha and said, "Here, Li'l Mama. Go on out to the truck. I need to holla at Mama-Mama for a sec."

Sacha took the keys from Taz, waved good-bye to Mama-Mama, and went and got inside of Taz's truck.

After she was out of the house, Taz asked, "Mama-Mama, do you like her?"

"She's perfect for you, Taz. That girl loves you, boy."

"Yeah, I know."

"The question is, do you love her?"

"Yeah, Mama-Mama, I do."

"What you gon' do about that white girl?"

Sighing heavily, he said, "I'm gon' have to keep it real with her. Tari knows everything about me. I've never kept any secrets from her, and I'm not about to start now."

"You know you gon' break that girl's heart, don't you?"

Nodding his head yes, he asked, "But what else can I do, Mama-Mama?"

"Nothin' I guess. Follow your heart, boy. I guess that's all you can do."

Smiling, he said, "That's exactly what I'm doing! Alright then, let me go. Oh, and don't worry about 'Neema. She'll be all right."

"Speaking of 'Neema, does Sacha—"

"One thing at a time, Mama-Mama . . . one thing at a time," Taz said as he gave his mother another hug and left her home.

Taz climbed inside of his truck and said, "You were a hit. She loves you."

Smiling brightly, Sacha said, "That's good. I really like your mom, Taz. She's so down to earth."

"Yeah, Mama-Mama's gon' always keep it real. Well, since you're now in with my Mama-Mama, all you have to do now is impress 'Neema."

"Your sister?"

Before he could answer her question, his cell rang. He flipped it open and saw a picture of Michael Jordan shooting a fadeaway jump shot over Joe Dumars of the old Detroit Pistons. He closed his phone and said, "Shit!" He reopened his phone and quickly dialed Keno's cell number. When Keno answered his cell, Taz said, "Dog, I just got hit by Won. Call the others and meet me at my spot. I'm out in Spencer, and I'm on my way there now."

"I'm on it, my nigga," said Keno, and he hung up the phone.

Taz turned toward Sacha and said, "Look, Li'l Mama. I gots to bounce outta town. I'm goin' to need you to do me a favor, okay?"

"Is something wrong, baby?"

"Nah. I just need you to take my truck to your pad for me, 'cause I'm not gon' have enough time to take you back to your spot. I'll most likely be gone for a day or two. I'll hit you when I know for sure."

"That's no problem, Taz, but is everything okay? You seem kind of bent out of shape."

"Everything is everything, Li'l Mama. I just gotta take care of some business and I'm on the clock."

Sacha didn't respond as she watched as Taz drove towards his house.

Oh, my God! I know this isn't this man's home! Sacha said to herself as Taz pulled into the circular driveway of his mini-mansion. He stopped his truck in front of his four-car garage, grabbed the remote control and pressed one of it's buttons. All four doors of the garage opened slowly, and Sacha gasped as she saw Taz's 2005 S Class 600 Mercedes-Benz in one stall. In the other stall he had an all-chrome Softail Harley-Davidson, and in the last stall there was a brand-new convertible Bentley Azure.

What the fuck? Sacha shook her head to make sure she wasn't dreaming. When she realized what she was staring at wasn't a dream, she said, "Taz, baby, what are—"

"Look, Li'l Mama, I ain't got time for questions right now. I gots to go get ready to get up outta here. I kinda got an idea of what's goin' on in that beautiful head of yours. Don't trip. I'll explain everything when I get back. Just trust me, okay?"

"Okay, Taz, but you definitely have some explaining to do, mister."

He smiled, gave her a quick kiss, and said, "Fa' sho! Now, let me go. I'll give you a call later on this evening if I can. If not, I'll call you sometime in the morning. I love you, Sacha."

"I love you, too, Taz."

They shared a quick kiss, and Taz jumped out of his truck and went inside of his home through the garage.

Sacha climbed over and got comfortable in the driver's side of his truck. After she adjusted the seat, she put the Denali in reverse and backed out of the driveway. As she turned onto the street, she stared in disbelief at what looked like a small fleet of all-black trucks driving past her and pulling into Taz's driveway: Keno's all-black Range Rover, Red's all-black Tahoe, Bo-Pete's all-black Navigator, Wild Bill's all-black Durango, and Bob's all-black Escalade. "Yeah, you're going to be explaining your ass off when you get back, Taz!" Sacha said as she drove away from his home.

Inside of Taz's house, the crew was waiting for Taz to let them know where they were going to now. Taz was sitting down in his den, tapping on the keys of his laptop. After about five minutes of this, he closed the laptop and said, "A'ight, it's like this. We're on our way to Chi-Town, boys. Keno and I are bouncing up outta Tulsa in two hours. Bo-Pete, you and Wild Bill are bouncin' up outta DFW, and Red, you and Bob gets to bounce up outta the City. The mission is set to go down tomorrow night, so we'll be spending at least a day out there. We're staying at the Courtyard Marriott in downtown Chicago. Our Barneys are intact so your rooms will be reserved. I'll hit y'all when we get in, and then we'll find out everything else. Any questions?"

"Yeah. What's the figures on this one?" asked Wild Bill.

"Oh, I forgot. Hold up," Taz said as he reopened the laptop and quickly tapped it's keys. After a few minutes of this, he smiled and passed the laptop to Wild Bill. Wild Bill smiled as he passed the laptop to Red. After the laptop had been passed to every member of the crew, Taz said, "Let's go earn our chips!"

Chapter Twelve

Later on that evening, Sacha was on the telephone with Gwen, explaining to her what she had seen earlier at Taz's home. "Girl, I'm telling you, that man has a fucking mansion! And the cars! Ho, he gots a damn Bentley!"

"Bitch, you lying!" yelled Gwen.

"I swear! What's the name of those loud-ass old type motorcycles them white boys be riding?"

"What, a Harley?"

"Yeah, ho, he even has one of those in his four-car garage."

"Four-car garage! Damn, he's got it like that, huh?"

"Yep. Oh, and did I mention the brand-new 600 Benz?"

"Stop it, bitch! You gone too damn far with that."

"I ain't lying. I'm telling you, Gwen, Taz is living large! My only question now is, how in the hell did he get it like that?"

"Didn't he tell you he owned a few restaurants and stuff?"

"Yeah, but ain't no way in hell can a nigga get money like he has with a few IHOPs and some rental houses."

"Why not? Shit, he might own way more than you think. Bitch, stop tripping out. I ain't never seen a woman who's mad 'cause she done found out the man she's in love with is rich. You are one silly bitch," said Gwen as she started laughing.

"Ho, I'm serious! You know I can't get caught up with no nigga who's into some illegal shit. I'd get disbarred. Ain't no man worth me losing my career over. I've worked too damn hard to let some shit like that happen to me."

"I hear you, Sacha, but didn't he tell you that he wasn't into anything illegal?"

"Yeah, but—"

"And you believed him, right?"

"Yeah, but—"

"But my ass, bitch! You're loving that man, so once he gets back, you ask him again just to satisfy your curiosity. Also, stress the fact that you can't risk being involved with someone who is into any illegal shit. If his answers are still the same after that, then you will have two choices to make. One, you believe him and move on with what y'all are trying to build, or two, you stop it right there and tell him that you just can't take the chance on him. It's as simple as that, Sacha," Gwen said seriously.

Before Sacha could speak, there was a click on her phone letting her know that there was another call coming in. "Hold on for a minute, ho," she said, and she clicked over to the next line. "Hello?"

"What up, Li'l Mama? You miss me yet?" asked Taz.

"Hey, Taz. Where are you?"

"Not too far. But check this out. I'll be back Friday evening. Do you want to get into anything particular, or do you wanna just chill at my spot?"

Sighing, she said, "Taz, we need to talk first."

"Hold up, Li'l Mama. I know you're out there thinking all types of shit, but I want you to think back to that time when we were at my IHOP. Remember what I told you what was a must for me, baby? Do you?" he urged.

Sacha thought back to that night for a minute and said, "Yes, I do, Taz."

"What was it?"

She smiled and said, "You said that it was a must that I believe you as well as in you."

"And do you?"

"Yes, but—"

"No buts, Li'l Mama. Do you or don't you believe me?"

"I do, Taz. I really do."

"Then don't trip off of any of the li'l shit. And believe me, all that you've seen so far is just that li'l shit. I told you from the beginning that I'm set financially for the rest of my life, so there's no reason for you to be letting your mind get you to trippin' out, thinking I'm *Scarface* and shit." He laughed, and then continued, "That's what you're doing, aren't you?"

Laughing herself, Sacha said, "I couldn't help it, baby. You know I can't risk ruining my career being involved with someone who's into some shady shit."

"I understand that, Li'l Mama, and you should know that I would never, and I mean *never*, put you or your career at risk. But look, I gots to bounce. I'll try to call you back later, after I finish handling my business."

"Taz, where are you?"

Laughing, he said, "Taking care of my business, Li'l Mama. I'll talk to you later. Now, tell me you love me before I bounce."

Smiling and blushing as if he was in the same room with her, she said, "I love you, baby."

"Good. I love you, too, Li'l Mama," he said and hung up the phone.

Sacha clicked back to Gwen and said, "Ho that was Taz."

"I figured that shit 'cause you was taking too damn long. The only reason I waited was because I wanted to know what he told your ass."

"He just reminded me of something he told me when we first met."

"And what was that, bitch?"

Smiling, she said, "That I should always believe in him, because he would never put me at risk."

"Do you?"

"Yeah, ho, I do. I love him, and my heart is telling me that he wouldn't do anything to jeopardize me or my career."

"Look at it this way. If he does, at least he has enough money to take care of your ass!" They both started laughing.

Clifford arrived at the office early in hopes of catching Sacha when she first came to work. He just couldn't get her out of his system. He wanted to be with her so badly that it actually hurt. *I have to convince her to give me another shot,* he thought to himself as he went into his office.

Sacha arrived at work in a really good mood. All was well, and she was in love! When she saw Clifford talking to one of the partners in front of her office, she almost stopped and went in the other direction. *I'm really starting to get tired of this nigga,* she thought as she held her head high and strolled confidently towards them.

"Good morning, gentlemen," she said once she was in front of Clifford and Mr. Whitney.

"Good morning, Sacha," they replied in unison.

"And a good morning it is, Sacha. I was just telling Clifford here that we're going to announce you becoming a partner at our annual Christmas party next week," Mr. Whitney said with a smile on his face.

Sacha beamed and said, "Really?"

"Yes, really. You will officially be a partner on the second day of the New Year. So, why not announce it at our party at the Westin's ballroom? So, you know the rules. Dress to impress, 'cause we're all going to have a real good time."

"Thank you, Mr. Whitney! Thank you so much!" she said sincerely.

"You've earned it, Sacha. You're one of the best attorneys in this entire firm."

"Congratulations, Sacha. This couldn't be happening to a sweeter person," Clifford said with a smile on his face.

"Thanks," she said flatly. "Well, if you two will excuse me, I have a court date in twenty minutes, and I have a few calls to make before I leave."

"Sure. Go get 'em, tiger!" Mr. Whitney said as he left her alone with Clifford.

Sacha went inside of her office, followed by Clifford. She went and sat behind her desk and quickly grabbed the phone. Even though she didn't have any calls to make, she dialed the number to her home, hoping that he would get the hint and leave her be, but her hopes were in vain. Clifford sat down in one of the leather chairs on the opposite side of her desk and waited patiently for her to finish. After letting her phone go to her voice mail, she finally hung up and asked, "Is there something that I can do for you, Cliff?"

Smiling, he said, "As a matter of fact, there is, Sacha. Could you please let me take you out Friday to celebrate your partnership?"

Sighing heavily, she said, "Cliff, look. We've been here before. Why do you insist on making this more difficult that it already is? I told you that I'm involved with someone, and it's serious. Can't you respect that and let it be?"

"To be completely honest with you, Sacha, no, I can't. I know that we were on our way to building something special, and I just can't get you or that night out of my mind. I really care about you. Can't you see that?"

"Yes, I do, Cliff. But you have to understand that what is done is done. Neither of us can go back and change what happened that night."

"I understand that, but can we at least try to move past that? Let me take you out to dinner Friday evening, Sacha. Come on, it's just a meal between colleagues."

Shaking her no, she said, "I have plans for Friday, Cliff. As a matter of fact, I'm going to the same club that started all of this."

"You mean to tell me that you've become a regular at that ghetto-ass establishment? Come on, Sacha, that's really not your style."

"Humph! It may not be *your* style, but my man and I seem to enjoy ourselves whenever we're there."

"Your man?"

"Excuse me, Cliff, but I'm running late. I have to be in court in a few minutes." She grabbed her briefcase and left her office with Clifford standing in her doorway, mad as hell. *Let that one simmer for a minute, fool!* she thought as she left the office building on her way towards the courthouse.

Mission complete, thought Taz as he sat back in Keno's Range Rover for the ride back to the City. As usual, their job was smooth and easy. Won had done it again. *Now that the crew is four hundred thousand dollars richer, it is once again time to go clubbin',* he thought as he grabbed his cell and called Sacha. He frowned as he heard her voice mail pick up, and he left a quick message: "I'm back, baby. Give me a holla when you get this message. I'm trying to be with you tonight. I miss you. Bye!"

Keno smiled and said, "Damn, my nigga! You're in love for real, huh?"

"Looks that way, dog. She's the real thing, homey, and I'm not letting her get away from me."

"I feel you, gee. Do your thang, boy!" They both laughed as Keno drove them back to Oklahoma City.

By the time Sacha made it home, she was dead tired. For the last two days, she had been in and out of court, and back and forth from the courthouse to the county jail. Her client, Tony Surefield was starting to get on her nerves with his snitching ass.

She slid off her shoes and went into her bedroom. After getting comfortable on her bed, she grabbed the phone and gave Gwen a call. "What's up, ho? I hope you haven't changed your mind about going to the club tonight," she asked as soon as Gwen answered the phone.

"That depends, bitch."

"On what?"

"On whether or not your man and his homies are back from their business trip. I'm trying to get me one of those rich-ass niggas for myself. Ain't no need in you having all of the damn fun, bitch!"

They both started laughing. Sacha said, "Ho, you're crazy for real. I haven't heard from Taz since last night.

But he did tell me that he'd be back sometime this evening and that he would meet us at the club. So, I guess it's on."

"That's what I'm talking about! Bitch, I'm going all out tonight. Wait until you see what I'm wearing."

Laughing, Sacha said, "Oh, my God! I know you're about to be on some hoochie shit for real."

"Nah, bitch, it's all about classy and fine tonight. Wait, you'll see."

"Whatever! All right, girl, I'll be over to pick your ass up around ten. Cool?"

"Cool," said Gwen, and she hung up the phone.

After hanging up the phone with Gwen, Sacha got up and went to her closet. "I might as well get sexy for my baby," she said aloud as she began to pick out what she was going to wear to the club.

The rest of the crew made it to Taz's house a little after nine p.m. They went inside and completed their ritual of checking their accounts. After seeing that everything was in order, they waited for Won's phone call. And as usual, he was right on time.

"What's up, Babyboy?" asked Won when Taz answered his cell phone.

"The same ol' same, O.G."

"Y'all checked them accounts yet?"

"Yeah, everything is everything."

"Good. Nothing's going to go down for the rest of the year, so you know how it goes. Enjoy, be merry, and most of all, be good! Out!"

Taz laughed as he told the crew what Won had said. "Now, I guess we can bounce on to the club so y'all clowns can do y'all's thang. I doubt if I stay too long, though. Sacha's going to bring my truck, so I'll be bouncin' up outta there with her."

"Damn, you sprung-ass nigga! You can't even kick it with your boys for a li'l while?" asked Bo-Pete.

"Nigga, I'll chill for a minute, but I'm trying to get my freak on with my broad. I ain't tryin' to be all up in the bunk-ass club, lookin' at you niggas all night."

"Whatever, dog! Come on, let's bounce. There's hoes to catch and liquor to be drank," Keno said as he stood up.

"I'm with you, my nigga," said Bob as he, too, got to his feet.

When they arrived at the club, Taz smiled when he saw his truck parked in his usual parking space. *It's good to see that the security at the club let Sacha park my shit where it normally sits,* he thought as he got out of Keno's Range Rover.

Bob parked his Escalade next to Bo-Pete's Navigator and climbed out of his truck. "Dog, I'm telling you, tonight I'm patching the baddest bitch in da club. I'm trying to go get my freak on somethin' awful," Bob said as he walked towards the entrance of Club Cancun.

"Whatever, clown! I'm tellin' yo' ass, I ain't with that carryin' you shit tonight, fool."

"The only person who's going to be carrying Bob tonight, is a bitch, nigga!"

Inside of the club, Katrina and Paquita were both busy hating on Gwen and Sacha. "I can't believe that bitch gots the nerve to be all up in here like she's the shit!" said Paquita.

"I know, girl. And look at her friend. She thinks she's flyer than a muthafucka in that mink wrap she gots on," added Katrina.

***

At their table, Sacha and Gwen both knew that they were looking especially fly. Their outfits spoke volumes to everyone around them. Several different guys came by and offered to buy them drinks, and they politely declined as they waited for Taz and his crew.

Sacha was dressed in a long, formfitting black Prada dress and red and black Prada pumps, while Gwen was just as sexy looking in a beige and brown suede jump-suit and a dark brown chinchilla fur wrapped around her shoulders. Her brown Manolos set the outfit off completely.

"Bitch, where the hell is your man and his homies? 'Cause if they don't get their asses here soon, I'm gon' start choosing some of these fine-ass youngstas up in this spot."

Sacha smiled and said, "They'll be here, ho. Relax."

Back by the bar, Katrina smiled and said, "Girl, there goes Bo-Pete and Wild Bill."

"So? I ain't feelin' that nigga Taz no more. I don't give a fuck about his entrance and shit," Paquita said as she sipped her glass of E&J.

"What? You mean to tell me that my girl has finally given up? Bitch, say it ain't so!"

"Don't get me wrong. I'm still diggin' that nigga, but I'm just not gon' be all on his dick, even though you know I'd love to."

They both smiled and watched as Bo-Pete and Wild Bill entered the club and went and posted up in their normal spot. And just like always, Red and Bob fol-lowed about five minutes later and went to their nor-mal spot. Then, finally, Keno and Taz came into the club.

Paquita's smile turned to a frown quickly when she noticed how Taz's eyes lit up when he spotted Sacha sitting at the table with Gwen. "I hate that bitch!"

Katrina didn't say anything. She just smiled at her homegirl and shook her head.

After Taz stepped to the bar and accepted the drink that Winky held out for him, he casually strolled over to Sacha and Gwen's table, followed by Keno. Once there, he said, "Damn, Li'l Mama! You're looking edible!"

Sacha smiled and said, "Hi, baby!" She stood, and they shared a long kiss, as if they were alone somewhere instead of in a jam-packed club. She pulled from Taz's embrace and said, "Whew! Do I get that every time you come back from a business trip?"

Taz smiled and said, "You better believe it! Now, introduce me to your friend."

"Oh, I'm sorry. Taz, this is Gwen. Gwen, this is my man, Taz."

Taz smiled and shook hands with the slim goody sitting in front of him and said, "Hello! I've heard a lot about you, Ms. Gwen."

Smiling herself, Gwen said, "And I've heard some fine things about you, Mr. Taz. And please, call me Gwen. That Ms. shit makes me feel old." They both started laughing.

"Excuse me, but I think you've forgotten about your homey, fool!" Keno said with a fake frown on his face.

Taz laughed and said, "My bad, dog! Ladies, this is my right-hand man, Keno. Keno, this is Sacha, my boo, and her friend, Gwen."

Keno shook hands with them and said, "It's nice to meet you both. Even though I've already met Sacha, your boo, it's still a pleasure."

"As you can see, he's a smart-ass, but I still love his ass," Taz said as he sat down next to Sacha.

"Well, y'all can excuse me. I see someone who wants to get better acquainted with me," said Keno as he left them to go chase a high yellow female with long hair, and a booty as big as Buffy the Body's.

Gwen frowned and said, "He's cute, but a li'l too cocky for me. Where's the rest of your homies, Taz? If I'm not mistaken, I was told that there were five of them."

"Damn, it's like that, huh?" asked Taz.

"Yep, it's like that," Gwen replied confidently.

Taz said, "All right then. Over there to the left are my niggas Bo-Pete and Wild Bill. See the real short one and the dark-skinned one standing right there?" He pointed to where Bo-Pete and Wild Bill were standing. "And over there to the far right are my niggas Red and Bob. The bigger one out of the two is Red, and the guy standing right next to him is Bob. So, those are your choices, Gwen. Which one would you care to meet first?" Taz asked with a smile on his face.

"Hmm, let me see. I love me some dark chocolate, so it's either going to be Bo-Pete or Bob," said Gwen as she looked back and forth from Bob to Bo-Pete. After about two minutes of deliberating, she said, "I want to meet Bob. He looks exciting."

Sacha and Taz both laughed and in unison said in a loud voice, "*Bob!*"

"That's right, bitch, Bob. I bet that nigga is packin'!"

Taz damn near spit out his drink when she said that. He wiped his face and waved over to Bob and signaled for him to come and join them.

Bob had a smile on his face as he came to the table. "What's up, my nigga? Hello, ladies."

"Dog, You seem to have been chosen by this pretty lady right here. Gwen, this is my nigga Bob. Bob, this is Gwen."

Gwen smiled wickedly and asked, "Tell me, Bob. How did you get that sexy-looking knot on your forehead?"

Bob smiled and said, "You like the knot, huh?"

"Umm-hmm! Love it!"

"Well, let's shake these two lovebirds for a minute so I can give you the history of the knot," Bob said as he winked at her.

As she got to her feet, Gwen smiled and said, "I'm with you, sexy."

Taz and Sacha were laughing so hard that tears were falling from their eyes as they watched Bob lead Gwen towards another table.

"Well, I'll be damn! She chose Bob! Of all niggas, she chose one of the freakiest niggas around!"

"Is that right? Well, I think Bob might have met his match tonight, 'cause my girl puts the capital F in the word *freak!*" They both started laughing some more. "Now, tell me, where were you, Taz? You never did tell me where you had to go and why."

He smiled at her and said, "I was in Chi-town, Li'l Mama. And like I told you, I went to take care of some business."

"For some of your properties?"

"You're not going to give up, are you?"

"Look, I trust you, baby. I really do. I just have to be certain that everything is on the up-and-up with you, that's all."

"I can dig that, but check this out. My business is complex and yet simple at the same time. Simple, because all I do in this state is make sure that my rental houses are in order and everything is straight. As for the IHOPs and the Popeyes chicken restaurants, my managers take care of them, so it's an easy process with them. I sign the checks and pay my taxes. I own close to fifty homes throughout the City. I even own a couple in your neighborhood. My yearly income in this state alone is close to two hundred thousand a year. So you see, Li'l Mama, I've never lied to you. I just chose not to speak on that shit 'cause I'm not with the braggin' and shit."

"Okay, I can understand that. I guess that's the simple part. But what about the complex part, Taz?"

Staring at her seriously, he said, "That, my love, is none of your business. Please don't press me about it, Sacha. Just try your best to understand what I'm about to say. If I tell everybody my business, I won't have any business at all."

Smiling as she shook her head from side to side, she said, "That's just too damn slick, Mister Taz."

"Nah, Li'l Mama, that's just keeping it real with you. So, like I said before, don't you worry about me ever putting you or your career in jeopardy, because that will never happen. Cool?"

"Yeah, we cool. Can I ask you one more thing, babe?"

Laughing, he said, "Anything baby . . . anything at all!"

"How many rooms do you have in that big-ass house of yours?"

He laughed even harder than he did about Gwen and Bob. After regaining his composure, he said, "That, my love, you'll find out later on. If you'd like, we can make love in every one of them when we get to my spot."

"That, Mister Taz, is something that I definitely would like to do!"

He smiled at her and said, "Yeah, I bet you would, with your horny ass!"

"You know it! You done got it started, so you better be prepared for it."

"As long as I stay ready, I'll never have to get ready, Li'l Mama."

"Good."

Clifford couldn't believe his eyes. Sacha and her best friend, Gwen, were chillin' out with those wannabe thug-ass niggas. "Ain't that a bitch! She done chose a nigga that's most likely going to be in federal prison before the summer's over. I can't believe this shit!" he said aloud as he sipped his drink. He had decided earlier to come to the club and see for himself exactly what type of nigga Sacha had chosen over him. And now as he stood in the back of the club and watched her, he just couldn't accept this shit. He set his drink down and stormed towards Sacha and Taz's table. He stepped straight to them and said, "What's up, Sacha?"

Sacha looked up and saw Clifford standing over her with a mean mug look on his face. She smirked and said, "What's up, Cliff?"

"So, this is your man?" he asked while pointing towards Taz.

Sacha smiled and said, "Yes, he is. What do you want, Cliff? As you can see, I'm enjoying my evening with my man, and you're interrupting us."

"Interrupting you! Ain't that a bitch! Come on, Sacha. I know you're not going to go out like that."

Before Sacha could respond, Taz felt that enough was enough. *It's time for this chump to be checked,* he thought as he stood up from the table and said, "Look, dog. Ain't no need for any drama tonight. My girl has told you what time it is, so you need to get to steppin'."

"Fuck you, nigga! I ain't going nowhere until we can get a better understanding out of this shit! And the 'we' I'm referring to is Sacha and myself! Not you, fool!"

Taz couldn't believe what he had just heard. He shook his head slowly from side to side and asked, "Are you sure you're trying to go that route, nigga? 'cause if you are, I want you to remember that this was your call," he said menacingly.

"Like I said, fuck you!" Clifford yelled. He turned his attention back towards Sacha and said, "Sacha, I really think we should leave this place so we can go somewhere and talk."

"*What?* Cliff, haven't you been hearing what I've repeatedly told you? This is my man, not you, so leave me the fuck alone!"

Her words were like a knife going straight inside of his chest. The pain was unbearable. Clifford didn't realize that he was reaching for Sacha's arm until he felt Taz's right hand on his forearm. "If you touch my girl, you're going to regret it, fool!" Taz said as he shoved Clifford away from the table.

Keno and Red were both talking to some females on the other side of the club when they noticed Taz's confrontation with Clifford. They quickly left the females they were conversing with and went to Taz's side. So did Bo-Pete, Wild Bill, and Bob, who had left Gwen out on the dance floor when he saw Taz shove Clifford.

Clifford saw that Taz's homeboys had him surrounded, and smiled. "Just like I thought. You ain't no man, nigga. You need your boys with you in order to help your soft ass fight. You're coward-ass nigga!"

Taz smiled and said, "That's funny, clown. But my niggas are here for *your* safety, nigga, 'cause they're the only ones who could stop me from serving your soft ass. Why don't you go on and bounce, dog? You're way out of your league," he said calmly.

Before Clifford could respond, Sacha said, "I don't know what the fuck's gotten into you, Cliff, but you really need to check yourself because you are way out of line. So, would you please leave us alone before someone gets hurt?"

Clifford was confused, hurt, and mad as hell, but he was no one's fool. He stared at Taz and his crew, smiled and said, "Yeah, I'll leave you alone, Sacha." He turned and faced Taz and said, "But I'm going to see you again when you don't have your boys, partna. Then we'll see how good your hands really are."

Taz was laughing as he watched Clifford leave the club.

Without a word being said, Keno and Red returned to the ladies that they were talking to before they had gone to Taz's side. Bo-Pete and Wild Bill went back by the bar where they had been standing before the commotion, and Bob grabbed Gwen's hand and said, "Come on, baby, they're playin' our song!" Gwen smiled and let Bob lead her back out on the dance floor.

Taz sat back down and asked, "What's up with that clown, Li'l Mama?"

"I honestly don't know, baby. We were going out for awhile, that is, until I met you and I told him that it was over. But I guess he can't accept it."

"He has no choice. And if he gets in my way again, he's going to get hurt."

"Come on, Taz, he's not worth it, baby," Sacha said as she grabbed ahold of Taz's hand. But as she looked into his dark brown eyes, she knew that if Cliff ever caused any more drama, he was in some serious trouble. She could tell that Taz was not a man to be fucked with.

Taz calmed himself, smiled, and said, "So, are you ready to shake this spot, baby? We do have some rooms at my pad that need to be touched, don't we?"

Sacha blushed and said, "Yes, we do, baby. I'm ready if you are."

Taz turned and waved toward Red and Keno. They came over to their table, and Keno said, "What's up, my nigga?"

"Dog, I'm out. Go holla at Bob and see if he's going to take Gwen home or what."

Red turned and went to go talk to Bob, and Keno said, "Dog, you might not want to leave just yet. Look who just came into the club."

Taz turned and frowned when he saw Tazneema and Lyla walking towards the bar. "Now how in the hell did they get in here? They ain't even twenty-one!" he said to himself louder than he intended to.

"Come on, nigga. Since when did you have to be twenty-one to get into any club in the City?" Keno pointed out honestly.

"Yeah, I know, huh? Man, go get her ass and bring her over here for me, gee."

"Gotcha," said Keno as he went over towards the bar.

"Who are you guys talking about, Taz?" Sacha asked as she tried to see who they were talking about.

Before Taz could answer her, Gwen and Bob came to their table and sat down. Bob smiled and said, "Sacha, I guess I owe you one, 'cause I think I'm in love!" They all started laughing.

Gwen shook her head and said, "Uh-uh, nigga! You ain't in love . . . yet. Wait 'til I put this thang on your ass! Then, you'll be in love!"

Taz shook his head and laughed. "So, I guess you're going to go on and take Gwen home for us, then, huh?"

"Nah, my nigga, I ain't taking her home. She's coming home with me!"

Taz stared at Bob as if he'd lost his mind. They normally didn't get down like that until after they were sure the females they were fucking with were straight. That usually took at least a month or so. That's why it had taken Taz so long to let Sacha know where he lived. Caution was a must with them. Taz was shocked at Bob's words, but he felt comfortable that Gwen was all good, so he didn't speak on it.

Keno brought Tazneema and Lyla over to the table and said, "Taz, guess who I've found?"

Taz turned and smiled at Tazneema and said, "So, you're hangin' in clubs now, huh?"

"I'm grown, Taz," Tazneema said with a smile on her face.

"Hi, Taz. I told your sister that you might be up in here, but she said that the club wasn't your thing," Lyla said, smiling at him.

Taz smiled and said, "Don't worry about it. It ain't no thang. 'Neema, I want you to meet someone. Sacha, this is Tazneema. 'Neema, this is Sacha."

Sacha smiled and said, "It's nice to meet you, Tazneema."

After they had shaken hands, Tazneema said, "Please, call me 'Neema." She stared at Sacha briefly and realized just like Mama-Mama had that they were in love with each other. It was written all over both of their faces. She smiled and said, "Ooh, she's your girlfriend!"

Taz started laughing and said, "Yeah, she's my Li'l Mama. Do you approve?"

Smiling brightly, she said, "Yeah, she's cool. But what about Tari? Oops! I mean . . . you . . . you know what . . . I . . . never mind. Look, I'm about to go over and get me something to drink, okay?"

With a frown on his face, Taz said, "Yeah, you go on and do that. Oh, before you go, I spoke with Mama-

Mama. You can go spend the holidays with Lyla and her family."

"For real? Thank you, Taz!" She gave him a hug and a kiss on his cheek, said good-bye to Sacha, and led Lyla towards the bar.

Sacha, who had caught what Tazneema had said, was frowning at Taz, who was trying to avoid eye contact with her. He looked up at Keno and said, "Dog, I'm goin' to need you to stay until the club lets out. Keep an eye on her for me, gee."

"Don't trip, dog. You know we got her. Go on and do you. See ya later, Sacha," Keno said as he left them alone.

Sacha tapped Taz lightly on his hand and asked, "Who's Tari, Taz?"

Taz sighed and said, "Somebody that you're about to meet. Come on."

Chapter Thirteen

When Taz and Sacha left the club, neither of them saw Clifford watching them from inside of his car as they climbed inside of Taz's truck. "Gotcha!" Clifford said as he quickly wrote down Taz's license plate number. Once they pulled out of the parking lot of the club, he smiled and started his car and went home feeling confident again about his and Sacha's future together.

Sacha was silent as she listened to Taz talk to someone on his cell phone. "Wake up, girl. I told you I'm on my way."

"Taz, why do you insist on waking me every time you choose to come over here?" whined Tari. "I do work, you know."

"Yeah, I know, but I need you to be up when I get there. I'm bringing someone for you to meet. And it . . . it's kind of important."

That statement grabbed Tari's attention. She sat up in her bed and asked, "A woman, Taz?"

He sighed and said, "Yeah."

Her tone changed to a more businesslike one when she said, "Okay, I'll be up by the time you get here. Good-bye."

After hanging up with Tari, Taz felt like his heart was going to pop outside of his chest. He couldn't remember the last time that he was this nervous. *Man, she's hot! I can tell,* he thought as he turned onto the highway, headed towards the city of Moore.

Sacha noticed that Taz was uncomfortable, and that made her all the more curious, but she chose to remain silent as long as he did.

After about twenty minutes or so, Taz said, "We're almost there. I'd rather have to say this once, because this shit is kinda hard for me, Li'l Mama. And please, don't trip out. This is something that I've been dreading since I realized how deeply I care about you. I've never lied, Li'l Mama, I just didn't exactly come completely clean with you. I hope that this won't hurt us or get in the way of our future," he said as he pulled into Tari's driveway.

"Well, I guess we're about to find out, Taz," Sacha replied with more attitude than she intended to.

Tari was standing at her front door as she watched Taz and Sacha get out of his truck. *Well, I'll be! He's finally found someone he can really love. Now ain't that somethin'!*

Taz stepped onto Tari's porch with Sacha's hand in his and said, "What's up, Tee?"

"It's late, Taz. Come on inside so we can get this over with." Tari turned her back to them and went back inside of her house. She was smiling as she entered her home—smiling because of how nervous Taz looked. She couldn't remember the last time she had seen him look so cute. *Ahh, my baby is nervous because he thinks he's going to hurt my feelings! That's so special!* she thought to herself. She turned and motioned for them to have a seat on her sofa and said, "I'd offer you both something to drink, but I have a feeling that Taz really wants to get whatever off of his chest. So, the floor is yours, babe." She sat down on the floor in front of her floor model 60-inch big-screen television.

Taz got to his feet and said, "Tari, this is Sacha, and Sacha, this is Tari. I really don't know how to say this shit without it upsetting either of you, so I'm just gon' spit it out." Turning toward Tari, he said, "Tee, I love this woman, and if she lets me, I want to be with her for the rest of my life."

Before Tari could respond, he turned towards Sacha and said, "Li'l Mama, Tari's been my friend, my confidante, as well as my lover, for a very long time. She will always be a major part of my life . . . always. But since we've hooked up, I've realized that it's you that I want in my life in that very special way. I love you, Li'l Mama. Now, I'll take a seat and let the both of you rip me apart," he said as he went and sat down next to Sacha, praying that this soap opera shit worked out in his favor.

Tari and Sacha smiled at one another. Sacha spoke first. "Tari, I want you to know that it is a pleasure to meet you. I have no ill feelings toward you or your relationship with Taz. I love him just as deeply, and if you are a major factor in his life, then I want you to know that you will mean just as much to me."

Intelligent, pretty, and sincere. I like that, Taz. I really do. You done good, babe. You done damn good! Tari said to herself. She smiled and said, "Thank you for that, Sacha. I do love this man, and I know for a fact that I always will. I don't know why he's so damn nervous, but I think it's so cute that he is. That shows me that he cares for me just as much as I've always figured he did. I've waited for years for this day to come. I've always known that I was not the woman for him. I am surprised that it has finally happened, though. For a minute there I thought our relationship, however strange it is, might just be able to make it. But now, I see the love you have for each other in the both of your eyes. I feel so happy for the both of you."

Taz sighed in relief, and Sacha smiled.

Tari continued, "I have only one thing to say to you, Sacha, and please don't take offense, because I'm speaking from my heart here. Don't ever hurt this man, whatever you do. Don't you ever cause him any pain. Because if you do, then you will see how unruly a white woman can be."

Sacha smiled and said, "Well, that's something that I'm really not looking forward to." They both laughed, and then Sacha said, "I respect everything you've said, Tari, and I give you my word that I'll love this man with all of my heart as long as he'll let me. And I'll never, and I mean *never,* hurt him." Turning toward Taz, she said, "But if you ever keep anything from me that is as important as this is, I might break your neck, mister!"

They all laughed, and Taz felt the tension leave his body in waves. He smiled at the both of them and said, "I love you two more than you both will ever know. Thank you, Tari, for not trippin' the fuck out on me. And thank you, Li'l Mama, for understanding. I didn't know how to tell you about Tari without pissing you off. That's why I had been procrastinating."

"So, what made you decide to get it over with?" asked Tari.

Before he could answer Tari's question, Sacha said, "His little sister let it slip at the club earlier."

Tari and Taz stared at each other momentarily, and then Tari said, "Ahh, so you've had the pleasure of meeting Tazneema, I see."

"Yes, I have, and she seems like a very sweet girl. She looks so much like this joker that they could pass for twins."

Taz smiled and said, "Well, I guess wc'll be getting outta here now, Tee. I know you gots to get some rest for work in the morning."

"Yeah, I do. Umm, excuse me, Sacha, but could I have a moment alone with Taz before y'all leave?"

"Sure. I'll be in the truck, baby. And once again, it was very nice meeting you, Tari."

"Same here, girl. Don't worry, we'll be seeing a lot of each other." Tari waited for Sacha to leave her home before she spoke. After the front door was closed, she said, "Love is a wonderful thing, isn't it?"

"Yeah, I guess it is. But to tell you the truth, I never thought it was for me. That is until I met Sacha. I'm tellin' you, Tee, the first time I laid eyes on her I knew that she was the one."

"That's good, baby. I meant what I said earlier, that if she ever hurts you, I'm going to hurt her something awful."

Taz laughed and said, "I don't think she'll ever get down like that, Tee. But it's good to know that you still got my back."

"Always. How much have you told her about your lifestyle?"

"Not much."

Laughing, she said, "Yeah, I can tell."

"She knows about the IHOPs, the rental houses, as well as the Popeye spots. But that's about it."

"Everything that's in the dark will sooner or later come to the light, Taz. If you love her, you're going to have to trust her."

"I know. But she's a lawyer. She can't afford to know what my real bread and butter is, at least not right now."

"True. Don't wait too long on telling her everything that's vital in your life, Taz. Or you'll risk losing her. It's been way too long since you've been able to love like this, so don't fuck it up," Tari said seriously.

"I won't. Now, give me a kiss so I can get the fuck up outta here," he said as he wrapped his arms around her waist and they shared a quick kiss.

"Damn! I guess that means you can't even come and break me off from time to time, huh?" Before he could answer, she smiled and said, "Don't worry about me, boy. I'm going to be all right."

Staring directly into Tari's eyes, he said, "I know, 'cause I'm always going to make sure that you're straight. Always. I don't think we're doing any traveling for the rest of the year, so everything is everything. I'll get at ya before we do bounce, though."

Tari yawned and stretched and said, "Alright. I hope my babies like Sacha, 'cause if they don't, she's in some big trouble, and so are you, for that matter." They both started laughing as Tari walked Taz to the door.

When Taz got inside of the truck, he smiled and said, "That lady is truly something special."

"I can tell that you two are really close. How long have you been . . . you know?"

He smiled and said, "From the days when I just didn't give a fuck."

"What's that supposed to mean, baby?"

Taz smiled and said, "Nothin'. I guess it's time for us to go touch those rooms, huh?" he asked, hoping she would let it go.

Smiling seductively, Sacha said, "Yes, I guess it is."

They arrived at Taz's home a little after three in the morning. During the drive back towards the City, Sacha decided that they'd better stop and get something to eat, so they had a quick breakfast at a local Waffle House.

Now that they were at home, Taz was excited. He was excited because his life finally seemed to have a purpose again; excited about being able to make love to a woman other than Tari at his home; and excited to actually feel alive again. *Damn! And it feels real good!* Taz thought as he showed Sacha around his home.

By the time they made it downstairs to the gym area, Sacha felt as if she was watching the *Lifestyles of the Rich and Famous* television show. *This nigga is living larger than I thought,* she said to herself as she dipped her foot into the Olympic-sized swimming pool. She frowned for a moment and said, "I thought you told me that you went to a gym when you worked out."

Smiling, he said, "I did. I just didn't tell you that it was inside of my home."

She punched him lightly on his arm and said, "Alright, mister, what else do you have in store for me?"

He grabbed her by her slender arms, pulled her close to him, and said, "First, you have to meet two more of my special loved ones. And after that, it's time for some of the wildest lovemaking you've ever had in your life."

Smiling, Sacha said, "I'm ready whenever you are, baby. Now, who are these two other special loved ones?"

Taz smiled and said, "Whether you believe me or not, they've been watching you ever since we came into the house."

"What are you talking about?"

He smiled and said," Heaven and Precious, come meet Li'l Mama."

Taz's two prized Dobermans came trotting out of the gym area as if they had been a part of the gym equipment. They had been observing their master and guest from a distance when they had first entered the house. Taz had them trained especially for stealth and stalking tactics. They were trained to kill at the slightest sign of danger to Taz, and anyone he deemed friendly. Both Heaven and Precious stopped in front of Sacha and raised their wet noses towards her hands.

Sacha was fascinated yet terrified. She couldn't believe that these dogs had been watching them the entire time they had been inside of the house. She reached down and patted them both on their heads and said, "Hey, Heaven! Hey, Precious!"

Taz laughed and said, "Heaven is on your left, and Precious is on the right."

"Oh, I'm sorry," she said as she turned to her left and said, "I'm sorry, Heaven." Then to her right she said, "Forgive me, Precious." She then rubbed both of them gently under their chins.

The Dobermans seemed to like Sacha, because the both of them began licking her hands and tried their best to keep her attention.

Taz smiled and said, "Well, it looks like you're a hit. Now that that's out of the way, are you ready to do the damn thang?"

Sacha looked towards Taz and said, "Whenever you are, lover! Whenever you are!"

Taz shook his head and said, "Protect us, Heaven. Protect us, Precious." Both of the Dobermans' ears became alert as they trotted out of the room. Taz said, "Come on, Li'l Mama. We're completely safe now, so let's go play!"

"Let the games begin!"

Chapter Fourteen

Sacha smiled when she opened her eyes the next morning. She smiled because she saw Precious and Heaven sitting by the door, alert and aware of their surroundings. *Taz didn't play around when it came to his safety,* she thought as she climbed out of his bed.

She went into the restroom and turned on the shower. While she was showering, she was trying to figure out a way to ask Taz to accompany her to the firm's Christmas party next week. She loved him so much, and she wanted her coworkers to meet him. Shit, she wanted the world to know about her and Taz! *But damn, Taz's platinum grille and all of the flossy diamonds he wore are just a bit much,* she thought as she lathered herself with a scented bar of Taz's soap. She made up her mind by the time she finished her shower. Taz was her man, and the grille and the diamonds were a part of him. "I love everything about that man, so who gives a fuck what my coworkers will think?" she said aloud as she wrapped herself in one of Taz's big fluffy, towels.

When she stepped back into the bedroom, Taz was still sleeping soundly. She smiled as she dropped the towel and climbed back in bed with him. She shook him lightly and said, "Taz, wake up, baby."

Taz had been awake ever since she first climbed out of his bed. He was so content with her being in his bed that it didn't make any sense. He opened his eyes, smiled, and said, "Good morning, sexy. How long you been up?" He played with a few strands of her wet hair.

"About twenty minutes. I just finished taking a quick shower."

"I can tell. Your hair is still wet."

"Baby, I need to ask a favor of you, okay?"

As he sat up in the bed, he asked, "What's up, Li'l Mama?"

"Well, next week the firm is having our annual Christmas party, and I'd really like for you to come with me. You see, the partners are going to announce my partnership, and I . . . well . . . It would mean a lot to me if you were there with me."

Smiling, Taz said, "I don't have a problem with that. When is it exactly, so I can make sure that I'm free?"

"Next Friday. It's going to be a real dressy-dressy type of an affair."

With a raised eyebrow he asked, "What's dressy-dressy mean, Li'l Mama?"

"You know, suit and tie stuff. You can do a suit and a tie, can't you?"

Taz smiled and said, "Yeah, I can clean up when I want to. Don't worry, Li'l Mama. I'll make sure we leave your peers with a positive impression."

"What do you mean by that?"

"Look, I know you were nervous about asking me to join you next week. It's written all over your face. And then you're probably worried about what your peers are going to think of you bringing a guy like myself to your party. But don't trip, Li'l Mama. Like I told you before, I'd never do anything to jeopardize your career. And I meant that. In fact, you'll be surprised at exactly how much I mean it."

"What's that supposed to mean, mister?" she asked, relieved that he wasn't offended.

"You'll see. Now, let me get up. The homies should be arriving any minute for our workout."

"Y'all work out on the weekends too?"

"Not really. Today is our running day. We're going to go run a few miles. Then we'll come back and chill out. Do you have any plans for the day?"

"Not really. I was going to call Gwen and see if she wanted to get into anything."

"That's cool. After I run, I was going to go check on a few of my rental houses. Then the rest of the day I was hoping we could chill out."

"That's fine with me."

"Have I told you that I loved you this morning?"

With a mock pout on her face, she said, "No, you haven't, Taz."

Smiling, he said, "Damn, I love it when you stick that bottom lip out like that! Come here, baby!" They shared a deep kiss for a full minute. Taz pulled away from her face and said, "I love you, Li'l Mama."

I love you, too, baby," she said, and they started kissing each other again.

Bo-Pete and Wild Bill pulled up to Taz's home, followed by Keno. Just as they were getting out of their trucks, Red, Bob, and Gwen pulled into the driveway.

"What the fuck is this?" asked Keno when he saw Gwen getting out of Red's Tahoe, followed by Bob.

Bob smiled and said, "What up, niggas? Y'all ready to get y'all's run on this morning?"

Wild Bill smiled and said, "Nigga, we might not be doing no damn running after Taz sees that you've brought a fuckin' guest."

"Shut the fuck up, li'l man! I just got off of the phone with him. He knows I brought my baby with me. She's hooking up with Sacha."

"Is that right? So, Sacha's inside, huh?" asked Keno.

"Yep. So I guess you guys better get used to us being around, 'cause we're going to be here awhile. Ain't that right, babe?" asked Gwen.

Smiling from ear to ear, Bob answered, "You damn skippy!"

"Damn, she must have really put that thang on that nigga!" said Bo-Pete with a smile on his face. They all were laughing as they went inside of Taz's home.

Taz, who had opened the door for them, asked, "What's so damn funny, clowns? What's up, Gwen? I see my nigga has made a good impression."

"Yes, indeed. Where's my girl Taz?" she asked as she looked around his spacious home.

"Here I am, girl. Come on up here so they can go on and get their run on. Baby, I'm going to take Gwen home. Then, after I change, I'll be back, okay?"

"Yeah, that's cool. Do you want to take the truck or what?" asked Taz.

Smiling mischievously, she said, "I'd rather take the Benz."

Taz laughed loudly and said, "Well, take it then. The keys are on the dresser, next to my jewelry." Turning towards his homies, he said, "All right, clowns, let's go do this."

Gwen gave Bob a kiss and said, "Give me a call after you're finished, lover. You know we gots some more work to put in later on."

"Without a doubt, baby girl," said Bob. They quickly shared a kiss.

The rest of the crew was laughing and clowning with Bob as they went back outside.

Sacha led Gwen upstairs to the bedroom and showed her around a little. "Damn, this nigga is living large! Look at the size of this place!" yelled Gwen.

"What's up with Bob? How's his place look?" asked Sacha as she sat down on the bed.

"It's real nice, bitch. Real nice. But it's nothing as fancy as this. Bob's more laid back, but you can tell he's got plenty of loot. He has expensive black paintings all around the place. And the bed! Bitch, the bed is the biggest bed I've ever seen!"

"You mean it's bigger than this one?" Sacha asked as she patted Taz's bed. "This is a California king–sized bed. This is, I think, the biggest they come."

"Nah, bitch, that there bed is small compared to my babe's. I'm telling you, bitch, when I say huge, I mean huge!"

"What! Come on, let's go downstairs so I can show you the rest of the house."

Gwen followed Sacha as she gave her the same tour of the house that Taz had given her the night before. By the time they made it to the gym, Gwen was completely speechless.

Sacha was smiling, because during the entire time she was showing Gwen around the house, Gwen hadn't noticed once that they were being followed by Heaven and Precious. Hell, the only reason why she knew it was because she'd spotted them coming out of the bathroom as they left the bedroom to go downstairs. *Damn, they're good!* she thought as she led Gwen towards the pool and Jacuzzi. "You like, ho?"

"I like! I like, bitch! Taz is the fucking man!"

They both started laughing. "Before we leave, I have to show you something. Now please, whatever you do, don't freak the fuck out on me, okay?"

"What are you talking 'bout, bitch?"

"Just relax, and watch." Sacha turned toward the gym, where she had watched Heaven and Precious enter after they had made it to the pool, and said, "Heaven and Precious, come and meet my friend Gwen."

Gwen's eyes damn near popped out of their sockets when she saw Heaven and Precious come trotting out of the gym. Once they were at her side, she stood frozen and scared shitless.

Sacha saw how nervous she was and laughed. "Girl, go on and pet them. They won't hurt you."

Gwen rubbed and softly petted the deadly Dobermans on top of their heads and watched, horrified, as they began to rub their wet noses on her hands. "O-okay, Sacha! Tell them to go bye-bye now, okay?"

Sacha smiled and said, "Protect us, Heaven. Protect us, Precious." Both of the Dobermans' ears rose at Sacha's command as they turned and trotted out of the room.

"Bitch, I done seen it all!"

They both laughed as they left and went back upstairs.

Chapter Fifteen

It was the night of Sacha's firm's Christmas party, and Taz was late. She couldn't believe that he would do this to her! Sacha was a nervous wreck as she paced back and forth in her living room. Here she was, dressed to fucking kill in a tight, formfitting Versace dress and matching Versace pumps, and Taz was fucking late! "I'm gon' kill him! I swear God, I'm going to kill him!" she screamed as she stormed back into her bedroom.

Just as she was coming back into the living room, there was a knock at her door. All of Sacha's anger evaporated when she opened the front door and saw Taz standing in front of her, looking like dapper don himself. He was dressed elegantly in a tailor-made Armani suit and black alligator shoes. The silk peach shirt and peach tie complemented his black suit perfectly. But what shocked her the most was his smile. When he smiled, she damn near felt faint. His diamond and platinum grille had been replaced with one of the most beautiful smiles she had ever seen. His white teeth seemed to sparkle, they were so bright.

"Damn, Li'l Mama! Are you going to let me in, or are you just going to stare at me all damn evening? We do have a party to attend, don't we?" he asked with that gorgeous smile of his.

"Baby, when you said you cleaned up good, you weren't lying!"

"I guess I should take that as a compliment, then, huh?"

Nodding her head yes, she said, "Yes, you should. Let me go get my purse. Then we can go, okay?"

"All right. I'll be outside in the car. I brought the Azure, or would you have preferred the Six?"

Smiling brightly, she said, "You know I would've preferred the Six, but the Azure is cool too. Ain't nothing wrong with pulling up somewhere in a Bentley."

Taz laughed and said, "Go on and get your stuff. I'll be in the car."

Once Sacha came and got inside of the car, Taz asked her, "Didn't you tell me that that clown nigga who was gettin' at you also worked at the same firm as you?"

"Shit! He does! Baby, I didn't even think about that. Please don't let Cliff ruin this evening for me. If he says anything, just ignore him, okay?"

"I can't make any promises, Li'l Mama. But as long as that fool stays out of arms' reach of me, he won't get the shit smacked out of his soft ass. That's about the best I can do for you."

Smiling, she said, "Fair enough."

Taz pulled the Bentley Azure in front of the valet parking at the Westin Hotel in downtown Oklahoma City. One of the young valets came and opened the door for the both of them. Taz stepped quickly around the car, and they entered the hotel with their arms linked together.

Sacha had a huge smile on her face as they entered the ballroom. Here she was, about to officially become a partner. All of her dedication and hard work had finally paid off. To make everything even sweeter, she had her man, Taz, by her side. This was definitely going to be a night to remember. She led Taz towards a table that she saw was reserved for them. After they were seated, she said, "Thank you for coming with me tonight, baby. This really means a lot to me."

"Don't trip, Li'l Mama. Tonight's your night to shine. I'm just glad that you have let me be a part of it."

Before he continued, a tall, immaculately dressed brother came to their table and said, "Mr. Good? How are you doing, sir?"

Taz looked up from his seat, smiled, and said, "Edward! How are you?" He stood, and they both shook hands. "I'm sure you know Sacha here."

"Oh, yes, she's one of the most talked about people at the firm nowadays. Good evening, Sacha."

"Hello, Edward," Sacha said as she glanced at Taz with a puzzled look on her face.

Edward noticed the look and said, "Don't tell me that Sacha doesn't know that you're one of the firm's most prized clients, Mr. Good."

Taz laughed and said, "Come on, Edward. I wouldn't go so far as to say one of the most prized clients."

"I don't see why not. Hell, I make a nice chunk maintaining all of your finances, Mr. Good. And I'm quite sure when Mr. Whitney and old man Johnson find out that you're here with Sacha, they'll be delighted." They all laughed. "Well, I'll leave you two now. I saw you when you two came in and thought I'd come say hello. Oh, congratulations on your partnership, Sacha. You deserve it."

"Thank you, Edward. Don't worry. Your turn is coming."

Smiling, he said, "I sure hope so. See you guys later."

After Edward had left their table, Sacha smiled at Taz and said, "One of Whitney & Johnson's most prized clients? Humph! I should have known. You are just too damn slick, Mister Taz!"

Taz started laughing and said, "Baby, it's a small town we live in. How was I to know that you worked for the law firm that I let handle most of my business? Are you mad at me, Li'l Mama?"

"No, I'm not mad. I just wish you would have told me. Taz, you make me sick sometimes, with all of your little secrets!"

"Secrets? Uh-uh. Remember what I told you about my business?"

"Uh-huh. If you tell me all of your business, you won't have any business at all. Bullshit!"

They both started laughing as a waiter approached them and asked them if they would like anything to drink. Taz ordered an XO for himself and an apple martini for Sacha.

While they were waiting for their drinks, several attorneys from Whitney & Johnson came over to their table and spoke to both Sacha and Taz. Sacha was shocked to learn that the firm she worked for handled all of Taz's business affairs, everything from the trust fund he had set up for Tazneema to his will. But what shocked her most was when Mr. Whitney and Mr. Johnson came over to their table and told them that they were extremely happy to see that they were an item. *My man is not only richer than I could have ever imagined, he's completely legal! Thank you, Lord!* she thought to herself as she accepted her drink from the waiter.

Taz was sipping his drink when he almost spit it all over Sacha's expensive dress. He set his glass on the table, wiped his mouth, smiled, and said, "Well, I'll be damn! Why didn't you tell me they were coming, Li'l Mama?"

Sacha smiled and said, "Bob made me promise not to. He wanted to surprise you." They both watched as Bob led Gwen towards their table.

"What's up, my brother? How are you this evening?" asked Bob, who was dressed just as clean as Taz was in a brown, tailor-made suit by Christian Dior. His Italian loafers completed the elegant but casual look he was sporting. Gwen was looking gorgeous herself, in a tan dress with her hair hanging past her shoulders.

Taz couldn't front. They were looking real good this evening. After they were seated, Taz said, "So, I see she's a keeper, huh?"

"Yeah, my nigga, she's here to stay," Bob replied confidently.

Sacha couldn't believe her eyes. Her girl Gwen was actually blushing. *Shit, I haven't seen her act like this since William,* she thought to herself as she continued to stare at her best friend. She smiled and then said, "You know what? This has turned out to be even better than I hoped it would be. My girl's all in love, and I'm in love. Shit, that's a wonderful thing!"

"Hold up, Sacha. Where is all of this all in 'love' shit coming from? I'm just loving your girl's sex game, that's all," Bob said with a serious expression on his face.

Sacha's face fell flat when she heard this. She turned towards Gwen to see what her reaction to that statement was going to be. Gwen smiled and said, "Bitch, don't pay that nigga no mind. He's just as gone for me as I am for his black sexy ass!"

They all started laughing as Bob smiled and winked his eye at Sacha. "Gotcha!" he said.

Nodding her head, she said, "Yeah, you did, and I will get you back for that one, Bob!"

The evening was going smoothly, and they were having a real nice time chitchatting back and forth with each other.

After dinner was served, Mr. Whitney and Mr. Johnson announced to everyone that Sacha was now a partner of the firm. She received a standing ovation from all of her peers, as well as their family members who had joined them tonight. *It feels really good to finally be appreciated,* she thought as she stood and waved her hands to everyone in thanks. *This night just couldn't be more perfect,* she thought as she sat back down.

Taz was so proud of his girl that he just wanted to grab her and hug her tight. But he knew that was just a little too much emotion for him to be showing out in public. Since he had been kicking it with Sacha, she brought out feelings inside of him that he'd completely forgotten about. It felt so good to be able to love again. But he knew that he had to be careful. He wasn't going to let this love end like his last love affair. He'd die before he let that happen to him again.

Just as it seemed the night was coming to an end, Clifford made his appearance inside of the ballroom, accompanied by Cory. They made an excellent-looking couple. Cory was looking good, dressed in a gown by Donna Karan, and Clifford was dressed neatly in a suit by Sean Jean. When Clifford saw Sacha, he went directly to her table and said, "Congratulations, Sacha."

Sacha smiled nervously and said, "Thank you, Cliff."

Clifford smiled at Taz and said, "So, the thug can clean up. How nice." Before Taz could move an inch, Clifford said, "I hope you all have a wonderful evening." Then he quickly stepped toward Mr. Whitney's table.

"That was close, Li'l Mama . . . real close," Taz said seriously.

Sacha smiled and said, "He didn't come within arms' reach, baby."

"As long as he doesn't, then we're good."

"What are y'all talkin' 'bout?" asked Bob.

"Nothin', fool. Relax."

"Are you good, homey?"

"Yeah, everything is everything. Don't trip, dog. Let's enjoy the rest of the evening." And enjoy they did.

Taz had Sacha out on the dance floor, song after song, dancing and laughing as if they didn't have a care in the world. Bob was right alongside them with Gwen in his arms. Everything was wonderful until Clifford came out on the dance floor with Cory and got a little too close to Taz. Taz turned and saw that it was Clifford who had just bumped into them and said, "Li'l Mama, it looks like this clown wants to play, after all."

"Come on baby, let's go. I'm getting kind of tired, anyway."

"You sure?"

"Yes, I'm positive," she said as she led Taz off of the dance floor. Gwen and Bob came to the table, and Sacha told them, "Thank you both for coming tonight. I really enjoyed your company. Me and my baby are about to—as he would say—shake this spot. Are you two good or what?"

"Oh, God, Taz! Do you hear how you got my girl talking? I think you've become a bad influence on her!" Gwen joked.

Smiling, Taz said, "Nah, if anything, she's became a bad influence on me. All she wants to do is go home so she can try to freak me crazy!"

"Taz! You know you need to quit that! But I am going to love you a long time tonight, mister!" Sacha said, and they all started laughing.

"Well, since y'all are about to bounce, I don't see no reason for us to still be here, baby. Let's shake this spot and go do the damn thing ourselves," Bob said with a smile on his face.

"I'm with that, sexy. Tonight's the night I plan on doing some freaky things with the knot."

"Is that right?"

"Yep!"

"What you got planned for the knot tonight, baby?"

"You'll see. Now come on, let's get outta here," said Gwen.

"Don't let her take all of your energy, my nigga. We do have to get our run on in the morning," Taz said with a laugh.

"Don't trip, gee. I gots this," Bob replied as he followed Gwen out of the ballroom.

"Well, baby, why don't you go on and say your good-byes and stuff, and I'll ease on by the door and wait for ya."

"Okay, baby. I'll be right there," Sacha said. She went to go say good-bye to Mr. Whitney and Mr. Johnson.

Taz left the ballroom and stood outside in the lobby as he waited for Sacha to get finished. A few people who he knew at the firm walked past him and said good-night. When he saw Clifford walk out of the ballroom, he said to himself, "If this clown-ass nigga tries me, it's on!"

Clifford was holding on to Cory's hand as they were leaving the ballroom. When he saw Taz standing in the lobby alone, he smiled and said to himself, "Now, let's see what you're really working with." He turned towards Cory and said, "Cory, go on ahead and wait for me outside by the valet. I need to talk to someone real quick."

"All right, baby, but don't take too long. I'm in the mood to get real freaky tonight."

"Don't worry. I won't," he replied, and he watched her walk away down the lobby. Once she was out of sight, he stepped towards Taz and said, "I think I remember telling you that I was going to see what you were working with whenever I got a chance at you without your boys around to protect your punk ass."

Taz smiled, took a quick look around, and said, "Well, it looks like tonight is the night you were referring to." *Now, come a few inches closer, nigga. That's right. Step into arms' reach, you bitch!* Taz thought to himself as he watched Clifford move into his arms' reach.

Sacha saw Clifford and Taz talking, quickly said good-bye to one of her coworkers, and hurried over to Taz's side. Just as she made it there, she heard Clifford tell Taz that he wasn't worth ruining a good suit. But he would definitely have his chance at him again one day. That infuriated her. "Damnit, Cliff! Why won't you leave us the fuck alone? I'm telling you, I'm getting sick and tired of this shit! And if I have to, I swear, I'm going to file a complaint with both Mr. Whitney and Mr. Johnson!"

"Sacha, I'm just trying to stop you from making the worst mistake of your life. This guy is a fucking loser!" Clifford said as he poked his index finger into Taz's chest.

Taz smiled as he stared into Sacha's eyes. He gave her a slight shrug of his shoulders and said, "Arms' reach, Li'l Mama!" Then with the speed of a boxer, he slapped the shit out of Clifford. He hit Clifford with so much power that the blow knocked him to the floor. "Now, be a man and show me that you're not all talk, you bitch-ass nigga! I've tried to be civil, but if it's gangsta shit you want, so be it!" Taz said as he towered over Clifford.

Clifford was trying to scoot away from Taz so that he could get to his feet.

Sacha came and stood next to Taz and said, "Come on, baby, don't do this. He's not worth it."

This gave Clifford the opportunity to get to his feet. He was so mad and embarrassed that he was literally shaking. "You wanna be thug-ass nigga! What, you gon' let a bitch stop you now?"

"*Bitch!* Cliff, you done lost your fucking mind! Beat the shit out of this nigga, baby!"

Taz smiled as he stepped a little closer to Clifford. Just as he was about to swing, Mr. Whitney, Edward, and Mr. Johnson all came running over to stop them from fighting. "What the hell is going on over here?" yelled Mr. Whitney.

Taz took a step back and said, "I'm sorry about this, Lee, but this guy has been asking for this for a minute now."

"That's bull, sir! He just assaulted me!" yelled Clifford.

"Is that true, Taz? If so, I want to know why," asked Mr. Johnson.

"Yeah, it's true, Jeff. This guy is interested in Sacha, and since she doesn't want to be bothered, he has issued several threats to me. Tonight was the last time that I was going to stand for any of them."

Before he could continue, Sacha said, "Mr. Whitney, sir, I don't know what's gotten into Cliff, but he needs to understand that Taz and I are together, and that there is absolutely no chance for us getting together. He's been acting extremely childish throughout the past few weeks."

"Clifford, this is a complete shock. But you have been assaulted, so if you want to press charges, the choice is yours. But I want you to know, and I'm confident that I'm speaking for both Mr. Johnson and myself here, that Taz is a very special client of the firm. He's been conducting business with us for years now. Some very good business. I think you should think about that before you make your decision."

"If he does press charges against Taz, I will file harassment charges against him, sir!" Sacha added vehemently.

Clifford realized that this situation had gotten out of control. The threat that Mr. Whitney had given him was crystal clear. Taz was special, and he was not. "No, sir, I don't feel that any of that will be necessary. I want to apologize to you, Sacha, for my behavior. I will not bother either of you again."

Smiling, Edward said, "I bet you won't! I saw how Taz slapped the mess out of you!"

"That'll be enough of that, Edward! Alright then, so, Mr. Taz, do you have anything that you'd like to say to Clifford here?" asked Mr. Whitney.

Taz smiled and said, "Nope."

"Come on, Taz, let's put an end to this issue, okay?" asked Mr. Johnson.

"Look, Jeff. This clown has been bothering me ever since he found out about Sacha and me. Now, he has said it's over and he'll stop. If that's the case, then so be it. But I will not apologize for my actions tonight. He pushed this issue, not me. And to be completely honest, I wouldn't give a damn if he pressed charges against me or not. He's very lucky that all he's received is a fuckin' slap. Make sure he stays away from me in the future, Jeff, 'cause the next time, I'm goin' to hurt him." He then turned towards Sacha and asked, "You ready to bounce, Li'l Mama?"

Sacha stared at Taz for a moment, then said, "Yes, we should be going. Good evening, Mr. Whitney, Mr. Johnson, Edward. It's definitely been memorable." She gave Clifford a frown as she grabbed Taz's hand and let him lead her out of the hotel.

Mr. Whitney smiled and said, "Clifford, you better make sure that you stay away from that man. He's one not to be messed with."

"That's right, Clifford. Not only does he spend close to fifty thousand dollars a year with the firm, he's a dangerous man," warned Mr. Johnson.

Clifford was so embarrassed that he was speechless. He said good evening to them all and went and caught up with Cory at the valet. Just as he made it outside, he saw Sacha and Taz climbing into Taz's Bentley. *Before it's all said and done, I'll get the both of you back for this night. Believe that!* he thought to himself.

Chapter Sixteen

The holidays flew by, and the New Year had started out strong for both Taz and Sacha. They were in love, and loving every minute of it. They became inseparable. And, they weren't the only ones. Bob and Gwen's affair seemed to have turned into something special also. Bob was becoming more and more interested in Gwen. They spent all of their spare time with each other too.

Gwen had shocked the both of them when she told Bob all about the loss of her beloved William, and her only child, Remel. Bob was touched deeply by what she had told him, especially when she told him that she thought she'd never be able to love again, that is, until she had met him.

For the first time in his life, Bob was in love, and it felt strange, but good at the same time. He had had a few flings over his lifetime, but nothing as serious as this one. Gwen gave him the impression that she wanted to ride for the long haul, and if that was the case, he was ready to accept her with open arms.

Bob pulled into Gwen's driveway with a smile on his face. Today was the day he was going to ask her to move into his place with him. He told his boys of his decision, and they all seemed to be very happy for him, especially Taz. Taz had told him that it was time for all of them to start settling down. None of them were getting any younger. Every member of the crew had everything that they ever wanted, but only Bob and Taz had found the one love of their lives. *"The game is starting to come to an end, so it's time that we all start preparing for it."* These words that Taz spoke stuck deep within Bob. His mind was made up. If Gwen moved in with him, he was going to ask her to marry him within six months. He was definitely in love.

When Gwen came outside and got inside of Bob's truck, she said, "Hey, you! How was your day?"

"It was straight. It's better now that I'm here with you. Let's go get our grub on somewhere. I gots some things I want to talk to you about."

"That's fine. Where do you want to go eat at, babe?"

"It don't matter. You choose."

"Let's get some fish from Bob Davis's, and then come back here and chill."

"I'm with that," Bob said as he started to pull out of her driveway. Once he had started driving down her street, his cell rang. He grabbed the phone and said, "What up?"

"Dog, Taz just got the word from Won. Meet us at the house in thirty," said Keno.

"Damn! All right, gee, out!" After closing his cell phone, he made a U-turn and told Gwen, "Baby, some shit has come up. I gots to bounce outta town. I shouldn't be no longer than a day or so."

"Where are you going, babe?"

"To be honest, I don't even know yet. I'll find out in a li'l bit. Once I do, I'll give you a holla and let you know what's what. Cool?"

"Yeah, I'm cool. But I am curious as to why you have to up and leave all of a sudden. But I ain't tripping, as long as it's not for some other female."

Bob smiled as he pulled back into her driveway and said, "Baby, you are the only woman I'm seeing. Fuck, you are the only woman that I want to see! Believe that! And when I get back, we'll have that talk I wanted to have with you tonight."

"About what, babe?"

Bob stared into Gwen's sexy brown eyes and simply said, "Us. Now, let me roll. Business gots to be handled." He gave her a tender kiss and watched as she climbed out of his truck and went back inside of her home. Once her door was closed, he pulled out of her driveway and punched it towards Taz's house. *Time to go to work!*

The crew was assembled inside of Taz's den, watching as he was tapping the keys on his laptop. After a few minutes, he closed the laptop and said, "Okay, boys, it's like this. We're on our way to L.A. Everything is set to go down in the morning. Me and Keno are leaving from here this time. Bob, you and Red are bouncing out of Tulsa, and Bo-Pete, you and Bill got Ft. Worth this time. Once y'all touch down at LAX, take a shuttle to the Budget Rent A Car spot right by the airport. Keno and I will already be there to pick y'all up. It's a timed op, so be ready because we're moving right from there. We should be back here sometime late tomorrow night. The pay for this one is a ticket apiece. Any questions?"

The room remained silent, as no one said a word.

"All right then, my niggas, let's roll!" Taz stood up and told Keno, "I'll drive this time, clown. And you better not bring that damn *Scarface* DVD!"

Keno laughed and said, "Dog, it's going to be a long flight out to Cali. What else am I goin' to watch?"

Taz smiled and said, "Here," as he gave Keno a DVD.

Keno opened the case, smiled, and said, "I can do this. Yeah, I can fuck with me some Fifty Cent. Where the fuck did you get this from? This shit just came out a couple of months ago."

"My nigga Big O hooked me up. You know that old nigga be having the hookups on bootlegs and shit. When he told me that he had *Get Rich or Die Tryin'*, I was like yeah, this might stop you from watching that old-ass *Scarface*."

Keno started laughing as he put the DVD inside of his carry bag. As they all were leaving Taz's home, he said, "Yeah, I'm gon' get into this one, but I'm still watching me some *Face!*"

Taz shook his head and said, "I just can't win fuckin' with you, can I?"

"Nope. Now come on, let's go get this money!"

Taz and Keno's flight arrived in Los Angeles a little after midnight. Since the rest of the crew wasn't due to arrive for several more hours, they went and checked into the Best Western Suites, where Won had a room already reserved for them. Once they were inside, Taz pulled out the DVD that was given to him by the manager when they had checked in. He quickly inserted the DVD and smiled when he saw a picture of Michael Jordan gliding through the air with a basketball gripped tightly in the palm of his hand. After about thirty seconds, Won's deep voice started speaking:

"Glad that y'all made it safely, boys. Now pay attention, 'cause like I told you, everything about this one is on the clock. The rest of the crew should be there by eight a.m. They should be at the Budget no later than nine. So, after you scoop them up, you are to get onto the 405 Freeway South and head out to Long Beach. Get off on the Carson Street exit and drive exactly one mile. You will see some apartments to your left and an auto body shop to your right. Park the truck over in the apartment's parking lot. Strap up and wait for a blue Mazda 626 to pull up. Once you spot the Mazda, start making your move across the street. A thick older lady should get out of the car and head towards the front of the body shop. Once she reaches inside of her purse to grab her keys, you should be on her. Take her inside and lead her to the back of the shop. After she's secure, two of you go straight inside of the office located on the far left of the building. There's a safe under the desk. The combo is 21 to the left, 11 to the right, and 99 back to the left. There should be approximately six million dollars in that safe. After the chips are secure, go back with the others and prepare yourselves, because this is where it's going to get tricky."

"Within ten minutes after you guys have entered the shop, two carloads of mean-ass brothers will be coming in. Force may have to be used, because these ain't no pootbutts. They're straight killas, so handle them as such. If need be, do what has to be done. All of your weapons are silenced for that purpose. One of the gentlemen will be carrying a case full of work. That's what has to be snatched next. After retrieving the case, secure everyone and get the fuck out."

"You are to then proceed back to the Budget rental spot and drop off the truck with everything you've acquired still inside of the truck. Your return flights are already reserved. You leave on the same flights you arrived on. Each of your flights departs between twelve and twelvethirty. You should all be back home no later than ten p.m. Your weapons and everything you will need for this mission are under the bed. Be precise, be prepared, and most of all, be careful. Out!"

The television screen went blank, and Taz and Keno went and got their tools for their mission. They made sure that each and every weapon was loaded and ready to fire. After that, they got the gym bags and plastic hand restraints in order for everyone else. Since they still had some time before they went to go pick up Bob, Red, Bo-Pete, and Bill, they decided to relax and get some sleep.

Taz called downstairs at the front desk and gave them a seven a.m. wake-up call for him. After he hung up the phone, he picked up his cell and called Sacha. Even though he knew that it was after two in the morning back in Oklahoma, he still wanted to hear her voice. When she answered the phone, he said, "Hey, Li'l Mama, I'm sorry I woke you."

"That's okay, baby. Is everything all right?"

"Yeah, everything's straight. I just wanted to hear your voice before I laid it down."

Smiling, she asked, "Where are you this time, baby?"

"I'm in L.A. I should be back tomorrow evening sometime."

"L.A.! Oooh, I wish I was with you! I could do some serious damage in those malls out there."

"Is that right? Well, I guess I'm going to have to get you back out here soon, so you can do all the damage you'd like."

"For real? Baby, you're so damn good to me. When can we go, Taz?"

Taz laughed and said, "Whenever you have the time, Li'l Mama. Now, go on and get some rest. I'll give you a call when I know exactly what time I'll be in tomorrow."

"All right, baby. Love you!"

Smiling, he said, "Love you too! Bye."

Keno was lying on the other twin bed in the room and said, "Damn, my nigga! It must really feel good to have someone to love again, huh?"

Taz smiled as he closed his eyes and said, "Yeah, my nigga, it does."

Keno and Taz pulled their rented Ford Expedition into the Budget rental parking lot just as the Budget shuttle van from the airport pulled in. Bo-Pete and Wild Bill were the first to climb out of the van. They saw the Expedition and stepped quickly towards the truck. By the time they were inside, Red and Bob stepped out of the van and went and joined the rest of the crew.

Keno pulled out of the parking lot and headed towards the 405 Freeway. While they were riding, Taz filled everyone in on how the mission was supposed to go down. After he was finished, Wild Bill asked, "Do you think we'll have to smoke any of those fools?"

"Ain't no tellin', so make sure that you're prepared to do whatever, feel me?"

"Don't trip, my nigga. If they make a wrong move, they're outta there," Wild Bill said seriously.

"I know that's right, homey!" added Red.

The rest of the ride was done in silence as they all prepared themselves for what had to be done. They were completely focused. None of them were scared, but their adrenaline was pumping big-time. *Time to go to work!*

Keno got off of the 405 on Carson Street and drove directly to the apartments that Won told them about. He parked the truck, and everyone inside began to check and recheck their weapons.

Keno pulled out a Black and Mild cigar and was about to light up until Taz stopped him and said, "No time for that, my nigga. There's the blue Mazda now. "Let's go!"

They climbed out of the truck slowly, looking both ways to make sure that there wasn't too much attention being paid to their movements. Once Taz felt that everything was good, he gave them all a nod of his head, and they quickly ran across the street.

The old lady who had climbed out of the Mazda 626 never had a chance. Just as she stuck her key into the front door of the auto body shop, Keno grabbed her by the back of her neck and said, "Don't turn around. Just keep doing what you were doing and you'll be fine, lady. Open the door nice and slow. Then step on inside." She did as she was told, and they all entered the auto body shop behind her.

Once they were inside, everything went on autopilot. Keno led the lady to the back of the shop and quickly put a pair of the hand restraints on her wrists and legs. Taz stood watch while Red, Bob, Bo-Pete, and Wild Bill went inside of the office. Red and Bob stood at the door of the office as Bo-Pete and Wild Bill went and opened the safe. Once their bags were filled and the safe was completely empty, all four of them came out of the office and stepped quickly to the back of the shop.

Taz checked his watch and figured that they had maybe three minutes tops before the killas arrived. He smiled and said, "Alright, the easy part's over with. Y'all get ready, 'cause it's almost time for us to earn our chips."

"You are some dumb young fuckers! Do you actually know who you're fucking with? You won't live a month after this, you damned fools!" screamed the restrained lady.

Keno smiled and said, "Don't worry about us, Ma. You need to be worrying about your boys, 'cause if they act up, not only will they lose all of that dope, but their lives are as good as bye-bye!" He smiled when he noticed the lady's reaction to his words. She shook her head slowly and said, "You all are still some walking dead men."

Bob, who had gone to the front of the shop to keep a lookout, suddenly turned around and said, "They're here!"

Taz gave Keno a nod, and they stepped to the right side of the shop with their weapons drawn. Bo-Pete and Wild Bill were on the other side of the shop, crouched low with their weapons aimed at the front door. Red stayed at the back with his hands wrapped around the old lady's mouth so she wouldn't be able to warn her peoples.

Since the auto body shop's lights were off and the room was somewhat dark, Taz felt comfortable that the advantage was theirs as he watched as two men came strolling through the front door, followed by three more. Once they were inside, one of the men said, "Why didn't Dee turn on the fuckin' lights?"

"Because she's a li'l tied up at the moment, gee," said Taz as he stepped in front of the first two who had entered the shop. He pointed his silenced weapon at their heads and continued, "Now, get down on the floor slowly."

The three men who had come in behind the first two tried to reach for their weapons, but Wild Bill and Bo-Pete stopped them. "Go on and pull out, nigga! You'll be dead with your gun in your hand," Wild Bill said as he put the barrel of his nine-millimeter to the side of one of the guys' head.

With a smile on his face, Bo-Pete had the other two held at gunpoint. "Make it happen, Captain! It's all on you. You want to live or die?"

All three of the men raised their hands in the air slowly.

"That's what I thought! Now, get your asses on the fuckin' floor!" yelled Bo-Pete.

Once they had them all on the ground and restrained, Taz had Keno and Bob take them to the back of the shop with Dee. Red watched with an amused smile on his face as the captives were led towards him.

"All right then, let's grab the work and shake this spot," Taz said as they sat all of the men down on the floor next to Dee.

One of the first two men who had come inside of the shop was staring real hard at Taz. *These fools are about to smoke us. How the fuck did they get onto us? This shit ain't right. Somethin' just ain't right. They ain't got on no masks or nothin'. Damn! They is goin' to smoke our asses!* he thought as he continued to stare at Taz.

Taz noticed him staring and said, "Don't trip, gee. Y'all gon' live. We gots what we came for." Then he gave him a big smile so he could see his platinum and diamond grille.

Some country niggas! Hell nah! You fools are dead! the man thought to himself as he watched in disbelief.

"Dog, go and get the truck. As soon as you're in front, blow the horn twice," Taz instructed Keno.

"Gotcha." Keno ran out of the shop and got the truck. By the time he blew the truck's horn twice, the crew was standing at the door, looking over their shoulders at the men and lady that they had secured in the back of the shop. They stepped out of the shop one at a time with a smile on their faces as they each climbed inside of the Expedition. They didn't have to kill anyone, and they were all one million dollars richer.

Taz came out of the shop and was about to climb inside of the truck when he noticed someone staring at him from inside of a red Escalade. He opened the door to the Expedition and asked, "What kind of car did those clowns pull up in, Bob?"

"That Escalade, my nigga. Why? What's up?"

"Fuck!" Taz screamed as he slammed the door and walked back inside of the shop. After he closed the door, he saw the guy inside of the truck talking to someone on his cell phone. "Damn, he gots to die!" Taz said as he opened the door to the shop quickly and charged the red Escalade with his pistol in hand.

The driver was so caught up with his phone call that he didn't even get a chance to yell. Seven bullets from Taz's silenced nine-millimeter crashed through the windshield of the Escalade, killing the driver instantly.

Taz opened the passenger's side of the truck, reached across and pulled the slumped driver over to him to make sure that he was dead. When he saw the three holes in his face, he grimaced and let the dead body fall back against the headrest. He closed the door and walked back to the Expedition. Once he was inside of the truck, he calmly said, "Let's roll out."

Chapter Seventeen

Sacha was sitting at her desk. Her intercom buzzed, and her receptionist told her that she had a call. "Hello, This is Sacha Carbajal. How may I help you?"

"Hello, ma'am, this is Tony Surefield. I just wanted to let you know that I'm out, and it looks like I won't be needing your services, after all."

"I see. So I assume that you were able to work a deal out with the U.S. assistant attorney, Mr. Surefield."

"Yeah, something like that."

"Okay, then, you better make sure that you keep your nose clean out there."

"I will, and thanks for your help anyway though."

"That's what you paid me for, Mr. Surefield. Have a nice day."

"You too," he said and hung up.

After Sacha hung up the phone with her client, she said, "Snitch!" Then she went back to reading the file on her upcoming trial.

Clifford was sitting in his office when he got a call from someone from his past. "Long time, C-Baby!" said the voice on the other line.

When Clifford heard his old nickname, he asked "Who is this?"

"Come on, my nigga, don't tell me you done forgot about your boy!"

Clifford couldn't help but smile when he asked, "Do-Low?"

"What's good, C-Baby?"

"When did you get out the pen?"

"Two days ago. I got your number from your moms. I need you, C-Baby. I need you bad."

"Look, I don't go by C-Baby any longer, Do-Low. You know that was a long time ago. I go by my government name now."

"Yeah, I know. But check it out, dog. We need to talk. You know about old times and shit. Come on, man, let's get together and kick it a li'l bit."

"What's up? You need some money or something?"

"Man, my problems are way worse than ends, my nigga. I'm dying, C—I mean Clifford. I got that thang, dog."

"What thang? What the hell are you talking about, Do-Low?"

"HIV, man. I got that package," Do-Low said seriously.

"How the fuck did you get that shit? I know you didn't go out backwards when you was in the pen."

"Hell nah! You know I ain't on that fag shit, fool. Remember when I got blasted back in '94?"

"Yeah."

"They had to give me a blood transfusion during surgery while I was down. I got called to take our yearly HIV test, and I tested positive. That was two years ago. This shit is starting to kick in on me now, dog. My days are numbered, and I'm not trying to go out without being able to leave something for my shorties, dog. Feel me?"

In a somber voice, Clifford answered, "Yeah, I feel you. How are your kid's anyway?"

"Man, they're big! Dionne is ten now, and she's almost as tall as her mother is. And the twins, man, they're the spitting images of me, gee," he said excitedly.

"That's cool. Yeah, that's real cool. Listen, I got a few things to take care of real quick. Give me a number and I'll get back at you in an hour or so." After writing Do-Low's number down, Clifford said, "Don't worry, dog. I'm going to make sure that you'll be able to look out for your seeds."

"Is that right? Come on, don't bullshit me C—I mean Clifford."

Smiling as he thought about Taz and Sacha, Clifford said, "You know me, Do-Low. I'd never play with you like that. Now, let me go so I can handle my business. I'll get at you in one hour."

"A'ight then, Clifford. One!"

"Yeah, later," Clifford said and hung up. "A nigga with nothing to lose. Perfect! Just fucking perfect!" he said aloud as he went back to work.

It had been a long time since Taz had actually had to use his weapon. It felt strange, but at the same time exciting. *Damn, this is some crazy-ass shit!* he thought as he relaxed in his seat as their flight prepared to depart out of LAX.

After their flight was airborne, Keno smiled as he inserted his *Scarface* DVD into his portable DVD player. Just before he plugged in his headphones, he asked Taz, "Are you all right, my nigga?"

"Yeah, I'm good. I'd be better if I didn't have to look at that old-ass movie again. I thought you were going to watch Fifty."

"I watched it when we left the City. It was cool, but gee, that shit just wasn't gritty enough for me. 'Face is a damn fool."

Taz laughed and said, "Whatever! Damn, dog! Bob slipped on us today. He was supposed to be on point with that clown in the truck."

"Yeah, I was thinking about that. What's up?"

"Nothin'. I'll get at him when we get back."

"Yeah, you need to, 'cause if that love-struck-ass nigga's gon' be slippin' like that on us, it's time for his ass to get the fuck out."

Taz closed his eyes and said, "I know, gee. I know."

After Clifford dropped Do-Low back off at his apartment, he sat in his car and thought about what he had just done. He was going to pay Do-Low fifty thousand dollars to take Taz's life for him. But he had to make it look as if it was a random robbery attempt. That way, Sacha would never link him to it. "I'll play the good, supportive friend with her for a few months. Then we'll gradually get closer. Then, everything will be good," he said to himself as he started his car and pulled out of the apartment complex.

Sacha and Gwen had just finished having dinner when both of their cell phones began to ring at the same time. Sacha smiled when she saw that it was Taz who was calling her. Gwen smiled also when she noticed that it was Bob who was calling her. After speaking to Taz for a few minutes, Sacha hung up her phone and waited for Gwen to finish talking to Bob.

When Gwen finally got off of her cell, Sacha said, "Damn, ho! He must have been telling you some real good shit. It took your ass long enough."

Smiling, Gwen said, "Yeah, bitch, he told me that he has something serious to talk to me about. I'm meeting him at his place in a couple of hours. I'm going to go home and get changed, and grab me some gear for tomorrow, 'cause I got a feeling it's going to be a real long night."

"What do you think he wants to talk about? I remember when you told me he said something about y'all getting closer and stuff."

"I think he wants me to move in with him."

"Stop lying! Ho, are you going to do it if he asks you to?"

"I might. Bitch, I'm sick and tired of being all by myself. It would feel real good to be able to wake up with someone every morning."

"I know that's right! But you have to remember, sometimes there will still be mornings when you'll wake up by yourself. You know how often they be going out of town."

"I know. What do they be doing when they leave?"

"I've tried my best to get Taz to tell me, but he just won't do it. No matter how mad I act, he refuses to tell me. He always comes with that 'it's my business' shit, or 'Don't worry, Li'l Mama. It ain't nothin'" she said as she tried to imitate Taz's voice.

"Do you think they're into some shady shit?"

"To be completely honest, no, I don't. Taz has shown me that he's legit, and I won't question him on it again. You know they're still caught up with their thug images and shit, so I've chosen to ignore that shit. The jewelry, the fancy cars, the gangsta shit, that's just who they are. I love Taz, and no matter what, I'm going to support him. As long as he's safe and I'm happy. Regarding his business affairs, no matter how sneaky they may seem, I'm rolling with my nigga."

"I hear you, bitch. But still, they could at least put our minds at ease."

"As far as I'm concerned, Taz has done just that. Don't worry about that shit, girl. I don't."

"Well, that's you. Bob and I are going to discuss this later on, and I'm going to make it a point to let him know that I want to know exactly what is going on. And believe me, bitch, he's going to tell me."

"Whatever! Come on, ho. Let's get out of here. I'm ready to see my man."

Taz and the rest of the crew were all seated in his den. They had just finished checking their accounts. After Taz got off of the phone with Won, he closed his cell and said, "All right, I guess everything is everything. Won wants us to stay ready, 'cause we might be bouncing as quickly as next week, so you know what it is. Stay ready so you won't have to get ready."

Bob stood and said, "All right then, my niggas, I'm out. I'm about to go get with Gwen and chill for the rest of the night. What's up for the weekend? Are we clubbin' or what?"

"It's whatever with me, dog. You know now that you and Taz are all in love and shit, y'all might not be able to come hang with us," Red said with a smile on his face.

"Fuck you, clown!"

They were all laughing as they filed out of Taz's home.

Taz stopped Bob before he had a chance to get into his truck and said, "Dog, let me holla at you for a minute."

Bob climbed into his truck and asked, "What's up, homey?"

"Tell me something. Do you feel that you're ready to get out of the game we're playing?"

"As long as we're safe and the chips are chunky, I'm in it to win it, gee."

"That's what I'm talkin' 'bout. But, dog, you slipped on us back in L.A. One of us could have gotten twisted."

"I was thinking about that shit on the flight back. I didn't pay attention once I saw the truck stop and saw the fools climb out. That was my bad, dog. It won't happen again, Taz."

"It can't happen again, Bob. I love you, dog, but before I let you put either of us in a jam like that again, I'll have to shake you, gee. We've been too strong for too long, my nigga. Ain't no room for getting sloppy now."

"I got you, dog."

"Do you? Is what you're feeling for Gwen causing you to slip, my nigga? This is some real shit, so I'm giving you some real talk. 'Cause we won't ever have this conversation again, gee. So don't take offense to my words. Feel every one of them."

Bob sat back in his seat and thought about what Taz had just told him. He smiled and said, "I ain't mad at ya, Taz. I love you and the rest of the homies as if we were all brothers. I fucked up in Cali, and like I said, it won't happen again. Thank you for catching my back, dog. And to answer your question, yeah, I love that broad. Dog, it's been a long time since a nigga has been able to feel some real love from a female. For once it ain't about the chips I got or the car I'm rollin' in. Dog, she's into me and I'm into her. It's real, dog . . . real as it can get. As a matter of fact, I'm about to meet her at my pad and ask her to move in with me."

Taz smiled and said, "That's cool, dog. I'm feeling just as deeply for Sacha as you are for Gwen, but I will never, and I mean never, let my thoughts or love for her interfere with the work that we do. So, make sure that you stay on your square, my nigga." Taz closed the door to Bob's truck, turned, and went back inside of his home.

By the time Bob pulled into his garage, Gwen was already parked in his driveway. He smiled as he climbed out of his truck, and his girl ran into his arms. "I've missed you so much, baby!" Gwen said as she kissed him passionately.

Bob pulled from her embrace, scooped her into his arms, and said, "I've missed you too. Let me take you inside so I can show you exactly how much." He then carried her into his home and straight to the bedroom. He dropped her onto his bed and started laughing when she threw her purse at him. "Ouch!"

"Don't get it twisted, nigga. I ain't with that rough shit!"

"I was just playin'! Damn!" He smiled as he sat next to her on the bed and said, "Check this out, baby. How would you feel if I asked you to move in with me?"

Smiling, she said, "That depends."

"On what?"

"On whether or not you're asking me, babe."

"Okay, let's do this then. I'm tired of being alone, and I love having you around me. I love everything about you, Gwen. You bring some balance into this crazy-ass life of mines. Will you move in with me, baby?"

"What about my house? What am I going to do with it?"

"You own it, right?"

"Yep."

"Well, rent it out. That way, you'll have some more income coming in, even though money will be the least of your concerns."

"Who's going to fix shit when something goes wrong over there?"

"Come on with that shit, Gwen. You know I'll make sure everything is straight. I love you, Gwen, and I want you to be with me. Let's do this for a while and see how things fall."

"What if they don't fall the way you expect them to?"

"I seriously doubt that will happen."

"But what if it does, babe? Then what?"

"Then, you can move back in and everything will be everything."

"I don't know, Bob. Don't you think that we're moving kind of fast here?"

"Baby, I don't give a damn about nothing but you. I love you, and I want to be with you. I want to wake up and see you sleeping in our bed. I want to spend the rest of my life with you, Gwen. Let's start with this, and once we've kicked it for a minute, let's make it official."

"Are you asking me to marry you, Bob?"

"You damn skippy! I love you and I want you to be wifey."

With a smile on her face, Gwen said, "Alright, babe, we can do this. I'll move in with you, and then we'll see if this is as special as we both seem to think. But I have a question that I want to ask you first."

"What's up?"

"I'm curious as to why you always have to go out of town so unexpectedly. What's up with the trips and shit, babe?"

"It's business, baby, that's all. We be having to go take care of certain things."

"So, why is it always a different place?"

"Look, you have to understand that our business ventures are spread all over the place. We're a team, and it takes all of our manpower to be able to deal with everything we have on our plates."

Shaking her head slowly, Gwen asked, "What exactly do y'all be doing out of town, Bob?"

"It depends. Sometimes there's business meetings that we have to attend, or sometimes we have to go look at several different sites that we're trying to acquire—business shit, baby. Now, what's up? Are you moving in with me or what?"

This slick, sexy-ass nigga of mines thinks he has all of the answers. Humph! He's forgotten that I'm a fucking psychiatrist. I'll let him off the hook for now, but sooner or later I'm going to find out exactly what the fuck they're into, she said to herself. She smiled at Bob and said, "Yeah, babe, we can do it. I love you, and I want to be with you just as much as you want to be with me." She took off her blouse and said, "Now, come here and let me show you how much I love you."

"Now, that's what I'm talkin' 'bout!" he said as he slid into her arms.

Chapter Eighteen

Taz and Sacha had spent the entire day together shopping. Now that they were finally finished, all Taz wanted to do was to go back to his house and relax and chill. But Sacha was in the mood for more. "Baby, we should go out to the club tonight," she said as she climbed inside of Taz's truck.

"For what? To look at the same old tired-ass niggas and shit? Nah, I'm good with that one, Li'l Mama," he said as he turned on the ignition.

Pouting, she said, "Come on, baby, it'll be fun. We haven't been out in a while. I'll call Gwen, and get her and Bob to go, and we'll have a nice evening."

"Why can't you just have them come on over to the house so we could chill out there?"

"'Cause that's no fun, baby! Let's go out and have some fun and drink and stuff," Sacha whined.

Taz sighed as he pulled out of the parking lot of the mall, and said, "If you want to go out that bad, I ain't trippin', Li'l Mama. But I'm going to have to see what Keno, Red, Bo-Pete, and Wild Bill are gettin' into. I never go to the club without all of my niggas with me."

"Why?"

"Security reasons, Li'l Mama. Beef never dies."

"What do you mean by that?"

"Let's just say that there are some people in this town that don't love Taz. And for that reason, I never go to any clubs without my niggas."

"But what if they don't want to go out?"

"Then neither am I."

"So, you're telling me that if your boys don't want to go out, then you're not going to go out with me?"

"Don't make this out to be somethin' against you, Li'l Mama, 'cause it ain't. It's just how I get down. Please don't try to make me go against the way I've been living for years."

"But that's so unfair, Taz!"

"Not really, baby, 'cause I don't really want to go to the club, anyway. The only reason why I gave in was because it seemed like you had your heart set on going out tonight."

"Anyway, go on and call Keno and the rest of your niggas, 'cause I'm trying to go out, and I want my man with me," she said sarcastically.

Taz smiled but said nothing as he grabbed his cell and called Keno. When Keno answered his cell, he said, "What up, dog?"

"What's good, my nigga?" replied Keno.

"Ain't shit. Just finished doing some shopping with Sacha. I'm on my way to the pad now. What you got planned for tonight?"

"Not much as of right now. I was thinking about rollin' by the club later on to see what was poppin'. What's with you?"

"Sacha wants to hit the club, so I was checkin' to see if y'all wanted to roll."

"I'm with it. It don't seem like there's much else to get into tonight. I'll get at Red and 'em, and I'll get back at you by the time you get to the pad."

"That's straight. Oh, and Sacha thanks you."

"For what?"

"Never mind, my nigga. I'll tell you about it later. Out!"

Sacha was just about to say something slick when for the second time that day she noticed that there was a black Altima following them. She turned a little in her seat so she could get a clear view in the rearview mirror on the side of Taz's truck. When she saw the Altima slow down a little and let a few cars get in front of it, she was positive that they were being followed. "Taz, I think someone has been following us."

"What? What are you talkin' 'bout Li'l Mama?" he asked as he checked his rearview mirror.

"About three cars back is an all-black Altima. I could have sworn I seen that same car as we left Crossroads Mall a few hours ago. I just noticed it again as we pulled out of Penn Square."

"Are you sure?"

"Positive."

"Okay, let's see then," Taz said as he accelerated. His truck gave a slight lurch as the speed increased from forty-five miles per hour to sixty quickly. He made a left turn onto May Avenue and slowed down a little as they came close to 63rd Street. "Don't look over your shoulder, Li'l Mama, but tell me, do you still see the car you was talkin' 'bout?"

Sacha checked the rearview mirror again and said, "Yep, about two cars back."

Taz slowed down and pulled into the parking lot of a Blockbuster Video store and hopped out of his truck. As he strolled slowly towards Blockbuster, he saw the black Altima pull into the parking lot of Ted's Mexican restaurant across the street. Taz turned around and stepped quickly back to the truck. Once he was back inside, he started the truck and said, "You're right, Li'l Mama. It looks like we do have a tail. Now, let's see who the fuck this is following us."

"H- how are you going to do that, baby?" she asked nervously.

"Don't trip, Li'l Mama. Everything is going to be alright," Taz said confidently as he picked up his cell and quickly dialed. A few seconds later he said, "Check this out, Won. I done picked me up a tail, O.G."

"Is that right? How long have you had it?"

"I'm not knowing exactly. At least a few hours."

"And you're just now getting at me?"

"Shit, I just figured it out."

"You're slippin', Babyboy. Can you get me the license plate number?"

"Yeah, I got 'em. GVM 214, Oklahoma tags." He had locked it into his memory as he walked back towards his truck when they were in the Blockbuster parking lot.

"All right, take 'em around the City for a li'l ride while I get on it. I'll hit you back in a minute."

"That's straight."

"Are you alone?"

"Nah, I got my boo with me."

"Your *what?* Since when did you have a fuckin' boo, Babyboy?"

Laughing, Taz said, "Don't you think we could get into that a li'l later, O.G.? This does need to be handled."

"My bad, Babyboy! Out!" Won said and hung up.

After Taz had closed his phone, Sacha asked, "Who is Won, baby?"

"A real good friend of mine." Before Sacha could ask him another question, he reopened his cell and called Keno back. When Keno answered his phone, Taz quickly told him about his tail and said, "I'm waiting on Won to get back at me now. After that, I'll hit you and we'll see what's what."

"How are we going to put something down when you got Sacha with you?" asked Keno.

"Don't trip. If we have to put a demo down, I'm going to go drop her back off at the mall. Then, I'll have Red or Bo-Pete come scoop her up while we handle this shit. For now, just stand by, my nigga."

"Gotcha," Keno said before hanging up.

After listening to what Taz had just told Keno, Sacha's heart rate seemed to increase rapidly. "Baby, what are you planning on doing?"

Taz stared at her briefly and said, "Whatever I have to do, Li'l Mama."

His comment was made so coldly that Sacha felt like she didn't even know the man that was sitting next to her.

Taz's cell rang just as he was getting onto the highway. "Talk to me, O.G."

"Babyboy, are you doing anything outta the normal out there?"

"Nah, why?"

"Are you sure?"

"Yeah, I'm sure. What's up?"

"You got the suits on your ass. That's a government vehicle. Now tell me, what the fuck's going on?"

"I'm tellin' you, O.G., I ain't doing shit! You know I don't get down like that. For what, some crumbs? This is some straight bullshit, Won!" Taz yelled with panic in voice.

"Calm down, Babyboy! Just relax. Go on and head to the house, and give me a call when you get there. We'll figure this shit out and put a stop to whatever the fuck is going on."

"Nah, fuck that, O.G.! I gots me a lawyer with me right fuckin' now, and I'm about to see what the fuck is crackin'! Exactly who the fuck is this? DEA or the Feds?"

"The Feds."

"All right, cool. I'll hit you back in a li'l bit."

"What the fuck are you about to do, Babyboy?"

"What needs to be done. Out!" Taz turned towards Sacha as he pulled off of the highway and said, "Li'l Mama, those are federal agents following us. Why? I do not know. But I'm about to find the fuck out. I need you to represent me. Are you cool with that?"

"You know I am, baby, but business hours are over. How are you going to get in contact with anyone?"

"Sit back and watch," he said confidently as he drove towards the headquarters of the FBI in Oklahoma City.

Taz pulled his truck into the parking lot of 50 Penn Place Mall. He smiled when he saw the shocked expression on the face of the driver of the black Altima as they passed by him on their way into the mall. Fifty Penn Place was not only an exclusive mall, but it also held the offices of the FBI.

Taz led Sacha to the elevator, and they quickly rode it to the third floor. When they stepped off of the elevator, Taz went straight to the receptionist's desk and said, "I'd like to speak to the duty officer, please."

"May I ask your name and reason, sir?" asked the receptionist.

"My name is Taz Good, and I'm here to find out exactly why your fucking federal agents have been following me!"

"Please, calm down, sir! There's no need for profanity."

"Fuck you! Get the fuckin' duty officer out here right fuckin' now!" he screamed.

The shocked receptionist quickly picked up the phone and called someone. A minute after she had hung up the phone, two white federal agents came into the waiting area.

"What seems to be the problem, Silvia?" asked one of the agents.

"This gentleman has come in here demanding to see you, sir. He seems to be very upset about someone following him."

The duty officer stepped towards Taz and said, "Hello, sir. My name is Agent Frank Johns. I'm the duty officer for today. How may I be of assistance?"

Taz took a deep breath to calm himself and said, "Look. I just figured out that I'm being followed by one of your agents, and I want to know why. I do not indulge in any form of illegal activity, so there should be no reason for this bullshit!"

"Please, calm down, sir! Maybe there's some misunderstanding. How do you know that it's one of our agents that is following you?"

Taz smiled and said, "Because I'm a nigga that is not to be fucked with. I have friends in very high fuckin' places. That's how I know. I had the license plate checked, and it came back to you all. So, like I said, I want to know why you got your people following me!"

"You need to watch your mouth, young man!" the other agent said to Taz.

"Man, fuck you! I'm grown! I have my attorney here with me just in case y'all want to try some bullshit. But I want some answers. And if I don't get them, I promise you that on Monday morning, there's going to be a lot of media in this bitch, 'cause I'm going to use everything in my power to put on a show this city hasn't seen since the muthafuckin' bombing in '94!"

Agent Johns stared at Taz briefly, and for some reason he took Taz's threats seriously. *This guy is too damn confident. He's not bluffing,* he thought to himself. "Please, come into my office so we can see if we can figure this out."

They followed the agents back into the inner offices of the FBI.

Sacha couldn't believe that Taz was talking to these people that way. She was excited both by how her man was checking these people and at the fact that he was showing no sign of fear whatsoever. She was actually getting turned on by his tirade.

After they were seated in Agent Johns's office, Sacha said, "My name is Sacha Carbajal. I work for Whitney & Johnson, and as you've already been told, I'm representing Mr. Good here."

"That's fine, Miss Carbajal. If you two would give me a moment, I need to contact my superiors. Hopefully we'll be able to find something out." Agent Johns then made a few phone calls and spoke to a couple of different people. After about ten minutes, he finally hung up with his last call and said, "Mr. Good, may I ask what you do for a living?"

Taz looked across at Sacha, and she gave him a nod of her head, giving him her consent to answer the question.

"I'm part owner in several small food chains here in Oklahoma City. I own over forty homes here, also."

"And that is your main source of income, sir?"

Taz smiled and said, "That's my only income."

"Have you ever been arrested, Mr. Good?"

"Nope."

"I see. Okay, here it is, sir. We have received information that you're involved in drugs. We admit that we have checked you and your background thoroughly, and you are clean. At least it looks that way. But the information we received came from a valuable witness, so we had to take it seriously. I've been told by my superior to inform you that we are backing off of this part of the investigation, and that you have our word that for now you will not be followed by anyone from our offices."

Sacha started to speak, but Taz interrupted her. "So, you're telling me that someone told you I was a dope boy?"

"Yes, sir, that's exactly what I'm telling you."

"And you believed him just because he's a valuable snitch? Y'all gots to be outta your fuckin' minds!"

"Come on, Taz. Calm down. There's no need to get too crazy. They're backing off for now, and that's all that matters. I'll check into this deeper on Monday. At least we've accomplished something out of this trip," Sacha said wisely.

Taz, whose thoughts were on who could have been telling the feds that he was a drug dealer, wasn't really paying any attention to her. He was too busy wracking his brain. After a few minutes, he snapped back to reality and said, "All right, I can accept that. But I'm telling you, I've never in my life sold any fuckin' dope. And if you really check deep into my past, you'll know why. I despise dope boys and anyone who deals with them."

"And why is that, if I may ask?" asked Agent Johns.

Taz smiled at Sacha, and then turned towards the federal agent and said, "You're the FBI, man. Figure it out. Come on, Li'l Mama, let's bounce."

As Sacha and Taz left the agents' office, Agent Johns told his partner, "He's as clean as a whistle, Tom."

"What makes you think so?"

"Too confident . . . too fuckin' confident."

"Yeah, I can tell. Did you catch what he called his attorney when they left?"

"What, the Li'l Mama thing? Yeah, I caught it. Not only is he confident, he has some very good taste, too."

"That's right. She's a looker."

Both of the federal agents started laughing as they resumed their duties for the evening.

By the time Taz had dropped Sacha off at her house and made it to his, he had explained everything that had just happened to Won and Keno. Won laughed and told him that he didn't have anything to worry about. Since everything was bullshit, he should maintain his composure and keep to his normal every-day routine.

Keno, on the other hand, was a little spooked. "What if they get into our business with Won?" he asked.

Taz didn't have an answer for that, so he left it up to Won.

Won smiled into the receiver and said, "Listen. Don't worry about our business. Everything is everything. As a matter fact, we won't be doing anything for at least a month or so, so relax, Keno! It's all good!"

"I hear you, O.G. I had to ask, you know?" said Keno.

"Yeah, I know. Alright, you two, be good. I'm out!" Won said and hung up the phone.

Taz pressed the button and cut the line to the speakerphone they were talking to Won on and said, "Dog, I really wasn't feeling the club at first, but now I am. Go get changed and get back over here. We needs to get to that club tonight, for real."

Keno smiled and asked, "All black?"

Taz stared at him for a moment, then said, "Call the homies. All black!"

Chapter Nineteen

Taz was dressed in a pair of black Sean Jean jeans, black T-shirt, and black Timberland boots. Keno, Red, Bob, Bo-Pete, and Wild Bill were dressed almost exactly as Taz. The only difference was that they had on other urban designer gear. But it was still all black.

When they made their entrance inside of Club Cancun, it seemed as if everyone inside of the club could feel the dangerous vibes coming from them.

Katrina and Paquita were standing by the bar as Taz came in and accepted his drink from Winky, the bartender.

Paquita watched him as he downed his drink quickly. "Girl, something is wrong with Taz. He never downs his entire drink like that. Shit, look at how all of them are dressed. Something's going to go down tonight."

"I know, girl, I've never seen Keno look so damn mean. Look how they're mean mugging all of the niggas in the club," said Katrina.

"Ain't that some shit? And those scary-ass niggas ain't even trying to make eye contact with them. I've heard some way-out-ass stories about Taz and Keno, but I've never actually seen them in action."

"Well, come on. Let's go get a table, 'cause from the way they're looking, we're going to see their work tonight," Katrina said, and they left the bar.

***

Taz scanned the club over and over, trying his best to make eye contact with any and every male inside. He was hoping to catch someone's eye to see if he could spot some fear. He was confident that if the guy who had told the feds anything about him was in the club, he would be able to tell if they made eye contact. Even if he didn't spot anyone, someone inside the club was going to get a beat down tonight. Tonight was statement night: *Do not fuck with Taz!* It was wrong and Taz knew that, but he was in a real fucked-up mood, and the only way he was going to feel better was if he got to put his hands on one of these soft-ass, wannabe thug-ass niggas.

Keno came to Taz's side and said, "Here comes your girl, dog."

"Damnit! I told her to stay her ass at home. It's time for this broad to get checked!" Taz waited as Sacha and Gwen came over to where they were standing, and said, "Sacha, why are you here?"

With a defiant look on her face, she said, "To make sure that you don't do anything that you might regret later on."

Her words had the exact effect on him that she had hoped for. She saw how his eyes softened a little. He smiled and said, "Thanks, Li'l Mama. I really appreciate that. But you have to understand something about me. When my mood becomes dangerous, there is nothing and no one that can stop me from doing what needs to be done. No one, Li'l Mama, not even you."

Before Sacha could respond, Tony Surefield, her client, walked up to them and said, "Hey, Ms. Carbajal! What you doing up in this piece?"

Sacha smiled and said, "How are you doing, Mr. Surefield?"

"Tony. Call me Tony."

"Okay, Tony. I'm here with my boyfriend, trying to have a good time. Taz, this is Tony. Tony, this is my boyfriend, Taz."

Taz stared directly at Tony for a few seconds, then said, "Yeah, I remember you. KK's li'l brother, right?"

"Yeah, that's right," Tony said as he quickly lowered his eyes.

Well, I'll be damned! It was that easy! This bitch-ass nigga is the one, Taz said to himself. He turned towards Sacha and said, "Excuse me, baby. Let me have a word with Tony for a minute."

Sacha noticed how timid Tony was acting, and knew instantly that her client was the person who had snitched on Taz. *Oh, God! Don't let Taz hurt that man!* she prayed silently. She knew better than to try and talk to Taz, so she told him that she'd be by the bar, and quickly walked away.

After Taz was sure that Sacha was out of earshot, he turned back towards Tony and said, "Dog, I heard you got scooped up by them peoples. You straight?"

"Y—yeah, I'm good. It wasn't nothin' but some bullshit. H-how did you find out about that?"

Taz hadn't heard anything. He just wanted to see if Tony had been in contact with any form of law enforcement. Now, he was absolutely positive that it was this clown-ass nigga who put them onto him. But, why? That was the question he was going to find out. "Dog, it ain't too much that goes on in the City that I don't know about. But I am curious, though. How the fuck did you get out? I know the feds didn't give you a bond. They don't get down like that too often . . . unless you told them somethin'."

"N—nah, I ain't get down like that. Th-the case was so w-weak that they th-threw it ou-out," Tony stuttered.

"Is that right? Check this out, gee. Do you have a problem with how I got at you the last time?"

"Nah, Ta-Taz, I understood you, gee. You don't get down. I was wrong for even gettin' at you like that."

"If that's the case, then tell me why the fuck you told the Feds you have been dealing with me, you bitch-ass nigga!" Before Tony could respond, Taz hit him so hard on his nose that blood splashed everywhere. Tony dropped to the floor as if he was hit with a sledge-hammer. Several people in the club came over and watched the action. Tony got to his feet and swung wildly at Taz, who easily sidestepped his wild punch. Taz smiled and said, "Calm down, Tony! You don't want to hurt yourself, do you?"

"Fuck you, nigga! I ain't no snitch, and I don't go for no nigga calling me one!" yelled Tony as he wiped his bleeding nose.

"So, I'm lying on you, Tony? You're calling me a liar, nigga? The only reason why you got socked in the fuckin' nose and not served properly is because of your brother, nigga! So, don't stand there and call me a liar, you cow-ard-ass nigga!" Taz said with venom in his voice. "Now, what else did you tell them, Tony? I need to know every fuckin' lie you told them peoples, nigga. And if you don't tell me, as God as my witness, I'm catching a murder charge tonight!"

Before Tony could respond, four of his homeboys came over to his side. This seemed to give him some courage, because he smiled and said, "Like I told you, nigga, I ain't no fuckin' snitch. I ain't never even fucked with your ass, so how could I tell them anythin' about you?"

Taz smiled and held up his hands to stop the security from interrupting them. He focused on Tony and his little crew and said, "I knew you were a dumb-ass nigga.

I just didn't expect for you to be crazy." He then turned towards Bo-Pete and said, "Dog, I want y'all to smash these niggas with Tony, so that he can see that they have no win what-so-fucking-ever with us."

Bo-Pete's response to Taz's words was his fist swinging. He dropped the first guy he hit with a hard left; then he charged the next guy who was backing away from him and caught him with a series of vicious blows to his face. Before either of Tony's remaining two homeboys could react, Wild Bill and Red were all over them. Red slapped the hell out of one of the guys and dropped him as if he had hit him as hard as Taz had hit Tony in the nose. Wild Bill, though small, was hitting just as hard as his comrades. He showed his strength as he hit one of the guys with a kidney shot that would make old Iron Mike proud.

Bob, who was standing next to Keno, said, "Dog, fuck all this shit! Let's take this nigga somewhere so he can tell us what we need."

Taz smiled and said, "Nah, we don't have to do that, do we, Tony? You're going to tell everyone in this club exactly what you told the Feds about me. Aren't you?" Taz stared Tony directly in his eyes, and once again asked, "Aren't you, Tony?"

Tony hesitated briefly and simply gave him a nod of his head yes.

With all of the commotion going on, the owner of the club had the lights turned on and the music turned off, so everyone in the club had heard what Taz had said to Tony.

"Now, get to talkin', bitch-ass nigga!" Keno said with contempt.

Tony turned towards his homeboys who were busy trying to tend to the wounds that Bo-Pete, Red, and Wild Bill had inflicted on them. He sighed heavily and said, "Man, I told them that I was plugged in with you, and that you were going to hook me up with some major weight."

Before he could say another word, someone in the crowd yelled, "You fuckin' snitch! Kill his ass, Taz!"

Taz ignored the comment and said, "What else?"

"That's it. They told me that they were going to put someone on you, and that they were going to bury you."

"So, that's all you told them about me, Tony?"

"Yeah, man, that's it, I swear."

"So, you want me to believe that all you said was that you were going to get hooked up by me, and they let you off on a Fed beef? Come on, nigga! I guess you are ready to die!"

"I'm serious, Taz. That's all I said about you."

Taz paused for a moment, then said, "Okay, so who else did you tell on, nigga?"

Tony stared at Taz, pleading with his eyes, and said, "Come on, Taz! Don't do me like that, dog!"

"I'm not your dog, snitch! It's been too many niggas like you puttin' a black eye in the game. That's why most of you dope boys are so fuckin' soft. Y'all ain't layin' these snitches down. So now, everyone is tellin' they asses off." He then stepped back from Tony, turned slightly so that he was facing the onlooking crowd, and said, "You see? This is how the game got punked in the City, 'cause of niggas like this coward. If I was a dope boy, he'd be dead! I know y'all be on some hating shit, but it is what it is. So, I have a question for you dope boys in here that have dealt with this nigga. What are y'all gon' do about him?" Taz started laughing as he stepped up to the owner of the club and said, "I'm sorry about this drama, Big Tim. I had to clear the air, you know?"

"I ain't tripping, Taz. You know I know how you and your boys get down."

"Good lookin'. Now here, take this and let everyone know that the drinks are on me for the rest of the night," Taz said as he passed Big Tim over four thousand dollars in one-hundred-dollar bills. "If that don't cover it, let me know when I come back next time and I'll take care of it."

Smiling brightly, Big Tim said, "Gotcha, Taz!" He then gave the DJ a wave of his hand to signal him to turn the music back on. The lights dimmed, and D4L's "Laffy Taffy" started playing loudly through the speakers.

Taz stepped toward a frowning Sacha and asked, "Are you alright, Li'l Mama?"

"That was my client you just humiliated, Taz!"

"Your client? You mean to tell me that you knew that he told the people on me?"

"Don't be stupid! But even if I did, I wouldn't have been able to tell you."

"Yeah, I know attorney-client privacy and shit. I ain't trippin', Li'l Mama. It's all but a memory now."

"You think? Humph! Let me see. Have you ever heard of obstruction of justice, assault, and a host of other felonies you have just committed? Taz, I'd be very surprised if the Feds weren't at your home first thing in the morning."

Taz smiled and said, "You think? At least I'll have the upper hand on them, Li'l Mama."

With a smirk on her face, she asked, "And how's that?"

"I'll already have my attorney present."

She punched him on his arm and said, "Ooh, you make me sick with your damn arrogance sometimes!"

"You love me?"

With a smile on her face, she answered, "With all of my heart."

He returned her smile and said, "Good. Now, let's go enjoy the rest of this evening."

Clifford and Do-Low stood at the back of the club and witnessed Taz's show with his homeboys. Do-Low frowned and told Clifford, "That nigga really thinks he's the shit, huh? I can't wait to serve that fool."

"Yeah, he does. Do you think he'll give you problems?"

"Did you just hear what I said? You know how I get down. It ain't no thang," Do-Low replied confidently.

"Good. When do you think you're going to take care of him?"

"If the time presents itself, I'm going to do it tonight."

"He has his boys with him now. I don't think that'll be wise."

"The night's still young, dog. You never know how things are gonna fall. Let's just wait and see," Do-Low said as he sipped his drink.

Bob and Gwen were sitting at a table, laughing and sipping their drinks, when Taz and Sacha came and joined them.

"Damn, bitch! Did you see how these tough guys handled their business? We got some straight gangstas in our lives, huh?"

After taking a seat, Sacha said, "Yeah, ho, we got us some real ones."

"Well, I'm glad to hear that our gangsta impresses y'all. I feel a whole lot better now knowing that," Taz said sarcastically.

Before either of the ladies could reply with a smart remark, Bob said, "Looks like our girl is really into clubbin' all of a sudden."

Taz turned and followed Bob's gaze towards Tazneema and Lyla and said, "Damn! What's with this girl?"

"Who are you talking about, baby?" asked Sacha.

Taz sighed and said, "Tazneema."

"Let her have some fun, baby. Your sister is still young."

He stared at Sacha for a minute, then shook his head. She just wouldn't be able to understand if he really told her why he was so concerned with Tazneema being in the club. He glanced toward Bob and noticed that he was following Tazneema's movements around the club. Bob gave him a slight nod, as if saying "Don't worry about it."

Keno saw Tazneema when she had entered the club also. He stepped over to her quickly and said, "Hey, baby girl! What you doing hangin' out in this dump?"

"Hi, Uncle Keno. Me and Lyla were bored and decided to come have a drink and chill out for a little while," said Tazneema.

"That's cool. If you need somethin', holla at me. Taz is sitting over there. You might want to go holla at him," Keno said as he pointed to where Taz was seated.

"Okay," replied Tazneema, and she gave him a kiss on his cheek and led Lyla toward Taz's table. When she made it to the table, she smiled and said, "Hey, Taz! What ya doing?"

Taz smiled and said, "Just chillin' a li'l bit. What it do?"

"Just came to hang out for a li'l while. We were bored, with nothing else better to do, so we came up here to chill too."

"How was your trip to H-town? Did you have fun?"

"Yeah, it was straight. Lyla's parents were real sweet. We had a really nice holiday."

"That's cool. Did you like your gift?"

"Did I! Thank you, Taz! You know I've been wanting that Dell notebook for the longest. Mama-Mama told me that it was too expensive. How did you talk her into letting you get it for me?"

Taz smiled at that and said, "You're not the only one who has a li'l pull with Mama-Mama. I just told her that you needed something like that to help you with your schoolwork. I knew she wouldn't trip out if I said something like that." They both laughed for a minute; then he said, "Well, go on and do you. Make sure that you—"

"I know! Be good! Bye, y'all!" she said as she grabbed Lyla's arm and quickly left them.

Sacha smiled and said, "You're very protective of your li'l sister, huh, baby?"

Bob and Taz exchanged quick glances with each other; then Taz answered, "Yeah. Next to Mama-Mama, she's all I got."

Sacha pouted and asked, "What about me?"

"You know what I mean, Li'l Mama."

She smiled, and they all started laughing again.

"Damn, my nigga! Look at that bad-ass young broad that just left that fool's table. That li'l bitch is right!" said Do-Low.

"I know," replied Clifford as he watched Tazneema as she led a white girl toward the bar. *She may be young, but she sure in the in hell is ready,* Clifford thought as he sipped his drink and focused back on Taz and Sacha. Just watching Sacha clinging to Taz drove him crazy. He hoped and prayed that Do-Low would be able to handle that fool as soon as possible. The sooner the better.

After another hour or so, Taz could tell that Sacha had gotten her club fix for the evening. Her eyes were a little glassy, and she had yawned at least twice in the past fifteen minutes. "Are you ready to shake this spot, Li'l Mama?"

Sacha smiled and said, "Yeah, baby, I'm getting kind of tired."

He stood and said, "Let me go get at my niggas real quick."

Sacha watched as he went and had a few words with Keno, Red, Wild Bill, and Bo-Pete. Gwen and Bob were still on the dance floor, acting like they didn't have a care in the world. Sacha smiled as she watched her best friend enjoy herself. *I'm so happy for her. She deserves all of the happiness she can get,* she thought as she finished the rest of her apple martini.

"I'm outta here, my nigga. What ya gon' do?" Taz asked Keno.

"I don't know about them, but I'm gon' chill until it lets out. I ain't got nothin' else to do," said Keno as he scanned the club for a victim for the night. His eyes stopped on Katrina and Paquita. He smiled and said, "As a matter a fact, I think I'm going to get with one of those rats for the night."

Taz laughed and said, "Don't tell me that you're slummin' tonight, my nigga!"

"Nah, I'm just in the mood for some of that good old-fashioned 'hood pussy! No strings, and no 'Can we get together again' shit. And that bitch Katrina is thicker than Thelma, so I'm tryin' to hit that tonight."

"That's on you, fool. What about y'all? Y'all straight?"

"I'm good," replied Red.

"Me too," added Wild Bill.

"Shit, ain't nothin' else to do. Might as well finish the night up here," said Bo-Pete.

"All right then, I'm out. Keep an eye on baby girl for me, huh?"

"Gotcha," they all replied in unison.

Taz left his homeboys and went over to the bar, where Tazneema and Lyla were standing. "I'm about to bounce, baby girl. Give me a holla tomorrow. Maybe we can do lunch or somethin'."

"Okay."

"Lyla, you make sure that you take care of her, ya hear?"

"Don't worry about it, Taz. I got her back," Lyla said with a smile on her face.

Taz smiled and said, "All right, you two. You be—"

"Good! We know, Taz!" replied Tazneema.

"Alright, smart-ass!" he replied affectionately. He gave her a kiss on her cheek and a brief hug, and went back to his table.

After Taz was back seated, Sacha said, "Gwen and Bob are staying, baby, so I guess we can go on and leave."

"Good. Let's go," he said as he stood up from the table.

"They're leaving, my nigga, and it looks like that nigga ain't taking his boys with him. I got him, gee," Do-Low said as he quickly stepped away from Clifford.

Clifford's heartbeat increased dramatically as he watched Do-Low leave the club right before Taz and Sacha did. *That nigga is about to die tonight, and soon Sacha will be all mines!* he thought to himself as he noticed that pretty young lady that Taz had spoke to before he left the club walk by him. She smelled so sweet that he had to speak. He reached out and gently grabbed her arm and said, "Hello, beautiful!"

Tazneema smiled and said, "Hi!"

"Since you already have a drink in your hand, I won't offer to buy you one. But I would be honored to buy you another one when you're finished with that one."

Tazneema stared at Clifford for a moment and then said, "Okay, maybe I'll let you do that." She stepped away, giggling with Lyla.

Damn! How did she get all that ass in them jeans? Clifford asked himself as he sipped his drink.

As Taz and Sacha stepped towards Taz's truck, they were completely unaware of Do-Low leaning against the front of his car, which was parked right next to the truck. Taz reached inside of his pocket, pulled out his keys, and hit the alarm button, which deactivated his alarm, as well as opened the doors of his truck.

Once the doors were open, Do-Low made his move. He pulled out a chrome 45-caliber pistol, pointed it at the couple, and said, "Don't move, tough nigga! You know what this is!"

Sacha gasped and fell back into Taz's arms. Taz wished she hadn't, because now he couldn't grab his nine-millimeter that he had in the small of his back. *Damn!* he thought as he gently pulled Sacha next to him. He wasn't about to let this clown hurt her. He'd die first. "Check this out, homey. If it's chips you want, don't trip. I got plenty for you right here," Taz said as he lightly patted his right pocket.

"You damn right I want the chips, nigga! The jewels too. Run everything, fool! One wrong move and your bitch gets it first!"

Taz took his platinum chain from around his neck and gave it to Do-Low. He then gave him his two diamond pinky rings. "Look, my nigga, I gots to reach in my pocket for these ends, so relax. I'm not trying to trip on you or do anything stupid."

"Whatever, nigga! Just run the ends 'fore you get blasted!" Do-Low said nervously as he quickly looked over his shoulder.

Mistake! Major fuck-up! Taz took that split second when Do-Low looked over his shoulder to push Sacha aside. He pulled out his weapon and shot Do-Low twice. The first bullet tore through Do-Low's face, and the second one caught him square in his chest. Do-Low fell flat on his back, dead as a doorknob.

Sacha screamed and ran into Taz's arms. He held on to her tightly as the security and a lot of people came running out of the club.

When Keno and Bo-Pete came outside and saw that Taz had his gun in his hand, they both pulled out their weapons and were by Taz's side immediately. "What the fuck happened, my nigga?" asked Keno.

Taz, who was still holding on to Sacha, said, "This fool tried to fuckin' rob us, gee! He slipped and took a look over his shoulder, and I nailed his ass."

"Are you alright, my nigga?" asked Bo-Pete.

"Yeah, I'm good. Look, get her out of here, dog. I'm going to be stuck dealing with the police and shit. She's seen enough."

"N-no, I'm fine, baby. I'm a witness to this so I need to stay," Sacha said shakily.

"Are you sure, baby?"

"Yes, I'm sure."

"All right then, go on back inside of the club while I get with these clowns first," Taz said as he pointed to some of the police officers as they were headed their way.

Gwen and Bob came outside, and Bob had Gwen take Sacha back inside of the club. He then went and joined his homeboys.

Wild Bill and Red were the last to come outside, and when they saw the body lying next to Taz's truck, they stared at each other briefly and then shook their heads at each other. They went and joined the rest of the crew to find out what the fuck had gone down.

The police had the entire club parking lot roped off. It was a crime scene now, and they weren't letting anyone leave for the moment.

The homicide detective took Taz's statement as well as his weapon. He sent his partner inside of the club to go get Sacha. After he received a similar statement from her, he told Taz that they were going to have to take him down to the station for further questioning.

"Whatever, man. Just let her go. I ain't trippin' off this shit. This was self-defense all the fuckin' way."

"We have Ms. Carbajal's statement, so she's free to leave. We'll get in contact with you if we need anything else, ma'am," the homicide detective said as he led Taz towards his car.

"Uh-uh! I'm his attorney, and I'd like to accompany him if I may."

"There's really no need, ma'am. We just want to make sure that his weapon is legal, and ask a few more questions, that's all. It's all pretty clear that this is an open-and-shut case."

"Well, if that's the case, you won't mind me accompanying him."

The homicide detective sighed and said, "Whatever you like, ma'am."

As they were walking towards the unmarked police vehicle, Taz saw Tazneema staring at him with a look of horror on her face. He stopped and called Keno.

Keno ran over to him and said, "What's up, my nigga?"

Taz pointed towards Tazneema and Lyla and said, "Get them the hell outta here. Now!"

"Gotcha, gee," Keno said and stepped over to Tazneema and Lyla.

Taz saw the tears in her eyes, and his heart felt as if it had stopped. *Damn! This is some fucked-up shit. Two bodies in less than two months.* He shook his head sadly as he watched as Keno led Lyla and Tazneema to their car.

What he didn't notice was Clifford as he stood there the entire time and watched in disbelief as the coroner covered up Do-Low's body with a sheet. The hatred he had for Taz had just been multiplied by 100.

Chapter Twenty

It had been a few weeks since the incident at Club Cancun, and Tazneema was still a little shaken by it. Even though she knew that Taz had done what he had to do, it still bothered her that he murdered that man in the parking lot.

On a brighter side of things, she was excited about her upcoming date with a guy she met that same night. She was excited because this was the first date that she'd been on in a long time. Usually, Taz wouldn't let her go out with any guys. With everything going on with him, she decided not to tell or ask him for his permission to go out tonight with Clifford. Clifford had asked for her telephone number that night at the club, and she willingly gave it to him because she thought he was so cute. She didn't expect to hear from him, but she was happy when he called her. She was even happier when he asked her out on a date.

So, here she was, all dressed up and ready to go. She couldn't remember the last time that she had been this excited. She chose her clothes carefully. She didn't want to be too dressy, but she wanted to show Clifford that she had class, so she went with a linen pantsuit and matching beige pumps. Her long hair was tied in a ponytail because there just wasn't much she could do with it other than to let it hang loosely past her shoulders. Even though her linen pants fit her loosely, she smiled when she noticed how they still displayed her thin waistline and fat booty. "All men love the booty!" she said to herself as she went into the living room to wait for Clifford to arrive.

Clifford smiled as he pulled into Tazneema's apartment complex. *Yeah, not only am I going to fuck this clown's sister, I'm going to make her love me,* he thought as he climbed out of his Mercedes.

That night at the club was a sad night for Clifford, but he still found something positive out of it. When he realized that Tazneema was related to Taz, he couldn't stop himself from smiling. Even though he was hurt behind losing Do-Low the way that he did, he still felt that it was better for him than suffering with AIDS and dying with no dignity. At least this way, he died the way he lived, in the streets. Clifford smiled when he remembered how excited he became when he heard Sacha's friend tell her boyfriend that someone should make sure that Taz's sister was okay. *His sister! Ain't that something! She's going to be mine, and ain't nothing that nigga gon' be able to do to change that after I get finish with her ass,* he thought to himself as he knocked on Tazneema's front door.

Tazneema jumped when she heard the knock. She took a deep breath and told herself to calm down as she went and answered the door. She opened the front door and said, "Hi!"

"Hello, beautiful! Are you ready?" asked Clifford.

"Yep," she said as she stepped out of the apartment with her purse in hand.

As they walked towards Clifford's car, he asked, "Do you have a special place you like to dine, or will I have the pleasure of choosing this evening?"

"I'm not picky. You choose, Cliff."

"Well, how about we do some Bricktown? I know a nice Italian restaurant that has the best veal in the City."

"That's fine."

Clifford opened the car door for her and closed it behind her after she was comfortable. He went and got inside of the car, thinking about how big and firm her ass was. He thought, *Man, I'm loving her already!* He then pulled out of the apartment complex.

Taz couldn't believe that that fool had actually tried to rob him, even though the shooting had been a few weeks ago. He just couldn't understand what would have made that clown think he could get away with some shit like that. This shit was crazy!

He went into his bedroom, changed clothes quickly, and called Sacha. When she didn't answer her phone, he decided to give Tazneema a call. After not getting an answer from her house, either, he dialed her cell phone.

"What's up, Taz?" she asked when she answered the phone.

"Nothin' much. What's up with you? Are you busy?"

"Kinda. I'm eating right now."

"All right. I didn't really want anything. I just wanted to make sure that you were straight, you know, with what happened at the club and all."

"Oh, yeah, I'm fine. I was worried about you, but I figured I'd wait for you to call. Are you okay?"

He laughed and said, "You know me. I'm good. Go on and finish eating. I'll get at you tomorrow or somethin'."

"Okay, bye, Taz," she said and hung up the phone.

"I need a break from this town. Fuck this shit!" he said aloud as he called Won. As soon as Won answered his phone, Taz asked him, "Do you think we have enough time for me to take a li'l vacation, O.G.?"

"As a matter a fact, you do. I thought it was going to get hectic for us, but my plans got screwed a li'l. Where are you planning on going, Babyboy?" asked Won.

"After all this drama, I was thinking about bringing my boo your way for a few days, and chill out in the sun, ya know what I'm sayin'?"

"That's cool. Come on out here and show her Hollywood and shit. I'm kinda curious as to what she's like, anyway. She has to be something special if she's captured your heart."

Taz smiled at that and said, "She is O.G., she is. Alright, let me get at her and I'll get back at you."

"That's straight. How's Mama-Mama and 'Neema doing?"

"They're good. I'll make sure I let them know you asked about them."

"All right then, out!" Won said.

After Taz got off of the phone with Won, he called Keno and told him that they had a break coming, and that he should let the others know what was up. He also told him that he was going to take a quick trip out to California with Sacha. "I need a break, dog. That shit at the club got me kinda trippin'."

"Why is that? That nigga brought that on himself, my nigga."

"Yeah, I know, but that fool should have known better. Every nigga in this town knows I'm not to be fucked with."

Keno laughed and said, "Well, for what I've heard, that clown was fresh out the pen."

"Is that right?"

"Yeah. And guess what?"

"What?"

"I heard the nigga had AIDS. You really did that clown a favor, my nigga. You took him out before that shit kicked in on his ass."

Taz laughed and said, "You're sick, fool!"

Keno laughed also and said, "Maybe, but it's the truth. You saved that coward-ass nigga some misery, gee."

"Yeah, I feel you. Let me roll. I gots to get at Sacha and see if she'll be able to take a few days off."

"How long are you goin' to be out that way?"

"Three or four days tops. I want to let her get her shopping on and shit. Then we'll just sightsee and kick it a li'l."

"Go on, dog, and get your mind right, my nigga," Keno said before he hung up the phone.

After Taz hung up the phone, he called Sacha on her cell and got her voicemail. He left her a message telling her to call him back as soon as possible.

After that, he went into his backyard and watched Heaven and Precious as they ran around the yard. As he watched his beloved Dobermans, he thought about what Keno had just told him. *Maybe I did do some good by smokin' that nigga. At least he won't have to go through all of that shit that comes along with AIDS,* he thought to himself. The ringing of his cell phone snapped him back to reality. "Hello."

"Hi, baby. I got your message. Is everything okay?" asked Sacha.

"Yeah, everything's good. I wanted to see if you could take some time off this week."

"Why? What's going on?"

"I wanted to take you out to Cali for three or four days."

"For real?"

He laughed and said, "Yeah, for real. So, can you go or what?"

She smiled into the receiver and said, "Baby, I'm a partner now. Hell, yeah, I can go! Plus, I don't have anything that pressing on my schedule, anyway."

"All right then, this is what I want you to do. Go home and pack a light suitcase. Then head on over here. I'll make the arrangements while you're getting ready. I think it's a flight out of Will Rogers that leaves a li'l after nine. If not, I'll check with Tulsa. That way, we'll be able to get out of here as soon as possible."

"Okay, baby, I'll be there no later than an hour or so."

"I said a *light* bag, Sacha!"

"I know, but I still have to make sure I have everything I need, baby."

"Sacha . . ."

"Alright, dang! You can't even let a girl be a girl!"

"Whatever! I love you, Ms. Carbajal!"

"I love you too! Bye!"

Taz hung up the phone and called Tari. "What's up, sexy lady?"

"Damn, it's been a long time, stranger," Tari said as she smiled into the receiver. She had been missing Taz's voice something terrible, and now that he called, she felt as if they were still together.

"I know. I'm down bad for not checkin' in on you, but I've been caught up a li'l. A lot of shit has been goin' on."

"Is that an apology, Mr. Taz?"

He smiled and said, "Yeah, it is. Do you accept it?"

"You know I do. Now, what's up?"

"Shit. I'm about to take a trip to the West Coast, so I'm goin' to need you to come take care of your babies and shit. Is that cool?"

"You know it is. But since things are different now, I'm going to have to charge you for my services."

He laughed and said, "Is that right?"

"Yep."

"All right then, what's your price?"

"Dinner."

"Dinner?"

"Yep. Dinner and a movie."

"Come on, Tee, you know I don't really be playin' the movies and shit."

"That's my price. Take it or leave it."

"Alright, Tee, you got that."

"As soon as you get back?"

"As soon as I get back."

"Good. Now, have a safe trip, and make sure that you call me as soon as you get back to this city, Mr. Taz."

"I will, baby. Bye," he said as he hung up the phone. He stood up and called for Heaven and Precious to come on in. He turned and went back inside of his house, followed by his dogs, so he could make his and Sacha's reservations for their flight to sunny California.

After dinner was over, Clifford took Tazneema for a walk down by the River Walk. They strolled casually hand in hand as Tazneema told Clifford all about herself. She felt so comfortable that she didn't even realize that she had just told him everything about herself . . . well, almost everything.

"So, how do you like going to OU?" asked Clifford.

"It's cool, but it's nothing like I thought it would be. I would have rather went to an all-Black college, but Taz and Mama-Mama would have both had babies if I would have tried that."

"Taz, that's your older brother, right? The guy at the club that night?"

Tazneema smiled sadly and said, "I'd rather forget that night."

"Oh, I'm sorry, beautiful. I forgot."

"It's okay." She glanced at her watch and said, "Well, it's getting kind of late, and I do have classes in the morning."

"All right, let me get you on home, then," Clifford said as they walked towards the parking lot.

Clifford walked Tazneema to her front door and said, "I want you to know that I had a wonderful time with you this evening, Tazneema."

"Call me 'Neema, Cliff. I'd prefer that."

He smiled and said, "Okay, 'Neema. I hope you'll give me another opportunity to take you out again."

She smiled brightly and said, "Sure. You name the time and place. I really like you, too, Cliff."

"Good. I'll give you a call in a day or so, when I'll have a grip on my schedule, okay?"

"That's fine," she said as she got on her tiptoes and kissed Clifford softly on his lips. "Good night, Cliff."

"Good night, beautiful," he said as he watched her go inside of her apartment. As he walked back to his car, he had a huge smile on his face. Phase one of his plans had just been accomplished.

"Damn, baby, don't stop! Oh, damnit, Taz! Don't you stop!" screamed Sacha as she bit her bottom lip. Taz was riding her like a bronco. Their lovemaking was so intense that it felt as if neither of them had had sex in years. "Ooh! I'm! Cumming! Taz! I'm cumming!"

"Me too, baby! Me to-o-o-o!" screamed Taz as they reached their climax simultaneously. Taz slid off of her and fell back onto the bed, out of breath.

They had arrived in Los Angeles late the night before. Since it was so late, they went and got a room and fell fast asleep.

Sacha had woken Taz up with one of the best blowjobs he had ever had in his entire life. That was around seven in the morning, and now it was after nine and they had just finished.

"Damn, Li'l Mama! You done fucked up your day of shoppin' now, 'cause I don't feel like doin' nothin' but staying in this damn bed all day."

Shaking her head no, Sacha climbed out of the bed and said, "Uh-uh! You better get yourself up. We got some shopping to do. You can rest while I take a shower. After I'm finished, then you'll come take yours. Then we're out of here, mister."

He smiled and asked, "Why can't I take one with you?"

She returned his smile and said, "Because then neither of us would get finished." She ran into the shower, laughing.

An hour later, they were riding in a rented convertible BMW. Taz figured that Sacha would have wanted a convertible so they would be able to enjoy the weather, and his assumption was correct. Sacha couldn't keep still. Everywhere they went, she kept oohing and aahing. She was like a kid on a field trip. He smiled at her as he drove towards the Lakewood Mall.

Sacha had seen a pamphlet that indicated where all of the malls were, and she said that she wanted to go to the Lakewood Mall first. They had a store called BeBe's that she wanted to go to. When they arrived at the mall, she went ballistic; she bought something in almost every store they went into.

Taz didn't mind. It was kind of funny to him as he watched her do her thing. He just pulled out his Black

Card and paid for everything she wanted. This was her time, and he was happy just to see that beautiful smile of hers. *This is what life's all about,* he thought as he lugged all of Sacha's bags.

"Oh, baby, let's go into that Zales jewelry store. I want to buy you something."

"Come on, Li'l Mama! You know I don't need no more jewels. I got damn near every new piece that's out," he said with a cocky smile on his face.

"Humph! Well, you don't have everything, mister. Come on," she said as she led him inside of the jewelry store. They went to the counter, and Sacha started looking at all of the different types of rings, bracelets and platinum chains the store had to offer. Her eyes grew wide when she saw a platinum bracelet with huge, canary-yellow diamonds inside of it. "That's it!" she yelled excitedly. "Excuse me, sir. May I see this bracelet right here, please?"

The jeweler came to the counter and grabbed the bracelet she had requested. She smiled as she held it in her hand. "Do you like that, ma'am? It's a new design from Jacob the Jeweler. We just got it in yesterday," said the jeweler.

"I love it! See, baby, you don't have any colored diamonds. This is nice. Let me see how it'll look on your wrist," she said as she grabbed Taz's arm and put the bracelet on him. Shaking her head yes, she said, "Yep, I knew it. That's the bomb, baby!"

As Taz stared at the bracelet, he had to admit that it was pretty tight. He asked the jeweler, "How much?"

"Five thousand eight hundred, sir."

Before Taz could say anything, Sacha spotted a pair of canary-yellow diamond earrings and asked, "How much are those earrings right there?"

"Those are eight hundred and twenty-five dollars a pair, ma'am," replied the jeweler.

"Okay, what will you do for me if I got the bracelet and a pair of earrings?"

The jeweler smiled and simply said, "You wouldn't want to just stop with the bracelet and earrings, ma'am. You'd have to complete the set with this." He then reached back under the counter and grabbed a small pinky ring with the same colored canary-yellow diamonds inside of it and said, "Now, this ring is thirty-five hundred dollars. As you can see, they have the same flawless canary-yellow colored diamonds inside. If you were to buy the bracelet, earrings, and this ring, I'd give them all to you for nine thousand dollars even. After taxes, it'll be around eleven thousand or so. The total price without my discount would be closer to thirteen thousand dollars for everything, so I'm saving you close to two thousand dollars."

Sacha smiled and said, "We'll take it!"

Taz started to say something, but she stopped him and said, "This is my gift to you, Taz, so please don't try to stop me." Then to the jeweler she said, "Could you please size my man for me, and we'll come back in an hour or so to pick everything up?"

The jeweler smiled and said, "No problem, ma'am!"

After the jeweler had gotten Taz's ring size, Sacha led Taz into yet another store. *Damn! This girl ain't playin', and this is just the first mall on her list,* he thought to himself as he shook his head and watched his girl continue to go wild with her shopping spree.

Finally after another hour or so inside of the mall, Sacha was ready to leave. "Let's go pick up your stuff from Zales, baby. Then we can go get us something to eat. I want to go to that soul food place called Aunt Kizzy's Kitchen. The brochure I read said it was one of the best soul food places in L.A."

"I'm with it, Li'l Mama, 'cause you're killin' me with all of this damn shopping!"

She laughed and said, "Will you come on, boy?"

As they were leaving the Zales jewelry store, Taz saw three guys staring at them. He didn't mind, because he knew that Sacha was a bad-ass female, so he took their stares as a compliment. But as they passed the three men, recognition snapped in both Taz's and one of the guys' eyes. Taz kept his cool and smiled as they walked by them. *Damnit! Of all places, I had to come to a fuckin' mall and bump into one of those clowns. Fuck!* he thought to himself as he walked towards the mall exit. *Think, nigga! You know you can't go outside. They'll move on you then.* He took a look over his shoulder and saw that the three guys were following them. He turned to Sacha and said, "Look, baby, let's go back into that Sam Goody's for a minute. I almost forgot that Keno asked me to see if I could find him some mixed CDs. That nigga loves West Coast rap," he lied.

"Okay, baby, but let's hurry, okay? I'm starving."

He smiled and said, "Alright." He then led her into the record store and started browsing as if he was really looking for CDs to buy. But, in actuality, he was trying to buy some time so he could figure a way out of this shit. The same guys he had robbed over a month ago were waiting right outside of the Sam Goody record store. He knew he was in some deep shit. He had killed one of their comrades, so he knew they had murder on their minds. He had no other choice but to call Won and see if he would be able to get him out of this mess. He didn't have a weapon, so basically he had no win whatsoever.

He stepped away from Sacha and pulled out his cell and quickly dialed Won's number. When Won answered the phone, he said, "O.G., you ain't gon' believe this shit, but I'm out here at the Lakewood Mall, and I done bumped into someone I met about a month in a half ago."

"Ah shit! Say it ain't so, Babyboy! Say it ain't so!"

"They're on me, O.G., and I'm strapless."

"Why in the hell did you go to the Lakewood Mall? Out of all of the fuckin' malls, you chose the one that's maybe ten minutes tops from where the work was put in."

"Dog, how the fuck would I know that shit? I'm from fuckin' Oklahoma!"

"All right, listen. You can't leave that mall 'cause they will do you."

"You think I don't know that shit? Tell me something I don't know, O.G.!"

"Stay close by security or some shit while I get someone out there to take care of this shit. Where is your car parked?"

"It's by JCPenny."

"What you driving?"

"A black convertible Beamer."

"A'ight, stay safe for as long as you can. Once my people are in position, I'll hit you back. Out!" Won said and hung up.

Taz closed his cell, stepped back next to Sacha, and said, "Check this out, Li'l Mama. Let's go to the food court and get something to hold us off for a li'l bit."

"But I thought we were going to get some Aunt Kizzy's, baby!" she whined.

"We will, but not right now. Now, come on," he said as he grabbed her hand with his free hand.

Once they had stepped out of this record store, one of the guys that had been following them said, "I never forget a face, cuz, and I damn sho' wouldn't forget a grille like yours!"

Taz stopped, let go of Sacha's hand and said, "Excuse me? Are you talkin' to me?"

"You know who I'm talkin' to, cuz. And you already know what time it is, so ain't no need to be tryin' to play dumb and shit, cuz."

Taz gave Sacha a confused expression and said, "Come on, Li'l Mama. These fools are trippin'."

The guy who did all of the talking said, "Yeah, we're trippin', cuz, but the best is yet to come."

Taz took a look over his shoulder and saw that the group of men resumed following them. Sacha saw that Taz was uncomfortable and asked, "Is everything all right, baby?"

Taz smiled at her and said, "Yeah, everything is everything, Li'l Mama."

They went to the food court, and Taz bought them a burger and some french fries from Wendy's. While they sat and were eating their food, Taz noticed the men that were following them had taken a seat about four or five tables away. They stared and smiled deadly looking smiles at him. One of them even went as far as taking his index finger and sliding it against his throat, indicating that Taz was a dead man. Taz shook his head and kept on eating his food.

Just as they finished eating, Taz's cell rang. "Hello."

"Head on out to your car. You know there won't be any way to do this without your girl getting up on it?"

Taz looked across the table at Sacha, sighed, and said, "Yeah, I know. I'll deal with that later."

"Okay, then do you, and hit me back when you're on your way. Out!"

Taz closed his cell and said, "Come on, Li'l Mama, it's time to go."

By now Sacha had figured out that something serious was going on. Taz's tone with her was just how it had been that night at the club. Someone was about to get hurt. She could see it in his eyes.

Out in the parking lot, Taz took a quick look to his right and smiled as he saw the opening doors of an all-black Lincoln Navigator that had just pulled up. He said, "Yeah, homey, I'm ready!"

Before the guy could reply, four gigantic men jumped out of the Navigator with automatic rifles in their hands. "Get your fuckin' hands in the air, now!" one of the huge men yelled as they stepped closer to the three men. The man who had given the order then told his partners, "Get them niggas in the truck." Two of the four big men then went and shoved the three guys towards the Navigator. Once they were secure inside of the truck, the obvious leader of the big men turned towards Taz and said, "It's all good, homey. You can go on and shake this spot. We gots this now."

Taz stepped to him, shook his hand, and said, "Thanks."

"Don't thank me. Thank your man, Won," he said as he turned and climbed back inside of the truck.

Taz followed him to the Navigator, peeped into the window ,and said to the three captives, "It's been real, gentlemen, but as the saying goes, you can't win 'em all!" Then he started laughing as he walked towards Sacha and the BMW. As the Navigator pulled away, he heard the one guy who had been doing all of the slick talking yell, "Fuck you, cuz!"

Taz just smiled as he climbed into the BMW.

Chapter Twenty-one

Sacha remained silent during the entire ride back to their hotel, but as soon as they entered their suite at the Marriott, she went ballistic. "Damnit, Taz! I want to know what the hell just went on back there, and I want to know right damn now!" She plopped herself onto the bed, folded her arms across her chest, and glared at him.

Taz sighed and said, "You're not goin' to let this go, are you, Li'l Mama?"

Her answer to his question was an even harder glare.

He shook his head slowly and asked, "Alright, what do you want to know? Why that shit went down at the mall, or why it happened in the first place?"

"Don't play with me, Taz! I want to know everything! Why that shit happened, what happened to the men that got put in that Navigator, and why the hell any of this shit happened in the first fucking place! But most of all, I want to know exactly what it is that you do when you go out of town. Because, I got a funny feeling all of the shit that happened today revolves around your trips."

"You're right," Taz said as he sat down on the bed next to her. "You have to understand that the life I lead is not a normal one, and you may not understand the things I'm about to tell you. So please, don't judge what I do, because I never meant for you to find out. You've pushed my hand, and I'm about to give it to you raw, only because I love you, and I don't want to lose you, Li'l Mama."

"I love you, too, Taz, and I have the right to know exactly what my man is involved in. Don't worry about me. Just keep it real with me, baby."

Taz took a deep breath and then went into detail about how he became involved in robbing people in other states. After about thirty minutes, he finished and said, "And that's everything."

"So, you mean to tell me that you've acquired millions from doing this stuff for Won?"

"Yeah. Seventeen point five to be exact. That's not counting the cars, my home, the jewelry, or the homes I own in the City. That's a completely different income."

"And the rest, are they in the same position as you are financially?"

"Yeah. We split everything six ways. You can never speak on any of this to them, because we've always sworn to never let anyone know our business. The only other woman who knows what I do is Tari, and that's because Won introduced us a long time ago."

"All right, I understand. But tell me, were those guys at the mall going to kill us?"

"They were going to try."

She sat there on the bed still and quiet for a moment. Then she asked, "What happened to them, baby? Are they dead now?"

Taz put his arms around her shoulders and said, "Don't worry about them, Li'l Mama. You're safe, so that's all that matters to me."

She put her head onto his shoulders and said, "*We're* safe. That's all that matters to *me.*"

"So, you're not going to leave me now that you've found out what I do?"

"I love you, Taz, and I mean that more and more every time I say those words. As long as your work doesn't affect mine, I will try my best not to let it bother me. But I know I'll be a nervous wreck every time you leave town from now on."

"You see, that's one of the reasons why I didn't want you to know about my business. But don't trip, because every time we get down, it's planned to the tee, and it's a cakewalk."

"How long do you think that will last, baby? Nothing lasts forever."

"Yeah, I know, but you don't know how Won gets down."

"I want to meet him, baby. I want to meet this spectacular man who saved our lives this afternoon."

Taz smiled and said, "That's funny, 'cause he wants to meet you too. Come on, let's go get something to eat at that Aunt Kassy's you was talkin' 'bout. Then we'll see what we can do about you meeting Won."

"Aunt *Kizzy's*, Taz!"

He laughed and said, "Oh, my bad! Come on, Li'l Mama."

Back in Oklahoma City, Tazneema had just gotten off of the phone with Clifford. They arranged to meet at the Red Lobster down in the City. She was so excited that she couldn't take the smile off of her face.

"Damn, girl! Why do you have that goofy-ass smile on your face?" asked Lyla.

"'Cause I'm meeting Cliff at the Red Lobster in an hour, and I'm happy as hell about it," Tazneema replied.

"Have you asked him if he has any attorney friends for me yet?"

"Your name has only come up once, and that was when I told him that you are my roommate. Wait until I see if this is going to go anywhere. Damn, you act like you're desperate or something."

"I'm not desperate. I'm just horny, girl! These little college boys out here act as if they're scared to talk to a nice-looking white girl like myself," Lyla said as she pranced in front of Tazneema.

Tazneema laughed and said, "If they only knew that you were a borderline nymphomaniac!"

"I know, huh? Maybe I should go pick a few players on the football team and invite them over for an all-night orgy. I'll bet I'd get their attention then!" Lyla said and busted out laughing.

"I know you're clowning, but then again, I'm afraid that you might actually be serious."

Lyla smiled and said, "You never know!" as she went into her bedroom.

Taz and Sacha were enjoying their meal at Aunt Kizzy's soul food restaurant when a tall older man approached their table. "Well, well! Look at my Babyboy! What it do?" asked Won.

Taz stood, and both men embraced each other tightly. "What's up, O.G.? Damn, you lookin' better and better every time I see you, old-timer!"

Won laughed and said, "Old-timer, huh? I'd run circles around you in any sport you name, Babyboy. I'm in the best shape of my life."

Taz laughed and said, "I can tell. Well, O.G., this here is my Li'l Mama. Sacha, I'd like you to meet Won. Won, this is Sacha."

Won reached out and shook hands with Sacha and said, "It is truly a pleasure to meet you, Sacha."

"Likewise, Mr. Won."

"Please, call me Won. That mister stuff ain't for us. You're now a part of this joker's life, so that makes us family."

Sacha smiled and said, "Okay, Won."

"That's better," Won said as he sat down at their table. "So, are you enjoying your stay in sunny, sunny land?"

"Oh, yes! It's been exciting, to say the least. I can't wait to see what's going to happen next in this wild and crazy town," Sacha said as she stared at Taz.

Taz smiled and said, "I put her up on everything, O.G."

Won raised his eyebrows and asked, "Everything?"

"Yep. Everything."

Won started laughing and said, "Well, I'll be damn! You really *are* in love then, aren't ya? That's good . . . that's real good, Babyboy." Won then turned his attention towards Sacha and said, "Since you already know what's what, I'd like to apologize for today's li'l. . . ah . . . festivities. That was something that was never to have happened. It was unexpected, and I apologize to you for it."

"There's really no need for apologizing, Won. After all, you did save us."

Won turned back towards Taz and said, "Yeah, I did, huh? I've been saving this guy here for a real long time now, but that's another story. Tell me, can you really accept what he does for a living?"

"Honestly, no. But I have no other choice if I want to continue to be a part of his life. I love him, and I will always have my man's back."

Won chuckled and said, "Oh, you're impressing me more and more, lovely lady."

Sacha stared at Won as she sipped her drink, and smiled. *This is one powerful man,* she thought to herself as she watched Won and Taz share words with one another. She took in his six-three frame and his conservative style of dress and wondered how many people he had killed or had had killed in his lifetime. His salt-and-pepper, short haircut gave him a sense of respectability, and his eyes were so warm looking she felt as if he could be her uncle or something. All in all, she felt comfortable around him, and that was all that mattered, because she could tell that Taz was really close to him.

"Sacha! Sacha!"

"Uh-huh? Oh! Excuse me, I must have been daydreaming."

"Well, I'm glad your back, Li'l Mama. Won wants to know if we'd like to join him out on his yacht tomorrow."

"Yacht? You mean as in boat?"

Won laughed and said, "Exactly, lovely lady. I have her docked out on Marina del Rey, not too far from here, actually. If you'd like, we could take her out and take a li'l ride out on the Pacific."

"I'd love to! I've never been on a yacht before."

"Well, it's settled then. I'll come pick the both of you up around noon." Won stood and asked Taz to step outside with him for a moment. "He'll be right back, lovely lady. I need to discuss a li'l somethin'-somethin' with him real quick."

"No problem, Won. I know business will be business. Plus, I haven't finished this scrumptious meal yet. Bye!" she said and started back eating her food.

After they had stepped outside of the restaurant, Taz asked, "What do you think?"

"She's definitely a keeper, Babyboy. I'm proud of you. But tell me, why did you tell her everything?"

"She wouldn't have it any other way. And I didn't exactly tell her everything. I told her enough, though . . . more than I thought I'd ever tell anyone."

"So, I guess it's safe to say that you trust her, huh?"

"With my life, O.G. . . . with my life!" Taz answered seriously.

"Okay, then, that's good enough for me. Now, check this out. We'll be ready to move most likely next Friday or Saturday. I'll know for sure by the time you leave. So make sure that the knuckleheads are ready."

Taz smiled and said, "They're always ready to get money."

"Yeah, I know. All right then, I'll see y'all tomorrow around noon. Out!" Won said as he walked quickly towards his car.

Taz smiled as he walked back into the Aunt Kizzy's Kitchen to finish dining with his Li'l Mama.

After dinner at Red Lobster, Clifford took Tazneema back to his place. They listened to some of his CDs and shared a bottle of white wine.

Tazneema was enjoying herself so much that she'd lost track of the time. When she glanced at her watch and saw that it was almost midnight, she said, "Oh, my! I didn't know it had gotten this late. I have a class at nine. I should be going home now."

Clifford got up from the sofa and said, "I'm sorry, Tazneema. I've been having so much fun with you that I didn't pay any attention to the time. Come on, let me walk you to your car."

Once they were outside in Clifford's driveway, Tazneema said, "Thank you for another wonderful evening, Cliff."

"No problem, Tazneema . . . no problem at all."

She grabbed his hand and said once again, "Please, call me, Neema. Everyone who's close to me calls me that."

Clifford smiled and asked, "Am I close to you, 'Neema?"

Her answer to his question was a long passionate kiss. When she pulled from his embrace, he said, "I guess that answers that question!"

She smiled at him and said, "Yep, I guess it does." She climbed into her car and said, "Cliff, I've never been in a serious relationship, so I really don't want to rush into anything. But I want you to know that I like you. I like you a lot. Please be patient with me, okay?"

Clifford bent his head so that his face was inside of the window of her car and said, "We have all the time in the world, 'Neema. I'd never rush you into anything."

"Thank you. Thank you so much for saying that. I promise you, once I'm ready, I'll be ready."

He smiled and asked, "What's that supposed to mean?"

She smiled seductively and said, "It means that when I'm ready to lose my virginity, you're going to be the one to take it. Bye!"

He was at such a loss for words that all he could do was nod his head as he watched her pull out of his driveway. *Well, I'll be damn!* he thought to himself as he watched her drive off down the street.

Chapter Twenty-two

Ever since their trip to the West Coast, Sacha and Taz's relationship seemed to have blossomed. Not only had they become closer, it felt as if they had become somewhat of a team. When it came time for Taz and the crew to take their trips, Sacha made sure that she kept herself busy so that she wouldn't have time to worry about Taz. She knew that if she didn't, she would drive herself crazy. She stayed at the house and enjoyed Heaven and Precious's company while Taz was away. A couple of times when Tari had come over to feed the Dobermans, they had sat and chatted with each other. The more Sacha got to know Tari, the more she liked her. They got along fine, and her life with Taz just couldn't get any better.

"What's up, Li'l Mama?"

"Hi, baby! Where are you?"

"I'm on my way in from Tulsa. I should be home in about forty-five minutes or so. You straight?"

"I am now. I've just finished for the day. I'll be at the house by the time you get there."

"That's cool. We have to take care of some things, but it shouldn't take that long."

"I know, I know, the last part of the business stuff. Don't worry about me. After I kiss that face of yours, I'll go back upstairs until you all are finished."

Taz laughed and said, "Damn! How did I get so lucky to catch a female like you?"

"I don't know. I guess God was smiling on you that night at the club," she said, and they both started laughing.

"I guess you're right. Alright then, baby, out!" he said and closed his cell phone.

"Love is truly a wonderful thing, ain't it, my nigga?" asked Keno.

Taz smiled and said, "Fuck you, nigga!"

Keno smiled as he drove Taz's truck towards Oklahoma City.

Sacha went directly to Taz's home and took a quick shower. After she was finished, she fed the dogs and went outside and watched them as they ran around the yard. As she watched them, she grabbed the cordless phone and called Gwen. "What's up, ho?" she asked when Gwen answered the phone.

"Nothing much, bitch. I'm sitting here bored as fuck. I'll sure be glad when my man comes home. I'm horny, and I want something inside of this kitty other than this plastic-ass vibrator."

"Ho, you nasty!"

"Uh-uh, bitch! Like I said, I'm horny!"

"Well, all that should be taken care of in a little while. They're on their way back now. I spoke to Taz about thirty minutes ago, and he said he'll be here within the hour."

"That's what I'm talking about! Bitch, let me go. I need to go take me a long hot bath so I can set the scene for this freak show."

"Damn, ho! You can't chill out and talk for a minute?"

"Bitch, haven't you heard me? I'm horny! Bye!" Gwen yelled and hung up the phone on Sacha.

Sacha shook her head from side to side as she set the phone next to her. *Gwen is happy, I'm happy, and everything and everyone in my life is happy. That is a true blessing!*

She called for the dogs to come on inside. Heaven and Precious obeyed her command and followed her back inside of the house. After refilling their water bowls, she went upstairs and pulled out her sexy little Vickie's Secret outfit she had bought while Taz was out of town. "Humph! Gwen's not the only one who's horny!" she said aloud as she started taking off her clothes.

About twenty minutes later, Taz and Keno pulled into the driveway, and Bob and Red pulled up right behind them. By the time they had made it into Taz's den, Wild Bill and Bo-Pete had entered the house.

Taz went upstairs to speak with Sacha real quickly before he made the call to Won. When he walked into his bedroom and saw Sacha lying on his bed in a short, sheer red nightgown, his eyes almost bulged out of their sockets. "Wha-what's poppin', Li'l Mama?"

Sacha turned towards him while lying on the bed so he could see that her outfit was crotchless, and said, "Nothing, baby. I'm just waiting for you to finish your business, so you can come take care of 'your business'!"

He smiled and said, "I know that's right! Keep it hot for me, Li'l Mama. I'll be back up here as fast as I can." He stepped to her and gave her a quick kiss with a little tongue, then said, "You know you're in trouble for this, right?"

She smiled wickedly and said, "I hope so!"

Taz laughed as he went back downstairs and into the den. "All right, dogs, let's check this shit," he said as he opened his laptop and checked his account. After passing the laptop around, he said, "It looks like we're quickly approaching 30 tickets, my niggas."

"I know that's right! But I'm trying to get a hundred of them bitches for me," said Bo-Pete.

"As long as we keep fuckin' with that nigga, Won, I don't see why we won't be able to get it, gee," Bob said with a smile on his face.

"Stay down, my nigga. Just stay down," said Red.

Taz's cell rang, and when he answered it, Won said, "I'm glad to see that y'all made it back okay. Have you checked the accounts yet?"

"Yep. And everything is everything, O.G.," answered Taz.

"Good. Now check this out. It's almost time for the big finale, so get plenty of rest, and make sure that y'all are prepared for a three-week trip."

"Three weeks?"

"Yeah, three weeks. When this is over, each and every one of you will have 200 million in those accounts of yours."

"Two hundred! Ain't that some shit!"

"What are you talking about, Babyboy?"

"Bo-Pete was just saying that he was tryin' to get a hundred tickets, and now you're talkin' 'bout two!"

"That's right. So tell Bo-Pete don't worry about a thang. It's all gravy, baby. You know how it is. Make sure you tell them knuckleheads I said enjoy, be merry, and most of all, be good! Out!"

Taz laughed and told everyone what Won had just told him. After he finished, he said, "Now, if y'all would excuse me, I have something very important to tend to."

Wild Bill laughed and said, "Come on, y'all. Let's bounce. That nigga is ready to get his fuck on." They all laughed as they filed out of the den.

Once they were outside, Taz told them, "Since it's the middle of the week, let's skip a workout. We'll hook up the day after tomorrow."

"Go on, you soft-ass nigga! We know you're not going to have any more energy after Sacha gets through with your ass!" yelled Bo-Pete.

Taz's response was his middle finger as he walked back inside of his house. Once he closed the front door, he bolted up the stairs towards his bedroom, screaming, "Here I come, Li'l Mama!"

Bob knew that something was up when he walked into his house and saw that all of the lights had been dimmed. He smiled as he stepped towards his bedroom. When he opened the door and saw Gwen sitting on the edge of his bed, completely naked, he said, "Damn, baby! Who you waitin' on?"

She smiled and responded, "Who the fuck you think? Sacha called and told me that you were on your way home, so I decided to get ready."

With a grin on his face, he asked, "Ready for what?"

"Ready to get real fucking freaky, baby! Now, come here!"

Bob stepped up to her and dropped straight to his knees. Without any hesitation, he started eating out her sex as if he was a starved man.

Gwen fell back on the bed with her small feet planted firmly on the floor, while Bob enjoyed her exquisite taste. She moaned softly as his tongue went deeper inside of her love walls. "O-o-o-o-h, baby! Let me feel the knot, baby! Let me feel the knot!"

Bob knew what she wanted, and he smiled as he pulled his tongue out of her sex and replaced it with the tip of the knot on his forehead. He applied just the right amount of pressure onto her clit and drove Gwen over the top.

"O-o-o-o-h, Bobbaby! Bobbaby, that's it . . . that's it . . . that's it! I'm cumming baby!" I'm cumming baby!" she screamed at the top of her lungs. Her orgasm hit her so hard that all of her words ran together.

After Gwen's trembling seemed to stop, Bob got up from between her legs, climbed on top of her, put his forehead towards her face, and said, "Now taste yourself for me, baby. Lick the knot and taste that sweet-ass pussy of yours."

Gwen smiled as she did as she was told. She licked Bob's forehead and enjoyed the tangy taste of her love juices.

Bob pulled away from her after she was finished, and took off his clothes quickly. Once he was undressed, he climbed back on top of her and started sucking her small breasts.

When his mouth touched her breasts, Gwen flinched slightly and said, "Uh-uh, baby. Come here. Put that dick in my mouth first. I want to taste *you* now."

Bob ignored her and shook his head while he continued to suck each of her nipples. The feeling felt so damn good that she relented and let him continue. She was so wet and hot that she felt as if she was going to cum again just from him sucking on her breasts.

Bob sensed this, pulled away from her ,and said, "You want this dick now, baby?"

"Yes! Yes! Give it to me, Daddy!"

Bob shook his head no and said, "Not until you answer a question for me."

"What is it, baby?" she panted as she squirmed and closed her legs tightly.

"Why do you tense and flinch every time I suck or play with your titties?"

"Yo—your imagining things, baby. Stop tripping and give it to me, Bob. Come on, baby, give it to me, please!" she begged.

Bob climbed off of the bed, shaking his head no again, and said, "Nope, you ain't gettin' this dick until you answer my question."

Gwen narrowed her eyes and said, "Stop playin', nigga! You better get your ass on this bed and come fuck this hot ass pussy!"

Bob started laughing and said, "You know what? I think I'm going to go on and make me something to eat. I'm kinda hungry."

Gwen sighed and said, "Damnit, Bob! Don't you do me like that! Come on, baby. Give me what I need, please!"

"Not until you answer my question. What's with you and your titties?"

Gwen frowned and said, "They're too damn small! I hate them! Ever since I turned eighteen, I've hated them. Now, are you satisfied?"

He smiled and said, "They may be small, but they're just right for me, baby!" He climbed back on top of her and gave her the ride of her life.

As soon as Taz ran into the bedroom, he jumped onto the bed and started kissing Sacha all over her body. He started at her toes, then slowly worked his way higher. When he reached her pussy, he slid his tongue onto her clit and worked it over feverishly.

Sacha felt as if she was in heaven as she held on to Taz's hair while he pleasured her. She came hard and screamed, "Ooh, yes! Oh! Yes! Yes! Yes, Taz! Yes!"

Taz smiled as he raised himself on top of her and slowly slid himself inside of her piping hot sex. With long, slow strokes, he slowly gained momentum as his strokes increased rapidly. Before too long, he was banging inside of her as if his life depended on it. The bed shook and rocked for the next twenty minutes.

By the time he reached his second orgasm, Sacha was in complete ecstasy. "My God! Oh! My! God! Taz! Baby! Don't! Stop! Please! God! Don't! Stop!" she screamed as she scratched his back with her fingernails and bit his shoulders. She felt as if his manhood was touching her deep inside of her stomach.

"Is it mines, baby? Huh? Is it mines?" asked Taz as he continued to pound away.

"Yes, baby! It's yours!" she screamed over and over again.

Upon hearing her answer his question, Taz felt his testicles tighten, and he surged forward with newfound energy. "If it's mine, then cum with me, baby! Cum with me!" he screamed as he unloaded what seemed like a gallon of his sperm inside of Sacha's pussy.

Sacha's orgasm was just as intense. She felt as if she couldn't breathe as her body rocked and trembled with so much force that she felt light-headed after her orgasm had subsided.

After taking a few minutes to recuperate, Sacha said, "Damn, that was intense! Where did you get all of that energy from, baby?"

Taz smiled lazily and said, "You did it to me, Li'l Mama. I was cool until I saw you all sexy lookin' in that li'l hookup you were wearing. Shit, after that it was a wrap!"

"If I knew that's what got you going, then I would have spent more money in Vickie's Secrets the other day. But don't you worry. I'm going to be spending a lot of money with them real damn soon!"

They both started laughing and held each other until they fell asleep in each other's arms.

By the time Bob and Gwen had finished sexing, they were both starving. Bob got up and took a quick shower, then went into the kitchen and made them both some breakfast. He fried some eggs and bacon, and popped a few slices of bread into the toaster for them. While they were eating their meal, he asked, "Baby, if you don't like the size of your titties, why won't you get some implants?"

"I've given it some thought, but I always chicken out. Plus, those fuckers cost a grip."

"Do you want me to get them for you, baby? 'Cause if you do, I'll give you the chips. Hell, I'll even go with you to get them done."

"You would? Oh, baby, that's so sweet!"

"What size are you going to want to get?"

Gwen smiled and said, "I want to go from an A-cup to at least a C-cup. That way, I won't look too crazy, you know, coming from something so small to something nice and right."

"Baby, I don't have a fuckin' clue 'bout no cups. Give me an example or some shit."

"Around the same size as Sacha's, Bob."

"Oh, okay, that's straight. So, when do you want to do it?"

"You're the one paying for them, so it's on you."

"Okay, this is what we're going to do. Since Taz don't want to work out in the morning, let's check and see if we can find someone here in the city that can do it. If everything works out, we'll set it up in the morning. And if we don't find anyone out here, we'll check out in Dallas. I know it doesn't take that long. I was watching that talk show *Tyra*, and she said that they basically have drive-thru spots for that shit nowadays."

Gwen smiled and said, "Thank you, baby, for being so good to me. I love you, Bob!"

Bob smiled and said, "As long as you're happy, baby, I'm the happiest man in this fuckin' world."

"Let's go back into the bedroom so I can make sure that you're completely happy tonight."

"I'm with that, baby!" he said as he got up from the table and followed her back into the bedroom.

Chapter Twenty-three

Clifford had decided that after a month of seeing Tazneema, he was in love. She was young, but she was perfect for him. He found himself thinking about her constantly all during the day. Whenever he had the time, he made sure that he gave her a call. And if he missed her, he would leave long sweet messages on her voicemail on her cell phone or on her answering machine at home. They went out to eat almost every other night. She was so energetic that she seemed to have breathed new life into him. All thoughts of Taz and revenge were gone. *Taz has Sacha, and he is happy. I have Tazneema, and I'm equally as happy. So, why not let bygones be bygones?* he thought as he pulled into Tazneema's apartment complex. He jumped out of his car and went to the front door.

Tazneema heard the knock at the door and smiled. "Right on time, as always!" she said as she went and answered the door. "Hi, Cliff! Come on in. I'll be ready in a minute."

"Hello, beautiful! Man, you're looking extremely sexy tonight. What's up? Have I forgotten something important?"

"What makes you say something like that?" she asked with a smile on her face.

"Come on, baby. You're looking too damn good tonight just to go back to my place and have dinner. Something's going on inside of that pretty head of yours. What is it?"

She smoothed down her dress and simply said, "You'll see!"

By the time they made it to Clifford's house, dinner was ready. He had put two steaks in his Crock-Pot and had been slow cooking them the entire day. When he got home from work, he put two potatoes into the oven and let them bake as he went out to Norman to pick up Tazneema. He prepared a quick salad, and dinner was served. They ate in Clifford's dining room and listened to some soft, soothing music by the great Luther Vandross.

The meal was perfect, the mood was nice, and Tazneema felt that the time was right for her to give that special something to her man. But first, she had to be sure that Clifford was in fact her man.

Clifford was clearing the table when she asked him, "Cliff, do you consider us a couple now, or are we still just friends?"

He smiled and said, "I'd love to say that we're a couple, but you wanted me to take it slow with you, so I've held back on asking you, 'Neema."

"Thank you for that. Thank you for respecting my wishes, Cliff. I want you to know that means an awful lot to me. I've fallen in love with you, and I want us to take this a step further this evening."

"Wha—what do you mean by that, 'Neema?" he asked as he set the plates he had in his hands down onto the dining room table.

Tazneema stood up from the table, stepped into Clifford's arms, and said, "I want you to have me tonight, baby. I want you to have my virginity, tonight."

"Are you sure, 'Neema? There's really no need to rush into this. I can wait as long as you want me to, baby."

She smiled and said, "You've waited patiently enough, Cliff. Tonight's the night it goes down." She stepped out of his embrace and slid the thin shoulder straps of her dress off of her slim shoulders, and let her dress fall to the floor. Her firm breasts stood at attention as she wiggled out of her black thong. She stood right in front of him completely naked and said, "Do you want me, baby? If so, come and get me, because I'm yours."

Clifford's dick was so hard that it felt as if it was about to burst out of it's skin. He took a deep breath and said, "Yes, beautiful, I want you. I want you now, and I want you for as long as you'll be mine."

They kissed slowly and hungrily. The passion between them was like a wildfire, getting hotter and hotter. Clifford scooped her into his arms, took her into his bedroom, and gently laid her down onto his bed. He took off his clothes and quickly joined her. He was so excited that he felt as if he was about to cum on himself any minute. *Calm down, boy! Calm down!* he thought, and reminded himself that this going to be Tazneema's first time. He wanted it to be a good memory, not a bad one. He kissed her earlobes, her neck; then he slid down to her breasts and put each one into his mouth one at a time.

Her erect nipples ached as he sucked them gently, then bit them lightly, causing her to shake all over. Her body trembled in anticipation of the next step. She was so wet that she felt as if she had peed on herself. She had heard plenty of stories about how the first time was always the worst time, and right then, she couldn't believe any of that, because Clifford was being so gentle with her that she felt like she was floating.

Clifford smiled as he slid down toward her pussy and started licking her all over it. She was shaved down there, so her smooth skin glistened as his tongue roamed all over her sex. He located her clit and started lightly nibbling on it.

Tazneema gasped and held her breath as feelings she had never felt before rocked through her entire body. "O-o-o-o-o-oh, that feels so good, baby!" she moaned as Clifford munched lightly on the sweetest taste he'd tasted in a very long time. *Eighteen years young, and the sweetest pussy in the world!*

When he felt Tazneema start to shake and shiver, he knew that her first orgasm was nearing, so he flicked his tongue faster and faster across her clit.

"Cliff! Oh, my God! Cliff, I'm cumming! I'm cumming!" she screamed.

Clifford let what felt like a small flood gush all over his face. He enjoyed her sexy aroma as he continued to lick all over her pussy. He pulled away from her and smiled when he saw how beautiful her face was. She was practically glowing as she blushed deeply. He reached into the nightstand drawer next to his bed and pulled out a condom. He tore it open and gently put it on. He then climbed on top of her and said, "Baby, you're nice and wet so it shouldn't hurt you that much. But there is going to be some discomfort for a minute. If I start hurting you, tell me, so I can take it nice and slow."

Tazneema was so caught up in the moment that all she could do was nod her head yes.

Clifford smiled as he slid himself inside of her. When he felt resistance, he pushed a little harder. *Damn! She wasn't lying! She is a virgin!* That excited him so much that he'd forgotten about what he had just told her and shoved harder than he had intended to. Tazneema screamed, and he came with so much force that he became dizzy. He never slowed his stroke as he continued to ease in and out of her.

As the pain somewhat subsided, Tazneema became more and more excited. *It did hurt, but it feels so-o-o-o good now!* she thought as she wrapped her legs around Clifford's waist and bucked back into his dick. This encouraged him to turn it up a little as he increased his pace. Now, they were both bucking back and forth and sexing each other like their lives depended on the outcome of their journey.

Tazneema felt that tingle again, and this time she was prepared for it . . . at least she thought she was. When her next orgasm hit her, it was just as intense as her first one was. She screamed out Clifford's name over and over and he penetrated deeper inside of her. By the time his own orgasm hit him, he was yelling just as loudly as she was.

Finally, their noisy lovemaking came to a halt, and they fell asleep in each other's arms, sated.

Taz was working out inside his gym by himself when he got the call from Won. He closed his camera phone and called Keno. "It's time to put in work, gee. Call the others," he said before hanging up. He then went upstairs and jumped into the shower.

By the time he finished, Sacha had come into the bedroom and was lying on the bed, watching television. He grabbed his clothes and quickly got dressed. While he was dressing, she tried her best to remain calm, but every time he went out of town she felt like that would be the last time she would ever see him again. That thought alone drove her insane. She didn't know what she'd do if she ever lost that man. She was in love, and her love was forever. "So, this is the three-week trip, baby?" she asked.

"Nah, Li'l Mama, that shit got put on hold. I should be back in a day—two tops."

She breathed a sigh of relief and, as calmly as she could, said, "Oh, alright. I'll make sure that everything is taken care of on this end, baby."

He smiled and said, "Yeah, I know you got me, you big old phony!"

"What are you talking about, baby?" she asked innocently.

"Don't even try to fake it, Li'l Mama. I saw how you were looking at me as I got dressed. I know you be worried about a nigga. I hate that I have to put you through this, but it's what I do."

The sincerity in his voice touched her heart deeply. She took a deep breath and said, "I know, Taz, and I will not try to stop you from doing you. Just please, be careful, baby. I'd die without you. I mean that."

He stepped over to her, kiss her, and said, "I know, Li'l Mama . . . I know. And I give you my word, ain't nothin' gon' happen to me. Every move we make is calculated to the very last detail. I don't slip, baby. Never have, and I never will. Now, let me bounce. The boys should be here any minute."

"Okay, baby. I love you, Taz."

"I love you, too, Li'l Mama," he said and went downstairs to wait for the crew.

After everyone was inside the den, Taz explained the mission. Bo-Pete and Wild Bill were due to leave Tulsa in the next two hours. Red and Bob's flight was scheduled to leave Dallas/Ft. Worth later on that night. Keno and Taz were flying out of Will Rogers Airport in forty-five minutes. Their destination was Houston. Once they all arrived in Houston, the details for the mission would be given to them by Won via DVD, as usual. This mission was going to make them all six million dollars richer. That put smiles on all of their faces as they filed out of the house.

***

Sacha hated what she was doing, but she couldn't resist the urge to listen in on Taz's conversation. After she had heard him tell everyone that they were going to be making six million dollars each, she put her hand over her mouth in fear that she would give herself away. She went back upstairs, closed the bedroom door, and watched as they all pulled out of Taz's driveway. "Six million dollars apiece! That's 18 million dollars! Who in the hell are they going to rob for that much money?" she asked herself aloud.

Taz and Keno arrived at Houston's Hobby Airport a little after ten P.M. Bo-Pete and Wild Bill would be arriving within the next twenty to thirty minutes. Since Red and Bob flew out of Dallas, they weren't due to arrive until close to midnight.

Taz drove their rented Ford Excursion to the Double tree Hotel in downtown Houston. He parked the truck, and they entered the hotel. After getting their room key, Taz asked the hotel clerk, "Do you have a package for me?"

"Yes, I do, sir. I was given strict instructions that you were to ask for it before I gave it to you," said the clerk.

"No, problem. Thanks," Taz said as he stepped away from the counter. As they stepped inside of the elevator, he told Keno, "Damn, my nigga! Six tickets! This shit is gettin' wilder and wilder, huh?"

"Nah, gee, it ain't getting' wilder. We're getting' richer!"

They both laughed as they stepped off of the elevator and went into their room.

Once they were inside of the room, Taz quickly inserted the DVD and listened to what Won had to tell them. Like always, a picture of the great Mike came onto the screen. After about thirty seconds, Won's voice came through the speakers of the television:

"Good evening, gentlemen. I trust all is well. As you already know, this is a money getter for you all, so pay close attention, because tonight you will be dealing with a whole lot of the greenbacks. Under your bed are the tools that you'll need for this mission. Your weapons of choice are there, as well as six army surplus duffel bags. Once everyone has arrived, you are to go down to the underground parking garage and get inside of the dark blue Tahoe. Taz and Keno are to drive this vehicle by themselves. The others are to follow in the rental that you already have."

"You are then going to take Texas Avenue to Main Street. After making a right on Main, I want you to take Main Street all of the way into North Houston. You'll know you're at your destination when you see a Platinum Jewelry store to your right on the corner of Main and Dewater Avenue. Pull around behind the jewelry store and park your vehicles. Then, proceed to the back entrance of the jewelry store. The doors will be unlocked, and the alarms will already be deactivated. Once you are inside, there will be six safes lined against the far wall. From right to left, the combinations are as follows . . ."

There was a pause while Keno and Taz both grabbed a pen and a piece of the hotel stationery. Just as they sat back down, Won continued:

"The first combination is 54 to the right, 61 to the left, and 19 to the right. The next one is 3 to the right, 26 to the left, then 71 to the right. The next one is 2 to the right, 19 to the left, and 70 to the right. The next one is 11 to the right, 29 to the left, and 50 to the right. The next one is 10 to the right, 14 to the left, and 69 to the right. And the last one is 7 to the right, 5 to the left, and 47 to the right."

"You all are to enter together and proceed straight to your designated safes. Once you get them open, take all of it's contents and fill each of your duffel bags. This is a timed op, so make sure that you're out of there within ten minutes after you enter. The alarms will reset at exactly two a.m. I expect for you to be in and out of there in no more than eight minutes, tops. If by chance you do stay inside over ten minutes, be prepared for heavy hostilities. Once the alarm is tripped, it will take no more than two minutes for the war to begin. This is what we're trying to avoid, so make sure that all watches are synchronized exactly. No room for error is allowed."

"After you have emptied the safes, you are to head back to the hotel and leave all of the bags inside of your room. Then, take your rental back to the airport and head back to the City in the Tahoe. I'll be in contact with you no later than four p.m. tomorrow afternoon. Do not try to contact me. Check your accounts by noon, and everything should be completed. Once again, do not try to contact me, because I will be dark for the time being."

"Good luck, gentlemen!"

The television screen then went blank.

Taz smiled and said, "In and out, just like that!" He snapped his fingers.

"I can dig it, my nigga! Damn, look at the fuckin' size of these bags! I can see why we're gettin' broken off so much for this shit. That nigga Won is gon' make a killin' tonight," said Keno.

"Yeah, and so are we," Taz said as he started to check and recheck their weapons.

***

As Taz drove towards the jewelry store, his mind was on Sacha. *Damn! Maybe it's time to get out of this shit. I can't be havin' my Li'l Mama stressed the fuck out every time I do me. Am I being selfish or what? Just hold me down a li'l more, Li'l Mama, and I promise, I'm gone make everything alright,* he thought to himself as he pulled in back of the jewelry store. He parked the Tahoe and climbed out, followed by Keno. They met the rest of the crew at the back door as they checked their watches. It was one forty-five a.m. exactly. They had ten minutes to get the money, and fifteen minutes total to be in and out of the store.

Taz took a deep breath and entered the store, followed by his homeboys. They were each designated a safe. Taz went to the first safe; Keno went to the next one, followed by Bob, who went to the third. Wild Bill went to the fourth, Bo-Pete went to the fifth one, and Red to the last safe.

When Keno had his safe open, he smiled and said, "Damnit, man! Look at all of these fuckin' chips!"

"Nigga, we ain't got time for lookin'! Clean that muthafucka out so we can get the fuck out!" whispered Red.

Each safe was filled to it's capacity with nothing but money. Taz couldn't believe his eyes as he quickly filled his bag. When he finished, he checked the time and said, "Seven minutes, gentlemen! How we lookin'?"

"I'm done," said Red.

"Me too," said Bob.

"Almost," said Bo-Pete.

"Done," said Keno.

"Got it," said Wild Bill.

"Good. Let's get the fuck outta here," Taz said as he led the way out of the jewelry store.

They made it back to the trucks without difficulty and departed just as quickly as they came. Mission completed.

Taz smiled as Keno drove them back to Oklahoma City in the Tahoe that Won had arranged for them. Bo-Pete and Wild Bill were in the back of the truck, sleeping, while Bob and Red watched Keno's damn *Scarface* DVD on the screen that was mounted on the seat's headrest. After they had dropped off the duffel bags full of money, they quickly stashed their weapons back under the bed and departed from the Doubletree.

Now that they were safely out of Houston and headed back home, Taz had to call Sacha. Even though it was close to four in the morning, he wanted to let her know that he was alright and on his way back home.

Sacha answered the phone on it's first ring. "Hello."

"What's up, Li'l Mama? What you doing up this late?" asked Taz.

"I was going over some files for my trial in the morning. How are you?"

"I'm good."

"Where are you?"

He laughed and said, "On the highway. I'm on my way home. I should be there by the time you're leaving to go to work."

Sacha smiled a relieved smile and said, "That's good. So, I guess everything went accordingly?"

"Always. I told you, Li'l Mama, every single move is calculated to a tee."

"Thank God! Good night, baby. I have to get some sleep, and now that I know you're alright, I'll be able to sleep peacefully."

"I know. That's why I called. I love you, Li'l Mama!"

"I love you, too, baby!"

After Taz closed his cell, he smiled as he relaxed back in his seat.

Red said, "You know what was the only fucked-up thing about this mission, dog?"

Taz turned around in his seat and asked, "What was that, gee?"

"We gots to drive all the way back out to fuckin' Dallas to get my truck!"

Bob started laughing and said, "*We* ain't got to do a muthafuckin' thang, partner! *Your* ass is on your own!"

They all started laughing as Keno drove on.

Chapter Twenty-four

Tazneema stepped out of the shower and walked into Clifford's bedroom with a towel wrapped around her. She smiled when she saw that he had left a note for her on his pillow. She let her towel fall to the floor as she quickly went to the bed and opened the letter.

Good morning, beautiful!

I'm sorry that I had to run off, but I was afraid that if I stayed and waited for you to finish your shower, I wouldn't have been able to make it to work this morning. (Smile!) No, seriously, I have a nine o'clock meeting that I can't be late for. I hope I'll see you this evening.

I really wish you would give some deep consideration on moving in with me. I love it when I open my eyes and the first sight I see is your lovely face. I know it'll be difficult for you with school and all, but for me, please give it some thought.

Bye, for now. Give me a call when you get out of class.

Love always, Cliff.

"Ooh, that's so sweet!" she said and began to get dressed.

Ever since their first night of lovemaking, Tazneema made it a point that Clifford made love to her at least twice every other day. She may have been a late starter, but now she considered herself a veteran. She had even given Clifford some head, and that was something that she thought she would never do. She smiled as she thought back to how excited Clifford's face looked the first time she had sucked his dick. Seeing him so happy made her feel even prouder of the fact that she could satisfy him. She was in love, and she wanted the world to know it. She knew that she would catch hell from Taz and Mama-Mama, but so what? *This is my life, and it's about time I started living it my way,* she thought to herself as she finished getting dressed. She had a man now, and they were just going to have to accept that fact.

Taz was breathing heavily as he climbed out of his swimming pool. He had just completed forty laps, and he was tired. He chose to push himself today, because he knew that any day now Won would be summoning them for the upcoming three-week mission. The thought of getting close to two hundred million was enough incentive for him. He didn't want to stress the crew, but something in the back of his head told him to make sure that he was on top of his game. Even though he trusted Won with his life, something about this next mission just didn't sit right with him.

He thought back to Won's words a few weeks ago, when he had told him that it was almost time for the finale. *Finale . . . finale to what?* he asked himself as he finished drying himself off.

He went upstairs to his bedroom and decided to give Mama-Mama a call. After speaking with his mother for a few minutes, he hung up and called Tari at work. "What up, Tee? You busy?"

"Not really, Taz, How are you?"

"I'm good. Look, can we get together after you get off? I really need to holla at you about some things."

"Sure. Do you want me to come over, or do you want to meet me someplace?"

"Yeah, let's meet at the Olive Garden, on me."

She laughed and said, "Oh, but of course! Tell me, is everything still going okay with you and Sacha?"

"Yeah, we're good. What I want to talk to you about doesn't concern her. It's more about Won."

"I see. All right then, I'll see you there around six?"

"That's good. And thanks, Tee."

"Don't thank me, joker. You know I'll always be there for you when you need me."

He smiled into the receiver and said, "Yeah, I know. Bye."

After he hung up the phone, he went and took a shower, still wondering exactly what the fuck he was tripping for. Won had never let him down before, so there was no reason for him to be second-guessing him now . . . or was there?

Tazneema called Clifford right after she left her last class for the day. "Hi, baby! What ya doing?" she asked as soon as Clifford answered his cell phone.

"Nothing much. I've just finished arranging a few meetings with some new clients, that's all. Just another boring day at the office. How about you? How was your day?"

"The same. I've just left my last class for the day, and I'm starving. Are you cooking tonight, or are we going out to eat?"

"Whatever you want, beautiful, you know that," he said sincerely.

She smiled and said, "Okay, I want some of your special pork chops and rice, with some buttered mixed vegetables."

"So be it! What time should I be expecting you?"

"I'm going to go get changed and pack me a light bag. Then I'm going to go see Mama-Mama for a little bit. Then I'll be there. So, be expecting me around seven. Is that okay?"

"You know it is, baby. I'll see you then."

"Okay, bye!" she said and pressed the end button on her cell. She jumped into her car, as happy as can be. *It feels real good having someone special to share your life with,* she thought as she drove towards her apartment complex.

"Damn! Baby, I'm loving them new knockers!" Bob yelled excitedly.

"Come on, baby, don't play with me. Do you really like them? They don't look too big, do they?" asked Gwen as she stared down at her chest.

"I wouldn't tell you they looked tight if they didn't look tight. I can't wait to get them inside of my mouth."

She smiled as she continued to stare at her breasts. Bob had remained true to his word and paid the seventy-five hundred dollars it had cost for her new breast implants. It took three and a half hours, and now here she was with a brand-new look. They had driven down to Dallas earlier that morning with a noon appointment. Now that they were finally finished, she couldn't wait to get back home. She wanted to know what Sacha thought about her new chest size. She was happy as hell that Bob seemed to love them, but she really needed to know what her girl thought, 'cause if Sacha didn't like them, she was coming back and getting them reduced immediately. She didn't want to look foolish to her best friend. Sacha's judgment was very important to her.

Ever since she had dropped out of college, she had always felt as if she had become inferior to Sacha. Once she went back to school and had gotten her degree, she thought she had leveled the playing field between them, but somehow over the years, she never overcame the insecurity she felt around Sacha. Even though she loved her as a sister, she just couldn't rid herself of those feelings.

"Come on, baby, let's get back to the City. I can't wait to show off my girl's new titties!"

"Bob, I'm still sore. It's going to be some time before I can go out. I can't even wear a bra yet."

"Don't trip, baby. You don't need no damn bra, anyway. Look how firm them thangs are. Shit, you're standing at attention, baby, and I want to show them joints off!" Bob said and started laughing.

Gwen laughed also and said, "You're crazy, nigga!" But with renewed confidence, she said, "If you want to show me off, baby, who am I to try and stop you? Come on, let's go home."

They left the doctor's office hand in hand, and with smiles on both of their faces.

Taz smiled as he watched Tari coming towards his table. *She's still one sexy white broad,* he thought, standing as she sat down. "What's up, Tee?" he asked after he had taken his seat again.

"Nothing much, really. You know, the same ol' same. What's up with you? That's the question."

"I've been doing a lot of thinking lately, and it's like I'm confused and shit."

"About what?"

"Everything."

Tari laughed and said, "Please, be a little more specific."

Taz then told her of his doubts about the upcoming mission, and how he had never doubted Won before, and how strongly he felt for Sacha. "Basically, this shit is all about her, I guess. Won has never given me a reason to ever doubt him, but now I am. He's made us all millions, and now just because I done fell in love, I'm starting to doubt my nigga. This shit is crazy. You know how I get down. I'm always cautious. But now that I have Sacha in my life, I'm spooked that something might jump off backwards, and I'll lose everything."

Tari smiled at her friend, her ex-lover, and said, "Love is a bitch, baby. But answer this for me. Do you still trust Won?"

"With my life," he said seriously.

"Do you want to stop doing you?"

"I've been thinking about it a lot lately."

She shook her head and asked again, "Do you want to stop?"

"Sacha becomes a nervous wreck every time I go out of town."

"What? She knows what you do?" Tari asked incredulously.

He smiled and nodded yes. "Yeah, we kinda got into a jam when we were in L.A., and Won had to bail us out," he said and told Tari all about what had happened when he and Sacha were in Los Angeles.

"Damn! This is deeper than I thought. Okay, but back to my question. Do you want to stop? Not because of Sacha, but because of you. This all revolves around your decisions, Taz. It's all about what you want. Either you do or you don't. When you can answer that question, everything else will fall right into place for you."

"Damn, how did you get to be so fuckin' smart?"

"I've been in this game a long time, Babyboy," she said, trying her best to impersonate Won's deep voice.

Taz laughed and said, "Yeah, I guess you have, huh?" He then waved for a waitress to come so they could order.

After the waitress had taken their orders, Tari said, "You need to hurry and find that answer, baby. All of you guys' lives will be at stake until you do. Don't take the chance by putting off what needs to be known."

Taz stared directly into her eyes and said, "I won't."

Chapter Twenty-five

Tazneema and Clifford were relaxing at Clifford's home, trying to see what they were going to get into for the weekend. It was Friday night, and Lyla had pitched a fit with Tazneema for leaving her to go be with Clifford. "I'm sorry girl, but that's how it is when you have a man in your life," Tazneema had told Lyla as she grabbed her overnight bag and left the apartment. Now, as she sat cuddled with Clifford, she felt as if everything in her life was just perfect.

She had finally built up the nerve to inform Mama-Mama about Clifford, and it wasn't as bad as she thought it would be. Mama-Mama was pretty cool about it. Her only concern was the age difference, but then she even took that kind of easily.

Tazneema smiled at Clifford and said, "You know you're going to have to meet Mama-Mama this weekend, don't you?"

He smiled and asked, "This weekend? I thought it would be in a couple of weeks."

"Nope. I told her that we would either come by tomorrow for lunch, or we'd be there for sure for Sunday dinner. So, which one is it going to be, baby?"

"Let's do lunch tomorrow."

"Are you sure?"

"Yes. It would be better for me. You know how I like to get my rest on Sundays before I start a new work-week. So, call Mama-Mama and find out what time she would want us to come over."

Tazneema smiled and said, "I don't have to do that. Mama-Mama will have everything ready, anyway. As long as we're there before four, we'll be on time for lunch."

"What do you mean by that?"

Tazneema laughed and said, "Mama-Mama prepares her meals for the day early in the morning, every morning. Her lunch for tomorrow will be ready by seven or eight A.M., so don't worry. Everything will be fine."

"Do you think she'll like me?" Clifford asked with a smile on his face.

Tazneema turned so that their faces were inches apart and said, "I love you, Cliff, and, baby, that's all that matters."

He smiled and said, "I love you, too."

After Taz and Keno had entered the club, Taz saw Katrina and Paquita, smiled, and asked Keno, "Did you ever hit that broad Katrina, gee?"

"Nah, nigga. You fucked that up that night, remember? You was on that murder shit that night."

"That's right. I forgot about that shit! I can't front, dog. She's over there lookin' kinda tight tonight."

Keno casually gave a glance towards Katrina and Paquita and saw that Katrina was indeed looking pretty damn good. He turned back towards Taz and asked, "You straight?"

Taz smiled and said, "Yep. I'm good."

"All right, I'll holla. She's mine tonight, my nigga," Keno said confidently as he started walking towards Paquita and Katrina's table.

"Go get 'em, tiger!" Taz said as he watched Keno go do his thing. He then gave a slight nod towards Bob and Red, then to Bo-Pete and Wild Bill. They dispersed from their normal spots and started mingling with the rest of the club goers. He then leaned against the bar and sipped his drink as he waited for Sacha and Gwen to arrive.

As Sacha pulled Taz's 600 Benz into Club Cancun's parking lot, she smiled when she saw Keno's, Red's, and Bo-Pete's trucks all parked side by side.

"Damn! I don't see why they wouldn't let us just ride with them. This shit don't make no sense," said Gwen as she checked her makeup in a compact mirror she held in her hand.

"That's just how they do things, ho. There isn't any need for you to be tripping, so relax."

"Relax? Bitch, I *am* relaxed! My titties are still so damn sore that I'm just a little irritable."

Sacha smiled and said, "But they look good, ho. I still can't believe you did that crazy-ass shit. What made you do it?"

Gwen, who was happy as ever that Sacha really seemed to be impressed by her bold decision to get her breasts enlarged, smiled and said, "I've always wanted bigger breasts, but I was scared to do it in the past. Bob convinced me when he realized that I was a little insecure about my chest. So I said, 'Fuck it! Why not?' and went down to Dallas and just did it. You like them for real, bitch?"

Sacha started laughing and said, "Ho, I didn't say that I like them. What, you thinking I'm on some pussy now? I think they fit you perfectly, if that's what you mean." They both laughed as they stepped towards the entrance of the club.

The line to get inside of the club was wrapped around the other side of the building, but that didn't bother

Sacha, as she walked straight to the front and told the security guard, "I'm meeting Taz." The guard smiled at her as he stepped aside and let her and Gwen enter the club. Sacha heard a few females say something slick, but she paid no attention to them as she led her best friend into the club. *Being Taz's woman has all types of little perks,* she thought to herself.

When Taz saw Sacha and Gwen enter the club, he smiled and waved for them to come and join him by the bar. As they were walking towards him, his smile turned into a look of shock as he noticed how big Gwen's breasts were.

Sacha stepped into his arms, gave him a kiss on his cheek. and said, "Close your mouth, baby. You act like you never seen any titties before."

He frowned slightly at Sacha's jibe and said, "Damn, Gwen! When you get them thangs?"

Gwen smiled brightly and said, "Last week. You like?"

"I wouldn't answer that question if I was you, Taz," Sacha said with a smile on her face.

Taz laughed and said, "You're looking real good tonight, Gwen."

"Thank you. Now, I'll leave you two lovers to do y'all for a minute. I see my boo smiling at me over there, so I gots to go. Get us a table or something, bitch. And you already know what I want to drink," she said as she went and joined Bob, who was at the back of the club, chilling out.

Sacha shook her head and said, "That girl is something else!"

"That, she is," Taz said, and he turned around and ordered two apple martinis for the two women. After he had given Winky the order, he turned back to Sacha and said, "So, when are you going to go get yours done?"

She slanted her eyes to mere slits and said, "You better start smiling to let me know that you're clowning, Mister Taz!"

Taz laughed and said, "You already know. You're just perfect just the way you are, baby. Ain't no need to try to improve perfection."

She smiled and said, "That's better. For a minute there I thought I was going to have to show a side of me that you're really not trying to see." They both started laughing as Winky gave Taz the apple martinis.

"Stop playin', Keno! You know damn well you ain't always wanted to holla at me. You think you can tell me anything and I'd go for it. You need to stop that weak shit and come better than that!" Katrina said confidently, and sipped her glass of hypnotic that Keno had bought for her.

"Nah, on the real, boo, you know a nigga be caught up on some other shit. But every time I be gettin' ready to holla at ya, it's like you either have a nigga all on you already, or some shit comes up and gets in my way. But I'm tellin' you, ain't nothin', and I mean nothin' stoppin' me from gettin' at you tonight."

Katrina smiled and said, "Is that right?"

"You better believe it, boo."

"Damn, Keno! What's up with your homeboy Red? He always comes to the club with y'all, but he don't be trying to get at nobody. What, he already gots somebody or somethin'?" asked Paquita.

Keno stared at Paquita for a moment and thought about dissing her, but he thought better of it, because he knew that she was Katrina's girl. Katrina was looking too damn good tonight, dressed in a blue and gold silk dress by Duro Olowu and a pair of blue strapped stilettos by Alessandro Dell'Acqua. Her long legs were looking so tempting to him that he decided to see if Red would play with him tonight. "Nah. See, my nigga just be on some laid-back time. What, you tryin' to holla?" he asked with a smile.

"You damn straight! That big, red, sexy-ass nigga needs a bitch like me in his life," Paquita said as she stared over to where Red was standing.

"All right, I'll be right back. I'm goin' to see if he'll come rock your world."

"Whateva!" yelled Paquita, and she and Katrina started laughing.

Keno stepped over to Red and said, "Check this out, my nigga. I need your help."

Red shook his head no and said, "Don't say what the fuck I think you're going to say, dog. 'Cause ain't no way I'm going to go over there and fuck with you and them rats."

"Come on, my nigga! Just entertain the bitch for me for a li'l bit. Once I know for sure that Katrina's going to bounce with me, then you can shake that broad. Come on, nigga. She ain't that fuckin' bad. She's thicker than a muthafucka. And, you never know, she might be down for the freaky-freaky thang."

Red smiled and said, "You think she'll be down for whatever, huh?"

"Come on, my nigga, look at that broad! She's answering that question herself right now. Look!" Keno said as he turned and pointed towards Paquita. She was staring at them, licking her lips with a seductive look in her eyes.

She may not be the prettiest female inside of the club, but she wasn't the ugliest, Red thought to himself as he smiled at her. After taking a deep breath and draining the rest of his drink, he said "Fuck it, nigga! Come on. But you're going to owe me for this one!"

Keno laughed as they strolled towards Katrina and Paquita, and said, "As long as I owe you, nigga, you'll never be broke!"

After Sacha and Taz had joined Bob and Gwen at the table that Bob had a waitress get for them, they proceeded to have a good time by getting nice and drunk. Bob and Gwen went back and forth out on the dance floor, while Taz and Sacha danced very little but drank a lot.

"Damn, Li'l Mama! You trying to get faded, huh?" asked Taz.

Sacha smiled at her man and said, "I'm enjoying myself, baby, that's all."

"I feel you, but at the rate you're going, you won't be enjoying much tomorrow."

She smiled, shrugged her shoulders slightly, and said, "Oh well! At least I know I'll be well taken care of, right?"

Taz grinned and said, "Always, Li'l Mama . . . always."

Bob and Gwen came back to the table and sat down. "Damn, girl! I ain't goin' back out there with your wild ass. You act like you trying to wear a nigga out before I can get your ass home and tap that thang!" Bob said, and he sipped his drink.

"Humph! You know damn well I'm going to be having your ass begging me to stop when we get home, nigga, so stop frontin' for Taz," Gwen said as she smiled lovingly at Bob.

"You two really need to quit that shit. Both of y'all are some straight characters," Taz said. He then noticed a little commotion over by where Keno and Red were standing. He got to his feet and said, "Bob, the homies are getting into somethin'. Come on."

Bob stood and followed Taz over to where Keno and Red were.

"Oh, shit! Here we go again!" Sacha said as she watched the men leave.

"Come on, my nigga. Ain't no need for any bullshit tonight. My nigga didn't know that this was your girl," explained Keno.

"I ain't his damn girl, Keno! I just got a baby by that broke-ass nigga! He thinks just 'cause he just got out the pen that he can come home and run me. Fuck him!" yelled Paquita.

Just as it seemed as if everything was going smoothly with the four of them, Paquita's baby daddy, Bump, had to come into the club, tripping. Once he saw Paquita all up under Red, he rushed right up to her and snatched her out of Red's big arms.

Red's first instinct was to start beating the shit out of Paquita's kid's father, but he was able to control that sudden urge.

"Nah, you check this out, partna. This bitch has my seed at home all by himself, when she should have her rat ass at the house taking care of him. I don't give a fuck who she fucks with, gee, but she's gon' respect me and take proper care of my seed!" yelled the angry father.

"I respect your mind, gangsta, so go on and chill, and I give you my word she'll go on and check on your seed. We're not trying to have all of this drama up in here tonight," Keno said wisely.

"Fuck you, Bump! My sister is at my house, watching my son! You ain't never done shit for him any fuckin' way! I don't see how your bitch ass has the nerve to come up in here and try to run shit! Yeah, he's your seed, but that's all! You ain't no damn daddy! You a fuckin' wannabe ass dope dealer, you broke-ass muthafucka!"

Before Keno could calm Paquita down, Bump slapped her so hard that she fell to the floor instantly.

"Come on, dog. Leave her alone," said Red.

Bump turned towards Red and was about to say something, but Taz stepped up and said, "What up, Bump? Back to your old antics again, huh?"

Bump focused on Taz, smiled, and said, "What up, Taz? Dog, it's been a minute, huh?"

"Yeah, It's been a minute. Why don't you let me buy you a drink or somethin'? Ain't no need for this shit, dog."

Shaking his head no, Bump said, "Nah, Taz, this bitch needs to be checked, and I'm goin' to make sure that she gets checked thoroughly."

Taz saw that Red was upset, and he knew that he had to get Bump out of the way before Red hurt him. "I can't let you do that, Bump. As you can see, Paquita is chillin' with my nigga Red here. So, why don't you let her make it tonight, huh?"

"Fuck this bitch, Taz, and fuck your nigga too!" yelled Bump.

Before Bump could say another word, Red stepped in front of him and punched him as hard as he could right between his eyes, and Bump fell to the floor, dazed. "Now, get the fuck up and show me how much you want to get down, you clown-ass nigga!" Red said angrily.

Taz helped Bump to his feet and said, "I told you to let this go tonight, Bump. Now, the rest of this shit is on you. As you can see, my nigga ain't for no bullshit. So, are you tryin' to see him or not?"

Bump saw the fire blazing in Red's eyes and knew that he had no win with him. He shook his head no and said, "Nah, this bitch ain't worth it." Then like a whipped dog, he turned and left the club.

Paquita smiled and said, "Thank you, Red! Thank you for checking that nigga for me!"

Red smiled and said, "Don't trip. Now, tell me. How are you going to repay old Red for lookin' out for you?"

Paquita stepped close to him and whispered something into his ear. After she finished, Red asked, "For real?" She shook her head yes, and he said, "I'm wit' that!"

Keno started laughing and said, "Damn, nigga! What did she say she's gon' do to your ass?"

"That's none of your business, Keno! You just worry about what you've gotten yourself into with me!" Katrina said with a smile on her face.

Keno smiled brightly and said, "No doubt, Ma!"

"Well, since everything is everything, me and Bob can go rejoin our girls. Be good, niggas," Taz said as he left the group.

Bo-Pete and Wild Bill went back to where they had been standing and resumed talking to a few females.

When Taz and Bob had sat back down at their table, Sacha asked Taz, "Is everything okay, baby?"

"Yeah, everything is straight."

"Damn! Can y'all ever go to the club without getting into some shit?" asked Gwen.

Bob started laughing and said, "It don't look like it, huh?"

They all started laughing and went on to enjoy the rest of their evening.

Chapter Twenty-six

Clifford and Tazneema arrived at Mama-Mama's home a little after noon. Mama-Mama was impressed immediately by Clifford's good looks, as well as his manners. She led them into the dining room and began to ask him all kinds of questions—everything from where he was born to what his religious beliefs were. By the time she finished questioning him, she was satisfied that Tazneema had picked a winner.

Mama-Mama smiled as she watched how Tazneema fussed over Clifford, making sure that his glass stayed filled with Mama-Mama's homemade lemonade, to keeping his plate full until he was completely stuffed. *She sure knows how to treat her man,* Mama-Mama thought to herself as she continued to watch their interaction. *My God! That boy Taz is going to have a fit when he finds out about this mess!* "So, when are you going to introduce Clifford here to Taz? You know Taz is going to want to meet him as soon as he finds out about you two's relationship," Mama-Mama said seriously.

"You know how busy Taz is, Mama-Mama. I don't see why I have to rush and bother him about something so minor."

"So minor? Humph! You go on with that mess, 'Neema! You give Taz a call as soon as you can, and just gon' and get it out of the way. I'm sure he's going to get along just fine with Clifford here."

At the second mention of Taz's name, Clifford once again realized that the odds of Taz liking him were like a trillion to one. *Shit! I don't even like him, so I can't blame the fool!* To Mama-Mama he said, "I really enjoyed lunch, ma'am. I can't remember the last time I enjoyed a meal this good."

"Why, thank you, Cliff! But you stop with that 'ma'am' mess and call me Mama-Mama like everybody else does, hear?"

Clifford smiled and said, "Yes, Mama-Mama."

"That's better."

"Excuse me, Mama-Mama. I'm about to go call Taz and see if he's busy," Tazneema said as she got up from the table.

"All right, girl, you go on and do that. We'll be in here getting better acquainted," said Mama-Mama as she smiled at Clifford.

Tazneema went into her old bedroom and grabbed the phone. As she was dialing Taz's number, she saw how her hands were shaking lightly. Once the phone started ringing, she took a deep breath and told herself that everything was going to be alright. As soon as Taz answered the phone, she said, "What's up, Taz?"

"Ain't nothin'. What's up with you, 'Neema?"

"Nothing. I'm over here having lunch with Mama-Mama."

"Yeah? What she cook?"

"The usual."

"That much, huh?"

"You know it! Fried catfish, rice, mac and cheese, her homemade corn bread, pies, and—"

Laughing, Taz said, "Enough! You're making me hungry up in here. I get the point!"

"So, what are you getting into today?"

"I really don't have much to do. I was going to take Sacha out to get something to eat in a minute. Other than that, I was goin' to chill out around the house. Why, what's up? You got somethin' on your mind?"

"Kinda. I think we need to have a talk."

"You think?"

"You know what I mean, Taz."

Taz laughed and said, "No, I don't, 'Neema. What do you want to talk to me about?"

"I'd rather talk about it in person, Taz. Could you come over here after you finish having lunch with Sacha?"

"Yeah, I could do that. We'll be over there in an hour or so."

"Okay. I'll tell Mama-Mama. Bye!"

After Taz hung up his phone, he turned towards Sacha and said, "'Neema wants to talk to me about something, and I got a funny idea it will have something to do with a nigga."

"What are you talking about, baby?" Sacha asked as she stretched and climbed out of the bed.

"'Neema was too damn nervous while we were talkin' just now. She says she has somethin' that she wants to talk to me about, and that she would rather do it in person."

"So, what makes you think it has something to do with a man?"

"'cause I know 'Neema. Whenever she thinks I'll be real upset with her, she gets real nervous and wants to talk to me with Mama-Mama around. She thinks I won't go off too bad 'cause of Mama-Mama."

Sacha laughed and said, "Smart young lady. I think I'll remember that the next time I have something I need to say to you that might piss you off."

"But what 'Neema doesn't realize is that not even Mama-Mama can keep me off of her ass," Taz said with a smile on his face.

Sacha's only reply to that was, "Oh!"

Taz laughed and said, "Go get dressed, girl. After we get something to eat, we're going out to Mama-Mama's."

She smiled and said, "Okay, Daddy."

He started laughing as he watched her enter the bathroom.

Just as Sacha and Taz had finished their meal at Leo's Barbeque, Taz's phone beeped to let him know that he had an incoming picture. He opened his cell and saw a picture of Michael Jordan holding up three fingers, indicating the Chicago Bulls' third NBA title. Taz closed his phone and said, "Shit!"

Sacha stared at him for a moment and then said, "It must be that time."

"Looks like it," Taz said as he reopened his phone and called Keno. When Keno answered his phone, Taz said, "Time to rock, my nigga. This is the one. Get at the others and meet me at the pad."

"Gotcha," said Keno.

Taz quickly paid for their meal and led Sacha out to his truck. They rode back to his house in silence. When he pulled into the garage, he told Sacha, "Look, Li'l Mama, when this trip is over, I'm gettin' at Won and lettin' him know that I'm done with this shit."

"Don't tell me that, Taz, just because you know it's what I want to hear. You don't have to do that, baby. I love you, and I'm not going anywhere. You know that."

"Yeah, I know it. Just like you should know that I would never tell you anything like this if I didn't mean it. It's over with, Li'l Mama. I'm ready to settle down and really enjoy some of this paper I've made. I want to go see the world, I want to relax and live for once, and I want to do that all with you. I want you in my life forever!"

"Are . . . are you asking me what I think you're asking me, Taz?"

"I know this isn't the most romantic moment I could come up with, but yeah, will you marry me, Li'l Mama?" he said as he pulled a ring box out of his back pocket and passed it to Sacha.

She opened the box, and her eyes bulged as if they were about to pop out of their sockets. She stared amazingly at an eight-karat solitaire diamond, mounted in all platinum. She was so stunned that she couldn't find her voice. All she did was nod her head yes over and over.

With a smile on his face, Taz said, "I guess your answer is yes, then, huh, Li'l Mama?"

"Yes! Yes! Yes!" she screamed.

He reached across the seat, gave her a hug and a kiss, and said, "I really hate to ruin this moment, but I gots to get ready. Keno and 'em should be here in a minute."

"I know. Come on, let's get inside so I can help you get yourself ready."

They climbed out of Taz's truck and walked hand in hand inside of his home.

The crew was assembled in Taz's den, waiting for Won's call. When the call came, Taz asked him, "Is this the one, O.G.?"

"Yeah, this is the one that's going to get us where we need to be, so pay close attention."

"First off, your flights are all arranged, as usual. Taz, you and Keno are leaving out of Tulsa in two hours. Bo-Pete and Wild Bill are leaving out of the City in about an hour or so. Red and Bob got Dallas/Ft. Worth again. I know they left this way before, but it shouldn't be a problem, because it's completely a different terminal. You guys' destination is Detroit. Everything will be set up inside your room, as always. You are to proceed to the Westin, located inside of the Renaissance Building in downtown Detroit, after you land. Each of your flights will land an hour behind each other."

"Once you all make it to your room, sit down and review the DVD that Taz will pick up once he checks into the hotel. Taz, don't look at the DVD until everyone has arrived. This is very important, because once again, everything about this one is timed. After you review the DVD, get strapped and head on out. As soon as this mission is over, you will be on a flight to your next destination, gentlemen."

"For the next three weeks, your stamina will be put to the ultimate test. Whenever you have the chance to rest, make sure that you take advantage of the opportunity. You will see as the days progress exactly what I'm talking about."

"After the initial flights out to Detroit, all of you will then be flying together on the same flights. After the last mission, you will then fly back the way you flew to Detroit."

"That's about it for now. If you have any questions along the way, Taz, you know how to get at me. Like I told you before, this is a two-hundred-million-dollar mission. After each mission, the money will be added to your accounts. Good luck! Out!" Won said before he hung up the phone.

Taz turned off the speakerphone button and sat down next to Keno.

"It looks like this is it, my niggas, the one we've been waiting for. Are y'all ready?" asked Keno.

"You damn skippy!" replied Wild Bill.

"Fuckin' right!" yelled Bo-Pete.

"Let's do this!" said Bob.

"I been ready!" added Red.

And finally, Taz said, "Yeah, let's go get this fuckin' money." He stood up, and they all filed out of his home.

Once again, Sacha was in her hiding spot, listening to the entire conversation that had just taken place. She went to the front door and watched as the man she loved and his friends climbed into their vehicles on their way to get two hundred million dollars. As they pulled out of the driveway, she went into Taz's den and poured herself a straight shot of his XO and quickly downed it. As it burned her throat, she stared at her engagement ring and said, "Two hundred million dollars! Well, I'll be damn!"

As Taz and Keno headed towards Tulsa, Taz remembered that he had forgotten to call Tazneema. He pulled out his cell phone and called Mama-Mama's house. When Mama-Mama answered the phone, he said, "Hey, Mama-Mama! What you doing?"

"Waiting on your butt, boy! What you think I'm doing?" she scolded.

"I'm sorry about this, Mama-Mama, but I have to go out of town."

"Well, why didn't you tell 'Neema about that when y'all spoke earlier?"

"'Cause something just came up. I was on my way out there when I got the call. Tell 'Neema that we'll talk about whatever she has to talk about when I get back."

"I'll do no such thing! You tell her yourself!" she screamed and dropped the phone.

A minute or two later, Tazneema got on the line, sounding relieved as she asked, "Is everything alright, Taz?"

"Yeah, everything is good. I just got to bounce out of town for a minute, though. So, we're going to have to postpone our li'l chat. Is that alright, or do you want to tell me what you have to tell me now?"

"Uh-uh. I'll wait until you get back."

"Is everything alright, 'Neema?"

"Yes, everything is fine, Taz, for real. It's just that I need to tell you some things that have been going on in my life, and I'd rather do it face-to-face."

Not wanting to be distracted during this upcoming mission, he said, "All right, we'll talk as soon as I get back, okay?"

"All right. Bye, Taz!"

"Bye!" He turned towards Keno and said, "'Neema has a boyfriend."

"*What?* Nah, not our favorite li'l virgin!"

"She hasn't come out and told me yet, but I know her, gee. Her nervousness has damn near confirmed it."

"Do you think she's lost her . . . you know?"

Taz sighed and said, "God, I hope not!"

Back at Mama-Mama's house, Tazneema and Clifford were preparing to leave. "I'd like you to know that it was truly a pleasure having such a delicious meal made by you, Mama-Mama," Clifford said sincerely.

Mama-Mama smiled and said, "Why, thank you, Cliff. Now, you make sure this girl brings you back over again real soon, hear?"

"I wouldn't let her talk me out of coming back over here if she tried!" He then gave Mama-Mama a brief hug and went outside to wait for Tazneema.

After Clifford had walked out of the house, Mama-Mama said, "I like him, 'Neema. I like him a lot. He's respectable and shows that he was brought up in a loving home. You done good, girl. You done real good."

"But what do you think Taz is going to say when he finds out about him?"

"Don't you worry about that boy none. He'll be bent out of shape for a li'l bit, but he'll be alright. Hell, he told me himself a while ago that you're grown now, and to let you start making grown-up decisions. You're a grown woman now, and much as I hate to admit it, he was right. I trust you and your judgment, and so will he."

Tazneema smiled as she gave Mama-Mama a hug and a kiss on her cheek, and said, "I love you, Mama-Mama!"

"I know, baby, and Mama-Mama loves you too. Now, gon' on with your man."

As Tazneema walked out of the house, Mama-Mama watched with pride as she got inside of Clifford's car and pulled out of her driveway. "That boy Taz is going to pitch a fit about this one!" she said as she shook her head sadly and went back into her favorite room of her house . . . the kitchen.

Chapter Twenty-seven

Forty-five minutes after Taz and Keno had arrived at their room at the Westin in Detroit, Bo-Pete and Wild Bill had joined them. They all sat around the suite, checking and rechecking their weapons as they waited for Red and Bob to arrive. As usual, all of their weapons came equipped with silencers, and even though they hardly ever had to use them, Taz felt comforted that they had them. He wasn't trying to kill anyone, but he knew that anything could go down, and they're Golden Rule was that as long as they stayed ready, they would never have to get ready. After they had finished making sure that their weapons were in proper order, they started talking about the upcoming mission.

"Why do you think that nigga Won is breaking us off this much fuckin' money?" asked Bo-Pete.

"Obviously because it's going to be a huge fuckin' take," replied Wild Bill.

"For real, I don't even give a fuck. Just as long as shit goes as smooth as it normally does, I'm wit' it," Keno said from the other side of the room.

"Yeah, I feel you, 'cause after this one, I think I'm out of this shit," said Taz.

"Yeah? You ready to lay it down, huh, homey?" asked Keno.

"Might as well, my nigga. We gots enough chips to last us a lifetime. Why push our luck?"

"I know that's right, but what the fuck are we going to do after we give up this shit?" asked Wild Bill with a smile on his face.

"I don't know about y'all, but I'm taking Sacha and marching her down that aisle, gee. And after that, I'm going to take me one hell of a long vacation. See the world and shit."

"That's straight, dog. I might not have a wifey yet, but I'm about to get on the fucking hunt and find me one, 'cause that shit you talkin' 'bout sounds real damn good to me," Keno said with a smile.

Before anyone could say another word, there was a knock at the door. "Go let them fools in so we can get this shit started," Taz said from across the room.

After Keno had let Red and Bob in, Taz pulled out the DVD and inserted it into the DVD player located under the television inside of their room. A picture of Michael Jordan shooting a fadeaway jumper over Karl Malone of the Utah Jazz came onto the screen as soon as Taz had turned on the DVD. A minute later, Won's voice came over the speakers:

"Glad that y'all made it safely. Now, it's time to go to work. You are to leave your hotel and take Jefferson Boulevard to the corner of East Grand Boulevard, make a right turn on Grand and take that all the way to Mack. On the corner of East Grand and Mack, you're going to see a funeral home, Swanson's Funeral Home, to be exact. You are to make a right turn onto Mack, and then pull into the back of the funeral home. The back door will be unlocked, and you are to proceed inside and go directly into the funeral director's office.

"Once you're inside of the office, move the funeral director's desk and you'll see a floor safe. The combination is 16 to the right, 16 to the left, and 16 back to the right. There will be a substantial amount of drugs as well as money. As usual, the ends are yours and the narcotics are mine.

"After each of you has filled your bags, then proceed into the chapel of the funeral home. There will be an open casket sitting right in front of the altar. Go directly to it, lift the pillows inside of it, and you will see some more money and drugs. After you have emptied the casket, you are then to head back to your room and leave all of what you've just acquired inside of your suite.

"Each of you is then to catch a cab back to Detroit Metro, check in at the flight counter, and get your tickets for your flight to Indianapolis. There will be a day's break before the next op, so make sure that you take this time to get some rest. When you get there, there will be a rental waiting for you reserved under Taz's Barney. Take that and drive to the W out in downtown Nap. Your instructions will be there as normal.

"Good luck, gentlemen! Out!"

After the screen had gone blank, Taz said, "Let's get to work!"

"Oh! Cliff! Give it to me, baby! Give it to me!" screamed Tazneema as she pulled Clifford as far as she could inside of her sex.

Clifford was amazed at how horny Tazneema was. As soon as they had gotten back to his place, the first thing she did was to take off all of her clothes and began ripping Clifford's off of him. Once she had him naked, she dropped to her knees and started giving him some of the best head he had ever received. After she let him come inside of her mouth, she led him into his bedroom, and that's where they stayed for the last two and a half hours.

After cumming way too many times, Clifford said, "Come on, 'Neema, you're killing me!"

Panting and almost out of breath, Tazneema said, "Come on, baby. One more time, 'k?"

Shaking his head no, Clifford said, "I can't do it, baby. I'm worn out. I have no more strength."

"Do you want me to suck it some more?"

"No!" he screamed as he jumped off of the bed and ran into the bathroom.

Tazneema laughed and yelled, "Come on, baby! I want some more!"

"I'm not coming out of this bathroom until you promise to let me get some sleep! You've turned into a sex maniac, and I can't take it!"

She laughed some more and said, "Okay, I promise. But you're going to have to give me some in the morning. Deal?"

Clifford opened the door to the bathroom and said, "Deal. Now, please go to sleep."

"'Kay," she said with a satisfied smile on her face.

Taz drove their rented SUV toward the funeral home. *Detroit's East Side is a wicked-looking place at night,* he thought as he made the left turn off of Jefferson and onto East Grand Boulevard. When he spotted Swanson's Funeral Home on the corner of Mack, he said, "All right, my niggas, it's time." He made a right turn onto Mack and then made a left turn into the back of the funeral home.

As soon as the SUV came to a complete stop, they all jumped out of the truck and headed straight towards the back door. Just like Won had told them, the door was unlocked. What Won didn't tell them was that as soon as they entered the back of the funeral home, they would come face-to-face with several dead bodies with plastic bags over their heads.

"Oh, shit! This is some creepy-ass shit!" Keno said as he followed Taz out of the preparation room.

"Don't pay that shit no mind, dog. We got a job to do, so let's do it," Taz said as he led the way into the funeral director's office.

Once they were inside of the office, Taz and Keno moved the funeral director's desk to the side so Wild Bill could open the safe. Red, Bob, and Bo-Pete stood by the door, making sure that there weren't any more surprises. Once Wild Bill had the safe open, he started filling up his bag. After he finished, he stepped aside so that Taz could start filling up his bag. After Keno had filled his bag, he said, "It's empty, gee."

"Good. Now, come on so we can get at that casket and get the fuck out," Red said as he led the way into the funeral home's chapel. Red opened the door to the chapel and saw the casket. He shook his head and said, "Dog, this is some morbid shit, for real."

"Come on, scary-ass nigga," said Bob as he went to the casket and pulled back the pillows that were inside of it. Just like Won had told them on the DVD, the casket was filled with money and drugs. Bob started packing kilo after kilo of cocaine into his bag. Once he had his bag filled, he stepped back so that Red could fill his. Bo-Pete came right behind Red and finished emptying the casket. After his bag was full and the casket was completely empty, he turned and gave Taz a nod of his head.

"Let's bounce," Taz said as he led the way out of the funeral home. When they had made it safely back inside of the SUV, Taz smiled and said, "God bless the dead!"

As they pulled out of the funeral home's parking lot, Red said, "You are one sick nigga!"

Every one of them laughed, and Taz said, "Maybe, but I'm also on my way to being one rich, sick nigga!" They all laughed again as Taz drove them back to the Westin. Mission completed.

Sacha couldn't sleep. Ever since Taz had left, she just couldn't stop herself from thinking about all of that money he was about to get. "This shit is like the movies. Whenever someone tries to stop doing wrong so they can live happily ever after, something always goes wrong. Please, God, don't let that be the case with Taz. Please!" she begged as she tried to get some rest.

Taz and the crew were on their way to the airport when he remembered that he hadn't called Sacha to let her know that everything was okay. He pulled out his cell and gave her a call. When she answered the phone, he said, "Hey, Li'l Mama! What you doin'?"

"Trying to get some sleep, but for some reason I can't keep my eyes closed. How are you?"

"I'm good. Everything is everything. I'm in a cab now on my way to another spot. I'll give you a call tomorrow, after I get up, okay?"

"All right, baby. I love you."

"Yeah, I love you too," he said and closed his cell.

"Dog, can I ask you a question?" asked Keno.

"What's up, gee?"

"Does Sacha know how we get down?"

Taz sighed heavily and said, "Yeah, gee, she does. I put her up on it after that shit went down out in Cali. I know I broke one of our rules, but I couldn't find another way out of it without exposing our hand. I even introduced her to Won."

"Ain't that a bitch! *We've* never even met that nigga, but your broad has. That's some cold shit, my nigga."

"Look, this is the last quarter of the game any fuckin' way, so why does it really matter?"

"It matters because you broke a rule, gee, a rule that we all swore we'd never break for anyone," Keno said seriously. "Just because you're in love doesn't justify your fuckup, my nigga."

"You're right, dog, and I apologize for my weakness for Sacha. But I love her, and whatever it takes to keep her sane I'm goin' to do it. After all of that shit went down in L.A., I had a decision to make, and I made it for my girl. I've asked her to be wifey, dog, 'cause she's the one. She's the one, my nigga," he said as he sat back and rode the rest of the cab ride to the airport in silence.

Chapter Twenty-eight

Monday morning, Sacha got out of bed feeling good. Ever since she had spoken to Taz the night before, she felt confident that everything was going to be okay. As she got dressed for work, her thoughts of Taz put a smile on her face. "Damn, I love that man!" she said aloud as she grabbed her briefcase and left for work.

Clifford saw Sacha as she walked inside of the office. He stepped quickly towards her and said, "Excuse me, Sacha. Can I have a word with you?"

Sacha glanced at her watch and said, "Could you make it kind of quick? I'm due in court in twenty minutes."

"Sure. I just wanted to tell you that I'm sorry for the way I behaved a while back. I was really hurt that I'd lost the opportunity to get close to you."

Sacha frowned at that statement and chose to remain silent.

"Anyway, I hope you will accept my apology, because it is definitely a sincere one. I've moved on with my life and I'm quite happy. I don't want to have any bad blood between us."

Sacha smiled and said, "Apology accepted, Cliff. I'm glad that you've moved on and that you're happy. That makes the both of us, see?" she said as she showed off the monstrous diamond ring Taz had given her.

"Wow! That's nice. So, you're taking the next step, huh?"

"Yes. We haven't set a date yet, but it most likely will be sometime this summer."

"Congratulations, Sacha. I'm happy for you. Well, I won't take up any more of your time. Have a nice day," he said as he turned and went into his office.

As soon as he closed the door to his office, he clenched his fist together tightly. "I hate that nigga! I can't believe that she's actually going to marry that wannabe-ass thug! Fuck!" he said aloud as he stepped toward his desk. After sitting down, he started wondering why in the hell was he so upset. He had Tazneema. He meant every word that he had just told Sacha. He was happy and had moved on with his life. But the thought of her marrying that nigga Taz irked him to no end. All of the old anger and passion he had had for Sacha came storming back tenfold. He shook his head sadly and said, "It just wasn't meant to be." He then grabbed some cases from his briefcase and started his workday.

"Damn, dog! We've been in this bitch over twenty-fo'. Why the fuck Won ain't got at us yet?" asked Red.

"Ain't no tellin', my nigga. Relax. When it's time to go to work, he'll holla," Taz said as he grabbed his cell and called Sacha. After getting her voice mail, he left her a quick message and closed his cell phone. Just as he had gotten off of his bed, his cell started ringing. He checked the caller ID and saw that it was Won. He smiled and said, "Looks like you done talked that nigga up, Red. This is Won right here. "What's up, O.G.?" he asked when he answered his cell.

"Everything is everything, Babyboy. I assume y'all have watched the DVD already, huh?"

"Oh yeah, we're ready whenever you are."

"Good. This is another day op. You are to move in approximately thirty minutes after we kill this call. You already have the directions, so you know where you're going. After everything is handled, come back to your room and drop off everything. I have already made y'all some reservations on a two o'clock flight out of Nap to Denver, Colorado. When you get to Denver, catch a shuttle bus to the Hertz Rental, and there will be a SUV already reserved for you. You are then to drive to the Doubletree Hotel on MLK and Monaco. After you're checked in, pick up your package and head on up to your room. You will be moving to your next op within an hour after you have checked into the hotel. Good luck. We won't speak again until you're out of Denver. Out!"

Taz closed his cell and said with a smile, "Time to get money, y'all!"

Sacha smiled as she listened to Taz's message on her voice mail. *He's so considerate,* she thought as she saved the message. Now that she was through with court, she had the rest of the day to herself. She didn't want to go back to Taz's big house all by herself, so she decided to call Gwen and see what she was up to.

Gwen answered her cell phone in a hushed tone. "Hello!" she whispered.

"Ho, what's wrong with you?" asked Sacha.

"I'm with a client, and we're watching a seminar on drunken drivers. Can I call you back in a little while?"

"Sure. I didn't want anything, really. Just wanted to see if you wanted to hang a little bit."

"Okay, I'll be out of here in an hour. I'll give you a call on your cell. Bye!"

Since Gwen was busy, Sacha decided to head on to her house. When she made it home, she smiled and said, "Damn! It feels as if I haven't been here in ages!" She walked around her living room, smiling. She was so happy. She knew that pretty soon she would no longer be living in this home anymore. Instead of this thought making her feel sad, she was elated. "I guess I'm going to have to contact a Realtor soon," she said as she went into her bedroom, feeling giddy about all of her and Taz's future plans together.

As Taz pulled out of the beauty shop's parking lot, he smiled and said, "Damn! It seems as if this shit is gettin' easier and easier."

"I know, huh? Those suckas was slippin' somethin' awful," added Keno.

They had just finished their mission in Indianapolis, and now they were headed back to their room so they could drop of their illegally gotten gains. Won had been exactly on the money again. His information about the beauty shop they had just finished robbing was perfect. Even though they had had to get a little physical with two of the men that were inside of the shop, the job still went off without a hitch.

"Denver, Colorado, here we come!" Taz yelled as he pulled into the parking lot of their hotel.

By the time Gwen had made it over to Sacha's house, Sacha had packed three suitcases full of her clothes. "Damn, bitch! What you doing, moving in with that nigga?" asked Gwen as she set her purse onto Sacha's dining room table.

Shaking her head yes, Sacha smiled as she stuck out her left hand so Gwen could see her engagement ring. "Does this answer your question, ho?"

Gwen's eyes grew wide when she saw the sparkling diamond ring on Sacha's wedding finger. She smiled and said, "That nigga done stepped up his game, I see. Congratulations, bitch! I'm so happy for you!"

"Ho, I can't lie. I never thought Taz was the marrying type, but when he asked me and I looked into those sexy-ass brown eyes, I knew he was serious. He loves me, Gwen, and I love him so much that it hurts to even think of my life without him in it. This is definitely the real thing."

"I know. I can see it in the both of you guys' eyes. Whenever we're together, I see how you two be looking at each other. I knew after the first day that I saw you two that your relationship was going to blossom into something real special. This shit is just perfect. You have found your soul mate, and so have I."

"*What?* Don't tell me you and Bob are planning on jumping that broom too!"

"Bitch, you're so late! When I moved in with him, he told me that he wanted to see if what we had was real, and if everything worked out the way he hoped it would, we would do the damn thing sometime this year. And so far, everything has been going just as we both had hoped for. So, you're not the only one who'll be changing their last name this year."

Sacha hugged Gwen and said, "Ho, I'm so happy for you! You know you deserve all of the happiness in the world."

"Yeah, I do, 'cause I've sure had enough pain. But come on with this corny shit. Our men are out of town, doing God knows what, and we're sitting here being all mushy-mushy and shit. Let's go on over to Taz's house and get blitzed off of some of that expensive-ass liquor he has behind that bar."

Sacha laughed and said, "I'm with that! Come on!"

Taz and the crew arrived in Denver right on schedule. After picking up their rented SUV, Taz gave Keno the directions to their hotel. While Keno drove, Taz called Sacha. "What you doing, Li'l Mama?" he asked as soon as Sacha answered the phone.

"Nothin'," Sacha answered with a slight slur in her voice.

"Nothin', huh? Sounds to me like you're doing somethin'."

"Uh-uh. Gwen and I are just chilling, baby. How are you? Is everything everything?"

Taz started laughing and said, "Yeah, I'm straight. Have you been drinking, Li'l Mama?"

"A li'l."

"What have you been drinking? Apple martinis?"

"Nope. Some of your XO."

"*What?* Now you know damn well your system ain't used to nothin' like that. What's gotten into you, Li'l Mama?"

"Nothin'."

"Somethin' must have, 'cause you're over there trippin'."

"No, I'm not, baby. Me and Gwen are just relaxing by the pool, sippin' on some of your good stuff. You're not mad at me, are you?"

He laughed again and said, "Nah, I ain't mad at ya. This shit is kinda funny, really. Check it out, though. I'm going to call you later, after my business is finished, okay? No, better yet, I'm just gon' call your drunk ass in the morning, before you go to work. I bet you won't have a problem gettin' any sleep tonight."

"I hope not."

"Tell me, how much of my XO have you two been drinkin'?"

Sacha grabbed the bottle of liquor out of Gwen's hand, saw that it was almost empty, and said, "Almost all of this bottle, baby."

"Sacha, take your ass upstairs and get in the bed! Tell Gwen I said that you two don't need to be down there by the pool! That shit is gon' kick in and lay the both of y'all down!" Taz said sternly.

"Uh-uh, baby. We know what we doing. We used to get drunk all the time when we was back in school."

"Do what I told you, Li'l Mama. Go upstairs now for me, okay?"

"All right, baby, I will."

"Do it while I'm still on the phone with you."

"Come on, Gwen. Taz wants us to take this party upstairs to the bedroom," Sacha said as she got to her feet.

"Ask Taz is my baby with him."

"Baby, Gwen wants to—"

"I heard her, Li'l Mama. Yeah, he's here. Go on and give the phone to her drunk ass," Taz said, and he passed the phone to Bob in the backseat of the SUV.

Bob accepted the phone from Taz and said, "Hello."

"Hi, you sexy-ass Black man! What'cha doin'?" asked Gwen.

"Taking care of some business. What's up with you?"

"Missing you."

"I guess that's a good thing then, huh?"

"You know it! Baby, did you know that Taz asked Sacha to marry him?"

"Yeah, he told us the other day. Why?"

"I was just wondering, that's all. Did you know that he bought her a big-ass diamond ring?"

"Nah, he didn't tell us that. What's up? You ready for yours yet?"

Gwen smiled as she sat down on Taz's bed and said, "You got that right, buddy!"

Bob laughed and said, "Don't trip. I gots you. Have you and Sacha taken y'all drunk asses upstairs yet?"

"Yep, we're in the room now."

"Good. Go on and spend the night, 'cause I know you are in no shape to be doing any driving. I'll get at you in the morning, okay?"

"All right, baby. Love you!"

"Yeah, I love your crazy ass too. Give the phone back to Sacha. Taz wants to holla at her."

"Okay. Bye!"

When Sacha got back on the phone, Taz said, "Alright, Li'l Mama, I'm outta here. I'll get at you tomorrow."

"Okay, baby. Be careful, Taz."

"I will, Li'l Mama."

"I love you!"

Taz smiled at that and said, "I love you, too!"

Chapter Twenty-nine

After a week of traveling and doing what they did best, Taz was starting to understand why Won had told them that this trip would be the ultimate test of their stamina. All of the flying that they were doing was starting to catch up to them. After they had left Denver, they drove to Colorado Springs and completed a mission there. After that, they flew to Memphis, where they took care of a quick mission worth a couple of million dollars. After leaving Memphis, they drove to a small town near Nashville, Tennessee, called Madison. They drove into the town and checked into the local Days Inn. After they had their rooms, Taz called Won as he was instructed to do back when they were in Colorado Springs. Won gave him the details to the next mission and told him that they had a flight to catch in five hours out of Memphis.

After Taz hung up the phone with Won, he went and checked under the bed and grabbed their weapons. *For the life of me, I don't know how this fool be doing this shit,* he thought as he pulled the duffel bag containing their guns and the rest of their equipment out from under the bed.

"All right, my niggas, it's like this. We are to drive over to this house off of Lovell Street. It's about ten minutes from here. We park the truck down the street from 307 B Lovell Street and walk the rest of the way. This is a home invasion raid, and it's all about in and out. No one is inside of the house, so it should go pretty

smooth. There are two safes in the bedroom. Keno and
I will go hit it while y'all watch our backs. We're getting
a ticket for this one 'cause there is a lot of drugs there.
Once we come out with the chips, Red, you, Bob, Wild
Bill, and Bo-Pete will then go in the back and grab the
work. Me and Keno will be standing point while y'all
are handling your business. After everything is everything, we'll then close the door and casually walk back
to the truck. The street is dimly lit, so there shouldn't
be a problem. Come on, let's do this."

   Tazneema and Clifford were having the time of their
lives. They spent a weekend down in Dallas, shopping
and wandering around the city. Clifford even took her
to Six Flags out in Dallas/Ft. Worth.
   Tazneema felt as if she was on cloud nine. No one
in her short life had ever shown her this much attention. Even though Taz had always been there for her,
he just wasn't the type to spend a lot of quality time
with a person. She understood that, and she had never
complained. She loved Taz, and no matter what happened, she always would. Being with Clifford showed
her an entirely different side of life, and she was loving
it. "Baby, when we get back home, I've decided to move
in with you."
   Clifford smiled and said, "Are you sure, 'Neema?"
   "Positive. I love you, Cliff, and I want to be with you
as much as I can, every single day."
   "Have you spoken with Taz or Mama-Mama about
this?"
   Shaking her head no, she said, "I don't have to. This
is my decision, and my decision only. I don't need their
approval."

He smiled and said, "Well then, let's get our butts back to the city then, 'cause we got some moving to do!" They laughed as Clifford started packing his bags.

As Taz parked the truck, he noticed how dark Lovell Street was and said, "That nigga Won wasn't lying. This street is dark as fuck. Come on, let's get this over with." He killed the ignition and jumped out of the truck.

As they walked down the street, they noticed that the street was damn near deserted. There were only a few houses on each side of the street. Taz scanned the houses until he saw the one he was looking for. "Three-oh-seven B Lovell Street. That's it right there, gee. The door should be unlocked, so we won't have to worry about making any noise kickin' it in," he said as he led the way towards the house.

"Shit, it wouldn't matter any fuckin' way. Ain't no-body around this bitch to hear us if we did have to kick it in," said Bo-Pete.

Taz stepped onto the porch and turned the doorknob to see that it was in fact locked. "Fuck! It's locked!"

"Kick the bitch in, dog, so we can do this shit and get the fuck out of here," urged Keno.

Taz gave a nod of his head, pulled out his weapon, and kicked the door hard right by the doorknob. The thin door busted open easily, and they all rushed inside with their guns drawn.

The first thing that Taz saw was a small lady sitting down at the dining room table. *Oh, shit!* he thought as he raised his gun, pointed it towards her, and said, "Be quiet, ma'am, and you will not be hurt. Now, is there anyone else in here with you?"

The small-framed lady shook her head no.

"Okay, then. Watch her, dog," Taz instructed as he led Keno into the back room. After moving some clothes out of his way, Taz spotted the safe concealed inside the closet. He quickly opened the safe and started filling up his duffel bag. After his bag was full, he stepped to the next safe and opened it also. He smiled when he saw all of the kilos of cocaine stacked neatly inside of it. After Keno's bag was full, they went back into the front and stood watch over the lady while Red, Bob, Wild Bill, and Bo-Pete went to the back room to retrieve the narcotics.

While they were standing watch, Keno stared at Taz and raised his eyebrows as if asking, what the fuck is going on? Taz's answer was a shrug of his shoulders, indicating that he didn't have a fucking clue.

A few minutes later, Red came back into the room, followed by Bob, Bo-Pete, and Wild Bill.

Taz said, "All right, ma'am, I'm goin' to need you to get on the floor. I give you my word that you will not be harmed. Just do as I ask."

For the first time during the entire incident the small lady spoke. "I'm not worried, son. Y'all done got what y'all came for. I know you ain't gon' do me nothin'. You better watch out, though, 'cause the boys be watchin' this house from across the street!"

Taz tried his best not to show any surprise in his voice when he asked, "What boys, ma'am?"

"Them boys who's puts those drugs in my house."

"Are you sure?"

"Positive."

"This changes shit, gee. Go get the truck and pull up in front of the house, K. Go with him, BP. You too, WB," Taz ordered, using the crew's initials instead of their names.

Keno, Bo-Pete, and Wild Bill walked out of the house with their weapons inside of their hands, cocked and ready, while Taz, Red ,and Bob stood at the door, watching the house directly across the street. All of the lights in the house were off, so Taz couldn't tell whether anyone was inside or not. It seemed as if it was taking Keno and the rest forever to come back with the truck, when in fact it had only been a couple of minutes. When Taz heard the horn blow, he turned and stepped out of the house, followed by Bob and Red. They jumped inside of the truck and sighed as Keno sped away from Lovell Street.

Mission completed, but Won has some fucking questions to answer! thought Taz as he relaxed a little.

By the time they had made it to Norman, Tazneema was asleep. Clifford shook her gently and said, "We're here, baby. Why don't you go on inside and get some rest? After I get off tomorrow, I'll come back and we can get your things."

"Okay, baby. I didn't know I'd be this tired. All I want to do is go to bed. Are you sure that you don't want to spend the night with me here?"

He smiled and said, "Yeah, I'm sure. Plus, it'll be nice getting a good night's sleep without worrying about being attacked in my sleep!"

Tazneema smiled and said, "Okay, I see how you are then! But wait until I move in. You're never going to get any sleep!" They laughed with each other, then shared a passionate kiss. "I love you, Cliff!"

"I love you, too, Neema. Now go on. I'll talk to you tomorrow."

"Bye!" Tazneema said, and she went into her apartment. After changing clothes, she went into the bedroom and pulled out the pregnancy test she had bought while they were in Dallas. She knew she was late for her period, and she was terrified of the results of the test she was about to take. "Please, God, don't let it be! Taz will kill me!" she prayed as she began to urinate onto the pregnancy test.

After waiting for the amount of time written on the instructions, Tazneema took a deep breath to see if she was in the blue or the pink. The blue would indicate that she was not pregnant, and the pink would indicate that she was. She stared at the test with a weird look on her face as tears slowly slid down her face. The test results were in the pink. *Damn!*

As soon as they were on the highway out of Madison, Taz pulled out his cell and called Won. When Won answered the phone, Taz quickly told him what had happened at the house on Lovell Street. After he was finished, Won asked, "Did you hurt her?"

"Nah, I tied her up and left the restraints kind of loose so she could easily slip out of them after we were gone."

"Good thinking. Damn! That was not suppose to happen!"

"Who the fuck you tellin'? You damn right that shit wasn't supposed to have happened! Don't tell me that you're finally slippin' on us, O.G."

"Nah, Babyboy, I'm on it. But like I've always told y'all, you will have to be ready for anything at any given time. As long as you are, if any surprises come up, y'all will be able to handle it."

"True, but you got us so damn comfortable with how we get down that we really ain't expectin' shit like this to pop off."

"I feel you. Go on and hit your next destination. Give me a call when you touch. I'm gonna make damn sure that everything is on point for this next one," Won said seriously.

"I hope so, O.G. I hope so!" Taz closed his cell phone.

Chapter Thirty

"Where are you now, baby?" asked Sacha as she tapped her fingers on top of her desk.

"In Baton Rouge."

"Louisiana?"

"Yeah."

"How long will you be there?"

Sighing, he said, "I'm not sure yet, Li'l Mama. What's with all of these questions? I was just callin' to let you know everything is everything. Damn!"

"Well, excuse me for caring! Bye, Taz!" she yelled and hung up the phone in his face.

Taz stared briefly at his cell before closing it. He got off of the bed and went into the bathroom of his and Keno's hotel room. They had made it to Baton Rouge early that morning, and to say they were tired would have been an understatement. The entire crew was completely exhausted. Taz had called Won after they arrived at the hotel. After retrieving the DVD, they sat and listened to Won's instructions with weary eyes. They all smiled when they heard Won say that the first of their two missions in Louisiana wouldn't be until late that night. That meant that they could get some much-needed rest. Even though they got to doze a little during their flights and brief road trips, there was nothing like getting some good old-fashioned sleep in a comfortable bed.

Everyone was in their rooms, sound asleep, at that moment—everyone except Taz. He couldn't stop thinking about how fucked up things had been in Madison. *What if they would have killed that old lady? What if the guys she had warned them about would have come out blasting?* These questions were running through his mind constantly.

He chose to call Sacha to try and keep his mind off of the Lovell Street mission. *And look what happened with that!* he thought as he smiled. *I done pissed my Li'l Mama off.* He grabbed his cell and called Sacha back. As soon as she answered the phone, he said, "I'm sorry, Li'l Mama. I'm tired as fuck, and I didn't mean to snap at you."

Sacha smiled and said, "I understand, baby. I can't help it if I'm overly concerned about your well-being."

"I know. But look, I really need to get some rest, so I'll give you a holla later on, okay?"

"All right, bye, Taz."

"Bye, Li'l Mama." He got back into bed and closed his eyes. As he finally started to fall asleep, his last thoughts were on Won. He hoped and prayed that he kept shit together. It was too fucking late in the game for mistakes.

Tazneema smiled as she unloaded the last of her stuff inside of Clifford's house. Clifford smiled at her and said, "Home, sweet home, baby!"

"You said it, mister! Now come here, because I have something to discuss with you." Clifford sat down next to her on the couch. "Cliff, what I'm about to say to you doesn't have to affect our relationship negatively. No matter what decision we make, I'm still going to love you. Do you understand?"

"Not really. Can you be a little bit more specific, 'Neema?"

She took a deep breath and said, "I'm pregnant." She stared at Clifford briefly, then continued. "I want to have this child, but if you're not ready, then I understand, and I have no problem with getting an abortion. I'm happy as long as I have you in my life. I would never do anything to hurt you, but more importantly, I want you to know that I never want to lose you. So, what you think?" she asked nervously.

Clifford smiled at her and said, "I love you, Tazneema Good, and I can't wait for our child to be born!"

Her face lit up as she asked, "For real?"

Nodding his head yes, he said, "For real. I don't know why you would think that I'd want you to have an abortion. I love you, and no matter what, I want us to be together also."

They hugged one another for a full minute, and Tazneema pulled from his embrace and said, "I'm going to have to tell Taz. He's not going to like this at all, but I'm sure after he meets you and sees what kind of man you are, you two will hit it off just fine. Taz can be hard sometimes, but he's a big softy when it comes to me."

"I hope you're right, 'cause your brother seems to be a little intimidating, from what I've heard about him."

Tazneema smiled and said, "Don't worry. I'll take care of him. Now as for Mama-Mama, that's another story."

"Oh, God!" Clifford said as he slapped his forehead.

They both laughed and gave each other another hug.

"Bitch, have you talked to Taz?" asked Gwen.

"Yes, I spoke with him earlier. What's up?"

"I've been trying to call Bob all damn day and he's not answering his phone."

"From what Taz told me, they were pretty tired, and they were getting some rest. Maybe Bob has his phone turned off," Sacha said logically.

"Uh-uh. If it was turned off, it would go straight to his voice mail. That nigga bet' not be up to no bullshit."

"Ho, go on with that silly talk. Bob is handling his business with Taz and the others. You don't have shit to worry about."

"How come all of the sudden you're not worried about what they be doing when they go out of town? Do you know something I don't?"

Sacha smiled and said, "Maybe I do . . . and maybe I don't!"

"So, it's like that, huh? We're keeping secrets from each other now, bitch?"

"Come on, Gwen. You know that if I knew something that was important, I'd put you up on it. I trust Taz, and I know he's legitimate, so I've stopped worrying myself about their business. And you should too. Bob loves you and you love him. Everything is just how it should be." Sacha felt bad for lying to her best friend, but she had promised Taz that she would never tell anyone of his secrets, especially Gwen, because if she said anything about it to Bob, he would have to answer to the rest of the crew for betraying them. So, here she was, lying to her best friend in the entire world for her man, her fiancé, the man she was planning to spend the rest of her life with.

Taz was just getting out of bed when his cell phone started ringing. "Hello," he said groggily when he answered it.

"I hope y'all got some rest, Babyboy, 'cause it's time to get busy. Have you already checked out the DVD?"

"Yeah, we took care of that as soon as we got here."

"Good. After you finish this op, you are to take the truck you have and head to Shreveport, check into any hotel you want to, and get some rest. Your next op will be early in the morning. Give me a call once you've made it there and I'll then give you the information for what needs to be handled out there."

"So, we need to keep the equipment with us from this last mission?"

"Nah. I don't want y'all making that drive dirty. Once you get at me, I'll have everything set up. Someone most likely will be bringing you what you need."

"All right, that's cool. Anything else?"

"This is the last leg of this mission, Babyboy. After y'all are finished in Louisiana, y'all will be flying out east to finish the last two ops."

"Good, 'cause this shit is starting to wear on a nigga's nerves. Mistakes can happen when we're this fuckin' tired, O.G. I've been staying on top of everybody, but still, all of this flying is tiring a nigga out," Taz said seriously.

"Hold on, Babyboy. This ride is coming to an end. Remember what I told you a long time ago, when we first started this shit?"

Taz smiled and said, "Yeah, you told me that when everything is everything, I would be rich and you would be in the position of power. And, as long as you had the power, I would have the power."

"That's right. My position of power has gotten stronger and stronger over these last few years. We're almost there. Just a little bit longer and everything I told you back in the day will become a reality. So, make sure you handle this shit for me, Babyboy."

"I got you."

"Out!" Won said and hung up.

Taz woke Keno and told him to call the others and wake them while he took a quick shower. It was time to go back to work.

After work, Sacha went over to Taz's house to relax. She smiled as she pulled into the driveway and saw Tari's Altima parked by the garage. She climbed out of her BMW and went inside.

Tari was out back, watching Heaven and Precious run around the yard. When she saw Sacha come outside, she smiled and said, "Hey, girl! How are you doing today?"

"I'm fine. How about yourself?"

"I'm alright. I had the day off today, so I came to spend some time with my babies. I didn't want them to think that I've forgotten about them."

"Those dogs are so spoiled. When I first started coming over here, they never showed themselves. But now, as soon as they smell my scent, they're all over me," Sacha said affectionately as she watched Precious and Heaven out in the yard.

"That's a good thing, though, 'cause if they didn't like you, you and Taz's relationship would have been doomed!" They both started laughing.

"Have you spoken to Taz lately?" Sacha asked as she slipped off her pumps.

"A couple of weeks ago, before he left, we met and had a talk."

"A talk? About what?"

Tari smiled and said, "You, what he does when he goes out of town, and Won."

"Whoa!"

"Those were my thoughts too. He doesn't know whether or not he wants to get out of the game he's been playing for so long. He's giving it some serious thought now because of you. But he's still unsure."

"He told you that?"

"Yep. I know how he thinks. Better yet, I know first-hand how Won thinks, and I know that even if Taz does decide to stop doing his thing, Won is going to try his very best to deter him from stopping. Won has something heavy up his sleeve, and Taz is a major part of his plans."

"What makes you think that Won won't let Taz stop?"

Tari shrugged her shoulders slightly and said, "I know Won, and I know the things that they've been doing for all these years are for a reason."

"What's the reason?"

"That's something that Taz and I have never been able to figure out. Won is the only person who can answer that question for you. And I highly doubt if he ever will."

Sighing heavily, Sacha said, "Taz asked me to marry him before he left, and he told me that he was going to get at Won and let him know that it's over and he wants out."

"Taz has always been his own man, to a degree. You have to understand that Won has done so much for Taz and never asked for anything in return. All he ever wanted for Taz was for him to be successful. Taz is financially secure for the rest of his life, and it's all because of Won. If and when Taz chooses to tell Won that he wants out, I'm 99.9 percent sure that Won will use whatever tactics he can come up with to keep Taz in the game."

"But why? If Taz wants to stop, why won't Won let him?"

Tari smiled sadly and said, "Because he gets to win!"

"Win what?" Sacha asked with a confused look on her face.

"Only Won knows the answer to that question, Sacha."

"That's so unfair!"

"That's how it is."

"So, are you telling me that no matter what, Won won't let Taz get out?"

"No, I'm not saying that at all What I am saying is that when Won is ready for Taz to get out, he'll let him out. But only after he has accomplished whatever it is that he's after. And, baby, believe me when I tell you this. People don't just call him 'Won' for nothing."

"What's that supposed to mean?"

Tari stared at Sacha briefly and simply said, "He always, and I mean always, has to win."

Chapter Thirty-one

Everything seemed to be back to normal. The missions in both Baton Rouge and Shreveport, Louisiana, went according to plan and without any problems.

As Taz drove their rented SUV out of Louisiana towards Dallas, he once again felt comfortable with their chances of completing these last two missions.

"So, we're flying out of Dallas/Ft. Worth, on our way to the East Coast, huh?" asked Bob.

"Yep. These are the last two missions," Taz said as he smiled at Keno, who was sleeping next to him in the passenger seat.

"Good. I'm tired of this shit, dog. All I want to do is get back to town and chill the fuck out."

"Stop whining, nigga. You ain't gone be tired when you see all of them chips in your account. You gots to work to get paid, fool," Red said with a smile on his face.

"Yeah, and the more we work, the more we get paid!" yelled Wild Bill from the back of the truck.

Bo-Pete smiled and said, "That's cold, though. We're so close to home and we gots to head the other fuckin' way."

"Yeah, I know. But don't trip, 'cause when we come back, we will be able to do whatever the fuck we want to," Taz said wisely.

Keno opened his eyes, scratched his two-day-old stubble, and said, "Nigga, we already can do whatever the fuck we want!"

Taz laughed and said, "I know, huh?"

Keno shook his head from side to side and said, "Bo-Pete, pass me my bag so I can put *'Face* in the DVD. It's time for me to get motivated."

Tazneema and Clifford went to Tazneema's doctor and confirmed what she already was certain of. She was nine weeks pregnant. Her doctor gave her a prescription for some vitamins and told her to make sure that she watched what she ate.

After they left the doctor's office, Clifford felt as if he was on cloud nine. He was about to be a father! He was in love with Tazneema, and he didn't give a damn whether or not Taz accepted it or not. There was no way in the world he was going to let Taz interfere with his child being born. "So, since I have the rest of the day off, is there anything special you'd like to do, 'Neema?" he asked as he pulled out of the parking lot.

Tazneema smiled sheepishly and said, "I want to go home and do it, Cliff. I'm horny."

"Damn, baby! Don't you ever think about anything else other than sex?"

"I'm still making up for lost time. Remember, I started late."

He smiled and said, "Okay, okay! But first we're going to go somewhere and get something to eat. I'm not about to let you wear me out on an empty stomach."

Tazneema smiled and said, "Thank you, baby. You're so good to me. And because of you being so good to me, I'm going to be extremely good to you as soon as we get home."

Clifford slapped his forehead with the palm of his left hand and said, "Oh my God!"

***

"Girl, why haven't you called that nigga?" asked Paquita as she sat down on Katrina's sofa.

"I didn't want him to think I was sweatin' his ass or nothin' like that. Plus, I wanted to see if he would get back at me first."

"Well, now that you've seen that he ain't, you need to be gettin' at his ass."

"Damn, bitch! Why you all up in mines any fuckin' way?"

"'Cause I want to see what's up with Red's big, sexy yellow ass. He hasn't gotten back at me either. I want to know if I impressed him or not."

"What did your freaky ass do with him, anyway?"

"Bitch, I ain't given you my secrets. That's for me and my baby, Red, only."

Katrina started laughing and said, "You and your baby, Red! Ain't that a bitch! What happened to you wanting Taz?"

"Taz is in love. You can see it in his eyes. I'm trying to get in where I fit in. I want Red to have that same kind of look that Taz has. You feel me?"

"Yeah, I feel you."

Shaking her head no, Paquita said, "Nah, you ain't feelin' me."

"What are you talkin' 'bout, bitch? I said I feel you, didn't I?"

"If you're really feelin' me, you'd be on the phone, dialing Keno's number right now."

Katrina didn't respond to her best friend. Instead, she picked up her phone, smiled, and started dialing Keno's cell phone number.

Once they arrived at JFK in New York, Taz led the crew through the crowded airport terminal. Since this

was their first time on the East Coast, Won had told
them that there would be too much traffic for them to
try and maneuver through in a rental, so he told them
to catch a cab to their hotel.

When they arrived at the Midtown Marriott, they
quickly checked into their reserved rooms. After putting their bags in their room, they met back up with Taz
and Keno inside of their room on the tenth floor.

Taz pulled out the DVD and inserted it into the television's DVD player. A picture of Michael Jordan came
onto the screen, showing the Great Mike slam-dunking
the ball over Charles Barkley. A minute later, Won's
voice came over the speakers:

"I know by now y'all are tired and about ready to get
back home. Don't trip. The Big Apple is your last stop.
But first, you have to do a quickie out in Jersey.

"Downstairs you have an SUV waiting for you that
is to be used for this mission, as well as the one out in
Brooklyn after you finish with Jersey."

As they sat and listened to Won explain their last
two missions, Taz was thinking about Tazneema. He
quickly shook her out of his mind and paid attention to
what Won was saying on the DVD.

After the DVD went blank, Taz turned off the television and said, "Alright, let's get this shit over with."

Keno reached under the bed and pulled out their
equipment. Once again, it was time to go to work.

"Are you busy, Mama-Mama?" asked Tazneema.

"Girl, even if I was, it wouldn't matter none. You
know I always have time for you. What's wrong?"

"Nothing. I just want to talk to you, that's all."

"About what?"

"A lot of things."

"Well, talk then, girl."

"I'd rather do it in person, but my schedule is kind of hectic right now. I'll give you a call later in the week and see when I can make it down to your house."

Concerned, Mama-Mama asked, "Are you feeling alright, 'Neema?"

Tazneema smiled and said, "Yes, I'm fine, Mama-Mama. Don't worry about me. I'm A-okay. I'll talk to you later, 'kay?"

"All right, baby. Bye now," Mama-Mama said before hanging up. "Humph! That girl done got herself into some trouble. I can feel it in my bones," she said aloud as she went back to work on the homemade biscuits she was baking.

By the time Taz and the crew had made it back to their rooms, it was close to midnight. That meant that it was close to eleven back in Oklahoma City. Taz sat down on the bed in their room and called Sacha. When she answered his phone, he smiled and said, "What's up, Li'l Mama?"

"Hi, baby. How are you doing?"

"I'm good. I'll be home within the next two days."

"For real?"

He laughed and said, "Yeah, for real. You miss me?"

"Now you know that's a silly question. Of course I miss you. I've been missing you ever since you first left me."

"How much do you miss me?"

"A lot."

"How much is a lot?"

"What are you talking about, Taz?"

Taz saw that Keno had fallen fast asleep, so he took his cell and went into the bathroom, closed the door, and said, "I said, how much is a lot?"

"A whole lot."

"Have you been horny since I've been gone, Li'l Mama?"

Sacha lowered her voice as if she wasn't alone and whispered, "Yes, extremely horny, baby."

He smiled and asked, "What you got on right now, Li'l Mama?"

"One of your wife-beaters."

"That's it?"

"Mmmm, hmm."

"You wanna do somethin' for me, Li'l Mama?"

"What's that, baby?"

"Play with it for me. I want to listen to you while you make yourself cum. Can you do that for me, Li'l Mama?"

She giggled like a schoolgirl and asked, "You want to have phone sex with me, baby?"

"Yeah, I want you to cum for me, baby."

"What are you going to do for me in return?"

"What you want, Li'l Mama?"

"I want you to stroke that big thang of yours while I stoke my kitty."

"I'm way ahead of you, Li'l Mama. I'm strokin' him already," he said as he continued to stroke his manhood with his right hand.

"Is it nice and hard for me, baby?"

"Yeah, it's hard, baby . . . it's real hard. Is my pussy nice and wet?"

"Yes! It's wet, baby! It's real wet," she said as she let her fingers manipulate her clitoris.

"You want this dick, don't ya?"

"Ooooh, yes, baby, I want it bad! Do you want this kitty?"

"You know I do, baby. I want it so bad it hurts," he said as his right hand started stroking himself faster and faster. "I'm almost there, baby! I'm almost there!" he panted.

"Oooh, me too, baby! Me too!" she screamed into the receiver.

"Cum with me, Li'l Mama. Let's cum together as if I was with you."

"I'm ready, baby! I'm ready!" she screamed.

"Me too, baby! Me too!" he yelled as he skeeted his semen all over his right hand.

Sacha moaned loudly as she gushed a large amount of her love juices all over Taz's sheets. After a minute of recuperation, she said, "Are you still there, baby?"

"Ye-yeah, I'm here, Li'l Mama. Damn, I've made a mess!" he said, and they both started laughing.

"That was crazy. I've never done anything like that before."

"To tell you the truth, me neither. It was cool, but nothin' beats the real thing."

"I know that's right, so hurry up and get your ass back home!"

He laughed and said, "Don't worry about a thang, Li'l Mama. I got one more mission to complete, and I'm on my way home for good."

"For good?"

"That's right, Li'l Mama, for good."

She laughed and said, "I can't wait!"

Chapter Thirty-two

"Damn! I told you I've been out of town, baby! Why you trippin' on me like that?" asked Keno with a smile on his face.

"'Cause you said you were goin' to get me the next day," Katrina whined.

Keno sighed and said, "Check this out, boo. I'll be back in town in a day or so. I give you my word that as soon as I hit the city, I'll give you a holla and we'll hook up. Cool?"

Katrina smiled into the receiver and said, "Alright, Keno."

"Look, I gots to bounce. I'll talk to you soon."

"Wait! Paquita wants to know if Red is with you."

"Yeah, he's with me, but he's not in my room right now. I'll tell him to give her a call when he has time."

"All right, baby. Be good."

Keno laughed and said, "I'm always good, boo, even when I'm being bad!"

"I know. That's why I'm diggin' you so much."

"I know that's right! Bye, boo," Keno said and hung up the phone. He turned towards Taz, who had a smile on his face, and said, "Don't even start, nigga."

Taz started laughing, raised his hands in the air as if surrendering, and said, "I don't want any problems, my nigga. It's just good to see that you've finally found someone that's able to hold your attention, playa."

Keno smiled and said, "Fuck you! Yeah, I'm feelin' Katrina a li'l, but that don't mean she's about to be wifey or no shit like that. I'm goin' to take it nice and slow and see if she's really worthy to be with a nigga, ya know what I'm sayin'?"

"That's the best thing, dog. Now, let's get some rest. It's on in the morning. Once we finish this last one, we can head on back to town and start living for once."

"So, this is the last one for real, then, huh?"

Taz nodded his head yes and said, "I'm gon' get at Won when we get back and let him know that this mission was our last one."

"Do you think he's goin' to trip out?"

"I doubt it. But if he does, so what? We ain't sign no lifetime contract with this shit. Nothin' lasts forever, and I'm tryin' to get out while everything is everything."

"I'm with you, dog. Whatever way you choose to go, I'm rollin' with my nigga."

"I know, gee. I know," Taz said as he got onto his bed and closed his eyes.

Sacha woke up the next morning feeling extremely happy. Taz was finishing up his last job, and then he was coming back home so they could start living a normal life together. That was a blessing from God, and she thanked Him silently as she started getting dressed for work.

Clifford had already left for work by the time Tazneema had awakened from a very comfortable night's sleep. She felt so secure when she was with Clifford that it was as if she was living with her knight in shining armor.

She stretched as she got out of the bed, and then ran to the bathroom and started throwing up. After she had finished, she wiped her mouth with a face towel, smiled, and said, "My first time having morning sickness!" While she was brushing her teeth, she thought about having to tell Taz that she was pregnant. "Damn, he's going to go ape on me! I just hope Mama-Mama will be on my side, 'cause if she's not, then I know I'm going to have hell convincing Taz to let me have this baby. Damn!" she said and rinsed the Colgate from her mouth.

Clifford was in his office, finishing up with a client, when he was interrupted by his secretary. "Excuse me, Mr. Nelson, but you have a call on line one."

"Thank you, Marcette. Put it through." He then thanked his client and quickly walked him to the door of his office. He came back to his desk and answered his call. "Clifford Nelson. How may I help you?"

"Hi, baby. You busy?"

He smiled and said, "I'm never too busy for you, 'Neema. You know that."

"I didn't want anything. I just wanted to tell you that I had my first case of morning sickness this morning, before I left the house."

"Are you all right? Do you want to go see the doctor?"

"No, and calm down before you have a heart attack. It was nothing really. I'm fine. As a matter of fact, I'm on my way to school now."

"Are you sure, 'Neema? Something might be wrong with the baby!"

"Don't worry, Cliff. If I thought it was something that serious, I would be calling you from the doctor's office now, instead of from my car on my way to class.

I should be done by lunchtime. Do you want to meet somewhere, or are you tied up today?"

"Sorry, baby, but I have to be in court at one, and I have a lot of paperwork here that needs to be taken care of. I don't think I'll be eating any lunch at all today. Let's go somewhere and have dinner later, okay?"

"That's fine. All right, I'll talk to you later. Bye."

"Bye, baby," he said and hung up the phone with a smile on his face.

By the end of her workday, Sacha was exhausted. For some reason she felt as if she was completely drained. That puzzled her, because she didn't do anything differently than she normally did.

When she made it back to Taz's house, she went and changed into her swimsuit, went downstairs, and got into the shallow end of the swimming pool. As she sat in the water, she smiled as she watched Heaven and Precious as they slowly walked around the pool, staring at her. *It feels so good to be protected and loved,* she thought as she watched the Dobermans as they continued to watch over her.

Just as she started to swim around in the pool a little, she had a queasy feeling in her stomach. She stopped, stood up in the pool, and grabbed her stomach. After her queasiness had subsided, she stepped out of the pool and went back upstairs to the bedroom. She went into the bathroom and splashed some water onto her face. Something was wrong, and she didn't know what it was.

She went back into the bedroom and climbed onto the bed. While she was resting, a thought came into her head and she smiled. "No, it can't be!" she yelled excitedly as she jumped out of the bed quickly and threw on a pair of shorts and a shirt. She grabbed her car keys and quickly left the house, feeling extremely excited.

Won woke Taz up early and said, "It's on for in the morning, Babyboy. After we finish talking, I want you to go downstairs and grab that bag that's in the backseat of the truck. You are to use them for this mission, because there's going to be a few people there, and they may be strapped."

"What are you talking 'bout, O.G.?" asked Taz sleepily.

"Vests. Y'all need to wear them for this mission."

"*What?* We ain't never needed no vests before. What's up with that, Won?"

"Safety measures, Babyboy. That's all. This is going to be an easy op, but then again, it's a dangerous one simply because there will be guards on point. But they'll be in front, and y'all are coming in from the back and the element of surprise is on your side. I would prefer for you to wear them just in case something goes down. At least this way y'all will have more protection."

"All right, I ain't trippin' or nothin'. That just threw me for a loop."

"I understand. Now listen. You are going to this clothing store called BB's. It's located in the Fulton Street strip mall. You are to take 42nd Street to the FDR, and take the FDR to the Brooklyn Bridge and exit in downtown Brooklyn on Fulton Street. Once you get on Fulton Street, drive around back behind the strip mall and park in back of the store. You will know it when you see it, because there will be a sign on the back door. Y'all are then to proceed into the back and empty both safes. The combinations are 29 to the right, 41 to the left, and 67 to the right. Both of the safes have the same combo, so that should save time for y'all. One of them is full of drugs, and the other is full of money.

"While you are emptying the safes, three of you should be on point by the door that leads into the front of the store. Like I told you, there will be armed guards in front. As long as you use your stealth abilities, you should be in and out without a problem. But if it has to go down, then you know how to handle your business.

"Now, what I'm about to suggest is optional. Y'all can do it the way I just suggested, or you can go in and rush the front and secure everyone, and then handle your business. The choice is yours, Babyboy.

"Once y'all are out of there, proceed straight back to your hotel and leave everything inside of the room. Y'all's flights are already reserved for a noon flight out of JFK. When you make it back to the city, check your accounts and give me a holla. This one puts y'all well over two hundred million, Babyboy."

Taz smiled and said, "I'm fuckin' with that!"

"All right then, do you. I'll holla at ya when you make it back to the city. Out!" Won said and hung up the phone.

After Taz hung up the phone with Won, he woke Keno and told him that he'd be right back. He then took the elevator down to the underground parking area and grabbed the bag out of the truck with the bulletproof vests in it that Won had told him about. After that, he went back to his room and ran the mission down to Keno.

"Damn, it's like that, huh? So, how we gone put it down? Won's way, or secure the spot first?"

"I think we should do it Won's way. What do you think?"

"It really don't matter to me, dog. Let's get at the homies and see what they think."

"All right, wake them niggas up and let's go get something to eat. We have the rest of the day to come up with how we're going to put it down, anyway,"

"That's cool. I wanted to go to Jay-Z's 40/40 Club, anyway. They say the food's expensive as fuck, but I ain't trippin'. I am a fuckin' millionaire too."

Taz started laughing and said, "I know that's right! And we might bump into B. She might choose a playa like you over the Jiggaman."

With a serious look on his face, Keno said, "Damn, gee! I didn't think about that shit. If Beyoncé is in the spot, she's definitely going to see that a nigga like me has way more flavor than that nigga Jay."

Taz shook his head but said nothing as he continued to unpack the bulletproof vests for their upcoming mission.

Chapter Thirty-three

Sacha's hunch turned out to be correct. She was pregnant. When she left Taz's house, she went to Walgreens and bought a pregnancy test. She then sped right back to the house and took the test. When she saw that the test came back positive, she was elated. "Yes!" she screamed as she ran into the bedroom and grabbed the phone. Her hands trembled as she dialed Taz's cell number. As soon as he answered the phone, she said, "I know you told me not to call you unless it's really important, baby, but I have something that I just have to tell you."

"Is everything all right, Li'l Mama?" asked Taz as he stepped away from the table. Taz and the crew were enjoying an expensive lunch at the 40/40 Club. He didn't want to disturb the others, so he stepped away and went and stood by the bar.

Sacha smiled and said, "Yes, everything is just perfect, baby. I have the most wonderful news for you. I'm pregnant!"

Taz was silent for a moment; then he asked, "Are you sure?"

"Positive. I just finished taking a pregnancy test, and it came out positive. I'm pregnant, Taz! I'm really pregnant!"

Taz smiled and said, "Damn! We're having a baby boy!"

"Whoa! Hold up there, mister! What makes you think it's going to be a boy?"

He smiled and said, "It has to be. It has to be!"

"I'm glad that you're as excited about this as I am. I was kind of worried that you might not want to have any children."

"Baby, I love kids, and I want to have plenty more, if it's alright with you."

"Three will be just fine. I don't think I could do more than that. But who knows? I love you, baby!"

"I love you, too, Li'l Mama! Look, I gots to go, 'cause we have something to take care of. When I get back, we'll sit down and talk about kids more thoroughly, 'cause I have some things that I need to tell you about."

"Like what, Taz?"

"I can't get into that right now. Don't trip. We'll talk when I get back."

"That will be tomorrow, right?"

"Yes, it should be. Now, let me bounce, okay?"

"All right, Taz. I love you!"

"I love you, too, Li'l Mama!" As he went back to the table to join the others, his only thought was, *Damn, we having a baby!*

After Sacha got off the phone with Taz, she called Gwen and said, "Guess what, ho?"

"What, bitch?"

"I'm pregnant!"

"Ooh, bitch, stop lying!"

"I just found out, ho."

"Are you keeping it?"

"Hell yes! Why wouldn't I?"

"Have you told Taz?"

"I just got off the phone with him, and he's just as excited as I am about the baby."

"I'm so happy for you, bitch! Congratulations!" Gwen said sincerely.

"I wish you could come over and have a drink with me, but I guess I can't be doing any more drinking for a while."

"You might not can drink, but that doesn't stop me from drinking! I'm on my way, ho. Get the XO out! I'll celebrate for the both of us!" Gwen yelled as she hung up the phone.

Sacha started laughing as she went downstairs and grabbed another bottle of Taz's expensive liquor.

By the time the crew had made it back to their rooms, they all decided to take it in early. Taz had explained to them the details for their next mission, and they were ready. More than ready, really. They just wanted to hurry up and finish the job so they could get back home. They agreed to do the job the way Won had suggested, but if anything got crazy, they were prepared for whatever.

"All right then, my niggas, go get some rest. We're out at five in the morning," Taz said before he got into his bed.

Keno walked the rest of the crew to the door with his cell phone in his hand and closed it behind them. He smiled at Taz as he dialed a number on his phone. "What's up, boo? What'cha doin'?" he asked when Katrina answered her phone.

Taz shook his head from side to side as he started to doze off to sleep.

The next morning, Taz got up at twenty minutes to four A.M. He took a shower and got himself prepared mentally for what had to be done. After he finished getting dressed, Keno went and took himself a shower. By the time he was finished, the rest of the crew had come into the room. Keno threw on his clothes, strapped on his bulletproof vest, and said, "I'm ready."

"Let's go to work," Taz said as he led the crew out of the hotel room.

They got into their SUV, and Taz drove them down 42nd Street. He followed Won's precise instructions, and twenty-five minutes after they had departed from the hotel room, he had them parked behind BB's clothing store in the Fulton strip mall.

Taz took a deep breath and said, "This is it, my niggas. Keep your eyes open and stay alert for any surprises. We should be in and out of this bitch in less than ten, but if there are any surprises, don't hesitate to do you. Our lives depend on how we watch each other's backs. Y'all ready or what?"

"You know I'm ready, my nigga," said Keno.

"I'm here," said Red.

"Let's get this fucking money!" yelled Wild Bill.

"It is what it is, my nigga," said Bo-Pete.

And finally, Bob said, "I was born for this shit, dog."

Taz gave a slight nod of his head and said, "Let's go!"

They all jumped out of the SUV and went to the back of the store.

Just as Won had told them, the door was unlocked. Taz turned the doorknob and opened the door slowly. Once the door was open, he led the way inside. He went straight to the safes, followed by Keno and Wild Bill. Red, Bo-Pete, and Bob stood by the door, watching the front entrance into the store from the back room.

Just as Taz opened the first safe, Red yelled, "Bob, watch yourself!"

A tall, dark-skinned man came walking through the door that led from the front of the store. When he heard

Red yell at Bob, he quickly pulled out a gun and started shooting.

Bob's reaction was a tad slow as he shot his silenced weapon twice. He hit his target twice in his chest, but during the process, he got shot in his stomach. He fell to the ground and moaned as he tried to remain focused on the door that the armed man had come through.

Red ran to Bob's side and said, "Hold on, my nigga! Hold on!"

Keno had his safe open and was busy cleaning it out as Bo-Pete and Red pulled Bob to the back door. Just as they had him close to the door, three more men came running into the back room, firing semiautomatic weapons at the crew.

Wild Bill turned just in time and started spitting fire with his silenced weapon. He caught one of the men with a bullet to his face, while Red and Bo-Pete finished the other two.

Taz and Keno never stopped filling up their duffel bags. Once they were finished, Taz said, "Red, Keno, get Bob to the truck. Bo-Pete, Wild Bill, come with me." His face was grim as he led them towards the front of the store. He opened the door cautiously and saw a woman on the phone, screaming to someone on the other end. "Someone's in the back with the shit! They're shooting the fucking place up! Get someone here quick!" she shouted.

Those were her last words, because Taz shot her from fifteen feet right between her eyes. He turned back and said, "Let's get the fuck outta here!" They then ran back the way they had come and climbed into the SUV. As soon as they were from behind the strip mall, Taz noticed several different types of cars speeding to the front of the store. Keno was in the backseat trying to calm Bob down, while Taz drove.

Taz pulled out his cell and quickly dialed Won's number. It took several rings before he answered. "Dog, the shit went haywire! Bob is hit!" Taz yelled frantically.

"Calm down, Babyboy! Calm down!" Won said calmly.

Too fucking calm for Taz's taste, he said, "What the fuck you mean, calm down? My mans is hit!"

"Where are you now?"

"I'm back on the Brooklyn Bridge! We gots to take Bob to a hospital, O.G.! He's bleeding like a muthafucka!"

"No! That's the last thing you want to do. Just stay on the same route that you came on. Someone will be calling you in less than five minutes."

"What the fuck are you talkin' 'bout? I gots to get Bob to a fuckin' hospital!"

"Don't panic on me now, Taz. Just trust me," Won said, and he hung up the phone.

Taz dropped the phone on his lap and yelled, "Hold on, my nigga! You're going to be alright!"

"All right, dog . . . alright, dog," Bob said weakly from the back of the truck.

"Damn, dog! Where the fuck is your vest?" asked Keno as he held Bob in his lap.

Bob winced from the pain in his stomach and said, "I . . . I forgot to put it on, my nigga."

Keno stared at Bo-Pete, and Red shook his head in disgust but said nothing.

Taz's cell started ringing and he quickly answered it. "Yeah?"

"Check this out, God. This is Magoo from the Bronx. Are you on the FDR yet?"

"Yeah."

"All right, son, stay on the FDR until you get uptown. Then, cross over to the Major Deegan and get off at

149th Street. You'll see some projects—the Patterson Projects. I'll be parked out front. Don't worry about your mans. By the time you touch down, a doctor will be on deck for you, son."

"Cool. How long will it take for me to get to you?"

"If you're already on the FDR, it should be no more than ten to twelve minutes."

"All right, I'll see you in a minute. Thanks."

"Don't thank me. You know who to thank. One!" Magoo said and hung up.

Taz turned around and yelled, "Hang on, my nigga! We're taking you to get some help now! You're goin' to be alright!"

Bob's eyes were closed, but he heard everything that Taz had said, because he shook his head slightly.

"Come on, Bob, baby! Open your eyes for me, gee! You can't close your eyes, dog!" Keno screamed.

Bob opened his eyes and weakly said, "I'm tired, my nigga. I'm real tired."

Shaking his head no, Keno screamed, "Think about Gwen, nigga! Keep your eyes open for her, dog!"

Bob smiled slightly, opened his eyes, and said, "I hear you, gee. I hear you."

Taz got off of the FDR on 149th Street and pulled in front of the Patterson Projects just like the guy Magoo had told him to. Magoo was standing in front of his red Cadillac Escalade as they pulled behind it. After Taz had parked the SUV, he jumped out of the truck and stepped up to Magoo and asked, "You Magoo?"

"Yeah, son."

"All right then, what now?"

Magoo turned his head and gave a slight nod. Three young Puerto Ricans with red bandannas on their heads came from behind a parked car and went straight towards the crew's SUV. "Don't trip, my nigga. I gots your man, Blood. He's in the good hands of some of the Bronx's best Damus. Y'all gots to get outta here now though, Blood. Won told me to tell you to stick to the script."

Shaking his head no, Taz said, "Nah, we can't leave my nigga."

"Everything is all good. My niggas are taking him up-stairs to one of our joints. A doctor is up there, and he'll make sure that your man is good. We got the painkill-ers and everything, son, so don't worry. We gots him," Magoo said confidently as he turned and followed his three young homies who carried Bob into the building.

Taz stepped back to the SUV and told the rest of the crew, "Won wants us to keep rollin', but I'm not sure if we should leave the homey. Magoo said he got Bob, and everything is goin' to be good. But we don't know this nigga, dog."

"If Won says we should keep with the program, I think we should go on and bounce. I don't think he'd say that unless he trusted this fool," Keno said wisely. "Come on, gee. We gots to keep some trust in Won."

"What if he's wrong, dog? What if something hap-pens to Bob and we never see our nigga again?"

"Then we come back out here to the Bronx and look at every nigga in these fuckin' projects! And then we look at Won's ass too!" Red said angrily.

Taz sighed and said, "Alright, let's bounce."

They climbed back inside of the SUV and went back to their hotel. After dropping everything off inside of Taz and Keno's room, the crew got back into the SUV and drove straight to JFK to wait for their flight back to Oklahoma City. They came into the Big Apple six deep but left one crew member short. *Damn!*

Chapter Thirty-four

Sacha and Gwen were still at Taz's house. Gwen had gotten so drunk the night before that she decided to stay over with Sacha. They stayed up late into the night, talking about their futures with their men. Sacha was so excited about her pregnancy that all she could think about was what room they were going to change into the baby's room in Taz's home. They laughed and joked until they both fell asleep.

The next morning, when Sacha woke up, she called in and told her secretary that she wasn't coming into the office, and to make sure that she rescheduled anything that she had on her calendar. After that was taken care of, she then took a shower and went downstairs to make some breakfast for her and Gwen. While she was making breakfast, Taz called. "Hi, baby. Is everything alright?" she asked him as she scrambled some eggs.

"Nah, Li'l Mama, shit is kinda fucked up. But we're good. I should be home in a few hours, though. You straight?"

"Yes, I'm fine. What's wrong, Taz? You don't sound too good. Are you feeling okay?"

"Yeah, I'm straight. We'll talk more when I get there. I just wanted to let you know that everything is everything. I gots to go now, okay?"

"Okay, baby. I love you."

"Love you too," he said and boarded the flight back home.

After Sacha hung up the phone with Taz, she finished cooking breakfast and took the food upstairs to where Gwen was still asleep. As she climbed the stairs, she wondered what was going on with Taz. She hoped and prayed that everything was okay. She couldn't take it if things weren't as perfect as they had been. She just couldn't take it!

Since they were all flying back the way they originally flew out, Red was the only one who flew alone. It felt strange to him as he sat in his seat without his partner, Bob, with him. *Please let him make it, God. Please!* Red prayed as he tried to close his eyes and get some rest on his long flight into Dallas/Ft. Worth.

Keno and Taz got comfortable as their flight to Tulsa International prepared to depart from JFK. They had watched as Red boarded his flight, and Bo-Pete and Wild Bill as they got onto the plane that would be taking them back to the City. Now that they were on their way back, Taz was thinking about everything that had gone down earlier that morning. "That shit was whack from the gate, dog."

"I know. But we had to do what we had to do," replied Keno.

"What the fuck was Bob thinking about by not protecting himself properly?"

"Ain't no tellin', gee. Look, don't stress yourself. He's going to be all right, my nigga."

"And how in the fuck do you know that?"

"I can feel it, homey. I can feel it in my bones. So relax."

Shaking his head no, Taz said, "Nah, gee, fuck that!"

As soon as their flight was airborne, Taz picked up the Skyphone from the seat in front of him and swiped his credit card. Once he received a dial tone, he called Won's cell. When Won answered the phone, Taz said, "What's what with Bob, O.G.?"

"Where are you, Babyboy?"

"We're on our way back to the house. We're in the air right now."

"Good. Listen, I don't really want to talk too long on this type of line. Give me a call as soon as you get back and we'll talk some more."

"All right. So, what's up with the homey?"

"He's all right. He had to have surgery, and it looks like he'll be wearing a shit bag for a few months. Other than that, everything is good. He should be able to be moved within a few days. I'm arranging for transport for him now. I should have something definite for you by the time you get back to the house."

"All right then. That's all I needed to know for now. I'll holla." Taz hung up the phone and returned it to the back of the seat in front of him. He turned and told Keno, "It looks like you were right, my nigga. Bob's straight. He had surgery and he's going to have to have a shit bag for a few months, but other than that, he's going to be good."

Keno smiled and said, "I knew it! I knew it, dog! Now that's what I'm talkin' 'bout!"

Taz smiled and said, "Yeah, I know." As he sat back in his seat, he gave a heavy sigh of relief and thanked God. His prayers had been answered.

It was a little after seven p.m. when the rest of the crew made it to Taz's house.

Sacha was full of smiles when she saw Taz and Keno walk in the front door. Taz gave her a hug and a kiss and said, "We have some loose ends to take care of, so you're going to have to excuses me for a li'l bit, Li'l Mama."

She smiled and said, "I understand. Gwen is still upstairs, so I'll go up and kick it with her until you're finished."

"Gwen? Why is she still here?"

"She got too drunk last night, so she spent the night with me, and this morning she was still out of it, so she's been sleeping it off."

"All right. But check this out. As soon as she wakes up, bring her down to the den. I need to talk to her about somethin'."

Sacha stared into Taz's brown eyes, and she knew instantly that something was wrong. Her heart skipped a beat as she asked, "Is everything alright with Bob, baby? Please, tell me everything is alright with Bob."

Taz shook his head and said, "He's fine, Li'l Mama, but he was shot in the stomach early this morning."

Before Taz could finish giving Sacha the details, Gwen, who was standing at the top of the stairs and had heard what Taz had just said, screamed the loudest scream that Taz had ever heard in his entire life. "No-o-o-o-o!" She fainted right where she stood.

Taz, Sacha, and Keno ran to the stairs and grabbed her before she had a chance to tumble down the steps. Taz carried her back upstairs into his bedroom, while Sacha went into the bathroom and ran some cool water onto a face towel. She then came into the bedroom and placed the cool towel across Gwen's face. While she was doing this, she explained some of Gwen's past to Taz and Keno.

"Damn, that's cold!" Taz said as he thought about his past and how much he and Gwen had in common. "Look, when she gets up, explain to her that Bob's going to make it, and I'll try and get a way for them to speak to each other before the night's up. Right now, I need to go downstairs and finish up things."

"Okay, baby. I got this. Go on and handle your business."

Taz and Keno went downstairs to the den and made the call to Won. Bo-Pete, Wild Bill, and Red came inside and sat down as they waited for Won's return call. Taz's cell rang a few minutes later, and he answered by pressing the speakerphone button. "What's up, O.G.?"

"I just got off the phone with Magoo. He has Bob secure at one of his spots. Here's the number, 'cause I know y'all want to holla at your boy: 212-252-9869. You might want to wait until the morning to give him a holla. He was sleeping soundly when I was speaking with Magoo."

"That's good lookin', O.G. You don't know how good that sounds to our ears."

"Tell me something. Why didn't Bob have his vest on?"

"I wish I could answer that one, O.G. I slipped on that one, because I should have made sure that everyone was ready. I take full responsibility for that shit," Taz said seriously.

"Nah, fuck that shit! It's my fault. I'm his partner, and I should have made sure that my nigga was ready," Red said angrily.

"It's no one's fault but Bob's, really, but I understand where y'all are coming from. Have you checked your accounts yet?" asked Won.

"Yeah, I did before I called you. Everything is everything."

"Good. It looks as if everything will be put on hold until Bob gets back on his feet, so I'll set things back for a minute."

"Nah, O.G., we're done. This shit is starting to get too crazy. We're out. Might as well while we're on top of the game," Taz said sincerely.

"Out? Babyboy, we're at the final stages of everything I've been working towards for the last five years. This shit ain't over yet. I understand that y'all are hurt by what went down with Bob, but it ain't over with yet."

"It is for us, O.G. We're done."

Won started laughing and said, "I'm going to let you go for now, Babyboy. But keep this in your head at all times. As a matter of fact, I want all of you to keep this in your heads. Don't ever think you're running shit in this, 'cause you ain't. I'm the head nigga. Always have been, and I always will be. So this shit ain't over until I say it's over. Relax and chill, and do whatever it is y'all be doing during our downtime. But as soon as Bob is ready to go again, we'll finish what we've started. Out!"

After Won hung up the phone, Taz stared at the rest of the crew and said, "I always hoped that it would never have to come to this, but it looks like we're going to have to go on one last mission, after all."

"I feel you, my nigga. That nigga Won has to be touched," Wild Bill said from the other side of the room.

"Exactly!" replied Bo-Pete.

"Definitely!" said Red.

"He's outta there!" said Keno.

Sacha and Gwen came into the den and joined the crew. After Gwen was seated, Taz explained that Bob had been shot, and that he had a number for her to call once Bob was able to get some more rest.

"Thank you, Taz! Thank you so much! But can you please tell me exactly what the fuck is going on with y'all? I have the right to know, don't I?"

Taz stared at the rest of the crew, and each one of them gave him a nod yes, so he told her exactly what it was that they did when they went out of town. He also explained in detail what had happened out in New York. "That's everything, Gwen. All of it. We're finished now, though. Our money is straight, and there will be no more missions for us."

"Are you lying to me, Taz?"

Taz shook his head no and said, "Nah, I'm givin' it to you 100. We're out."

Before Gwen or Sacha could say anything else, Taz's cell phone started ringing. When he answered it, Tazneema said, "Taz, I need to speak to you. Please tell me that you're back in town."

"Yeah, I'm at home now. What's up, 'Neema?"

"Could you come out to Mama-Mama's house? I'm over here now, and we have some serious things to talk about."

Taz sighed and said, "Can't this wait until tomorrow, 'Neema? I have a lot of shit on my plate, and I'm tired as hell right now."

"No! I need you, Taz. Can't you see that?" she screamed and dropped the phone.

Mama-Mama picked the receiver up from the floor and said, "Taz Good, you get your ass over to this house right now! Do you hear me?"

"Yeah, Mama-Mama, I hear you," he said and closed his cell. He turned towards everyone and said, "I gots to go out to Mama-Mama's house. Somethin's goin' on with 'Neema."

"Do you want us to roll with you, dog?" asked Bo-Pete.

"Nah, y'all go on and get some rest. I'll get at y'all in the morning. Sacha, do you want to roll with me?"

"Yes. Let me go get my purse."

"What about you, Gwen? You straight?"

"Yeah, I'll be all right. I'm going home to try and get some more sleep, 'cause that XO of yours ain't no punk." They all started laughing. Then she said, "Seriously, I'm fine. I want to be well rested when I speak with Bob in the morning."

"All right then, I guess I'll get at y'all later, then," Taz said and left the den.

After everyone had gone, Taz and Sacha climbed into his truck, and Taz sped out of his driveway. "Is everything alright with Tazneema, baby?" Sacha asked.

"She seems real upset, so I guess not, Li'l Mama," Taz said as he turned onto 63rd Street.

They made the twenty-five-minute drive out to Mama-Mama's home in less than fifteen minutes. As soon as the truck stopped in Mama-Mama's driveway, Taz hopped out of it and marched directly inside of the house. Sacha followed him, praying that this wouldn't get ugly. When Taz opened the door, he saw Tazneema sitting on the couch, being consoled by Mama-Mama. He took a deep breath and asked, "What's wrong, 'Neema? Why are you crying?"

Tazneema raised her head off of Mama-Mama's lap, smiled sadly, and said, "I'm pregnant, Taz."

Taz was so stunned by her news that he was speechless. He just stood there staring at her as her words kept repeating themselves over and over inside of his head.

Sacha had come inside of the house just as Tazneema told Taz that she was pregnant. She knew then that this was definitely going to be an ugly scene. She grabbed Taz's right hand and said, "Calm down, baby. Please don't get too crazy right now. More than anything, Tazneema needs your support, not your anger."

Taz shook his head, took a deep breath, and asked, "By who?"

A defiant look came into Tazneema's eyes as she said, "His name is Clifford, and he's a very nice, respectable man, Taz. Ask Mama-Mama."

Taz glared at Mama-Mama and asked, "So, you've met him?"

"Yes, I met him a while back."

"And you didn't tell me about this, Mama-Mama?"

"It wasn't much to tell. 'Neema brought him over to meet me, and I cooked them both a meal."

"But why didn't you tell me about this?"

"Don't you raise your voice at me in my own house, Taz! It wasn't my place to tell you. I told 'Neema that she had to tell you. She called you and asked you to come over, but you had to go out of town. So don't you be blamin' me about this mess, boy!"

Turning his attention back towards Tazneema, he said, "You're too young to be havin' any kids, 'Neema."

"I'm eighteen years old, Taz! I'll be nineteen later this year! I'm grown, and you can't make this decision for me!"

Taz shook his head and said, "The decision's been made, and you are goin' to have an abortion."

"Taz, you should—"

"Hold what you got, Li'l Mama!" he said angrily. "Let me deal with this in my way. Please, don't get in my way right now."

"Taz, if 'Neema wants to have this child, you have no right not to let her," Mama-Mama said as she got up from the couch.

Taz's head was spinning so badly that he felt a little dizzy as he went and sat down next to Tazneema. After getting his bearings together, he said, "Okay, you're right. Where is this clown at? I want to meet him."

"He's not a clown, Taz! He's my man!" Tazneema screamed.

"Your what? Raise your voice to me again like that, 'Neema, and I swear I'll—"

"Taz! Don't you dare threaten that there girl!" screamed Mama-Mama.

"I think everyone needs to take a deep breath and calm down. There will be no way to resolve this intelligently with this much anger in the air," Sacha said wisely.

"All right. Now, where is this Clifford at? I want to talk to him. Do I have that right, Mama-Mama?"

"Watch yourself, boy! You're not that grown! I'll still pop you upside your head!"

Taz smiled at that and said, "I'm sorry, Mama-Mama. You know I'll never disrespect you. But this has to be dealt with accordingly."

"He's on his way over now. He should be here any minute," Tazneema said as she wiped her nose on the sleeve of her blouse.

"How long have you been messing with this guy, 'Neema?" asked Taz.

"Ever since that night you shot that guy at the club."

"Shot? Club? Boy, I thought your crazy days were behind you! What the hell have you been gettin' into out there?" screamed Mama-Mama.

"It was self-defense, Mama-Mama. A dude at the club tried to rob me and Sacha, so I shot him."

"Lord! Taz, you know this stuff is going to have to stop one day. You can't keep on living this crazy life you've been living. It's bad enough this girl's moth—"

"I know, Mama-Mama . . . I know," Taz said, cutting Mama-Mama off.

Before anyone could say another word, Sacha heard a car pull into the driveway. "I guess that's your boyfriend now," she said, and she stepped to the door so she could get the first look at Tazneema's boyfriend. She gasped and felt as if she had been hit in the stomach by a two-by-four when she saw Clifford getting out of his Mercedes-Benz. She shook her head a few times to make sure she wasn't seeing an illusion. When she focused on Clifford as he walked up to the front door, she said, "Oh my God!"

Taz got up from his seat and asked, "What's wrong, Li'l Mama?"

Sacha was speechless. All she could do was point towards the door.

When Clifford walked through the front door, Taz's eyes grew as wide as saucers as he yelled, "Oh, hell nah! I know God damn well this ain't the nigga that has gotten you pregnant, 'Neema! Please, baby girl! Tell me this ain't the nigga!"

With a confused expression on her face, Tazneema got up from the couch and said, "Yes, that's Cliff, and he's my man, Taz."

Before Taz could speak, Clifford said, "Look, Taz. I know this looks kind of crazy, but ever since I meet 'Neema, I've been in love with her."

"Nigga, if you don't shut the fuck up, I swear to God, I'll blast you right here in my mother's fuckin' living room! You know damn well you don't love her! You're just trying to do this shit to get back at me for taking Sacha away from your sorry ass!"

"*What?* What are you talking about, Taz?" asked Tazneema.

"Baby girl, this clown-ass nigga you've been callin' your man don't fuckin' love you! He used to be all caught up with Sacha until she dumped his ass for me!

Can't you see? This nigga is just trying to get back at me! Just like I've always told you, you have to stay out of the way, 'cause niggas out there would one day try to use you as a tool against me. And that's exactly what this nigga is doing. He don't love you, 'Neema! He's been using you!"

"That's not true! We've been living together for the last two weeks. I know this man. I share a home with him. He does love me, Daddy! He does!" screamed Tazneema.

"*Daddy?*" Clifford and Sacha yelled out at the same time.

Taz smiled and said, "Yeah, nigga! Daddy! 'Neema's my daughter, you punk muthafucka! My fuckin' seed, fool! So, do you really think I'm goin' to let you get away with this shit? Huh? Do you?" yelled Taz.

Clifford said, "Listen, Taz. It doesn't matter that she's your child. What does matter is that we both love her and want nothing but the very best for her. And I'm willing to do whatever it takes to prove that to you. I know you don't like me, and I know you think it's some type of conspiracy going on here, but you are wrong. I love Tazneema, and I'd die for her!"

Taz grinned and said, "Nigga, you don't know how true those words you just spoke are!"

"Taz! Watch yourself, boy!" Mama-Mama threatened.

Shaking his head no, Taz said, "Nah, Mama-Mama. This is my baby, and you know that ever since MiMi was killed, I swore that nothing and no one would ever hurt my baby. This nigga has got to go, one way or the other!"

Clifford knew that this could possibly turn into something ugly, and that's why he came prepared. He stepped back towards the door, pulled out a chrome 380. pistol, and said, "Look, Taz. I don't want any problems with you, but there is no punk in me. I'm not letting you take the woman I love away from me."

Taz stared at the small-caliber gun in Clifford's hand, smiled, and said, "So, you ready to play gangsta, nigga? You gots me twisted if you think you will ever have a child by my seed, fool. So, if you gone bust your gun, you needs to get to bustin', 'cause as far as I'm concerned, you are already a dead man!"

"If I lose 'Neema and my child, I might as well be dead, because she's all that I have," Clifford said as he raised his pistol and aimed it directly at Taz's face.

Taz smiled as he glared at Clifford and said, "Go on, coward-ass nigga! Do it! *Do it!*"

Clifford was so scared that he was literally shaking.

Mama-Mama was so shocked at what was happening that she felt as if she was going to faint.

Sacha, on the other hand, was neither scared nor shocked. She was flat-out angry. "Damnit, Cliff! This isn't the way to go about handling this! Put that fucking gun down!"

"No! He took you, and I accepted that. But he's not taking my 'Neema away from me! I'll kill his ass before I let him do that to me!"

With her hands in the air, pleading, Tazneema begged, "Please, baby! Don't hurt my daddy! If you kill him, it won't do anything but hurt us both. I'll lose my father, and I'll lose you, too, 'cause you're going to go to jail. Put the gun down, baby. Please!"

Shaking his head no, Clifford said, "I love you, 'Neema. You have to believe me. But your father will never let us live our lives. Look at him. Look at how he's staring at me now. Can't you see the hatred, baby? Can't you see it?"

"That's right, nigga. Pump yourself up to do it. Don't let no female stop you, you coward. You're right. I'm never going to let you take my seed away from me. Do you hear me, coward? Never!"

Tazneema screamed, "No-o-o-o-o!" and pushed her father out of the way just as Clifford pulled the trigger on his weapon. The small pop hit Tazneema in her upper torso, and she fell to the ground.

Taz got off of the floor and stared in disbelief at his daughter lying there unconscious. He stepped to her and cradled her in his arms as tears streamed down his face.

Mama-Mama fainted, and Sacha ran to her to see if she was alright.

Clifford stood in the doorway, speechless. "Lord, God, what have I done?" he said to himself as he turned and ran out of the house.

Sacha screamed for Taz to call an ambulance, but he couldn't hear her. He was in too much pain.

Author's Note

This is my first attempt at writing a two-part book. I hope that the readers are feeling this story so far. I guarantee that you won't be disappointed in *Gangsta Twist 2*. I will answer all of the unanswered questions, such as: What is Won really up to, and why? And what happened to Tazneema's mother, and why? This will also give the readers a better understanding as to why Taz does the things that he does where Tazneema is concerned.

The twists have just begun, so hold on for a few until I can get back to the lab and bring it all together for you all.

I want to thank every homie who has let me use their name for creative purposes. I hope I haven't upset anyone too badly by how I displayed their character. Remember, gee, it's just fiction. All make-believe! (Smile!)

So, once again, please stay tuned for the next and final installment of *Gangsta Twist*.

ONE LOVE,

SPUD